W9-CTC-294

BEATING
RUBY

Also by Camilla Monk

SPOTLESS
Spotless Series, Book 1

SPOTLESS BOOK 2

BEATING RUBY

CAMILLA MONK

This is a work of fiction. Names, characters, organizations, places, events, and incidents are either products of the author's imagination or are used fictitiously.

Text copyright © 2016 Camilla Monk
All rights reserved.

No part of this book may be reproduced, or stored in a retrieval system, or transmitted in any form or by any means, electronic, mechanical, photocopying, recording, or otherwise, without express written permission of the publisher.

Published by Montlake Romance, Seattle

www.apub.com

Amazon, the Amazon logo, and Montlake Romance are trademarks of Amazon.com, Inc., or its affiliates.

ISBN-13: 9781503952027
ISBN-10: 1503952029

Cover design by M. S. Corley

Printed in the United States of America

This book is dedicated to Benoît, who's still not allowed to read it, to Roberta and Marie, who went above and beyond their duty as Beta readers, and Annette, who hopes, one day, to stroll into a French bookstore and casually ask them if they got the latest Camilla Monk.

Table of Contents

A PROLOGUE OF SORTS

"Destiny feverishly pressed her perfectly sculpted body to Colt's. He growled, the evidence of his untamable desire a heat-seeking missile against her panties. 'I love you, baby. I got you under my skin! I'll fight them all for you, honeypots, even your father!'"

—Natasha Onyx, *Muscled Passion of the SEAL #2: Blitzlove*

I used to be very critical of this particular volume of *MPOTS*, on the grounds that I didn't think they should be going at it in the helicopter while those FBI guys from the CIA—I keep confusing them—are still chasing after them. That's being an engineer for you: safety first! I've since come to revise my opinion, because I realize I can relate to almost everything Destiny experiences, save for the bra-ripping heat-seeking-missile part.

For one, she has a wavy auburn bob, just like me, and hazel eyes. We're both tall—yes, five foot three is tall, shut up—and we both have a sculpted body, albeit mine is in the shape of a stick. My name is Island Chaptal, which is just as stylish as Destiny Heartwind, and I too ended up being consumed by the blazing flames of passion in the arms of a dangerous man. Thank God he had an extinguisher and didn't let things go too far . . .

Indeed, my own Colt Brannigan was too much of a gentleman to rip the panties off a twenty-five-year-old virgin after kidnapping her. We spent five days racing from Paris to Tokyo in search of a two-billion-dollar diamond . . . and I got abandoned in a hotel room with my underwear still intact and my heart broken in a zillion pieces.

Now, I know what you're thinking: six months spent eating Ben & Jerry's, a mountain of tissues, increasingly gloomy Facebook posts, all leading to a botched suicide attempt with cough syrup. I'm better than that. I did spend a week surviving solely on Mounds bars, I nearly overdosed on romance books, and there were, indeed, tears and sad J-pop for a while, but my descent stopped there. The cough syrup thing is just a story my new boyfriend told me—happened to one of his little sister's schoolmates after some punk dumped her on Twitter. High school, these days . . .

In any case, that poor girl survived a scathing "#UJustAKid #WerInDifrntPlces" and half a bottle of Theraflu, just as I survived falling hard for an OCD-ridden hit man whose real name I didn't even know. March, most of the time, but also Mr. April, May, June, July . . . You get the idea.

By the way, if March had actually possessed a Twitter account, I suspect he'd have sent me the same message, only with more vowels.

Oh well, like the Beatles said: life goes on . . .

Sort of.

If you paused on the words "hit man" in the above sentence, by now you've guessed that said life was a little more complicated than your average computer engineer's. Well, to quote one of the most goal-oriented assholes I ever met in my life, "We're only getting started."

ONE

Countdown

"Sexy billionaire, philanthropist, genius hacker: How many faces did Drake possess?"

—Jennie Kyler, *Black Hack #1: Pulled*

I looked up from the thousands of lines of code scrolling on my laptop's screen. The last of my colleagues had just left, leaving me alone in the darkened open space of EM Tech's R&D department. My hands slid away from the keyboard, and I leaned back in my chair, gazing at the skyscrapers surrounding our building, sparkling checkerboards illuminating a mild night in April. It was eight thirty, and Alex's plane had landed in JFK half an hour ago, after a weeklong business trip in Cambodia, punctuated by increasingly longing text messages.

I grabbed the smartphone resting on my desk, opening the messages app with a swipe of my thumb. A youthful face framed by messy brown locks and sculpted by a week's worth of stubble appeared on screen. Under a picture of Alex, grinning at my phone's camera during our second date two months prior, were the last messages he had sent before leaving Phnom Penh: a pic of skewered, roasted cockroaches surrounded by plates of other miscellaneous entomological nopes, a mention that he hadn't slept much last night . . . that he thought of me.

My hand let go of the phone to bunch the cotton of my dress. I stared down at my lap, as if the navy paisley might hold the answers I was looking for. *Maybe not . . .* I eventually slammed my laptop shut, shoved it inside my black tote, and left my desk. Once in the silent hallway, I scanned the long row of perfectly similar frosted glass doors.

Through one of them, a dim light still shone.

———

Even though he was EM Tech's director of R&D, and therefore my boss, I never needed to announce myself before entering Thomas Roth's office, because no one else knocked the beat of "The Imperial March" at his door.

"You should be home. Come in."

A smile stirred the corners of my lips at his laconic greeting. I pushed the door open and went to plop myself in one of the chairs across from him, taking in the piles of papers, scientific magazines, and odd gadgets cluttering his desk—few of my acquaintances could boast of possessing a last-generation NAO robot or an accurate LEGO model of the *Millennium Falcon*.

He seemed to ignore me at first. His entire attention was focused on the dual screen in front of him, long fingers scratching sparse and short blond hair, when they weren't busy constantly readjusting his small round glasses over and over. I didn't mind; I knew he meant no contempt. Many at EM Tech regarded Thom as this secretive, Gollum-like figure who spent most of his time curled up in his office, hiding behind the piles of résumés he received from young engineers desperate to join his team. As his Dotar Sojat, though, I was allowed past the curtain of his introversion and therefore enjoyed a different perspective of the man behind the LEGOs.

Thom had handpicked me two years prior, freshly out of Columbia Engineering. Back then, I'd been—and still was, to some extent—a machine: few friends, no life, and the winning (gap-toothed) smile of an overachiever who craved validation from teachers and superiors. I would work up to fourteen hours a day if fed enough doughnuts, and show up even for the meetings no one wanted to show up to—which eventually led me to conduct an entire keynote alone in front of ten empty chairs.

That was in early November, by the way, a few weeks after my adventure with March. I had seen my entire existence unravel in less than a week, and I had yet to fully recover from the ordeal. Physically, of course, but also emotionally, since I still thought of him 24-7. Took me fifteen minutes to realize there was no one in the room, and I finished my presentation anyway . . .

I know it sounds bad when I put it like this, but the truth is, those months spent working like a zombie to better forget March paid off. Thom progressively entrusted me with all critical algorithmic kernels in EM Tech's most ambitious project: Ruby, a new program designed to put online banking systems' security to the test. From breaking into dummy accounts to simulating complex data-hacking scenarios, Ruby was to become the end-all of financial software security testing. Once we had a functional beta, anyway. Said beta was to be presented a week from now, during a public demo in front of EMT's entire board and a measly couple hundred journalists. Needless to say Ruby had better impress, because the solution had been sold to half a dozen major banks already.

So yeah, R&D had been working under some modicum of pressure lately. That being said, if we managed to pull it off, this demo would become the pinnacle of Thom's entire career so far—and incidentally, mine as well.

Thom's eyes never left the screens as I leaned to rest my elbows on the cool glass of his desk. "You should be home too, playing with your son."

On the keyboard, his fingers faltered, and I saw him punch the Back key several times to correct something. Once he was done, he massaged his forehead with his palm for several seconds. "Tobias is asleep. He went to sleep seven minutes ago. It's because Emma took him to the park after five. Playing outside after five will cause him to fall asleep thirty-two minutes earlier on average . . . I have data . . . I—"

I shook my head. "You're ranting. You really need to take your mind off Ruby and get some rest."

His fine, ever-anxious features pinched, creating deep wrinkles around his mouth, pale blue eyes narrowing behind his glasses. "I'm not sure I can do that. Not tonight."

"What's so urgent that it can't wait for tomorrow morning? We still have bugs—you know that, I know that, and they'll be fixed on time for Ruby's demo," I said with an encouraging smile.

At last, he unfolded his tall frame to look past the bright glow of his screens and directly at me. "I hope so."

He sounded remote, like he didn't believe it himself. And yet I knew that this was the most enthusiasm he'd voice about our project. Even once we were done and the execs showered him with champagne, Thom would probably just readjust his glasses and soberly comment that things were headed in the right direction.

I flicked my head toward the screens. "How about I help you wrap up whatever you're onto and we leave together?"

Thom usually didn't mind discussing his code with me, even more so since we shared the same quiet, nerdy nature. So I was a little unsettled to see him shake his head in response to my offer. "No need for that."

"It's okay, I can stay a little longer and help you."

That next try was met with several seconds of silence—something frequent with Thom. His brain would sometimes take wild tangents, causing him to space out and stare at people until the gears were done rotating. Then his hands gripped the keyboard almost protectively. "It's just . . . administrative tasks. I won't keep you up all night checking expense requests." His eyes hardened. "It's not your job."

I raised my hands in surrender. "Okay, you're the boss."

"Weren't you supposed to see your boyfriend tonight?" he asked, rearranging pens I knew he didn't need.

My lips twisted sideways; I sighed. *You're stressed out of your mind, grumpy, and you want me out. Reading you, five . . . over.* "Alex is probably on his way here from JFK. I guess I'll just go."

A series of muffled chiming sounds rose from my bag as if to confirm this statement. I dug up my smartphone. Alex was on Broadway, asking me if I was still at work, and if I wanted him to pick me up.

I felt Thom's gaze on me. In those pale blue irises shone the understanding of a fellow nerd who had successfully made it out of the virgin zone and unlocked the wife achievement with a history teacher a few years ago. He knew that there was, in fact, a life beyond our screens. "Go."

I glanced down at my phone, then back up at Thom. "Are you sure you'll be okay?"

There was something I couldn't fully decipher in his expression as he answered—not so much raw exhaustion as a form of tender sadness. "Yes."

TWO

The Bra

"As soon as their eyes met, torrents of honey suddenly flooded the secret well of ecstasy concealed under her shift."

—Ovidia Houghton, *Scandalous Victorian Nights*

It wasn't cold—the night air was in fact rather warm and humid for that time of the year—but I shivered. I wrapped my arms around myself, tucking my cardigan closer to my body as I paced in front of EMT's building on Greenwich Street. Every time a car slowed down, my heart would jolt a little. Even after two months, I still experienced this odd mixture of anxiety and childlike anticipation whenever I saw Alex. I figured it had to do with how he was my first real boyfriend, and that made every single interaction between us a tentative step in the dark. On an ice rink. With ski shoes.

Alex was the one who had taken that first risky step, messaging me on Yaycupid one lonely night in February. Back then, I still thought I'd never get over March. My first exchange with Alex had turned into a suicide mission of sorts, during which I'd bluntly admitted to being this horrible aging virgin who had spent the past months nursing a broken heart and reading romance books to forget a man no suitor could ever replace.

For Alex to message me again two days later had been a spectacular and unexpected development—Joy said only Jesus would have come back for more, and that I should check Alex's palms for stigmata should he offer further interaction. He *had*, in the form of an actual date at the Museum of Natural History, complete with a stop at a Greek joint. I could still remember the crunchy, squishy feeling of freshly salted snow under our feet as we shared falafels and discussed the romance scenarios in *Mass Effect 3*. He'd steal glances at me and just smile, almost to himself, like he understood some sort of vast mystery I didn't. It was then and there, as I stared at Alex's ruffled hair and his old sweatshirt advertising an ice fishing contest in Wisconsin, that I had been hit by an epiphany. Regular, decent guys were in fact available.

And maybe I had been so busy dissecting every second of my past failures that I had missed this crucial detail. Of course, March had played in an entirely different league: mysterious, dangerous—okay, sexy too—and yet so goddamn flawed and tender. But he wasn't a regular guy . . . and if I was honest with myself, he wasn't even a decent one, judging by the fact that he had chosen to knock me out while we were kissing, and sneak out in the middle of the night, instead of leaving with a proper good-bye. Or just a fricking *note*. He couldn't be there for me. Would never be.

Alex had been raising his younger sister alone in Washington's suburbs since their parents' death in a plane crash six years prior. He worked his ass off for a big expatriate insurance company—which at least gave him the opportunity to travel a lot, although mostly in third-world countries. He struggled to keep boys away from sixteen-year-old Poppy, didn't like to cook, and enjoyed going out with friends, but was often too tired on the weekends to do so. He'd read and play video games instead, or message girls on Yaycupid in hopes for an actual relationship rather than the vicarious delights of the clumsy love letters he sometimes received from his sister's schoolmates.

And so, one afternoon he had driven all the way from Silver Spring, Maryland, for our first date. Because he liked me. Because there was room in his life for someone. Because *he* was ready.

"Are you ready?"

My heart slammed against my rib cage, and I spun around. "Sorry, I didn't hear you—"

My voice faltered, swallowed by his embrace. Alex nuzzled my hair, ignoring the few passersby walking past us on Greenwich Street. I buried my face in his neck, breathing in his light cologne. Something homey, not very sophisticated, made sweet and soapy by hours of travel and a little sweat. This was one of the many things I loved about him: the way he was so warm, so uncomplicated—that and the fact that at five foot eleven, he remained within marginally accessible heights for me. My fingers played with the light blue cotton of his shirt. Worn jeans, no tie, not even a jacket—typical Alex. I registered his voice, barely above a whisper against my earlobe. "I missed you . . ."

I shifted away a little to look up at him. Taking in his gentle cinnamon gaze and thick eyebrows, I couldn't help but think of March's guarded blue eyes and faint crow's-feet. Alex had experienced loss, had made sacrifices to take care of Poppy. Yet, unlike March, who had grown up in poverty and spent almost half of his life killing, Alex still retained an air of innocence, as if he hadn't been bombarded with life's lemons yet . . .

His palms cupped my cheeks. "Earth to Island. Are you still with me?"

"Yeah . . . I just . . . I guess I spaced out. Sorry about that."

"Something bothering you? Too much pressure at work?"

I relaxed at the caress of his thumb, combing locks of hair away from my face. "No. The stakes are high, but I think we're on the right track. We'll be ready. I'm sure we will."

"Good. You know what I think you need right now?"

I smiled. "No, but you're gonna tell me?"

"The same thing I need—something to drink and any junk food that could pass as dinner," he said with a wink.

"I'm in. Where are we going?"

"Well, my hotel has this bar, kind of steampunk, with a piano lounge. I'd tell you they serve great Belgian beers, but I know you don't like beer. I can, however, bait you with the promise of a gin-and-strawberry cocktail and the best *pommes frites* you've ever had."

Normally I'd have melted at his adorable English accent when pronouncing French words. Being half-French, the language carried a particular sense of nostalgia to me—something sweet and vaguely comforting, like the buttery scent of a Petit Lu. At the moment, however, I was stuck on two words. Insignificant and essential.

My hotel.

Alex's hotel. As good as his place, really—even more so since I suspected he had never invited me to his house because he had no idea how to juggle a relationship with the demands of his role as Poppy's substitutive parental unit. Except Alex wasn't a parent, but rather a healthy twenty-eight-year-old male posing as a responsible and somewhat conservative authority figure.

I felt his hands linger on my arms in an absent caress. My brain conjured the memory of our last date, a couple of days before his trip. After an awesome picnic in Central Park, Alex had driven me home and parked in front of my building. We both knew I wouldn't invite him upstairs, since Joy, my roommate, best friend, and occasional therapist, was home. So he and I had chatted for a little longer. There'd been some playful flirting, and the inevitable kissing. The taste of a mocha Frappuccino lingering in his mouth, his stubble prickling my Cupid's bow. His palm, so warm on my knee. Then just a little higher, venturing for the first time under my dress . . . until I'd squirmed away from his touch with some lame excuse that I was tired.

It had been two months, six days, eight dates, and eighty-four chat logs. And I still couldn't, for the life of me, figure out if *I* was ready.

"You vanished on me again."

I snapped out of my considerations to see that Alex had picked up a black sports bag from the ground and flung its strap on his shoulder. "I . . . No! I was listening. Your hotel. We're going . . . to your hotel."

Alex grinned in affirmation and pulled a key fob from his pocket. The lights of a beige Ford SUV flashed twice behind us. Last time his rental car had been a Hyundai. He opened the trunk, threw his bag into it, and unlocked the passenger door for me to climb in. I sat down, my fingers playing with the worn leather strap of my tote bag. I thought he'd start the engine, but instead he turned to look at me, with a calm, knowing smile. The corners of my lips quivered up in response, and I shrugged a little in a silent reassurance that everything was totally fine, and look at that, I'm oozing confidence and stuff!

Alex's hand found mine, and he shifted in his seat, leaning toward me until our foreheads were touching. His lower lip brushed my upper one in an almost chaste kiss. "Baby . . ."

Funny how even after two months, I wasn't used to that particular term of endearment yet.

"If you don't want anything to happen, nothing will."

Oh, right, I forgot to mention that Alex was an expatriate insurance expert . . . and a mind reader.

I returned his kiss tentatively. "What if I just don't know?"

Alex's grin turned impish. "Then I'll kiss you until you do."

That one made me blush pretty much all over, until I realized that his eyes were looking past me and into my mirror. I craned my neck to check it, but I saw nothing out of the ordinary, save for the fact that a black Mercedes sports car had slowed down and appeared to be parked a dozen yards or so behind us.

"Is something wrong?"

"No. Nice car, though."

"I didn't picture you as a sports car kind of guy."

Alex laughed as he started the Ford's engine. "You don't know me yet."

———

Don't pretend you're not trembling with anticipation, a long trickle of drool running down your chin as you wait for the filthiest details. Were the *pommes frites* that good? Indeed yes, crisp on the outside, soft on the inside. Did I drink myself under the table? No, but there was definitely more gin than strawberry in my glass(es).

By the way, I'm not blaming anything on the gin. I mean, it *did* warm me up a little, but I knew what I was doing. When our hands started roaming under the table, I looked down at our fingers, laced on the leather of the seat, then up at Alex, with his messy brown curls and hopeful smile. And I made up my mind. I was five months away from my twenty-sixth birthday, in a healthy, wholesome relationship with a great guy . . . Goddammit, I could do this!

Now, allow me to seize this opportunity to debunk a hoax that maybe has been told to you too—I know Joy told it to me, that's for sure. So, it goes like this: if a mommy and a daddy love each other very much and they get together in an elevator at the appropriate time for that love to express itself in its purest form, they'll push the stop button and bang each other silly against the walls of said elevator until their nether regions start to chafe. Well, I can think of at least one hypothetical case where this isn't true: when an old couple enters the elevator as well.

Those seemed like the longest, tallest ten floors of my entire life. Alex and I stood side by side, looking straight ahead and feigning disinterest, while the tip of his fingers teased mine and the tension between us grew to the point where I feared we might set the lady's bun on fire before the elevator reached his destination. As fate would have it, their room was on the same floor as his, so we had to behave until they were out of sight.

Then we didn't behave so much. Alex's lips crashed on mine the second their door closed behind them, and roughly twenty seconds later, we stumbled into his room. He didn't bother with giving me a tour, or even turning on the lights. I didn't mind; the dark made me feel safer. I figured it'd conceal my fumbling, my hesitations, even to myself. Hungry kisses were raining down my neck and I felt dizzy, maybe because of the gin after all, or those zings of electricity that seemed to sparkle all over my body. It was happening. I was in this nice room, facing the shimmering top of the Chrysler Building, and it was *really* happening. I actually had to place my hands on his shoulders to call a break, because it all felt a little too much.

Alex cupped my cheek in his palm. "Are you okay?"

"I'm . . . I'm good. Just getting a little worked up."

"That's the whole idea." He grinned, pulling me closer again.

I stood there for a moment, shivering in his arms, trying to catch my breath. He gave me time, stroking my back, and when our lips met again everything seemed to slow down, hurried touches turning into sensual, explorative ones. I realized that one of his hands had lifted my dress and was now grazing my thighs. I tried to return the favor, inhaling that sweet cologne lingering on his shirt as I undid the first buttons. My fingertips met warm skin, and I think that's when it became real to me. The notion of sex had been almost abstract in my mind until then. I wanted it, but "it" was little more than a word carrying vague implications and scary promises. Once he started undressing me, though, said implications reached a whole new level.

I remember that Alex kept saying I was beautiful, kept calling me *baby*.

I registered the whisper of clothing falling to the floor. My dress. His fingers left a trail of goose bumps on my ribs, my sides, traced the edge of my bra.

It was happening. It was really happening.

THREE

The Polly Pocket Shoe

"Traci stared at his massive organ, which was glowing in the dark.
Her instincts had been right—Oxo wasn't from this world."

—Maxie Skye, *The Dur'yân Chronicles*

"Oh my God! Yes! Yes!"

I jerked awake in my bed at the sound of something slamming against the bathroom wall and Joy soaring toward felicity.

6:07 a.m.

You know what's worse than being a virgin? Being a virgin *and* getting woken up before dawn on a Tuesday morning by people having loud sex in a tub you know you'll *have* to step into afterward. I was reaching for my phone on the nightstand when I heard the bathroom door closing, along with a series of giggles past my bedroom door. Vince-the-cutest-photographer-in-the-world had performed his morning duties, and Joy would be in a good mood for the rest of the day.

As for me . . . I was in the mood of a girl who had freaked out and fled her boyfriend's hotel room because she couldn't take off her bra for him.

I'll spare you the embarrassing details of how I went to hide in his bathroom under the pretext of an overwhelming need to pee. There, the bluish foil of a condom peeking out of his toiletries bag made me panic completely. I'd said I was sorry about a million times. He'd tried to hug me, kiss me, stroke my hair . . . told me it was okay—even though I could almost taste the frustration on his lips. I'd said I just needed time, promised to call, to text. And less than ten minutes later, I was three blocks away, running breathlessly up Broadway past homeless guys hauling bags full of cans.

As you can imagine, I hadn't slept much, replaying my evening with Alex over and over again to figure out *why* I had collapsed in front of the obstacle. Well, technically I knew why: my bra had come loose, I had pictured him touching my breasts, touching everything else . . . and my body had pulled the brakes on that shady arousal business, screaming that I wasn't ready. What I truly feared was the deeper reason behind this failure. Unspeakable things happened in my *Star Wars* PJs at night, when I closed my eyes and remembered the feel of March's naked body against mine during that last night in Tokyo, his scent, a combination of the mints he ate like a junkie and something that was just *him*, all that silky chest hair . . . But there appeared to be a considerable gap between dreams and reality. Alex, the hotel room, the condoms—this had been reality, and I hadn't been able to handle it.

I stared at the ceiling, vaguely aware of further sighing and giggling in the hallway. I didn't want to consider the possibility that March had invaded and broken for good some tiny part of my psyche, and that I'd never be able to give myself to someone else . . .

Dismissing this depressing thought, I grabbed my smartphone on the nightstand and started scrolling through my e-mails, wrapped in my flowery comforter like a Swiss roll. There was a chat notification from Alex, sent around one, telling me he was sorry things had moved too fast, and offering to take me somewhere for lunch before he returned to Washington. Overcoming the butterflies partying hard in my stomach—they had kind of been pushing the limits of their lease agreement lately—I agreed to meet him in Zucotti Park at twelve thirty.

My fingers froze when I reached the most recent e-mails: a series of automated alerts from Ruby's test servers, pointing to a massive crash around three a.m. I swore under my breath. Ruby would recover from the crash itself, that was no problem, but it meant that, six days away from our big reveal, it still wasn't stable. I could already guess I'd arrive at EMT to find Thom hunched over his keyboard, wearing yesterday's shirt and scratching his head compulsively. I rubbed my eyes and sent him a reassuring e-mail that I'd show up even earlier than usual to investigate the incident and help him set Ruby back on track.

I crawled out of bed and dragged myself to the living room, where I was greeted by the rich aroma of coffee. On our old green couch, Joy and the new love of her life were snuggling and dipping Oreos in their double espressos—a repulsive habit only they understood, and which contributed to bringing them closer. Joy pushed a heap of blonde curls from her left shoulder and appraised me with bashful cornflower eyes. She was wearing Vince's shirt—something I understood to be mandatory when you've slept with a man—meaning he, of course, was only wearing silk boxer shorts, as usual. I didn't care. Vince was cute enough, but he was also a pompous jerk in need of a haircut, and who shaved what little chest hair he had.

With my leg razors.

Yeah, I know. In North Korea, people get executed for that kind of stuff.

"Sorry about the—" Joy waved a dismissive hand and had the good grace to blush.

Vince didn't. Slanted black eyes scanned the stormtroopers on my PJs as a grin lit his angular face, revealing teeth that seemed even whiter against his bronze skin and coal stubble. "Oh, so you were listening?"

Like I had a choice. I fought a scalding blush and, from the corner of my eye, noticed that Joy's foot was kicking her boy toy's calf in a bid to prevent any further descent into assholism.

"No . . . It's . . . Never mind." I averted my eyes, went to fix myself a bowl of Apple Jacks, and sat on a wooden chair by the window. I loved nothing more than that peaceful moment when I'd eat my breakfast watching the darkened street.

Behind me, squeals suggested that Vince was about to ravish Joy on the couch. My window-daydreaming time now ruined, I got up and glanced at the two of them just long enough to see his hand retreat from under the wrinkled gray shirt.

Joy's voice stopped me halfway to the kitchen as she let go of Vince to join me and carry both their cups toward the sink—where they'd make a nice addition to our rapidly growing pile of dishes. "How did it go last night with Jesus?"

I cringed. "Please don't call Alex that."

"You came home pretty late . . . but you came home," she replied with a wink.

"We just had a drink at his hotel's bar."

How foolish of me to think that Joy wouldn't pick up on that particular detail. As her eyes lit up, I could practically see the report writing itself in her mind.

> The defendant loaded herself with strawberry gin cocktails and agreed to follow Mr. Morgan to his hotel room at 10:49. To have **wild, rampant sex** all over the furniture.

I took a wary step back. "It wasn't like that."

"Aw, come on! You and Alex aren't kids!" Joy groaned.

On the couch, Vince finally expressed interest in our conversation. "Does he have, like, a problem with his dick? I knew this guy who had stuck a Polly Pocket shoe in there in first grade, and after that, he couldn't—"

"No! I don't think . . . I mean, I'm sure it's working fine!" I pictured myself hurling my dirty bowl at Vince's face.

Joy seemed to consider rinsing the cups for a second, before abandoning them to their fate and walking out of the kitchen. "I need to get ready for court, but tonight we'll have to further investigate the issue."

Family lawyer, sexologist, urologist—was there anything Joy couldn't do? Yeah, the dishes. I shrugged and rinsed my bowl, because March had made me a new and better person. Meanwhile, she flung herself back on the couch and into Vince's waiting arms with a catlike grin. I frowned down at the war zone in our sink and the lime building up on our faucet.

"Joy?"

She disentangled herself from Vince with a squeak of delight. "What?"

"You still don't want to try those free cleaning hours?"

"The ones from Maid-shit-whatever?"

"Yeah. Maid Magic."

"I dunno, I don't like the idea of someone coming into my place when I'm not home," she said, her nose wrinkling in disapproval.

I left the kitchen and padded across our living room to the long black sideboard on which Joy and I had made a habit of throwing anything that came either from our handbags or the mailbox. I went through the pile of receipts, ads, and unopened mail sitting on it. Indeed, between my cell phone bill and a flyer advertising a Hello Kitty–themed after party at some bar, I found a coupon book for free housecleaning hours we had received a few days ago.

"Are you sure you're not interested? I mean, we got"—I counted the coupons—"ten of these. And their letter says we won a free trial for the VIP service with laundry, ironing, and antibacterial cleaning included."

"But I don't want these weirdoes snooping around my house. It looks like some kind of scam. I didn't even register for any contest," Joy groaned.

Vince nodded absently while massaging her shoulders.

"Maybe you don't remember," I countered. "Or maybe it's one of these websites where you click 'Yes' to read an article on the hairiest baby in the world, and they tell you that you just entered to win a golf cart."

She sat up. "I *want* a golf cart. I don't want a cleaning lady."

I gazed at the coupons longingly, remembering how immaculate our apartment had been the morning after March had broken into it. He had cleaned our entire place while I slept off a migraine—admittedly sparked by his repeated threats to torture me until I gave him the Ghost Cullinan—nothing huge, just the biggest natural diamond in the world, stolen a decade ago . . . by my late mother. For some tentacular criminal organization, a bunch of malevolent assholes who called themselves "the Board." Because she had never been a French diplomat, but rather some sort of glamorous international spy and superthief.

Hey, I warned you that my life was weird.

Anyway, there was something to be said about the way the man had turned his cleaning disorder into a gift for housekeeping, and he had branded me irremediably; I would start cleaning my apartment. Soon. Not today, but real soon.

Behind me, Joy had resumed making out with Vince on the couch, and she struggled to speak in between noisy, slurpy kisses. "I vote no . . . to Maid Magic!"

"We'll see about that. I need to get ready," I said, heading toward the bathroom. Sweet Jesus, I prayed these two had rinsed the tub well. Wouldn't hurt to rinse it again.

———

There were two undeniable perks to leaving for work at the crack of dawn: I was on a first-name basis with EM Tech's morning security team, and once in a while, I actually caught glimpses of Hadrian *fricking* Ellingham, super billionaire, legendary stick-in-the-mud, and CEO of

EM Group, our parent company. He and his brother, Maximilian, had inherited an industrial empire, of which EM Tech constituted a small but nonetheless highly profitable part.

EMT ∈ EMG. You get the idea—pretty logical.

I had in fact gotten so used to those brief encounters that when I reached Greenwich Street that morning and saw what I now recognized as his limo driving past me, I barely spared it a glance. I buried my hands in my jeans pockets and looked down at the mice on my ballet flats, imagining them gossiping about Ellingham's love life.

I didn't realize something was off until I was standing twenty yards or so from the entrance. In the brownish windows of EMT's building—an architectural faux pas warranting its nickname as "the Kit Kat"—bright red and blue lights were reflected. Police car lights. My walk slowed down. Whatever was going on had to be pretty serious, as no less than four NYPD cars were stationed in the street, not far from the entrance, along with a black SUV that looked straight out of a government conspiracy. Indeed, I soon watched with increasing worry as a steady stream of policemen in uniforms and suited guys came in and out of the building, performing what could best be described as cop stuff: talking into phones and walkie-talkies, eating bagels, drinking coffee, and occasionally flashing their badges at the Kit Kat's security officers.

In the distance, I noticed two guys I knew from HFT entering the building, so I bunched my fists and took a few cautious steps toward the revolving doors as well. Just so you know, HFT stands for "High Frequency Trading," aka the Ninth Circle—in charge of developing those trading robots that break Wall Street entirely with a bazillion simultaneous transactions once in a while. I heard they test applicants with holy water there, to make sure they have no soul.

As I approached the doors, I was able to catch bits of the cops' conversations. Jumper . . . west side . . . fifth floor. A suicide? Maybe it was someone important. But the fifth floor was the mainframe's floor, basically a ten-thousand-square-foot clean room. No VIPs there, just a team of engineers maintaining EMT's servers 24-7 in a climate- and static-controlled environment—while slowly turning into ghouls from the lack of natural light.

Right after I had passed the security gates, I had to hand my tote bag to one of the security officers for searching. I watched him fumble with little conviction into my usual mess of keys, candy wrappers, and tampons before he let me access the lobby. I barely had the time to take a few steps on the granite floor and inhale the morning bouquet of coffee and detergent when I heard a breathless call from the other end of the hall.

Sheltered behind a massive circular aluminum desk sat Prince Grimaldo, part of the Kit Kat's morning security team, and to some extent my bro—he and I shared the sort of complicity only people whose parents named them at random can understand.

I ignored the stares from the policemen guarding the elevators, ran toward him, and slipped behind the desk, a privilege I had earned after two years of undying loyalty. Prince's ample body was sprawled in his leather chair, squeezed into a navy-blue uniform that was anything but flattering. He combed a hand through the shoulder-length black hair he had been reminded on numerous occasions was against company policy and looked up at me, eyes wide with apparent distress. I opened my mouth to ask about the commotion around us, but before any sound could come out, Prince struggled up from his chair and pulled me into an awkward hug. He was crushing me, and I was distracted by the smell of candy clinging to his jacket.

"Thom is dead. They say he killed himself."

I think I didn't hear him speak, or maybe I did but the words didn't register. There was this buzzing in my ears. I felt numb, confused.

He repeated the words, louder this time. "Island, he killed himself."

The hall spun around me, and for a few seconds, there was nothing solid, nothing tangible to hold on to anymore. The floor under my feet,

Prince's body, it all felt like warm molasses engulfing me. I squirmed out of his embrace and staggered back.

"I need . . . I need a moment. I'll see you later."

I saw his hand reach out, perhaps to help me stand, but I turned away. I could feel eyes on me, no doubt observing my reactions. I just wanted to be alone. I walked toward the elevators like a zombie, showed my employee badge to a woman apparently in charge of making sure no one would access the clean room until the police were done. It seemed to take ages for the car to reach the ninth floor—R&D, and therefore my floor. I remember that I pressed my palms against the metal walls because the cool contact made me feel a little better. The hallway and open space were plunged in an eerie silence.

Thom should have been there to greet me, because even when I made it in before seven thirty, he was always the first to show up—when he didn't just cheat and spend the night in his office. Attendance was one of the many games I could never beat my mentor at.

I registered movement in my field of vision at the other end of the hallway. Cops were guarding the door to his office, and there were some hushed conversations. I gathered they were searching his things. Seeing their uniforms, I felt the reality of what had happened finally seeping into me, like ice inside my bones, rocks in my stomach. My eyes were starting to water, and I could barely stand. I made a beeline for the ladies' room. As soon as I was in one of the large stalls, I let myself fall on the toilet seat and allowed quiet sobs to shake my body, tasting salty drops on my upper lip.

It all seemed unreal. Sure, Thom had been tired last night, and we were all under pressure, but Ruby's final development phase had been going well overall. We would have been done fixing the few minor glitches by demo day. He couldn't possibly have killed himself over a goddamn piece of software; he had been stronger than that. Focused. Driven to the point of obstinacy sometimes.

I wondered if something could have happened in his marriage that would have led him to do such a thing. Had Emma cheated on him? Hard to believe, since Thom's wife worshipped the very ground he walked on, as far as I had been able to tell. Like most computer-illiterate Muggles, she believed her husband to be some sort of hacker genius, capable of installing an antivirus or even filing a tax return online. Bits of conversation and scattered memories flashed in my mind, one after another. I was hyperventilating. I couldn't process this. Couldn't make any sense of it.

A few deep, calming breaths later, I came out of the stall and stared at my reflection in the mirror; tears had left damp stains on my teal sweater, my eyes were red, and my face looked ashen under the fluorescent lights.

My hand reached inside my bag almost like a reflex. Joy would be in court all morning; I'd need to wait at least a few hours before I could confide in her. But maybe Alex . . . I needed to tell him, to hear his voice. My stomach knotted at the first ring. Two more rings, until it all stopped. He had declined the call. I thought of texting him; I didn't. I felt nauseated, weary, and suddenly angry at everything—at Thom for dying, at myself for having spent twelve hours a day with him and failing to detect his distress, even at Alex, who always picked up when I called, except today. I shoved my smartphone back into my bag with trembling hands and slammed my palms against the counter.

A soft tapping sound and a male voice coming from the other side of the restroom door made me jump. "Are you all right?"

Joel—fellow developer, *Minecraft* enthusiast—had seen me run to the bathroom, and I still looked like a zombie. I tried to tame my short curls with trembling fingers, rinsed my face, dried it with a paper towel, and stepped out.

"Yeah, sorry . . . I guess I'm just a bit shaken." I sighed, scanning the colorful jungle pattern on his sweater. I was still in shambles, looked the part, and I didn't feel ready to meet his eyes yet.

A forced smile cracked through his bushy ginger beard. "Come. We need a Dr Pepper."

I massaged my temples with my thumbs to fight the dull throbbing that threatened to turn into a migraine later. A goddamn *Dr Pepper*? There it was again, that surge of pain and anger laced together, making me feel helpless, crushing my lungs.

Thom's death was a problem no amount of Dr Pepper would solve.

FOUR

Equivalent Exchange

"No, I mean, it's not that it was too small, or, you know . . . not up to the job. That wasn't the problem with Hadrian."

—Nina Rivera, *Women & Styles*, May 2013 issue

The first thing Joel and I found when turning on our computers was a memo Kerri Lavalle, our CEO, had sent to the entire R&D department. Tedious corporate bullshit for the most part, poorly concealing the fact that neither she nor anyone on EMT's board knew Thom all that well. The words *deeply saddened*, *thoughts and prayers*, and *immeasurable loss* floated around in an improbable soup describing Thom as a cheerful and enthusiastic team leader, on top of being a visionary security expert.

That last part at least was true. Too bad they had missed everything else, the mosaic of skills and ideas that had made him so unique. I thought of Emma, and the last picture of their son she had posted on Facebook. Twelve hours ago, the biggest problem in her life had been that two-year-old Tobias had stuck her MetroCard in their Blu-ray player.

For a second, I saw my mother again, remembered the vertiginous sense of loss I had experienced in the first few days; back then I had believed the weight in my stomach would never go away. This was the kind of pain Emma was in at the moment. My eyes threatened to water again, and I wanted to call her. She was probably still speaking to the cops, though, and I didn't know what I'd say. I decided to wait a few days. I knew from firsthand experience that nothing I could say or do would change anything until she had overcome the initial shock.

I collapsed in my chair, and my eyes fell on the last paragraph of Kerri's e-mail.

I blinked.

I reread it and typed in my credentials to connect to our test server . . . only to get kicked out.

As Thom's brutal disappearance significantly challenges EMT's short- and mid-term R&D strategies, the following projects will be temporarily put on hold, pending the appointment of a new director and review from the executive board:

—Ruby Core 1.0 49, Beta

—Ruby API suite 0.1.7, Alpha

All related server access privileges will be revoked as of Tues. 2015-04-12 05:00:00.

I checked the time the e-mail had been sent—5:13 a.m. What the hell was going on here? What little I knew so far—along with this e-mail—suggested that Thom had jumped out of one of the fifth-floor windows sometime during the night. Then Lavalle had fired off her rubbish e-mail . . . and also decided to shut down the Ruby project entirely, with no clear mention of when—or if—development would resume.

That didn't sound like her. The very reason why engineers didn't like the woman much was her carefree personality; she was the one who had sold Ruby to several major banks before the project's feasibility had even been assessed. In fact, this way of dealing with the incident sounded a lot more like Ellingham—opaque and ultra-cautious. Which suggested that the shockwave provoked by Thom's death had reverberated all the way up to EMG's board in a matter of hours.

"I'm telling you he *did* something. They've locked the fifth floor. I heard there're cops guarding the clean room and everybody got kicked out!"

I looked up from my screen. Joel and Vishal were back from their mandatory Dr Pepper break—I had cut mine short because the knots in my stomach wouldn't allow for anything to go down.

Joel walked toward my desk. I winced when I realized that Vishal, one of our Product Owners, was following him. The guy always showed up with a close shave and wearing impeccably cut Italian suits, but the way he'd stare at people with wide, round eyes always weirded me out. I hadn't yet recovered from the shock of Thom's death; I wasn't ready for a *Simpsons*-eyes session.

Joel casually leaned against my desk and, *God*, Vishal's gaze fell on me, black eyes widening, widening like two creepy saucers as a way to greet me.

"Feel better?" Joel began in a compassionate tone.

"Yeah, thanks. I don't understand, though. I *just* don't . . ."

"There's been talk of corporate espionage."

Joel and I both looked at Vishal. Apparently content that he now had our full attention, he brushed some imaginary lint off his charcoal pants and went on. "My personal theory is that he was stealing data from EMT's servers, and he took his own life when they caught him."

"Bullshit! Thom wasn't like that, he—"

Vishal's eyes bulged out until I feared they'd fall off and roll across my desk like marbles, effectively silencing my protest. "He planned everything. I heard cops saying he cut the power in the west wing so the cameras wouldn't record what he had done."

"But what did he do, exactly?" Joel didn't sound convinced.

Vishal nodded to himself. "Corporate espionage."

"Way to cook up rumors out of thin air!" I grunted.

One detail stood out in this ridiculous story, though: the power had been cut on part of the fifth floor. Did this mean no one had actually seen or recorded Thom jumping? Around us, more developers were starting to come in and sit at their desks. We greeted them and watched as they too read the memo and attempted to access Ruby's server in vain. Soon, the entire open space was filled with an increasingly anxious hubbub. Even our managers had no idea what was going on, and from the looks of it, none of us would be working anytime soon.

It was almost eight-fifteen, and the rumor had reached stage two—aka "We're all getting let go; I saw someone from HR in the hallway"—when I noticed Kelly Skepps, our HR director, near the open space entrance. She was accompanied by a thirtysomething woman in a black pantsuit with a long ponytail, and an older black guy wearing an equally black trench coat.

Kelly clapped her hands three times to gather everyone's attention. In all fairness, she didn't need to do that. Save for myself, the open space was exclusively populated by male engineers under forty, and Kelly stood on five-inch heels whose beige shade matched that of her tight-fitting pencil dress and sandy blonde bob. She already had the entire R&D department's undivided attention, as always.

"Good morning, everyone. I know that this is a very difficult time and we're all shaken by what happened last night. I really want to thank you guys for bearing with us while we sort the situation out and find someone to help EM Tech make even better R&D in the future! I'm here with Officers Murrell"—she flashed a tense smile to the man in the black trench coat—"and Di Stefano." A gesture in Ms. Ponytail's direction this time.

The two cops stood like wax figures, staring at us impassibly. Kelly went on, forcing a sad expression onto her doll face, because that's how you talk to developers: like to a bunch of kids watching *Dora the Explorer*, and—*Oh no!*—Boots killed himself! "Officers Murrell and Di Stefano need to ask you guys a few questions, because it's really important that we understand what happened and make sure every-body is safe here at EM Tech. Please keep in mind that this is a routine procedure; no one is being accused of anything!"

What happened, huh? She wouldn't even say Thom's name out loud. Like the cops had been called over someone spilling a can of juice on the carpet. I hated the way they seemed to have swiped Thom under the rug already, so everything would resume as usual.

Kelly took a breath and pulled out a white smartphone from the pocket of her dress. "So I'm gonna call your names in alphabetical order, and when I do so, I'll ask you to follow Detectives Murrell and Di Stefano. Each interview will take ten minutes tops, and when you're done, you can go home. Kerri has decided to grant you all a week of paid leave so you can get over this tragedy and take some well-deserved rest."

A collective murmur rose in the assembly. *Paid leave.* The magic words. I'm not gonna try to draw tears by pretending that EMT was some kind of dark, dingy mine where we'd work half-naked and be flogged daily. Still, an entire week of extra paid leave was, indeed, a con-siderable event, one that had me wondering just how badly our bosses were panicking, to shut down all operations for that long.

Kelly cleared her throat and called the first name in a loud voice. "Joshua Amberg."

We all watched as Joshua left the safety of his little group of Scala enthusiasts to walk bravely toward the officers. He waved at the cops with a smile, but they didn't react. It appeared they hadn't come here to fraternize with young engineers who wore their checked shirts over their jeans and coded with cutting-edge languages no one understood but them.

As soon as the three of them were out of sight, I turned to Joel and Vishal. "I think I'm going to take advantage of the fact that my name starts with a C and go to the ladies' room. I'll see you guys later."

Vishal's eyes started bulging out again, but I walked away before he could give the full measure of his talent.

———

I worked in the "small tower" (the Kit Kat), as opposed to the "big tower"—on Broadway, and also referred to as "the Castle." It basically went like this: EM Tech was stuck in a little brown building dating from the seventies while our mother ship, EM Group, a huge holding operating in a variety of sectors, got a sixty-story glass skyscraper, because there were only four hundred of us, and that amounted to less than 0.5 percent of EM's total workforce worldwide.

Things weren't that simple, though. EMT's meager staff might have been but a drop of water among EMG's eighty thousand employees, but it nonetheless brought in almost 11 percent of the group's net revenue, mostly through the sale of overpriced super-high-tech financial software like Ruby. The relegation of EMT to the ignominious Kit Kat was therefore perceived as an injustice—if not a direct provocation—and the five hundred yards EMT execs had to cover in order to attend Hadrian Ellingham's annual charity cocktail for the leper kids didn't help.

As part of the insidious war raging between the two buildings, my colleagues discussed all kinds of crazy rumors about the Castle, such as the fact that EMG employees were treated to truffle-and-Parmesan Pringles imported straight from Europe, or that the executive toilet was flushed with champagne. Which leads me back to . . . Prince, who dutifully elaborated and spread most of these rumors.

When the elevator doors opened to the lobby, he was still there, hunched behind the large desk—no doubt spying on some pretty girl from marketing through the surveillance cameras. He waved at me. "Hey, hey . . . Island!"

I crossed the hall and entered his territory. Hidden under an impeccable glass counter, his actual desk was a mess, as usual. A row of screens delimited his kingdom, all covered with Post-it notes about every single thing that went on in EMT's walls. A small stack of brand-new security badges waited near his keyboard—which he would need to distribute—and there was enough food stored everywhere around us to supply a small nation. Prince had passed the four-hundred-pound mark a couple of months ago, and he had yet to heed his grandma's encouragements to start a diet.

He patted the empty chair next to his with a tentative smile. "You feeling better?"

I watched two of my colleagues sip sodas near a vending machine on one of the surveillance screens. "Prince."

"Isles?"

"Did you see . . . I mean, do you guys have Thom jumping . . . on the security recordings?"

He cleared his throat. "No. Someone cut the power in the west wing. The security cameras were down when he . . . fell."

My scalp prickled. "*Fell?* Not jumped?"

Prince reached for a mini Reese's cup in an open bag. "Look, I heard some of the cops . . ."

I shook my head when he pushed the bag toward me. "What are they saying? Do they suspect someone murdered Thom?"

There was some more intense throat-clearing, and his brown eyes avoided mine. "I can't say anything. You know I'm bound by confidentiality."

Goddammit. "Prince, this is serious. Thom fricking *died* and no one will tell me anything!"

He shrank on his chair, looking left and right, as if the cops still guarding the lobby might hear us. "Officially, everybody is still calling it a suicide."

"But?"

"But I'm getting the feeling that there's more to it. You see that car, the black one?" He jerked his chin in the direction of the SUV stationed in front of the building. "The cops in that car, I can't figure what they are. They came with the NYPD, but no one knows which unit they're from. I heard cops saying that orders came from above and maybe they're Feds."

What the hell would Feds be doing on the scene of a suicide? Vishal's rant about some sort of breach of security regarding Ruby echoed in my mind. EMG and EMT had shut down the entire floor, frozen the Ruby project, all in the span of a few hours . . . and now Feds were investigating Thom's suicide?

"So even the NYPD is kept in the dark?" I asked.

"Totally. They keep bitching that they're being ordered around by the young one . . . Joe Jonas."

"Joe Jonas?"

He grabbed his Post-it block and checked it. "Liz Weng from accounting confirms their boss looks like Joe Jonas. It's verified intel."

"O-kay . . . What about Ruby? Have you heard anything about that? They've locked us out of the servers, and Lavalle said in her e-mail that the whole project might get canceled."

"I think that's what those Feds are here for. There's a rumor something happened in the clean room, some kind of data theft." He pointed at one of the screens displaying the entrance to the clean room. "I've seen them go in there twice already."

Data theft? So there could be some truth to Vishal's crap? I bit one of my nails, watching the closed doors on the screen. I'm not gonna pretend I inherited my mom's skills and was the new Mata Hari, but I did have a Spidey sense of my own, and said sense was on high alert at the moment. Someone had intentionally disconnected the fifth floor's surveillance cameras before Thom's death, at the same time that Ruby's server had possibly been accessed and compromised. I *needed* to get to the bottom of this.

"Prince."

"Isles?"

"If you get me inside the clean room, I'll tell you about Hadrian Ellingham's girlfriend."

FIVE

The Operation

"Rica knew she was risking her life . . . and her heart."

—Kerry-Lee Storm, *The Cost of Rica II: Ramirez Strikes Back*

"Oh my God!"

Prince's hands were trembling so badly he had to put the mini Reese's he had been reaching for back into the bag. *"Oh my fucking God!"* His voice broke. "You're shitting me!"

I plastered a stoic expression on my features. "I saw her getting out of his limo. Twice."

"But . . . *Jesus* . . . Nina Rivera broke up with him! I read all her interviews in *OK!*"

"It was someone else. A younger one."

Before me, EMT's most dedicated security officer was collapsing. An emotional, physical disintegration of his very self. Here, tantalizingly out of reach, brushing the tips of his fingers like the velvety wings of a butterfly, was the hottest, nastiest piece of gossip he had ever come across. But the price was high. Oh, so very high.

I was almost certain Prince would break, though. Hadrian Ellingham's short-lived romance with the statuesque Nina Rivera—Brazilian, former VS angel, five foot ten, 33–22.5–35, fake boobs—had turned this filthy-rich but otherwise ordinary stiff-lipped bourgeois into a complete Internet legend. Prince would never pass up the opportunity to learn more about Ellingham's rebound and perhaps anticipate the next buzz.

For those of you who've lived under a rock for the past decade, I'll recap the facts quickly: Long ago, in a galaxy far, far away, lived a prince charming with a cold heart, who was too busy running his empire and swimming in his billions of dollars to look for love. Also there was this persistent rumor that he was even colder in the bedroom than in public, and that sleeping with him was kind of like a Pap smear that would last an hour. One day, though, he met this beautiful model and fell madly in love. He gave *People* interviews; she gave *People* interviews; they cuddled in public; it was awesome. This man was Hadrian Ellingham.

But then Princess Nina got the lead role in a dark, gritty theatrical adaptation of *Snorks*, and she dumped Ellingham for her costar, a beefy MMA champion. Still, she needed to promote that movie, so she started sharing her impressions of her ex's sexual performances and peculiar approach to intercourse. Her publicist did so under the form of a "Bad Sex Sloth" meme, which went viral, got copyrighted, spurred all kinds of questionable merchandise . . . and basically turned our already stiff hero into some kind of embittered Gargamel-like figure. I'll let you be the judge:

I know, right?

So, like I said, the probability that Prince would want—crave—the slightest bit of intel related to Bad Sex Sloth's latest victim was . . . high, to say the least.

He kept swallowing and licking his lips, kneading his fleshy thighs with a white-knuckled grip. "How do I know you're not lying?"

"You don't. But I guess you'll see when he announces their engagement."

"En-engagement?"

"Yeah, she had this big ring." I mimicked a rock the size of an egg on my ring finger.

He buried his face in his hands. "Oh . . . *Jesus Christ!*"

I patted his back impatiently. "It's okay, Prince, now just tell me how to get inside the clean room."

It took him a little while to recover—that and quite a few mini peanut butter cups—but Prince eventually managed to focus. A formal agreement was made that I would provide every single bit of intel I had on the mystery fiancée if Prince managed to sneak me into the room hosting Ruby's servers. External risk factors were to bear no consequence on our deal. I swore to not only exonerate him, but also fulfill my end of the bargain, even if I went to jail.

"We got two problems to solve here," he began, lacing his fingers with a frown of intense concentration.

I gave a firm nod.

"First problem is that access to the stairs is restricted, and I don't have control over the elevator. They've reprogrammed it so no one can reach the fifth floor without a key. I think only a couple of execs and the cops were given one."

"Okay." So far, so bad.

"The second issue is that, even if I could get you up there, I can't get you inside the clean room itself. I still have access to the security cameras, but that's it, I can't unlock the doors. And"—he pointed to one of the screens—"the floor is basically empty right now, but there's a cop guarding the only access to the room."

"All the other doors have been locked already?"

"Yeah. Only rats and cops up there."

"Rats?"

Prince shrugged, a move that caused his wide chest to wobble a bit. "In the air vents sometimes."

In my mind, a terrible idea formed.

"How big are they?"

He brought his hands together, mimicking a small shape in the air. "Like this."

"No, I mean the vents."

He seemed to read my mind. "You're too fat—you'll never get in!"

"I thought those were designed so that maintenance technicians could crawl into them if necessary," I snapped back.

He blanched. "It's . . . it's different. They're all little people!"

I practiced my cold-killer stare on him, which I had learned from March. "Bullshit. How do I get into the air vents?"

"It's like, the worst idea—"

"How?"

Before my eyes, Prince crumpled for the second time of the day, sweat running down his cheeks and dampening the neck of his shirt. "You could . . . *Jesus* . . . We could cram you in the freight elevator—this one isn't monitored—then there's a vent in the north hallway, but—"

"Excellent," I announced, clasping my hands together.

He crossed himself and we huddled in front of the fifth floor's surveillance screen, hidden behind the lobby's desk like conspirators.

"I don't have it on-screen because cameras usually point at the doors, but the vent is here, somewhere to the right," he whispered when a cop walked past us, showing me a blank wall. "Here." He pointed to a set of low metal doors encased in the opposite wall. "You got the freight elevator. No cops around there. I'm the one who's supposed to watch over this part of the floor from here, so I'll be able to monitor your progress. You'll have to be quick. If anyone comes in, we're both screwed."

"Roger that."

"Once you're inside the vent, just crawl straight ahead. This one ends up directly in the clean room. Be careful when you open the grid. I think there's some kind of filter you have to remember to put back."

"No problem."

"You'll also need this—" He contorted to reach a drawer on his right and opened it, retrieving a red screwdriver. "The air vents have these special star-shaped screws so people won't just go and open them."

I took the precious tool and stared at the screen for a few seconds, the fingers of my left hand drumming on Prince's cluttered desk. This could cost me my job. But then again, *Thom* had given me that job in the first place. I needed to find out what had really happened to him.

"Okay. I can do this. Take me to the freight elevator."

He risked a peek at the cops in the lobby. They were chatting with one of the security guards. No one would notice Prince's absence if we were quick enough. He gave me a fearful nod and maneuvered his large body out of the desk. I followed him, and we both kept our shoulders hunched as we tiptoed to a service door a dozen feet away.

Prince led me down a narrow hallway whose concrete walls were painted a dull gray. Soon we were standing in front of a set of low brushed-steel doors similar to the ones I had seen on the security footage. The freight elevator was normally used as a fast means to deliver small equipment and packages such as computer screens, mail, or catering without moving your ass. Of course I had sometimes wondered what it'd be like to ride inside it. I mean, who wouldn't?

Near me, Prince whined as he used his key to unlock the elevator. "Oh God, this is such a shitty idea!"

He pressed a big green button on the concrete wall to call it. A few seconds later, the car stopped at our floor with a creaking sound. I won't lie—when the doors slid open with a faint chime, I did consider chickening out. God, it looked dark in there. And cramped. I took a deep breath and folded my body to climb in. Notwithstanding the fact that this looked like the premise for some terrible B-horror movie, I was, indeed, small enough to fit in.

I contorted a few times until I was sitting in a crouching position. Prince looked at me questioningly, his hand lingering on the elevator button while drops of sweat beaded on his forehead. I answered his worried gaze with a vigorous thumbs-up gesture; he pushed the button.

Funny how it was only when the doors closed that I truly got scared. I was suddenly engulfed in complete darkness, my only bearings the faint sounds of metal scraping against metal and the feeling of my stomach heaving a little as the car sped up. After a few seconds, I felt the elevator slow down. It stopped with that same faint bell sound, the doors sliding open to reveal a white and silent hallway.

The bright light bursting into the tiny space proved equal parts blessing and curse. It was marginally better than crouching in that pitch-black shoebox, but I was now terrified that the floor might not be empty after all, and someone might see me exit the car. In my jeans' back pocket, I felt my smartphone vibrate. I extracted it with great care, afraid that a single noise might betray me. It was a text from Prince.

Go, go, go!

Thank God, he could see me with the security cameras. My heart racing, I wiggled out of the car and fell onto the soft taupe carpet. No one in the hallway. I inspected the opposite wall. A man-sized vent was there, as promised. Game on.

Unlocking that damn grille proved a tedious challenge. At first, the star-shaped screws resisted the magic screwdriver Prince had given me. I struggled for a few seconds, blood drumming in my ears, faster and faster every time the blade slipped. When the screws loosened up at last, I let out a long sigh of relief; I was starting to get cramps in my forearms. I carefully placed the metal grille and the four screws at the tunnel's entrance with the intent of putting everything back in place when I was done. Now all I had to do was wiggle my way into the vent.

This, at least, was the easy part—there weren't even any rats. I silently crawled straight ahead in the dark tunnel, toward a faint light I assumed came from the clean room. Of course, there had to be a catch: it turned out the tunnel I was crawling into crossed a vertical one, forming a wide hole in the passageway. It was manageable, but the few seconds I spent contorting to pass that particular obstacle had my chest constricting in near-panic. Against my belly, I could feel the slight breeze coming from the vertical vent, blowing under my sweater and reminding me that I was perched precariously above a five-story-deep rabbit hole.

Once I was on the other side and only a few feet away from the clean room's grid, I registered male voices. *Dammit!* If there were still people working inside the room and so close to the air vent, I'd never be able to sneak in and reach Ruby's servers. I crept closer, my breath coming in short pants. I rolled to my side so I was able to see where the voices came from. Less than three yards from where I lay hidden, two men were sitting on the white floor, surrounded by laptops all connected to the same server rack. Ruby's.

The older of the two was a short, fiftysomething man with a neat suit and a shaven skull. I squinted to better see his face through the grid. Small rectangular glasses, potato nose. I knew this guy; I had seen him with Ellingham and Kerri Lavalle at a press conference a few months prior. The other guy was a young Asian with long hair, round glasses, and a cool Teenage Mutant Ninja Turtles T-shirt. His face looked sort of familiar, but I had no idea who he could be. I was pretty sure I'd never seen him inside EMT's walls before. Some nerd cop, perhaps?

I heard a door open somewhere in the clean room. Then the sound of footsteps approaching, closer and closer, until a pair of khakis entered my field of vision. I jumped and stifled a squeak of surprise when they brushed the vent's grille. Paralyzed by fear, I clasped a hand on my mouth to muffle the sound of my breathing. The pants shifted away, revealing brown boots partly covered by bright blue overshoes. Worn leather, no shine. I knew those pants and those boots.

The newcomer walked to the two men working on Ruby and knelt beside them. And when he did, it took everything I had not to scream. My chest constricted until I thought I'd suffocate, my ears were ringing, my heart seemed to be ramming against my ribs as if to tear through bones and muscles and escape.

Alex.

Alex was in the clean room.

Past the shock, there were a few seconds during which my brain went into overdrive trying to rationalize this. Alex worked in insurance. Maybe he didn't specialize only in expatriate contracts, and someone had stolen something in EMT's building. I had seen in movies that sometimes they might send an insurance expert to investigate, and maybe he had tried to tell me he was coming, but my phone hadn't rung and he had forgotten to call back because he was busy with insurance contracts . . . and stuff.

Or maybe . . . not. He was with those Feds. For some reason he worked with them.

A cold sweat dampened my back as he spoke. "So? What gives?"

That young Turtle fan greeted him with an apologetic look. "Not much. The only thing I'm sure of is that Roth is the one who launched the program. I can place him in the clean room during the time frame, and it's his security pass that was used to unlock the doors."

Wait . . .

"Besides him, Chaptal was the last one to connect to the server. She disconnected at 8:34. Whether she actually helped him prepare the attack, that part I'll leave to you."

Wait, wait, wait. *What attack?* And what was this guy implying about me and Thom?

Alex's expression darkened. Gone were the gentle, ever-amused brown eyes sparkling under thick and expressive eyebrows. Something tore in my chest, because it seemed I was seeing him, really seeing *him* for the first time.

"What about the attack itself? Did you find anything?" he asked Turtle-boy.

His colleague shrugged. "Nope. The app normally generates extensive backlogs in a NoSQL database that would contain every single bit of data sent and received, every method executed, when—"

Alex cut him off sharply. "In English, please."

His tone made me shudder a little. Turtle-boy, on the other hand, appeared used to it. "All tracks got erased right after Ruby was shut down. It's a complete disaster. All I can tell you is that Roth copied Ruby on a distant server around midnight, then the local version got launched at 2:41. From there, several terabytes of data got exchanged. Then it was shut down at 3:37, and someone wiped all logs, all remote backups, and physically destroyed all the disks where Ruby had been installed. Totally degaussed them—that requires some serious hardware," the young guy explained, pointing at several racks that seemed to have been disassembled.

Holy shit. What exactly were these three accusing Thom of? Stealing Ruby before destroying every single trace of the program in EMT's mainframe?

Alex turned his piercing gaze to Ellingham's subordinate. "Is EMG done assessing the losses?"

"Yes. Ninety-seven bank and trading accounts accessed. Six hundred—" The bald guy's voice faltered. "Six hundred and ninety-eight million, four hundred and seventy-three thousand, five hundred and ten dollars . . . and eighty-two cents missing."

I clenched my fists until my knuckles hurt. Ruby had been used. Unbridled. On actual bank accounts. And nearly seven hundred million bucks had been stolen. I couldn't believe this. It wasn't possible. Well, it *was*, but only if someone had bypassed all security systems to replace Ruby's simulation scenarios with real targets. None of this made sense, though. Why would Thom have done such a thing? He had never shown any sign of being greedy, and the Ruby project was his *fricking* chef d'œuvre!

I focused my attention back to the three men in the clean room, where a long sigh had just escaped Alex's lips. "And we have no idea where that money has gone?" he asked, his gaze traveling back to Turtle-boy.

"Nope. Ruby hammered the banks' systems, and once it got in, it performed thousands of micro transfers to some obscure offshore banks, and just as many dark pool transactions. By the time the banks' security systems started automatically blocking the accounts showing suspicious activity, the money had already been transferred so many times it was untraceable."

Alex raked a hand in his messy brown curls. "All accounts belonged exclusively to EMG?"

There was a brief pause, during which I heard the bald man breathe in and out several times, until he seemed to find the courage to speak again. "Yes. Ruby targeted very . . . specific accounts."

"What he means is that EM's saving several billion dollars each year through tax evasion schemes, and all the accounts targeted were located in tax havens," Turtle-boy supplied with a smirk.

"So they can't go public about those losses," Alex concluded.

Turtle-boy laughed. "That'd be in bad taste, to say the least. And then, of course . . ."

The bald man clasped a trembling hand around Alex's arm, who seemed unaffected by his interlocutor's tension. "Agent Morgan, I hope you understand that *no one* must know about what happened here. If the general public learns what Ruby proved capable of . . ."

Agent? FBI then? Provided their agents were allowed not to shine their shoes. But if so, did he know about me, March, and my family? Was it why he had lied to me about his job? But why go so far, then? I felt tears brimming at the corners of my eyes at the memory of his hands holding me, his lips caressing mine as he tried to reassure me last night. I swallowed them back.

After a few seconds spent listening to EMG's exec prophesying a financial Armageddon, Alex schooled his features back into that warm smile I knew so well. "I get it. Investor panic, wide-scale market losses, public hearings . . . the whole nine yards."

"Yes." The bald guy said in a gasp.

"All right. You two try to recover whatever you can. We still have employees to question. I'll see you later." With this Alex got up on his feet and seemed to be ready to leave.

The tension in my muscles eased a little, and that was when I noticed that something was tickling my hand.

I looked down.

A dark mass. Fur.

I promise I'm not kidding—that rat was bigger than a raccoon. I jumped back in panic and hit my head against the metal walls imprisoning me. The clanking sound seemed to echo indefinitely in the narrow tunnel, laced with my squeal of pain. I clasped my hands over my mouth in horror. The fifteen seconds that followed were something halfway between *It* and *Alien*. Blood pumped furiously in my ears, my chest hurt from the effort not to scream, and I could see Alex's legs approaching the vent slowly . . . while that twenty-pound—no, make that thirty-pound—rodent returned to nibble on the little leather ears of my mouse ballet flats.

Behind Alex, Turtle-boy had heard the noise too. "What is it?"

All I could hear was my own shallow panting, the beating of my heart, as I watched Alex crouch down to examine the air vent. I saw his face appear inches from mine, familiar yet terrifying, the only barrier between us that small grille.

A soft expression, belied by that intense cinnamon gaze. A tilt of his head. A smile.

"It's nothing. Just a rat," he announced before getting up with the ghost of a sigh.

My heartbeat settled as he walked away, and I jerked my leg to kick the beast away. It ran down the tunnel with a series of protesting squeaks. I curled up and massaged my temples for a few seconds, struggling to process what had just happened. Alex couldn't possibly have seen me. He worked with them; he'd have said something. Plus it was dark in here. He wouldn't have been able to make out anything through the grille, right?

But he had *smiled*. That gentle, enigmatic smile I now knew to conceal a great many layers. What would I do if he knew? He had just given me a temporary reprieve, but for how long?

No need to stay to see if he'd come back and check again. With excruciating care, I turned around and started a slow crawl back toward the light of the hallway, a distant white square whose edges appeared blurred—or maybe I couldn't see straight because all I could think of was that under my palms and knees, reality seemed to have collapsed. Thom had broken past Ruby's security systems and reprogrammed it to steal Ellingham's money. Alex was some kind of federal agent—or even worse, I realized, remembering what kind of countries he traveled in— and had been lying to me from the day we had met. My head was spinning. I stopped a meter or so from the air vent's exit, suddenly scared that perhaps someone might be waiting for me out there.

My breath little more than a faint whistle, I waited, every muscle paralyzed, eyes wide. I strained my ears to pick up the slightest whisper that might indicate that someone stood in that damn hallway. Nothing came but the low hum of the air-conditioning system and the occasional buzz of fluorescent lights on the ceiling. I inched forward. A sticky sweat caked the vent's grayish dirt on my palm. I couldn't even find the strength to swallow. And all that tension made me want to pee. Badly.

I squirmed as silently as possible in an effort to get some sort of vantage point of view to the hallway. When I was 100 percent certain no one was waiting out there to pounce on me, I darted my nose out, breathing in fresh air and thinking of *Fantastic Mr. Fox*'s tale. You know, that part where not only do the farmers manage to get Mr. Fox out of his burrow, but they shower him with bullets, shoot his tail off, and destroy everything with bulldozers. That stuff traumatized me when I was seven.

It took me almost a minute to dare climb out of the vent, and by the time I stood alone on the taupe carpet again, the mad beat in my rib cage progressively slowed down. Best cardio of my life. Putting the vent's grille back in place was a torturous process, since I had to deal with a bad case of clammy, trembling fingers. Dammit, those little screws kept slipping out of my hands! Once I was done, I drew out a calming breath and looked up at the security camera.

I hadn't received any texts for a while, but Prince was probably still watching. Behind me, the freight elevator's steel doors opened with a muted metallic sound. I folded myself back in and balled my fists as darkness engulfed me.

I can't even begin to describe how relieved I was to see Prince's pudgy fingers reach out for me when the elevator doors opened again. That second ride had made me nauseated; I struggled out of my shoe box with almost frantic movements.

At first I didn't realize something was wrong. Then I registered how short Prince's breath sounded, as if he had been the one trapped in there. He hadn't said a word since helping me out of that car. I saw him shake his head. I blinked and looked around.

Next to us, patiently leaning against the wall with his arms crossed, stood Alex.

A jolt of electricity that I recognized as panic contracted my muscles. My legs flexed of their own volition in a familiar feeling: the need to run. I was trapped between four walls and couldn't reach the exit door without making it past him, though. And Prince . . . *Nah*. Behind me, he remained frozen by fear. He had been caught red-handed by "Joe Jonas" and looked like he could barely stand as it was.

I couldn't read Alex's expression as he moved to take a few steps toward me. This shuttered, impassive face was foreign to me. He didn't look mad, but there was no trace of compassion either.

"Miss Chaptal . . ."

I gulped.

"We need to talk."

SIX

The Puffer Fish

"'I wish I could clean my heart of you, Asher! I wish I could scrub it with this sponge,' Peyton sobbed."

—Izzie Shepherd, *The Cardiologist's Christmas Surprise*

When I was twenty-two, I tried to go to a frat party because I was stalking this cute guy from Joy's family law class. I padded my bra with the firm intent to seduce him, but that didn't work because the tissues I had crammed in there fell into the punch bowl when I bent down to fill my glass. Right in front of the guy.

On an awkwardness scale of one to ten, I rated that particular event a solid eleven.

Now, on a similar scale, I'd rate it around a forty-six for me to be arrested by my boyfriend and end up sitting across from him, ready to be questioned. Alex had dragged me into a small, nearly empty office used to store stacks of undistributed copies of *EMG Magazine*. Hadrian Ellingham and Kerri Lavalle's photoshopped faces smiled at us, while Agent Morgan's fingers rapped against the brown melamine of the desk between us.

I didn't say anything at first, and he remained silent as well, observing me with predatory patience. I found it difficult to collect my thoughts, sort them out, and decide what aspect of this debacle needed to be discussed first. I studied his features, the hawkish eyes and tightly sealed lips. In control. Unreadable. He was the one who eventually broke the silence, faint rustling sounds echoing in the room as he reached inside his brown leather jacket. I looked down at the wallet he had opened and laid on the table for me to see. A blue ID card bearing a round seal and eagle hologram.

It's a possibility that my adventures with March and everything I'd learned about my mother's past had made my skin a little thicker, or maybe it was just that I had been readying myself for this since the moment I had realized that a regular federal agent would have likely had no business in Cambodia.

I massaged my temples. "CIA, huh?"

He nodded.

A memory flashed in my mind. I was in Paris, alone with March's ex. We were in her bedroom, resting and confiding in each other—yeah, she had been the nice ex type. A rare species, according to Joy.

"Since he started his . . . business, March has often accepted wet jobs from the CIA. It's an easy way to stay on the US government's good side. He gets things done for them, and in exchange they'll overlook the rest of his activities as long as he chooses his clients wisely. Of course, they never trusted him much, so a few years ago this guy called Erwin came up with the idea to try to put one of his agents in March's bed. That sounded like the best way to keep a close eye on him."

Spoiler alert: that particular plan hadn't ended well. The aforementioned agent, a woman named Charlotte Covington, got captured and burned alive during a mission in Ivory Coast. March struck a deal with Erwin to come to her rescue, but he made it there too late. There was nothing left to do. He killed Charlotte to end her suffering, and it took him three years to sleep well again in the wake of that intense trauma.

My hands gripped the edge of the desk so hard I feared my fingers might snap, and in the storm roaring inside my skull, something struggled to surface, bubbling with anger. Now I knew where to start. "You'd have—" I swallowed, forcing the word out of my throat. "You'd have *fucked* me."

I knew we had somewhat more urgent issues to address, but this realization overwhelmed me, made me physically ill. If I had let him, he'd have used my body the same way Charlotte had used March's. He'd have taken my virginity, that tiny chunk of myself that meant so much. All because it was his job. My skin itched; I felt violated by what had nearly happened just a dozen hours ago.

"Island, this is not the best time—"

"*Not the time?* Really? You *touched* me!" I yelled, wishing I could now scrub my skin clean until it was raw. I was so throwing those panties away. Hell, the dress was going in the bin as well.

Alex jumped out of his chair as if he had been stung, and his fists banged on the desk. "Island, your boss is dead. He let loose a goddamn cyber disaster. Seven hundred million dollars is missing from EMG's accounts, you're the last person who saw him alive, and I just found you in a fucking air vent, spying on a classified investigation!"

When he sat back, I remembered how to breathe. "Thank you for the recap. So you're gonna make it all fall back on my shoulders? What really happened to Thom?" My nails scraped the melamine repeatedly, the only outlet for my anger at the moment. "I heard . . . rumors . . . that you have no actual recording of Thom jumping, that someone cut the power in the fifth floor's west wing right before—"

His tone was direct, clinical: "Thom was dead before he touched the ground."

I took the blow with a clenched jaw. "How?"

"The coroner found traces of TTX in his blood. It paralyzed his diaphragm. Cause of death is asphyxia. We have evidence of two men entering the building via a maintenance tunnel around two thirty.

Accomplices, likely. They killed him sometime after he was done wiring the money and destroying the servers."

TTX. Tetrodotoxin. Paralysis; loss of sensation. A painless yet horrifying death. As a kid, puffer fish had been among my favorite animals until an old encyclopedia taught me that they were—quite literally—full of that shit. I struggled to focus back on Alex. My voice sounded muted, distant to my own ears. "Will it be made public? Will you tell his wife?"

His lips curved; his gaze softened. Not really a smile—a silent apology. "You know we can't. Death has been ruled a suicide."

"I see. And I suppose it's a complete coincidence that you're the one investigating all this. I mean, you must be bored already. Greenwich Street doesn't sound nearly as exotic as your usual destinations," I said bitterly.

Lines appeared on Alex's brow that I wasn't sure I had ever noticed before. He seemed equally tired and conflicted, and when he spoke again there was an edge to his voice. "Don't play with me. I know you're smarter than that. The CIA is involved because US interests are threatened, and *I* am involved because *you* are threatened. My boss gave me the job because he knew I could never stand watching someone else—"

"Treat me like this? Locking me in a room for interrogation?"

"Yes," he admitted.

I looked away. "You're lying. All you've done is lie from the start, anyway."

"As you lied to me," Alex gritted out. "If I recall, you told me your mother had been a French diplomat. I must have missed the part where you mentioned her job as a spy."

I wondered, as he said this, if he knew about the Cullinan affair as well, or even . . . Dries.

He was the other surprise package my mom had left for me to discover after her death. You see, she never delivered the diamond after she stole it, and was murdered before she could reveal where she had hidden it. What the Board would learn only a decade later was that she had double-crossed them with her lover, and incidentally my biological father, a supervillain hell-bent on world domination and known as Dries. No wonder my mom had chosen the nice American banker she had shared a brief fling with to raise me, instead.

Here is where things get even trickier: she was supposed to give Dries the Cullinan, but for some reason she decided against it and vanished off the grid in Tokyo with me. Dries, however, belonged to a little club called the Lions, a secret fraternity of deadly and incredibly arrogant South African assassins who seemed to believe that the rest of us were maggots and the world was theirs for the taking. Said fraternity often took care of the Board's dirty jobs: they got summoned to catch my mother and recover the diamond. Very convenient, as you can imagine.

Except that on the day Dries was supposed to kidnap us, one of his men went rogue and shot my mom while she was driving, without any valid explanation, save for some bullshit about a faulty aim. I should have died too, but Dries's favorite disciple, a young assassin he brought everywhere with him, turned his back on his "brothers" to save my life.

That young man was March.

I was fifteen, he was twenty-two, and unbeknownst to us both, he had set in motion a chain of events that would change our lives forever, like they say in movies.

March left the Lions after that, and went on to fly solo, "cleaning" people on his own terms and becoming some kind of legendary criminal wildlife regulator, mostly for the Board, but sometimes also for the US government itself. I didn't even remember him, until one fine night in October, he came knocking at my door—well, breaking in, really—for that goddamn rock . . .

I figured I'd better not ask Alex if he knew any of this, and risk getting myself in even more trouble than I was already in.

"What did you want me to tell you? I don't even know that much about her. Don't try to deflect this shit on me, Alex. I omitted a part of my life I felt it was too soon to tell you about; you *made up* an entire fricking life!" I snapped, getting up from my chair.

He imitated me and walked around the desk. I stepped back until my shoulders hit the room's locked door. "Don't come near me. If I'm getting arrested anyway, I want to be handled by someone else. I won't say anything to you."

God, I was trying to sound cool, but each intake of air betrayed my increasing panic. Alex's brow lowered in a mask of barely controlled anger as he marched toward me. Without thinking, I raised my hands to shield myself as he lunged forward. His hands slammed hard on each side of my head against the door, trapping me. A faint whiff of his good-guy cologne floated in the air between us.

I stood paralyzed. This man was a stranger who looked like Alex.

"Island, I didn't have the *right* to tell you!" he hissed. His eyes searched mine for a couple of seconds, and he drew a long breath through his nose. It dawned on me that the intensity I had mistaken for anger sounded in fact more like desperation. "No one knows about my job, not even Poppy. After we chatted and I offered to take you out, they screened you. It's mandatory; we're discouraged from engaging in relationships outside of the Agency."

His gaze had softened, and in spite of myself, my own animosity started to ebb; I knew what was coming.

"The screening raised a number of red flags . . ."

I went limp against the wall, overcome by a sense of mental exhaustion. "How do I know you're not lying? That you weren't just trying to bed me so you could better spy on me?"

To my astonishment, this time his features relaxed, revealing the gentle expression I was accustomed to. His right hand left the door to caress my hair. I fought a shiver. "Look, I know this is gonna come out wrong, but—" He seemed to fight a smile. "Your file wasn't big enough to warrant a seduction mission."

I pursed my lips, unable to find the right answer to this. Should I voice some degree of irritation at his clumsy statement? At the fact that in spite of my family tree, I was nothing but an ordinary girl he had picked up on Yaycupid? Or should I just be relieved that this wasn't the storyline of *Fatal and Sensual Ukrainian Nights* after all?

Still, I could spot a couple of loose ends in Alex's version of events. "Why did you date me anyway, after the CIA screened me and said I was bad news?"

He shifted closer, his eyes shining with warmth, a tender certainty I didn't dare to name. "Because you were intriguing, and I liked you. I thought that whatever you were hiding, I could deal with. The more I got to know you, the more I wanted to protect you."

I averted my gaze. I couldn't withstand the look in his eyes, those softly spoken words caressing me the same way his hands were. Alex was telling me exactly what I wanted—needed—to hear, and I was scared by the contradictory emotions fluttering in my chest. In that moment, I just wished I could have turned into a bubble and burst in his arms, free of all tension.

"I'm not sure I believe you," I finally said.

At this, he bent down with slow, controlled movements—likely because he knew he had scared me and I was still shaken—and pressed a delicate kiss to my forehead. His lips moved to graze my ear, his voice down to a suave whisper. "And yet here I am. There are two agents waiting for you on the other side of that door, and I'm with you, baby."

No, I corrected him inwardly.

Agent Morgan was with me.

SEVEN

The Caterpillar

"'How cheerfully he seems to grin,

How neatly spread his claws,

And welcome little fishes in

With gently smiling jaws!'"

—Lewis Caroll, *Alice's Adventures in Wonderland*

Alex had been right. When he opened the door, Classy-Trench-Coat Murrell and Mrs. Ponytail Di Stefano were waiting for us in the lobby with blank faces. Prince was no longer sitting at his desk, and I prayed he hadn't been fired—or worse.

I looked up at Alex anxiously; he placed a hand on my shoulder in response. "Island, there's someone who wants to see you. It won't take long. Do you mind coming with us?"

Like I had a choice . . .

"Yes. Can I just take my bag—"

"It's already been taken care of," Di Stefano announced. She and

Murrell took the lead, while Alex followed, sandwiching me on our way to a nearby elevator.

We all stepped in, and Di Stefano pressed the Basement 2 button. I peeked up at Alex. "Where are we going?"

"I can't tell you that, but don't worry, everything will be all right." He patted my shoulder, and his hand lingered on my shoulder blades until it traveled down to my waist, squeezing it. That's when I realized that my knees had turned to jelly and he was in fact supporting me.

His hold loosened when the elevator stopped, doors sliding open onto a small lobby that led to the garage itself. Again, Murrell—whom I now realized smelled faintly of tobacco—and Di Stefano stepped out first before letting me out with Alex close behind, assuming their sandwich formation all the way to one of the black SUVs I had seen in the morning, parked next to an equally black minivan.

We weren't alone in the garage. Turtle-boy stood near the vehicles, next to a fortysomething blond guy who appeared to be helping him load equipment in the trunk. Gray suit, black coat—there seemed to be some sort of dress code going on around there, but Alex, with his wrinkled clothes, worn leather jacket, and unpolished boots, hadn't gotten the memo.

I'm not sure what came over me, but upon seeing Turtle-boy again, bits of the conversation I had witnessed in the clean room flashed in my mind, and I was swept by the irrepressible urge for a nerd in distress to reach out to another nerd.

"I think the logs that got destroyed were the recent ones. Our old servers looked still intact," I squeaked, avoiding Alex's curious stare.

I saw the older blond guy's hand move to his pocket. I gulped.

Turtle-boy took a step back from the trunk. "So, we could recover older simulations? See how the operation got planned?"

"I think so. We used to store command and simulation logs on other servers during development, but we switched to those Opterons two weeks ago."

This was one of the many times I wished I could have shrunk like Antman and disappeared. They were all staring at me, and at least one of them was ready to shoot me. No, make that two, I thought, noticing how Di Stefano was reaching for something behind her back.

I felt a touch on my shoulder. Alex's. "I find it hard to believe that Thom could have missed such a crucial detail."

I batted his hand away and spun on my heels. "You don't know that he did anything! Maybe it's proof he's innocent. Whoever did this apparently had no idea the servers were new ones!"

His composure faltered, but not in the way you'd expect. That shadow passing over his features wasn't so much surprise, or even anger, as a spark of excitement. He pinned me in place with a hard gaze, until his head jerked in Murrell's direction. "She'll ride with me."

Murrell answered with a nod and climbed into the SUV while Di Stefano took the wheel.

Turtle-boy and that blonde agent left in their turn, and I found myself alone with the "new" Alex . . . whose dominant behavior and sometimes cutting tone reminded me a lot of March's bad side. Don't even get me started on his *very* bad side; let's just say that few people lived to tell about it. Still, riding with Alex sounded marginally better than being smuggled in a CIA van with a bunch of armed men in black.

"Let's go," he said, pulling out a key from his pocket and pressing it. A beeping sound echoed in the garage, and a gray Corvette's lights flashed twice.

I sauntered closer to examine it. "It's not really your car, *right*?"

He unlocked the passenger door for me. "Why?"

"It's just—" My eyes scanned the silvery paint, the two large red stripes in the middle of the hood, and the twenty-one-inch wheels. "It looks like something straight out of *Fast & Furious*. I mean, this is ridiculous—there's even a spoiler!"

I settled in the black-and-red bucket seat. I could practically feel hair growing on my chest as I buckled up.

Alex flashed me a smug smile. "So? Is it that bad? Girls usually like it."

I bristled at the implication of his words. *Girls.* The *other* girls. The ones he had shown his true self to. How many, anyway? Under my butt, I could feel the engine roaring. I stiffened. "Well, I guess I had gotten used to those dad cars you always showed up with. Shouldn't the CIA give you something less flamboyant, though? Like a regular sedan or whatever?"

"That's exactly why I didn't choose the FBI," he said, shaking his head.

In front of us, traffic was already pretty dense, but still manageable. Alex slipped between two cabs with practiced ease, moving fast down Broadway and toward Battery Tunnel.

I fidgeted in my seat and peered at his profile while he drove. The peaceful expression I knew was back, as if being content were some sort of default mode for him. I found some modicum of comfort in the thought that this, at least, had been real. "Are you seriously going to pretend this is a standard vehicle for CIA agents?"

"It's not. Let's call it a well-negotiated bonus."

"I bet you took all the options because you weren't paying," I huffed, secretly reveling in the feel of the seat's black suede under my fingertips.

"You have no idea . . ."

My throat went dry. "Are we talking underbody lights here?"

"Among other things."

Sweet Raptor Jesus . . . This was like *GTA!* I fought the urge to squish my nose against the window, hoping to verify his claim. I think my mind went a little into overdrive at that point, perhaps because of the stress. As we plunged—terrible choice of word—into the tunnel and got enveloped in its golden-orange hue, I thought of how it had been flooded by ninety million gallons of water during Sandy—almost a billion soda cans, people!—and then I wondered how often Murrell smoked, and if he had ever set someone on fire with his lighter like James Bond does to Sanchez at the end of *License to Kill*.

"So, what were you doing in that vent?"

My chest heaved, as if he had pulled the brake, sending the disjointed thoughts in my head to collide and shatter like glass. Alex—or rather Agent Morgan—was one sneaky asswipe. I folded my hands on my lap and looked in my mirror. Di Stefano and Murrell were following us closely. "I-I have the right to remain silent. Also I want to speak to a lawyer."

"You're not under arrest, Island," he said, as we came out of the tunnel.

"Are you kidding me? You—" I paused upon realizing that the car had taken several turns in Red Hook and we were now somewhere on Brooklyn's docks, surrounded by brick warehouses and a long, dilapidated concrete building that looked like an old factory. My pulse quickened. "Oh my God, this is starting to look like a bad kidnapping scenario. Am I getting cement shoes or something? Do you guys have the right to do this?"

Alex chuckled. "Relax, baby. We just wanted a little privacy."

I gritted my teeth. It couldn't be that bad. After all, less than twelve hours ago, Alex had still been the perfect boyfriend, and back in the storage room he had heavily implied he intended to remain so. Plus EMT had allowed him and his colleagues to question employees, and they seemed to be working hand in hand with our top management. Surely they wouldn't waive procedures and waterboard me in an empty warehouse, even if they were CIA, *right*?

In any case, I'd know soon; the Corvette had stopped in a deserted parking lot. With each frantic thump of my heart I thought of my mother. What would she have done in a situation like this? Perhaps flashed Alex a friendly smile of her own and asked him if he got off playing with people's nerves in clichéd film noir settings?

I shrank in my seat as I heard the Corvette's doors unlock with a faint click.

"Baby, no one is going to hurt you."

Shudders coursed through my body when he took my hand and stroked my palm with his thumb, the tender gesture at odds with the warning I could read in his eyes. Outside, Murrell had gotten out of his own vehicle and came to open my door. Once I was out, he stepped back, allowing Alex to escort me instead. I tensed at the feeling of his right hand brushing my waist, alertness and relief playing a constant game of tug-of-war within me whenever he got too close.

The air was warm, the ground still humid from a light spring drizzle, and the scent of ocean and diesel floated in the air. I scanned the run-down buildings surrounding us and spotted a third car at the other end of the parking lot—some sort of long sedan. Alex guided me across the lot and toward it, his hand never leaving the small of my back—whether to comfort me or just to prevent my escape, I still wasn't sure. Once we were close enough, it became clear that whoever awaited us did so in a Cadillac limo. Pissing all over my rights and buying luxury cars. With my tax dollars. Nice, government, nice. Alex opened the rear door and ushered me inside.

As soon as we were seated on the black leather seat, I heard the doors lock, and my nostrils were assaulted by the strong smell of cigar smoke. Reclining in the opposite seat was a gray-haired guy smoking a cigarillo. At first he reminded me of the senior execs I'd sometimes encounter within EMT's walls: lean build, well-cut dark suit, douchey poker face, like he was bored already. My gaze lingered on the deep creases around his mouth. That was the moment he chose to blow a fricking smoke ring, and my mind was made up: I was sitting face-to-face with *Alice in Wonderland*'s Caterpillar. Call me insane, but picturing the guy sitting on a giant mushroom helped me get my nerves back under control.

Near me, Alex seemed just as relaxed, acknowledging our host with a slight duck of his head.

The cigarillo finally left the Caterpillar's lips. He spoke in a low baritone voice. "Miss Chaptal, I understand you are the last person who saw Thomas Roth alive."

Wow. Near-kidnapping, no greeting, no introductions? My jaw clenched, and as a second ring of smoke dissolved in the air, I felt the remnants of my fear give way to a growing irritation. "*Good evening* to you too, *sir*."

I heard Alex stifle a laugh.

The Caterpillar's nostrils flared. He spoke again, this time enunciating each word slowly. "When did you last access Ruby?"

Okay, maybe I did chicken out, after all. "My last connection was yesterday night. I logged out around eight thirty. I did not attempt to access any of EMT's servers until this morning, except for my e-mails; my phone makes automated connections to the mail server every minute."

He smirked. "The face of innocence. And yet I understand that you went to speak to Mr. Roth immediately after you disconnected. Any thoughts on this?"

"I was the last one in the open space. I did see Thom before leaving, but it was nothing pressing—I just wanted to chat. He was working on Ruby, and he was worried that we wouldn't be ready for our demo." I swallowed. "He seemed tense, and he told me to go home. But I had no idea—"

One of his shoulders jerked in the faintest shrug. "Why did Agent Morgan find you spying on our personnel in an air vent?"

Okay, from where these guys stood, things looked bad, but did everybody have to make such a big deal of a tiny little . . . felony? I cleared my throat several times, looking for the best words to plead my case. "I didn't do anything wrong. Well, I *did*, but I was upset by Thom's death and also the way EMT was shutting down the entire Ruby program. And then I heard those rumors about someone cutting the power on the fifth floor at the time of Thom's death, and how they didn't have actual footage of him jumping . . . I just couldn't believe it was a suicide. I wanted to learn more."

"That you did. Classified information, mostly, I'm afraid."

My fingers twisted in my lap. "I didn't really hear anything. There was this huge rat in the vent, and I—"

The Caterpillar dismissed my bullshit with a flick of his hand. "I'll leave it to your boyfriend to hear this fascinating tale." He flashed a pointed look at Alex. "I have other concerns. Tell me, Miss Chaptal." He paused to take a long drag and blow a cloud of smoke through his nose. "When was the last time you left US soil?"

Blood drained from my face, leaving an icy sensation underneath my skin. Did he know about March? Alex hadn't seemed to be aware of his existence; all he had mentioned was my mother's file. "I . . . Uh . . . My father took me to London in January. We spent a week there, together with his wife."

Yep, that trip to the UK three months ago was the last time I had *legally* left the country. My skin prickled at the memory of the fake passport March had purchased from his mobster friend Paulie to smuggle me out of the US during our hunt for the Cullinan.

The Caterpillar appraised me with narrowed eyes for a good thirty seconds. I stole a glance at Alex. He was looking at me too, those soft cinnamon irises shining with something I couldn't quite place, like a blend of tender amusement and pity. Inside me, something broke. He knew. He had known all along.

The faint whisper of smoke being exhaled drew my attention back to the Caterpillar, who spoke in a suave voice. "Miss Chaptal, you're being offered a parachute. I can only recommend you use it, as the opportunity might not present itself twice. If anything out of the ordinary happened in the past months, now is the best time to talk."

My breathing grew uneven, soon coming in shallow intakes of air. This choice of words sounded a lot like an explicit threat to throw me off a plane. I looked down, almost hypnotized by the ghastly pallor of my hands against the dark blue of my jeans. The choice itself boiled down to a simple alternative: telling the truth to save my ass, and betraying March . . . or lying for him, and facing the consequences. The only question was: How hard would I crash without my stars-and-stripes parachute?

In retrospect, I wonder if I even chose. "I don't understand what you mean. Are we still talking about what happened with Ruby?" I asked, swallowing a tremor in my voice.

The Caterpillar straightened in his seat and reached for what looked like a black leather folder lying next to him on the seat. Alex shifted as well, inching closer to me. I clasped my hands so they wouldn't tremble. I watched as the Caterpillar opened the folder to reveal a tablet. His fingers danced on the sleek glass surface for a couple of seconds before he handed me the object.

I took it gingerly, and as soon as I registered what, or rather *who* was now pictured on the screen, I felt my stomach heave. Fine, angular features, forty at best, but with graying wavy hair. It looked like some kind of mug shot, and he seemed younger than when I had met him for the first time. The long scar on his left cheek, which had been inflicted by March in Colombia, seemed to be missing as well.

Creepy-hat.

Well, Rislow, to be precise—I never knew his first name. Sent by the Board to kidnap and torture me until I gave them the Ghost Cullinan, he had double-crossed them and teamed up with Dries instead. Bad idea. March put an end to a long-lasting feud between them by severing his spinal cord with a scalpel as swift retribution for having attempted to dissect me alive on an operating table. Creepy-hat's life as a quadriplegic was a short one; Dries showed up later that night, equally displeased by the table thing, and shot him in the head. I know, it made me cry a little too; even supervillains can be dads, after all.

At the moment, however, there was no time to reminisce. Alex and the Caterpillar quite obviously knew Creepy-hat, and they knew that

I knew him too, and that I knew that they knew . . . You get the idea. Things didn't look good.

"Island, have you ever seen this man?"

I looked up to find myself sucked into Alex's tranquil gaze. I shook my head negatively, holding the tablet with a white-knuckled grip.

He sighed and extended a hand to swipe across the screen. When the second picture appeared, I'm pretty sure I gasped, even though I tried to stifle it. Every single hair on my body stood on end as I stared at the SUV Rislow's men had used to kidnap me. The pic appeared to be a still from some sort of traffic camera. The car could be seen driving along a river—likely the Hudson—and there was a timestamp in the top right corner. Sat. 2014/10/27 14:27:21. I had been sitting gagged and handcuffed in the backseat at the time.

Trust the CIA to come up with an early and unique birthday present: footage of your own kidnapping. I averted my eyes and pushed the tablet back into Alex's hands. "I've never seen that car. Sorry."

The Caterpillar brought the cigarillo to his lips again. He blew another smoke ring. I gazed at it until it had completely dissolved, half mesmerized by the rich, roasted aroma floating in the air, half desperate for something to focus on, to carry me through this hellish interrogation game. The feeling of warm fingers wrapping loosely around my left hand jerked me back to reality.

Alex was touching me. I looked down where his hand now held my arm, his thumb brushing the underside of my wrist, sending shivers up my arm. "Island, you shouldn't say things you're not confident you could repeat during a lie detection test."

I didn't understand immediately. I mean, I understood his words, but I didn't connect them with the careful pressure on my wrist or the sympathetic stir of his lips when my eyes darted to his face. Under his thumb, I felt my pulse flutter.

He was the lie detector. That bastard was checking my fricking pulse!

I snatched back my hand as if I had been burned, burying it into one of my pockets with a glare.

"I've said all I have to say!" I snapped. I also tried to pump my chest, but I don't think anything actually happened because I have no muscles there.

The Caterpillar crossed his legs and stubbed out his cigarillo in the car door's ashtray. "Listen to me, Miss Chaptal. I have yet to decide whether you're a talented actress or just some exceptionally unlucky airhead who's always in the wrong place at the wrong time—but I'll find out soon enough."

I opened my mouth to lash back at him, but he cut me off before any sound could come out, going on in an increasingly cold tone. "We'll see each other again. Until then, you will assist Agent Morgan in his mission to recover EM Group's money."

"I'm sorry . . . I *what?*"

"I understand that your contribution was crucial to the Ruby project and that you knew Mr. Roth well. I can't see anyone more qualified to help us, especially since you might be his accomplice," he concluded with the faintest smirk.

"*Hey!* How can you—"

"Island." Alex's voice was still soft, but I didn't miss the warning undertone. I wasn't allowed to say out loud that his boss was full of himself and, as a direct result, full of shit.

"I'll take you back to EMT. We have a lot of work to do," he said.

Already ignoring us, the Caterpillar reached inside his jacket for a silvery cigarette case, by way of dismissal. A muted clicking sound indicated that the doors had been unlocked; Alex opened his and helped me out. He was about to close the door when the Caterpillar's deep voice echoed one last time from inside the car.

"Island. Choose your friends carefully. I'd be sorry to see you end up like Léa."

In spite of everything that had happened—his lies, the broken bond between us—I was grateful for Alex's presence and his gentle grip on my arm. Under my feet, it seemed the ground had collapsed, and there was this pressure in my chest, like I was free-falling.

The Caterpillar had known my mother.

Alex slammed the door shut, and the Cadillac's engine started. I watched it drive away across the parking lot and past the SUV inside which Murrell and Di Stefano still waited. Alex waved in their direction and walked me back to the Corvette, hand still hovering behind my back, occasionally brushing my shoulder blades. We climbed in as the SUV left in the same direction the Caterpillar's limo had.

As we drove away from the docks, I mulled over the events of the morning. Part of me was dying to ask Alex what he knew about the Cullinan affair and March, but that would basically be admitting I had lied to his boss back in the limo. Not only that, but I was pretty certain Alex would lie to me again. There was a bitter taste in my mouth as I came to terms with the fact that he was more skilled than I was at the spy game . . . and couldn't be trusted. Ever again.

I rubbed my eyes. The aftereffects of the constant stress I had been subjected to since dawn were creeping in. I felt exhausted, a little sluggish, and my temples were starting to throb unpleasantly.

I looked through the window and focused on the cars gliding past ours in Battery Tunnel, unwilling to meet Alex's eyes as I finally spoke. "So . . . I gather that Poppy exists, but what about the rest? Was it all lies? Like, do you even live in Silver Spring?"

There was a beat of hesitation, a low sigh, and to my amazement, he answered. "No, I live in Washington."

I shifted in my seat to look at him. "Does that house you told me about exist? With the garden, the lilacs, and the dog?"

"Yes, it was my parents' house, but there was no dog. Poppy and I live in an apartment."

I pondered this. Alex's parents had been killed in a plane crash in Egypt six years prior. He wouldn't say much about it, but, unable to resist my curiosity, I had spent hours combing the net for some details—I wondered if he knew about that too . . . At any rate, some pieces of the puzzle were starting to click together. I could see how the event had branded him so deeply that he'd made the choices he had, and unconsciously weaved the happy family portrait of his childhood into the web of his lies.

I let out a weary sigh. "Now, at least, I understand why you didn't want me to come to your place. What would you have done if I had insisted?"

He ducked his chin, lips curling in a sheepish smile. "I guess I'd have invited you—I actually wanted to. I figured I'd tell you we had moved and the dog had been run over."

"Okay, so the real Alexander Morgan likes sports cars, doesn't live in a suburban house with a white porch, doesn't have a dog . . . Anything else major? An actual girlfriend waiting in Washington, maybe?" I had meant to say this casually, but as the words escaped my lips, I cursed myself for their cutting edge.

I saw the muscles twitching in his jaw, and the Corvette sped up, passing several cars. "*You* are my girlfriend, Island."

I closed my eyes as EMT's building came in sight. Was I?

EIGHT

The Chicken

"'Clara, without you, I'm like a chicken: I have wings, but I can't fly.'"

—Emmy Lee Jolly, *The Pioneer's Last Chance at Love*

When we stepped into the garage elevator and I saw Alex use a key and press the button for the fifth floor, I got this strange feeling, as if just being allowed up there the regular way was even worse a transgression than my little stunt in the air vent. Then I remembered Prince. "Can we stop at the lobby? There's someone I'd like to see."

He seemed to ignore my request, allowing the elevator past the first floor without stopping. "Prince Grimaldo?"

My throat went dry. "Look, the air vent thing was my idea. He's not gonna get in trouble, right?"

"We have no interest in him at the moment."

I welcomed the news with a sigh of relief. The elevator stopped, steel doors sliding open on the fifth floor's pristine hallway. As we walked toward a set of doors guarded by a policeman, a young engineer came out, escorted by a second policeman. They walked past us and toward the floor's open space, from which Thom was supposed to have jumped.

The guy's shoulders were hunched, and one of his hands kept smoothing wrinkles from the front of his shirt. Having to work under the constant scrutiny of a cop—I could relate to that kind of tension.

The cop allowed us inside the clean room, and right after we had put on our overshoes, I peeked up at Alex. "Does EMT know that I have to work with you?"

He gave a quick nod while we made our way through a maze of alleys lined by dozens of server racks encased in tall black glass cabinets. "Yes. EMT's top management has been made aware that you'll collaborate with our investigation, as one of Thom's closest collaborators." He paused. "The . . . details of your situation haven't been disclosed to anyone, though, and will not be brought up as long as you cooperate fully and help us recover that money."

I tried to answer with the same professional, remote tone he was inflicting on me. "Thank you for your discretion. I appreciate it."

"Hey!"

Alex stopped; I jumped and spun on my heels, searching for the source of the youthful voice I recognized. A black-haired head popped out from behind a cabinet at the end of the alley. Long bangs, round glasses. Turtle-boy. He walked toward us, hands tucked into the pockets of really skinny jeans. He didn't exude the same sort of confidence Alex did. Scratch that—once he was standing right in front of me, he looked frankly intimidated. Which was odd, given that he had at least three inches and ten pounds on me. Plus he was CIA: a nerd heavyweight of sorts.

I gave him a timid smile, which he returned with equal uncertainty. "Great to see you again."

"Same here. I think we're gonna work together, right?"

He seemed a little fidgety. "Yeah. I'm Colin."

"Just Colin?"

His eyes darted to Alex, who nodded in response. "Colin Jeon."

Holy macanoly. Now I remembered where I had seen this guy before.

On TV. And on the Internet. And fricking everywhere for a couple of weeks, actually. "Oh my God! You're the Wall Street Avenger, right? We discussed your method in my network security class, back when I was in grad school."

Turtle-boy scratched his head. "Ah . . . yeah."

Not very enthusiastic for a guy who had once managed to get trading suspended for two of the country's largest banks after hacking into their networks and publicly sharing more than two hundred thousand confidential e-mails and documents.

"And now you're working for the government?"

He looked at Alex and winced. "Didn't have a lot of options."

Okay, the CIA clearly had him by the balls. "Well, that's . . . cool, I guess."

I gave him a thumbs-up to cheer the mood; my heart went out to this fellow prisoner.

Our jailer interrupted this emotional bonding sequence. "So, Colin, you were checking the servers Island mentioned? The ones Roth didn't destroy?"

He walked to an open cabinet. "Yeah. You were right. I recovered logs and data up to April 8. But I found nothing interesting so far. Just standard backups, simulations with nothing in common with the scale of the attack he led."

"Which makes sense, in a way. Let's say I believe Thom did this—he wouldn't have been stupid enough to perform a large-scale simulation and leave obvious tracks," I confirmed.

We all knelt in front of the server rack, and Colin handed me one of his laptops, showing the results of his investigations so far.

I felt Alex move right behind me, peeking at the screen over my shoulder. "Island, do you think that's why Roth didn't destroy those servers? Because there was nothing useful on them?"

"I'm not sure. Maybe he just wanted to make it look like this . . ."
I browsed through the files with a frown. "You're right, Colin, the

simulations here are the ones I already knew of. Limited ones, on fake accounts we generate with a secondary application."

Alex's sigh of disappointment breezed against the nape of my neck, making me shiver a little. I tried my best to block his presence and focus on the files. "Hey . . . these—"

Colin tilted his head at the couple of well-hidden files I had just isolated. "SVG pics?"

"Yeah."

I clicked on the first one. Another sigh, followed by the sound of Alex scratching his stubble.

"Well, it's that chicken from *Family Guy*, right?" Colin ventured.

"Island?" Alex's voice made me jump. It was still gentle, but he sounded increasingly annoyed.

My eyes narrowed. "Look at the size of the files."

Colin cracked a victorious smirk. "One point seven megabytes. A little heavy for a chicken."

I opened the SVG file to examine its source code. "There's additional code hidden inside."

Near me, Alex shifted. "It doesn't look like code, more like . . . gibberish."

"It's encrypted."

"Can you decrypt it?" he asked.

"Without the key? Depends. How many years do you have?"

Colin chuckled at Alex's visible despair.

"If I helped you build the database, could you do a dictionary attack?" I asked Colin.

"Don't insult me," he said with a wink. His fingers started dancing rapidly on the keyboard. I read the lines of code piling up on screen. Yup, he could. He definitely could.

Alex's gaze traveled back and forth between Colin and me. "What's a dictionary attack?"

I pointed at the encrypted files on the screen. "Well, when you want to crack a password, one of the most common approaches is the brute force attack. It means you just try billions of random combinations one after another. But Roth's encryption key is apparently using Scrypt—"

Colin completed the explanation for Alex, whose mouth hung slightly open in the cutest fashion. "It's an encryption system relying on sequential memory–hard key derivation functions. It multiplies exponentially the time and hardware resources you'll need to crack the key."

When his mouth opened some more, I decided to end his suffering. "It means the encryption is theoretically invulnerable."

Colin chimed in. "But the weak link is often not the machine—it's the human. So, what we need is a smaller database—a dictionary—that would contain words, dates, names, everything relevant to our subject."

Alex seemed pleased with the idea. "Some sort of more targeted and less systematic approach."

"Precisely," I said, before turning to Colin. "Thom often said that the kind of passwords that are easiest to remember and hardest to crack are complete sentences with punctuation. He encouraged us to use those when choosing our credentials. Could you access his personal devices? Kindle, iPad, that kind of stuff?"

He grinned. "No problem. I've got my personal farm of zombie machines. I can run them all against the encryption key simultaneously. Will get us done faster."

Zombie farm . . . What could I say? I wasn't going to complain that he hacked thousands of computers on a regular basis, since he was using them for our benefit at the moment. Next time your computer gets infected by some backdoor worm while you're watching *Barely Legal College Lesbians Party* on Porntube, you can thank Colin and go to bed with a clear conscience, knowing you and your machine have served this country well.

After a few minutes, a green window on the screen indicated that

Colin's attack had succeeded, and before my eyes flashed words I knew well: *My doom has come upon me.*

Alex cocked an eyebrow. "Island?"

"This is taken from Homer's *Iliad.* It's the part where Hector is about to die," I said. "Thom spoke about that book often; it fascinated him."

"And it's the key he used to encrypt his data," Colin announced.

I thought of Thom's choice of password, as the previous mishmash of random letters and numbers on the laptop's screen morphed into readable code. This hadn't been about money; he had known something would happen to him. I felt Alex's hand squeeze my shoulder. "Island, what's in the file?"

This should have tasted like victory, but it didn't. My throat tightened more and more with each line I read. I had wanted so hard to believe that Thom had nothing to do with the hacking of EMG's accounts . . . yet what scrolled before my eyes was a large-scale simulation—if you could even call it that when the accounts seemed very real—combined with an ingenuous overlay to deactivate all of Ruby's security restrictions, giving it unlimited access to external networks and free range to attack any kind of banking system.

My eyes met Alex's. "It's what you were looking for. But these files only contain the target accounts. I can't see any parameters for the wire transfers. Maybe those were entered at the last minute to preserve secrecy." I frowned. "At this point, judging by the way this was coded, I can confirm Thom engineered this . . . 'simulation.' But I can't tell you the money's final destination."

Colin gestured to his laptop's screen. "Yeah, like I told you, he split the cash and had it transferred thousands of times through offshore accounts and ghost funds to cover his tracks."

A sudden anger coiled inside me at the way he assumed Thom was the mastermind behind the operation. "You're saying that like he did it for himself. Just in case you forgot, Thom is dead!"

Colin cowered. "I'm sorry. We know someone was there with him, likely overseeing that he'd launch Ruby as planned. They also cleaned up after him: his phone was missing when his body was found, and I haven't been able to track it. My best guess is that it got destroyed."

I listened to his explanations, my fists clenched tightly on my lap. Alex took my hand. "Island, I'd like you to come with me to check Thom's office again, see if there might be something we missed."

As I nodded my agreement, I felt his thumb linger on my wrist for a second. It reminded me of what he had done in the Caterpillar's car, but this time I could tell Alex wasn't trying to check my pulse. A tingle traveled up my arm; I pulled my hand away carefully. "It's okay, I'm fine. Take me there."

NINE

The Coupons

"Ramirez sleeked his thick mustache lasciviously. 'My beautiful Rica . . . Did you think I wouldn't recognize you under a French maid disguise?'"

—Kerry-Lee Storm, *The Cost of Rica II: Ramirez Strikes Back*

I guess I watch too much television, because when Alex, Colin, and I entered Thom's office, I expected to see tons of yellow police tape all around the room, but there was nothing like that. Since the whole episode had already been ruled a suicide and the paperwork was done, there was no "crime scene" left, just an empty room. Not that some tape would have made much of a difference. Now that Alex's colleagues were done questioning my colleagues and everyone had left, EMT and the police had basically put the entire floor under a lid, the same way they'd locked down access to the fifth floor. The handful of people still allowed in there operated under tight surveillance, as evidenced by the presence of a cop to monitor all movement in the hallway and the silent open space.

Alex flung his jacket on a guest chair, and Colin sat in its twin, opening his laptop. A bleak morning light bathed the sparse white furniture and the sea of books, folders, papers, and LEGOs covering Thom's long glass desk.

I couldn't stop myself from walking up to the window and looking down at the street below, where Thom's body had been found after his killers had thrown it from one of the fifth-floor windows. The Kit Kat was sandwiched between Greenwich Street and Washington Street. The glass building across the street did have a clear view of ours. In the middle of the night, however, there had probably been no one there to witness the murder.

I moved away from the window and scanned Thom's desk. I could see him again, sitting in his chair right before I had left, unaware that this was the last time I'd speak to him. I had never been big on displays of affection, but I wished I had told him, at least once, just how much I admired him and how happy I had been to work at his side. I turned to Alex and Colin with a heavy sigh. "What do you want me to check? His computer?"

"Could be a start. Colin says he didn't use it to launch Ruby, but maybe you'll see something else."

A faint buzzing interrupted our conversation, and I watched Alex reach for his phone in his back pocket. He checked what appeared to be a text, typed a brief answer, and shoved the device back in place.

I didn't dare ask, but he spoke anyway, as if in afterthought. "Island, I need to go take a look at something with Agent Murrell. I won't be long. Can I ask you to stay here with Colin?"

I froze, and behind me I could sense Colin was staring. My eyes darted to the hallway. "Agent Morgan? Can I speak to you alone?"

Alex nodded and opened the glass door for me, before closing it behind us. Farther down the hallway, the policeman guarding the open space's entrance glanced at us from the corner of his eye.

"Why would you do that?" I whispered.

He tilted his head, faking a surprise the curve of his lips belied. "You mean trust you?"

"*Yes*. Alex, are you testing me or something?"

"Not really." He reached behind his back and under his shirt; I heard a clicking sound.

I recoiled as he pulled out a Glock 21. Yeah, after my time with March, I'd spent a lot of time on Wikipedia researching the fascinating subject of modern firearms; also, it was written on the barrel. Unaffected by the fact that the cop might still be watching us, Alex racked the gun, spun it around with deft fingers, and handed it to me, barrel facing him. "*Now* I'm testing you."

God, I didn't like the intensity in his gaze. I shook my head, palms rising in a defensive gesture. "Look, I—"

"Good." In the blink of an eye, the weapon was safely back in its holster and under his shirt. "You passed."

I could have punched him for that, but I was still trying to calm my heart's frantic beat. "*Please* don't do that again. I've seen this documentary about a guy who accidentally shot himself in the face while robbing a Walgreens, and doctors were trying to graft a chimpanzee's jawbone on his face—"

My ramblings were interrupted by his hands moving to cradle my face delicately. I felt my cheeks flame up as he bent down, closing the distance between us and studying me with those hypnotic cinnamon eyes. "Island. The safety was still on . . . and that guy deserves a Darwin Award."

I knew I should have pushed him away, now that he was nothing but a stranger I had met a few hours ago, but I could still see, still feel the old Alex, his outline blurred with the new one in something akin to a watercolor portrait. I babbled the first thing that came to my mind. "He can't have a Darwin Award; he's still alive."

His lips quirked. "I expected no less from you."

I freed myself from his hands and looked down at our shoes, at the tiny curls in the gray carpet. Did he feel it too, that our geeky banter wasn't working anymore, and each word exchanged between us now rang strained, stilted?

"Alex."

"Island?"

"Don't play with me like that again. This is difficult enough as it is."

I registered the cotton of his shirt grazing my forearms as he moved closer, felt his drawn-out sigh breeze against my forehead. "I'm sorry. This isn't easy for me either."

Alex's hand brushed mine—perhaps a substitute for the kiss he knew he couldn't risk with people watching us—and he walked past me toward the elevators.

I heard the doors slide shut with an odd mixture of regret and relief.

———

Colin and I were, in many regards, the same. For example, when I have a problem with someone, I never dare to bring it up; I just keep stealing anxious glances at them until either they react or I give up and go eat some brownies. Which was exactly what Colin was doing at the moment. No need to ask whether he had seen Alex play trust games with his gun and touch my cheeks earlier; the answer was written all over his face.

When his eyes darted to me for the hundredth time in five minutes, I abandoned my scrupulous analysis of the activity logs on Thom's Mac and spun my chair around to face Colin. He seemed to shrink in his own chair and allowed his long black bangs to fall in front of his glasses in an attempt to conceal his discomfort. Too bad I already knew this technique—it was my favorite one too.

"Did you find anything new?" I asked casually.

More shrinking.

"Is there something you'd like to say?"

Raisin-level shrinking.

"About Agent Morgan, perhaps?"

Subatomic particle–level shrinking. Before my eyes, the Wall Street Avenger was now threatening to disappear. A low gasp indicated he was trying to force words out of his throat. "No . . . I mean—" Slender fingers left the laptop's keyboard to play with the black cotton of his T-shirt. "Look. I know . . . I've heard you guys were sort of . . . close. But I think you should be more careful around him."

I stole a guilty glance at the hallway, where I knew Alex might show up at any moment. I knew Colin and I were alone, but I whispered anyway. "What do you mean?"

"They had an eye on you, even before this Ruby thing," Colin hissed back.

I shook my head, half-relieved. "It's okay, I know about that. Alex and that old guy—they made it clear that they have a file on me. That's actually why I have to work for them. I guess . . . I guess my life is a little complicated."

Colin's eyes widened in apparent outrage. "*A little complicated?* You're the South African's daughter!"

A prickling sensation spread across my cheeks as if I had just been slapped. The only man I had ever heard being called that was March. But we were clearly talking about Dries, my biological father. I looked down at the laptop's keyboard, unnerved by Colin's intense scrutiny. "I'm *Simon Halder*'s daughter."

"No, you're not. I managed to access part of your file. You're his daughter. The older South African, I mean—" I noticed his hands were trembling a little, but that energy radiating out of him seemed more like childish excitement than fear. "And the *young one*, his disciple . . . You've met him too, right? What's he like in real life? I mean, I've read some crazy stuff."

The first words my brain conjured upon hearing this were "bazooka" and "sniper rifle." I mentally cringed. March was, indeed, capable of some crazy stuff.

"Do you know what the NSA's code name is for him, the young one?" Colin asked, his tone turning conspiratorial.

"Um, no."

"The Tomato Guy."

I gave him a wary look. "Do I want to ask?"

The grimace twisting his mouth was an answer in itself. "Have you seen *The Goonies*?"

"Oh *no* . . ."

"Oh *yeah*. They actually have him on some old Russian surveillance tape doing that . . . Well, they're pretty sure it's him, anyway. You can't really see his face."

Against my best efforts, my brain conjured up the infamous scene that had scarred my—and quite a few kids', it seems—childhood. I felt my stomach heave as I pictured Mama Fratelli threatening to put young Chunk's hand into a blender and mixing a couple of tomatoes to demonstrate. The kid's crying, the blender's ominous noise, all that juice . . . I prayed it was someone else on that NSA video. I didn't want my number one fantasy to be ruined by visions of bloody fingers being pureed next time my own hands took a trip under the covers.

I took a deep breath. "Look, Colin. Whatever you've heard, it's not what it seems." *God*, I sounded like Bill Cosby. "I-I hardly know them, and, uh . . . I don't want to discuss this."

"Discuss what?"

Colin blanched, and at the same time my spine turned to a Popsicle. Alex was back. And he apparently possessed ninja skills on top of a gun.

"Nothing!" I said, turning around with what I prayed passed as a confident smile. "Colin and I were just chatting. About . . . stuff." My ears were red. I could tell they were.

Alex tilted his head, his eyes narrowing ever so slightly. "If you say so . . . Murrell got results from the lab. They were able to connect some fibers we found on Thom's body to an army surplus store in Queens. Buyer hasn't been ID'd yet, but we have a physical description and a license plate. If we're lucky, they might even still be in town."

"But you don't think they are?" I asked, reading the slight twist of his lips as he said this.

He shrugged. "Decent pros will usually vanish once they're done. Our best hope is for those guys to have some sort of business left in New York. Might make them easier to trace."

"What about DNA?" I inquired—yeah, *CSI* made me a supercop, just like everyone else.

Alex seemed to fight a smirk. "We're not dealing with guys who leave hair and fingerprints everywhere, Island."

Figured. I remembered the way March always wore his black leather gloves, how he kept his light chestnut hair in a short Caesar cut and sported a close shave all the time. Those probably weren't just fashion choices.

"Island, are you done checking things in here?" Alex asked.

"Almost. We didn't find anything unusual in his files or his papers, but I wasn't done with his e-mails and chat logs."

Alex looked at Colin over my shoulder. "Thank you for your help, Colin. You can leave with Di Stefano if you want."

The offer was made with one of those good-cop smiles Alex seemed to have mastered to perfection, but it was clearly an order rather than an invitation. I watched as Colin packed his laptop and the various pieces of equipment he had brought in a large metal case. I still wondered what Alex had overheard a few minutes prior and how badly it might affect Colin's own detention regimen. I felt guilty.

There wasn't much I could do as he walked past me. I placed a hand on his forearm to stop him. "Colin. Thank you, for everything you've done."

He responded with a quick nod.

Di Stefano stood in the hallway. He followed her, parting with one last wave of his hand, and as they disappeared into the elevator, I wondered if this was the kind of future awaiting me: a human commodity for the CIA to place where they saw fit.

A pawn.

I don't know about you, but I have this internal clock for burritos when I'm working. It's set to twelve thirty. So you can be sure that around that time I'll stop whatever I'm doing to think of burritos. It doesn't necessarily mean I'll have one for lunch, but I'll think about them anyway. That's how I could tell lunchtime was overdue without even checking the clock—I was getting increasingly frequent mental flashes of black beans and guacamole.

Alex and I had remained alone in Thom's office after Colin and Di Stefano's departure. I was sitting cross-legged in one of the guest chairs, stomach rumbling while I finished reading Thom's latest e-mail. My heart sank when I reached our exchanges. It was an indescribable feeling—an elusive mix of pain, guilt, and nostalgia—to read myself telling him that all the servers had crashed during the night, but surely it wasn't anything huge, maybe a memory leak, and I'd be there soon. Next to me, Alex was swimming with a look of mild exasperation in the capharnaum covering Thom's desk.

He abandoned his inspection of a pile of résumés to rub the bridge of his nose with a long sigh. "Nothing, right?"

I looked up from the screen, shaking my head. "Not really. Seems like he kept saving his work on those fake image files we found, and even the code he was working on last night has been wiped from the logs. Looking at his Mac, you'd believe he barely worked at all. All I got are his e-mails—everyday stuff, nothing out of the ordinary. Not that he'd have been stupid enough to use his EMT mail address to contact whoever made him do this."

Alex walked around the desk to stand behind me and take a look. I pointed at a particular list of folders. "We also got some files related to the department's administrative supervision. But there's no code here either. Not a single line."

I heard him scratch his stubble as he always did when thinking. The only time I had ever seen Alex with a close shave he had looked eighteen, and I could tell he'd missed his precious whiskers, because he kept stroking his chin unconsciously, looking for them in vain. "I see. Those chicken files . . . What was the exact date they were created?"

I checked again. "They were first saved on March 14, basically right after Thom got back from—"

"Zürich?"

Alex had reached across the desk to grab Thom's beloved quantum physics cat memes calendar. On March's page, under the picture of a kitten playing with strings, several days had been circled with a red pen.

"Yeah, he was at Mach-T."

"Mach-T? What is that?"

"Machina Tomorrow," I explained, getting up and setting the laptop aside to fish for a colorful brochure on the glass desk. I showed it to him. "It's the biggest machine learning conference. They do it every year in a different country, and EMT Switzerland was the principal sponsor this year, so they organized it in Zürich. I was supposed to go too—I went last year—but this year Thom said he needed me here to finish our beta."

Alex's eyes lit up. "So he went alone, and right after he came back, he started tweaking with Ruby's code in secret. Looks like we're finally going somewhere."

"To Switzerland?"

"Yep. And you'll be coming too."

My jaw dropped. "You mean . . . with you . . . there?"

"Is that gonna be a problem?"

All I could do was shake my head lamely.

"Not really where I planned on taking you for a surprise getaway, but I guess the cheese wheels will have to do," he concluded with a sheepish wink.

"A surprise getaway?"

"Well, before all this"—he made an all-encompassing gesture at Thom's desk—"I'd been thinking of taking you to Ferris Lake. Ever been there?"

"No . . . where is it?"

"North, in the Adirondacks. One of my friends has a cabin there, in the woods—not too far from the road," he added quickly as he took in my expression of doubt.

I wasn't much of an outdoor enthusiast, more like that annoying friend who falls into every possible hole, gets mysterious rashes and giant blisters, and keeps checking her phone for 4G coverage and bear sightings. If I was being honest with myself, though, the slim chance of getting chased and killed by Confession Bear over a tuna sandwich was not the real issue here . . .

I found myself staring once again at the pieces of a puzzle scattered in front of me, and whatever image slowly emerged was neither just "Alex," nor Agent Alexander Morgan. So he had meant to take me on a surprise romantic getaway—or a romantic survival trek—in a cabin in the woods, owned by a "friend," who might be another agent for all I knew. Would he have kept up the act even then? Or dared to show me a little of his true self?

I was still grappling for the best answer to this non-invitation when he spoke again. "It's okay. I understand—" He tilted his head, and there it was again, that look of frustration, like we stood on opposite sides of a miles-deep gap. "Let's take care of Ruby first. Maybe we can talk about this again when we're back from Zürich."

I couldn't meet his eyes. "Maybe."

"Good. There's something else I'd like to do before we pack."

"What is it?"

"I'd like to search his apartment again. With you." Concern warmed his gaze. "Do you think you can?"

Physically, yes, of course I could. But the idea of searching Thom's things, now that he was gone . . . it almost felt like a violation. "I guess . . . but I thought you guys would have done that already."

"We did. And our agents came back empty-handed, but now I've got an ace up my sleeve." The corners of his lips curled up. "You."

I didn't think I deserved such high praise. "I'll do what I can," I said lamely.

I exited Thom's office to go pick up my tote in the open space—someone had placed it back on my desk at some point, no doubt after a thorough search. When I flung it on my shoulder, I felt a vibration against my hip. I fished for my phone in one of the many inner pockets under Alex's suspicious gaze. Private number. I picked up anyway, slightly anxious at the idea that somewhere, someone might be listening to the call.

"Island Chaptal speaking."

On the other end of the line, a youthful, nasal voice greeted me. "Hi, Island, this is Shauna from Maid Magic. I see you haven't returned our subscription form yet, and I was wondering if you'd have a minute to discuss our services."

Murder, hacking, theft, CIA, and now . . . telemarketing. How much worse could this day get?

"I . . . uh . . . I'm sorry, we're interested, but this is not the best time—"

She went on. "The form was attached to our coupon book. Maid Magic is pleased to offer you a free ten-hour trial for our VIP service, with laundry, ironing, and antibacterial cleaning included!"

My eyes darted to Alex, who was staring at me, one of his eyebrows raised in question. "Thank you, Shauna. Like I said, I *do* plan on using my coupons, but I'm at work right now, so I can't really take care of the subscription."

"But I can't schedule intervention hours until you've returned the form," Shauna insisted.

I sighed. "Look, I promise I'll get back to you as soon as possible. I have to go."

Concern—and some level of scandal—rose in her voice. "Island, there's mold around your sink. That kitchen is a serious health hazard!"

A chill cascaded down my spine. "What the hell? *How* do you know?"

Next to me, Alex tensed; his eyes narrowed.

Shauna, on the other hand, seemed to completely ignore my shock, resuming her sales pitch in a casual, businesslike tone. "You were recommended to us by one of our clients. Apparently it was a case of immediate emergency."

"Uh . . . recommended?" I tried to lower my voice. "I thought this was a contest."

She answered with a steady voice. "Must have been a typo in the letter."

Okay, things were getting weird. I could feel sweat dampen my neck, and I fought the urge to raise my voice so Alex wouldn't suspect anything. "Thank you again, Shauna. I don't have time right now, but I'll definitely call back. Good-bye."

Once I had hung up, I stood there for a couple of seconds, overwhelmed. Someone had called Maid Magic to tell them Joy and I needed cleaning hours. Someone who already knew how messy our apartment was . . . I turned to Alex. That twitch in his jaw spoke volumes: he didn't like what had just happened.

"Telemarketing," I explained with a shrug. "They're getting worse and worse these days—borderline creepy."

He seemed pensive for a couple of seconds before his smile slowly returned. "I know, I sometimes get those too."

As he said this, an inelegant gurgle rising from my stomach officially heralded lunchtime and interrupted this awkward moment.

Alex chuckled. "Why don't we go get ourselves something to eat?"

I gave a quick nod. It seemed I was reaching a point in my life where only a burrito could help.

TEN

The Contest

"Derek's long and huge car raced past her, the roar of the powerful engine pumping the fuel of desire into her most secret tank."

—Alannah Prost, *Formula 1: Racing for Love*

Under any other circumstances, this would have been one of the high points of my biography: I was going to Chipotle. In a sports car.

As you can guess, though, a few technicalities dampened my enthusiasm. My eyes darted at Alex's profile while he drove us up Liberty Street. I examined the dark bristles outlining his jaw. I had always liked them; up close, they looked a little shiny. It was hardly the best time to indulge in the strange infatuation with androgenic hair that March's glorious chest hair had awakened in me, but Alex's whiskers were the only topic able to take my mind off that damn phone call.

In the meanders of my brain, the rambling of a crazed saleswoman who probably called a hundred people a day had sparked this wild scenario where March decided to come back for me. He would sweep me off my feet, call me "biscuit"—the nickname he had given me in Paris—and he'd fold and sort my panties by color like he had before.

I guess that was the sweet side of his OCD issues. Or maybe the really dark one. Not sure.

Yeah. Except that the most reasonable hypothesis was that my dad had been the one to call them. I'll have to check this with him later. From my diet, to my cell phone contract, or even my dates, he needed to stick his nose everywhere, and he perfectly embodied the concept of a mother hen. Well, more like a grumpy father hen. With a serious temper.

My "tryst" with March had only made his parental anxiety worse. From my father's point of view, I had run off to the other end of the world with a (possibly) deranged stranger, stopped answering my phone for five—five!—days. All this to come home and start asking questions about my mother's past—a past he had made considerable efforts to hide from me. According to Janice, my stepmom, that evening we had spent sorting out our family issues and yelling at each other had nearly caused him an ulcer.

At any rate, the case was closed—for my dad, at least—and he was back to his overprotective self. In spite of his initial wariness, he had welcomed my relationship with Alex rather favorably, and I shuddered at the idea of him learning half of what had happened so far since this morning . . .

I stole another glance at Alex, noticing the way his lips were pressed together. He seemed distracted. No, more than that—he was . . . worried?

"What's going on?" I asked.

He checked his mirror with a somber look as we turned right on Williams Street and drove past Chipotle without stopping. "I think we're being tailed."

I twisted on my seat to look behind us, only to be stopped by his hand on my shoulder. "Don't. Just check the mirror. Black Mercedes, behind the two cabs."

Following his instructions, I sat still and glanced sideways. Barely visible behind two yellow cabs was indeed a low sports car whose large emblem on the ventilation grille was the only thing allowing me to tie it to a Mercedes; everything else was just sleek, aggressive lines wrapping around large wheels, like Alex's car.

Oh crap. I was pretty sure I knew that car. It looked every bit like the one that had parked behind us the night prior and caught Alex's attention. We glided down Barclay Street and toward the massive Ionic columns of Saint Peter's Church, a Greek temple oddly planted among skyscrapers. At that point, my eyes were glued to the mirror, trying to determine whether Alex and I were right, or if the recent events were making us both paranoid. That Mercedes *was* technically following us, but this was New York after all, luxury cars weren't rare, and we were driving on a one-way street, so it's not like the guy had much of a choice. Maybe he had meant to go to Chipotle too and couldn't find a spot to park.

"Island. Relax and lean back in your seat."

I glanced at Alex, and my mouth opened to form a question, but when he turned on Church Street and shifted from second to fifth gear with a quick movement of his wrist, I experienced a split second of weightlessness that left me breathless before being pinned to my seat in a deafening roar. I distinctly heard my internal organs splatter against my rib cage and saw the whole street around me turn into a blur of brick buildings and cars. I shielded my eyes with my hands and felt nausea rising in my stomach when Alex started slaloming through the traffic, each acceleration of the Corvette's engine sending powerful vibrations up my legs and spine.

Then we were on Sixth Avenue. And I didn't understand how we could already be there. I tried to force words out of my mouth in a series of rapid pants. "Alex! Please slow down. I don't . . . I don't like this at all!"

"It's gonna be okay, Island. Just breathe." Gone was sweet Alex; this voice was confident but rough with adrenaline.

My eyes squeezed shut when we flew past a fricking bus, its wheels inches from ours. The drivers around us rewarded our performance with some furious honking and outraged shrieks. The Corvette wasn't slowing down, though, and when a close rumble finally registered in my brain through the noise of our own engine, I looked into my mirror with a strangled gasp, my nails digging into the red harness securing me against my seat. The black Mercedes was tailing us, no doubt about that; you don't swerve at full speed to slip between two trucks unless you have some sort of emergency.

Not only that, but it seemed to be catching up fast. I watched with gritted teeth as that monster effortlessly passed a cab and a couple of sedans to cruise at our level, getting closer and closer to my side. Dammit, those black tinted windows screamed "bad guy."

"Alex, it's coming—"

"I know, baby. Hold on!"

I would have commented on the deeply rooted machismo influencing male behavioral patterns and forcing guys to buy muscle cars and call women "baby," but Alex took a violent left turn that caused the car to drift, tires screeching on the asphalt, smoke rising behind us, and, well, I just squealed in panic instead. Not to be outperformed, our pursuer imitated him, barreling after us on West Thirteenth Street while, in the distance, the first howls of police sirens echoed. Not that it would do any good; their sedans were likely no match for Alex's or that guy's car.

There was another series of sharp turns, more buildings and cars flying past us. Road code and basic courtesy were ruthlessly shat on, and I caught a glimpse of a street sign indicating that we were now racing on West Forty-Fourth Street and toward Times Square. I twisted my neck to look behind us. Two more police cars had just made a failed attempt to join in the fun, and the black Mercedes was still tailing us with a persistence I had to say was admirable.

When we reached the corner of Forty-Fourth Street and Seventh Avenue, I heard tires screeching again and felt my torso being projected forward, my head jerking as Alex slammed on the brakes at a red light. I felt his hand squeeze mine. "It's gonna be okay," he said.

No, it wasn't. "Alex, what's going on? Why is he doing that?"

"No idea, but we need to lose him."

I looked around in panic. One car away from us, the Mercedes . . . had stopped as well, engine growling impatiently. *What the hell?* I pushed my hair out of my eyes and blinked at the avenue in front of us. Glass buildings, lights, lights everywhere, theaters, M&M's, old people . . . It took me a few seconds to make sense of the scene unfolding before my eyes and understand why Times Square was virtually paralyzed. A bunch of guys disguised as M&M's were busy promoting the theatrical release of *Cars 6: Ponies under the Hood.* Terrible crossover, by the way—I heard some parents left the theater with their kids when the Hummer villain runs over Twilight Sparkle.

Anyway, they were having this street marketing thing in Times Square that was part advertisement for "*Cars* Limited Edition" M&M's, part community service. They were helping tourists and old people cross the street, and waving racing flags for the cars to drive every time people were done crossing, thus rendering the traffic lights useless.

It was completely surreal. Two M&M's were helping an old lady limp her way across the street, while in front of our car, a yellow M&M waved at us and played with his checkered flag. Cars were rapidly piling up behind us and the Mercedes, equally trapped. On Seventh Avenue, three police cars were trying to maneuver through the dense traffic and undisciplined passersby, ready to intercept us and our pursuer when we were finally able to drive.

And the light was now green, but we were still waiting.

Like decent road users.

And that bad guy was waiting too, because even when you've devoted your life to crime and drive an entirely black car to make a statement about that choice of career, you just don't plow into old ladies and M&M's. Gotta have some standards.

That grandma and her knight in saccharine armor were almost at the sidewalk. I felt Alex's warm hand leave mine to return to the gear-shift. I released a trembling breath.

"Trust me," he said quietly.

Beneath me, the engine's roar intensified. I don't think that yellow M&M really understood what was going on—then again, I gather he's the stupid one in the ads. He kept hopping happily and raised his flag. Those black-and-white squares were all I could see. I heard Alex swallow. I gripped the harness on my shoulders, blood pounding in my neck and temples, beads of sweat forming on my brow. The police cars were now lined up to our right, thirty yards away, their rumbler sirens pulsating and sending ominous chills down my spine.

We *had* to make it through that crossing, away from the black Mercedes and past those cops.

Or did we?

It dawned on me that maybe this was no longer about being tailed. After all, we could abandon the Corvette to block the traffic completely and lose that asshole in Times Square's crowd. Alex could go speak to those cops, show them his badge. I looked at him, my eyes widening in realization. In my peripheral vision, the old lady had just safely reached the sidewalk.

"Alex. What are you trying to prove? Are you two—"

His breath was a little short. His hands gripped the wheel tighter. The corners of his lips curled up in a near-snarl. "Don't worry. Guy has no idea what to do with his engine."

The flag went down. The road was clear. In the space of a heartbeat, tires howled on the asphalt, and as I slammed back into my seat under the strength of the Corvette's acceleration, I had a moment of sudden clarity. My life was being risked in a dick-measuring contest. Also, I was participating in a car race organized by M&M's.

I wasn't given the opportunity to voice any of these concerns. Both cars cometed through the crossing under the passersby's bemused eyes. I registered some flashes in my field of vision; our exploits were likely going to end up on a quite a few social media platforms, along with ridiculous captions. The police cars had been ready all right, but once again, it all boiled down to who had a V-8 engine capable of reaching 190 miles per hour and who didn't. We bulleted past them, swerving to avoid a more daring vehicle attempting to block our way. The Mercedes, however, seemed more hindered by that particular cop car than we had been. In my mirror, I saw it drift around the obstacle, losing ground on us.

By the time we were on Sixth Avenue again, the blaring of the sirens had become distant. I looked through my window; I could no longer see the black car. The Corvette sped up one last time as we reached Central Park, and once we were driving on Central Drive, surrounded by the soothing scenery of blossoming trees and green lawns, everything slowed down.

I slumped in my seat and let the air out of my lungs in a long exhale, the sight of a rickshaw cycling by our side bringing me a ridiculous amount of relief. "Is he gone?"

"Yes, we've lost him."

Alex's right hand left the wheel to caress my forearm; I covered his fingers with mine without thinking. When I saw him smiling at me, at our joined hands, I pulled away gingerly.

"What did he want?" I asked. "Do you think he might have something to do with the people who killed Thom? It looked like the car we saw last night."

"Could be. You're the last person who saw Thom alive, so maybe they were watching you too. Could mean we've made more progress than we thought."

I was about to reply to this when I remembered the obvious. "You were *racing* with him!" I groaned, slapping his shoulder. I wondered how many years you could spend in jail for hitting a federal agent, even if he was technically your boyfriend.

That warm, mysterious smile returned to his lips, and already I feared I wouldn't be able to stay mad at him. "But I won."

"Are you for real?"

Alex welcomed my outrage with an easy laugh as he drove us toward the East River. We'd be able to catch the FDR and be on Roosevelt Island in less than half an hour if traffic cooperated. As we turned on West Fifty-Eighth Street to reach the Queensboro Bridge, I noticed that behind us a long white truck had stopped on Second Avenue, preventing the other cars from following us. I heard some honking and someone asking with a touch of impatience if that truck driver fucked like he drove. I thought nothing of it, but Alex checked the mirror with a frown. I could understand how he'd still be on edge after what we had experienced less than ten minutes ago.

Then it went very fast.

Coming from a street on our right, less than a hundred yards away, I heard an ominous roar. I saw Alex's left hand tighten on the wheel while his right one reached for the gearshift, readying to fly us away from the trap. That goddamn black Mercedes rushed into view, racing toward us. My eyes screwed shut, I anticipated the impact with gritted teeth; it didn't come. Alex swung the wheel, and we dashed into a small underground parking garage on our left, just before the guy could ram into us.

We plunged into the darkened ramp and crashed through the barriers under the eyes of a panicked employee. I started feeling more and more like this was a terrible idea, and I think Alex knew it too, but I gathered we were momentarily out of options. A near-empty parking level came into view. The evil Mercedes didn't seem to be following us, but I wasn't so sure that was good news. I scanned our surroundings for some sort of exit. A surge of terror rushed through me when I realized that the only access to sublevel two was barred by a heavy steel gate.

"Alex!" I gasped, even when a rational part of me knew that reminding him that we were trapped was perfectly useless—he knew it better than I did.

He reached out to push my head down. "Stay down. It's gonna be all right."

Too bad that the moment he said this, faint shocks came from under our wheels, as if we had just driven on a series of tiny bumps. I registered the sound of something flapping; the Corvette shook a little and slowed down. The tires. Something—someone?—had deflated them. Alex swore under his breath, and pulled hard on the brakes. My stomach twisted into knots when I saw him take out his Glock and arm it. A few seconds of thick silence ensued, our tense breathing the only perceivable sounds in that concrete tomb. I struggled to take big gulps of air, inhaling the stench of exhaust fumes permeating the air.

Then that noise. The velvety purr of an engine slowly approaching. The black Mercedes was here. Blocking any possible escape. The chase had just been a way to bring us *here*. Right in the center of the spider's web. I felt Alex's hand graze my hair for an instant, the ghost of a caress, almost at odds with the cutting edge of his voice. "Don't move."

A door opened. Footsteps on the cold concrete, echoing in the garage.

I think the worst part was when I heard Alex's breath falter. Or maybe it was his low hiss, through gritted teeth. *"Fuck."*

ELEVEN

The Emu

"A man is nothing if not the extension of his business card. Aim for **entrepreneurs, doctors, lawyers**: you'll never be disappointed, because what they don't have, they can buy anyway."

—Aurelia Nichols & Jillie Bean, *101 Tips to Catch Mr. Right*

The footsteps had stopped. The guy was probably standing a few feet away from Alex's car. I assumed the Corvette's windows had to be bulletproof and might be able to sustain some damage, since Alex gave no sign of wanting to leave the car, and our mysterious pursuer wasn't making any attempt to shoot into the windshield either.

A draw of sorts.

Alex released a long breath that ended in a chuckle before his index finger settled on the gun's trigger. "Baby, if we survive this, I'm having a missile launcher installed on this car."

Still down, I curled into an even tighter ball. "Don't say we're gonna die. And *don't* call me ba—"

"Get out of the car, please."

The voice was deep, calm, resounding in the garage with a familiar accent that reverberated through my entire body. In my chest something sweet and painful exploded.

"March!"

I lunged at my door handle, felt the brush of Alex's fingertips as his hand reached out to stop me, but I tumbled out of the Corvette before he could. My feet bumped against the door's threshold, causing me to lose what little balance I possessed. I landed face-first and hit my forehead on the ground.

I was a little dizzy, and around me, everything felt blurry for a second. A pair of brown oxfords ran toward me, clapping on the dusty concrete. Spit-shined, impeccable, as always. Then the jeans, the black corduroy jacket—same kind as my grandpa's—the immaculate white shirt. Not one fricking wrinkle. How did he even do that? And then I didn't see anything, because I was in his arms, and he was holding me tight. He smelled of laundry and of those goddamn mints he munched all day long like a junkie. He was squeezing me a little too hard, but he was warm, and most of all . . .

He was here.

"Get the fuck away from her!"

I looked up from March's chest with a start, simultaneously taking in the look of fury in his dark blue eyes, and Alex, who now stood near the Corvette, his gun aimed at March. It looked like he'd shoot in the next second, if the snarl revealing white incisors was any indication. Still huddled against March, I didn't miss the cool and hard object poking my right arm. Blood rushed to my temples. Whatever was going on here wouldn't end well.

I moved away from March, fighting the reflexive tightening of his fingers around my arms. His tongue clicked in annoyance as he let go, probably unwilling to risk bruising me. I struggled back up on my feet to shield him from Alex's gun. Behind me, March had gotten up too, his hands brushing my hips like a discreet safety net.

"Alex, don't!"

I saw Alex's index finger tighten on the trigger. "It's gonna be okay, baby. Get back in the car. *Now.*"

"You don't underst—"

Air wheezed out of my lungs when a strong grip on my shoulder hauled me backward. I staggered, and before either Alex or I could react, March had moved in front of me, standing inches from the gun's barrel. "It's a pleasure to meet you, Agent Morgan. I assume there's no need for me to introduce myself?"

Alex's lips twitched in a bitter smirk. "Your reputation precedes you. Now, I said: Get. The fuck. Away. From her."

All I really saw was the black corduroy adjusting itself on March's right shoulder, that imperceptible shifting of his posture betraying the fact that he had reached the limits of his courtesy. Then his right arm moved in a blur, grabbing the Glock's barrel without hesitation and spinning it. I remember breathing in, breathing out, and the gun was in March's hands, its barrel pressing firmly between Alex's eyes. Alex now stood pinned against the Corvette's side, teeth gritted, eyebrows drawn together in a defiant glare.

I lunged at March, gripping his forearm with all I had. "No! *Please* calm down!"

"I'm perfectly calm, Island."

You know what's the worst part? He was right. The muscles my fingers were digging into were hard as steel, and there was no way I could have prevented him from shooting Alex in the face had he meant to. But there was in fact no rage in his eyes, and he hadn't even broken a sweat through the whole ordeal. Something else bothered me that I couldn't quite place. It was only when he deliberately moved the gun away from Alex and thumbed a button near the trigger, causing the magazine to drop safely in his left hand, that I understood: ever since he had trapped us in that garage, March had made no attempt to draw out his own gun. I stared at him, my own hand still lingering on his sleeve as he handed a befuddled Alex his weapon back.

At this point, it dawned on me just how bad the situation must have looked to Alex, what with me running into the arms of a guy who had casually disarmed him and held him at gunpoint. I let go of March's arm, my initial shock giving way to confusion. "What's going on? You were . . . You *chased* us!"

"I was merely *following* you. Until Agent Morgan attempted to abduct you."

Agent Morgan—so he knew Alex already? I thought of that same black Mercedes parking behind us the night prior. Call it feminine intuition—I had no doubt it had been him all along, tailing Alex and me, in the shadows. And now he had come to my rescue, because he had learned I was in trouble and thought I was being kidnapped when Alex raced to lose him.

I raised my palms in a pacifying gesture. "No, March, he was just—"

Alex took a menacing step toward March. "What the hell are you talking about? You could have gotten her killed! Is this some sort of joke for you?"

"I'm known to have a limited sense of humor, Mr. Morgan," March retorted coolly.

Taking a step back, Alex placed a hand on my shoulder. "Listen to me. This is not the DCB, and I don't give a shit about your résumé or whatever VIP treatment you think the Company owes you. She's a person of interest in *my* investigation, and therefore under *my* protection—" His gaze slanted. "For obvious reasons."

March's eyes never left mine as he answered Alex. "A *person of interest*? Is that what you call it, Mr. Morgan?"

My throat tightened. If he had seen me with Alex last night, there was a subtext in that comment whose ramifications I didn't want to explore . . . "It's true," I confirmed. "But it's not like I really had a choice. Something happened at EMT. My boss is dead, and now I have to collaborate with them in their investigation. He wasn't trying to kidnap me. I think—" My eyes darted to Alex. "I think there's a lot of misunderstanding going on here."

A quiet fury seemed to return to March's eyes. "There certainly is. Well, Mr. Morgan, perhaps it is time your mentor teaches you that there are *rules* to our business. Rules one does not breach without facing heavy penalties."

Rules? What did he mean by that? Also, what was that DCB thing?

"Are you threatening me?" Alex asked flatly.

"Call him," March ordered.

One of Alex's eyebrows rose. "Call *who*?"

"Don't test me, Mr. Morgan."

My gaze kept traveling between the two of them as if I were in the stands at Wimbledon, and to be frank, I had no idea what they were fighting about. Who did they mean by *"him"*? The Caterpillar? Unlike me, Alex seemed to understand. His hand left my back to reach inside his jacket. He pulled out his smartphone and tapped the screen twice with his thumb. I heard one ring, and when his interlocutor picked up, he pressed the speaker to his ear, preventing me from eavesdropping any further.

"Sir, we have a problem." The tone was curt, matter-of-fact.

I expected Alex to start reporting on his little racing contest with March, but on the other end of the line, the voice seemed to keep talking, and when it was Alex's turn to speak, his left fist was clenched so tight the knuckles had turned white. "Yes. He's here with us, sir . . . Sir, I don't think . . . I . . . This is unexpected . . . With all due respect, sir, I should have been informed of this development . . . This is not . . . I understand . . . I understand, sir . . . I will."

After Alex hung up, he remained silent for a few seconds. His tongue darted to wet his lips, as if he meant to speak but couldn't find his words. At last, he shook his head with an expression of utter disbelief. "Struthio Security? *Really?*"

I looked back and forth between them. "Struthio? What's that?"

For the first time since our reunion, March seemed to relax; the gentle smile I had missed so much curved his lips, pinching two adorable dimples. "Phyllis and I have launched a new business venture in the security industry." He paused and took a breath before reciting in a scholarly tone: "We provide high-end services to companies or individuals facing critical security issues and immediate threats to goods and personnel. Here's our leaflet."

Alex stiffened when March reached inside his jacket to fish out two small brochures with an ostrich picture on the cover. He handed us one each with a self-satisfied nod. I looked down in perplexity at the document in my hands and started reading.

The sales pitch informed me that "struthio" meant *ostrich* in Latin, and that this noble and peaceful creature's sharp senses and brilliant intelligence, combined with a top speed of forty-three miles per hour—making it the fastest two-legged animal on earth—made for a perfect allegory of the high professional standards and nonlethal efficiency Struthio Security strove to achieve. Following were a bunch of technical paragraphs regarding the types of missions Struthio could undertake, along with a surprising amount of seemingly legit federal accreditations and quality certifications. The pitch ended with a detachable $20,000 coupon for new customers and the company's contact information, including a website and their headquarters address in New York, on 111 Central Park West.

I blinked at March several times, a strange warmth spreading in my chest. "You stopped—" My voice faltered. "What you used to do?"

His eyes softened. "Let's say I needed a change of air."

Alex stepped between us, holding the brochure in front of March accusingly. "But it's not an ostrich on the cover. It's an emu!"

March's jaw twitched in apparent irritation. "My PA suggested we experiment with a new commercial iconography."

I raised a dubitative eyebrow at the balding emu gracing the document's first page, its creepy orange glare bearing promises of senseless violence and surprise butt sex.

March glanced at the cover with a dejected sigh. "Phyllis liked the emu better."

"Whatever. This is grotesque. You won't have me believe that a guy like you suddenly decided to turn into some kind of Good Samaritan," Alex said.

"Sadly, no one cares for your opinion, not even your own superior, it seems, Mr. Morgan," March retorted with a smirk.

Alex's posture changed, shoulders squaring and heels digging into the ground. Cockfight, round two: coming up next on the Espionage Channel. I stepped between them and shot March a warning look. "Stop it. Both of you."

Confident I had their full attention, I turned to March. "I'm lost. What's going on with you following us? Why did you tell Alex to call his boss?"

He sent a pointed look in Alex's direction before returning his attention to me. "Following the Ruby incident and Thom Roth's . . . *demise*, Struthio was hired to protect EM Group's best interests during the current investigation. I'm here to ensure that EMG's money will be recovered at any cost, as well as to keep them updated on any progress made to this end."

My jaw went slack. "What the—"

He cut me off with the ghost of a smile. "It is my understanding that Mr. Morgan already identified a prime suspect."

I glowered at him. "You people need to stop banging at my door every time something gets stolen somewhere on this goddamn planet!"

"Well, I do see a pattern here . . ." Alex winked at me.

"So do I." March concurred. "Congratulations on being my first returning client ever, Island."

TWELVE

Contemporary Romance

"I need to know, Swanella. Do you love Djahkobh?"

—Lory Deesire, *Accidentally Married to the Billionaire Sheikh*

My fingertips were tingling. I could feel it again in my skin, just like that day in a deserted garage in Tokyo—the hot rush following the contact of my palm with his cheek, the lingering pain. That surge of emotional distress, inseparable from the physical relief after I had slapped March for having lied to me about his involvement in the Cullinan affair, lied to me about everything, from the very beginning.

And God, I wanted to slap him again. Hard enough to wipe that little smile off his face. *Congratulations on being my client again.* Really? *Fricking really?* Not "Hey, biscuit, I missed you too," or "Sorry I ditched you like an asshole, but now I'm back for you." Nope. Just the good ol' "How about I follow you around, but whenever you get too close, I'll act like a douche and disappear?"

Yeah. How do you like that, Island?

My eyelids fluttered shut and I balled my fists, willing my composure back in a long exhale. When I reopened them, March's smile was gone, replaced by a quiet watchfulness.

"You know, you could have just *e-mailed*," I gritted out.

This was neither the place nor the time to have that conversation; we both knew it. March seemed to acknowledge the warning in my eyes. "Island and I need to sort a few things out. I suggest we do so on our way to lunch," he said, at the same time that he pulled out his smartphone and replied to an incoming text message.

"Lunch?" Alex inquired, breaking his self-imposed silence.

"We've been invited by my employer to discuss our new arrangement over a plate of sushi," March clarified, raising the screen for us to see.

I squinted at the terse message. It was signed "H. E." As in . . .

"Sweet Jesus! Hadrian Ellingham is inviting us to Mesa!"

I felt Alex's fingers wrap around my wrist. "There is no arrangement. And she doesn't leave my sight."

March's lips stretched into a threatening smile as he glanced at the silvery caltrops scattered on the floor that had destroyed Alex's tires, then at his own black coupe. "Are you certain of that? Why don't you find yourself a cab, Mr. Morgan? I'm afraid I only have one seat to offer."

I glowered at March. "Stop being like this. Let's just find a solution—"

"Island, you *can't* go with that guy. You *owe* me an explanation!"

The distress in Alex's voice registered in my brain before the sharp pain in my arm. Around my wrists his fingers had tightened, cutting off my blood flow and digging into my skin. By the time I yelped, March had lunged forward and I saw his right hand fly past my shoulder and grab Alex's throat. The grip around my arm eased immediately, and I staggered back in shock, just as March stepped forward, his face inches from Alex's.

"*Never* do that again, Mr. Morgan."

I panicked at the sight of his fingers digging into Alex's skin. "March, please stop! He didn't mean—"

There was no need to insist. His hand left Alex's throat immediately after the warning had been issued, and on Alex's neck reddish marks had appeared, mirroring the ones around my wrist.

I knew what March was capable of—I had seen him kill people in ways I didn't even know existed—but there was something disturbing about this burst of pure aggression. This wasn't him. Even when he had maimed Creepy-hat because I had been hurt, or when he had engaged in a bare-handed fight with Dries, he had retained a thin thread of control; those had been *decisions*. I had read enough novels about biker alpha males who pissed around the heroine to mark their territory—sometimes literally so, if we're talking about dog shifters—to know that this was a *reaction*.

I stepped closer to Alex. I didn't dare touch his neck for fear I'd make it worse; I merely allowed my hand to graze his arm in an awkward gesture of comfort, something halfway between a hesitant pat and a platonic caress. "Are you okay?"

"Yeah, don't worry."

I cast March a disapproving look. "That was unnecessary."

To be fair, I think he knew that already and felt perhaps a little embarrassed about his primitive display. He readjusted his cuffs with a cool glare in Alex's direction. "I'm certain it won't need to happen again. Now, please get in the car, Island."

Behind me, Alex was already reaching out for my arm again, this time more carefully. I moved to stop him, placing my hands on his shoulders. "I know this is complicated, but I swear it'll be okay. March won't hurt me; he just wants to talk."

He seemed conflicted. "Island, you can't ask me that. I'm not supposed to let you go with him—and I don't want to."

"You want me to trust you. I need the same from you. You have to trust me on this," I insisted.

The corners of his lips quirked up, but his eyes told a different story. "I get it. You want space. I'll give you space. But sooner or later we're gonna have to talk about this."

It was no threat, just a fact. I nodded. "I know."

I stepped away from Alex. March took it as a cue that he had won this round, and flashed his adversary a contemptuous smirk. "Feel free to report this to your superiors as a bona fide kidnapping, Mr. Morgan. I'll see you at Mesa in thirty minutes. Do not be late."

All traces of sadness and betrayal vanished from Alex's features, and he responded with a smile of his own that was definitively Agent Morgan's. "Drive safely, *South African*—that's my girl in the front seat."

A blush spread to my cheeks, and I didn't miss the way March's right fist clenched at this explicit reminder. He kept his cool this time, however, choosing to pull out his car key and press it to unlock the Mercedes doors instead. For all my determination, I couldn't look at Alex as I got into the car. I needed that time away from him, just as I needed to talk to March, but I couldn't shake the sense of guilt seeping under my skin.

———

The atmosphere in March's Mercedes as we drove toward Central Park South was tense, to say the least. There was a lot of traffic, and at some point we got completely stuck, so I leaned my forehead against the window to stare at the carriages lined up along the street, their horses waiting patiently for tourists to climb in.

It felt weird to realize that after six months of thinking of him, March was right next to me, that I could feel his presence, smell the mints, and I had no idea where to start. I shifted to look at him—the familiar chiseled features and aquiline nose, those faint crow's-feet . . . His hair had grown a little. It was still pretty short, but tiny waves were starting to emerge along his hairline.

"Why?" I asked.

His fingers drummed on the wheel as we waited at a red light. "Why what?"

"All this!" I sighed in frustration. "I thought I'd never see you again, but you were here all along, in New York. You've been to my place, right?"

"Only once," he mumbled.

"March, you can't do this! You can't . . . hover above my life. You have to let me move on!"

"With Mr. Morgan?"

His tone had noticeably cooled down as the car started moving again. I had hoped this conversation would take us in another direction. "How long have you known? I'm pretty sure I saw your car on Greenwich Street last night."

"I checked on you a few weeks ago. I merely wanted to know how you were doing. I discovered you had met someone. I was happy for you." The way his hands tightened around the wheel as he said this belied his words.

"So happy that you ran a background check on Alex?"

"It was in your best interest. He hid a lot of things from you, Island."

I thought of the Caterpillar, of how he and Alex seemed to know everything about me, from my ties with March to my mother's past, and even the fact that Dries was my father. One piece was still missing from the puzzle, but I was almost certain I knew what it was by now. "Alex's boss, the guy who smokes cigars—his name is Erwin, right?"

March averted his eyes from the road for a second. "I didn't know Kalahari had told you that much, but yes, it is. I used to work for him, and I assume there's no need to explain to you why allowing one of his agents to . . . *court you* under a false identity was absolutely unacceptable."

"Because it meant sticking his nose in your private life again?"

"Something like that," he said quietly.

"What's the DCB, by the way? Alex mentioned that, back in the garage."

"It's a department Erwin relies on frequently. DCB stands for Dry Cleaning Boutique. Need I elaborate?"

"No, I think I get the idea. And I suppose it's no coincidence EMG hired you to help recover Ruby and their money?"

"I did pull some strings," he admitted. "Given the circumstances, it was the least a friend could do."

His words tore through me, sizzled across my skin, and in that moment, even if it was not the best time—would it ever be?—I decided that I *needed* it all off my chest.

"You're not my friend, March. You'll never be."

A thick silence welcomed this statement. Outside the car, a light breeze had started to rise; I watched it stir Central Park's elms from their slumber, their leaves like green shoals.

When he finally answered me, his gaze was straight, and his voice sounded cold, remote, which I knew to be his way of expressing anger. "I understand. I apologize for this misunder—"

"Stop that! You know exactly what I mean!" I had to catch my breath because I could feel my eyes watering already. "You're not my friend because you broke my heart. I spent an entire week crying; I couldn't focus on anything. You were in my mind, and you were in my fricking life all this time! I can *never, ever* think of you as a friend."

I looked at him as he drove, searched his features for any sign he had actually heard me. I found none, and this silence was even worse than the previous one. I feared I had gone too far this time, embarrassed myself by coming off as some enamored teen, and in the process broken March's limited ability to cope with human emotions.

Hope returned when I noticed his lips had moved in a visible effort to formulate a coherent sentence. His Adam's apple twitched as he swallowed and gave it another try. "I've been . . . I just finished reading that book you told me about, *Accidentally Married to the Billionaire Sheikh*."

My mouth fell open in shock. "You *have*? So, um, did you like it?"

"It's a little predictable, and very explicit, in an oddly lyrical way. I can only imagine how disappointed female readers must be when facing the reality of—" He cleared his throat. "Well, in any case, I'm not certain Hedwardh is a good match for Swanella. I feel the author was forcing them together toward the end."

"Why? I think it's made clear that they have this irresistible attraction and all," I countered.

"An unhealthy attraction." He frowned. "Swanella is inexperienced, and she throws herself in the arms of an older man without *ever* considering the possibility that he might hurt her."

"But why would he hurt her? There's a happy ending; she even gets pregnant!"

"Because he pushes for them to have this child. Hedwardh is very controlling, and his love for Swanella borders on obsessive. I think that scene in the limousine clearly shows he cannot restrain himself once he's given in to his . . . urges. And by the way, the refractory period doesn't work like that," March concluded with a snort.

I shrugged. "I know, after thirty it's like a day or even two."

He stopped at a red light and averted his eyes from the street to stare at me for several seconds. He wasn't saying anything, but his nostrils flared, and he looked as if I had played with his radio or thrown a candy wrapper in his car: beyond outraged.

"What?"

He sighed as we exited Columbus Circle to stop in front of the Time Warner Center's futuristic twin towers. "Nothing. But I rest my case: the relationship portrayed in this book is not healthy. Hedwardh knows he can't make Swanella happy, and still he can't stay away from her. *That* is his fundamental problem."

March drove toward the parking entrance, and I gazed at the shoppers hurrying into the place, fighting a smile. "Maybe. But when Sheikh Djahkobh holds her captive in his palace, Hedwardh comes to save her. I think that's all that matters in the end."

The car had stopped. March remained quiet for several seconds, his hands still on the wheel. "Biscuit . . ." His voice was low, laced with the tenderness I had missed so much. I held my breath. "Simply because Djahkobh is bad for Swanella doesn't mean Hedwardh is a better choice."

There was this ache in my chest, as if it would collapse on itself. I sat up straighter and swallowed. "You know what? You're right. Swanella deserves better than this," I snapped, opening my door and stepping out of the Mercedes.

I heard March's door slam shut and his footsteps behind me as he followed me toward the exit without a word. I never looked back on our way to the elevators; I couldn't face him yet. My heart was pounding, and I knew that if I turned to look at him, I'd say something stupid, something that would cause him to retreat even further back in his shell and hurt me. Again.

I looked at the tip of my ballet flats on the garage's dull gray paint. How could a man who had read *Accidentally Married to the Billionaire Sheikh* for my sake be so totally, infuriatingly, painfully blind?

THIRTEEN
The Kraken

"Give Trenton a chance, Jess! For Christ's sake, he's bending over backward for you!"

—Lane Tempest, *Wrapped Around Me: The Octopus Shifters Series #6*

Given all the rumors about his icy and controlling character, I could see why a guy like Ellingham would enjoy the Time Warner Center. The whole thing felt austere and monumental, with its massive incurved atrium enclosed on one side by a glass curtain, smooth gray stone columns, and steel cables holding the structure together. A perfect showcase for the trendy shops lining the floors.

We made our way across the lobby toward the elevators and stepped into one of the cars, along with a couple of Asian tourists carrying shopping bags. March pressed the fourth and last floor's button, and soon we were rising toward the top of the huge hall, the elevator's glass doors a window to this modern temple of self-importance. It was a nice view, though, and I'm sure March enjoyed it too, until a pair of brown boots appeared in our field of vision. Khakis. Rugged leather jacket. The rest of Alex's body was progressively revealed as the car slowed down and stopped at Mesa's floor.

He stood in front of the doors with his arms crossed, one eyebrow cocked at us. "Did you enjoy your ride?"

Next to me, I felt March shift. I took a step forward in case there might be more throttling coming. "Alex, let's go."

The three of us made our way across a minimalist hall toward Mesa's entrance, marked by a sober black *noren* curtain bearing two white kanji forming the restaurant's logo.

目先

A long corridor with dark wood walls led to the dining room, where a young Asian woman stood near a waiter and a few burly-looking guys in dark suits. Alex and I probably didn't fit the dress code in this den of super-elegant Zen; the hostess did. Her silky, straight black bob, high cheekbones, and impeccably cut short-sleeved red dress—designer stuff, no doubt—felt almost intimidating.

"Miss Chaptal, Mr. Morgan, and Mr. November?" she asked with a suave voice. Dammit, that beige lipstick was so perfectly applied it looked tattooed on her lips.

We all nodded, and I saw Alex cock an eyebrow at March upon hearing his "name." Oh well, if we were going to work with March, Alex would get used to those aliases like I had, eventually. Since my first encounter with him in October, I had heard March introduce himself with half a dozen different months, and there was at least one thing I was almost certain of: I'd never hear his real name—if the man even had one.

The young woman stepped aside to reveal a long sushi bar with a wooden counter. "Mr. Ellingham has been waiting for you."

Now, my dad was a banker, so he was pretty wealthy. After more than a decade spent killing people for two hundred grand a day, March was frankly rich (but I had been told he saved most of it and lived in a cubicle house). Finally, Dries, my biological dad, I filed in the category of the supervillain-rich, and he had no qualms about showing off a little. None of that was billionaire-rich, I realized upon scanning the barren dining room with beige walls and minimalist black furniture.

No. Billionaire-rich is when you can privatize the most expensive restaurant in New York on a whim. The place was empty, and I assumed that those big guys with the crew cuts acted as bodyguards for the blond man in an anthracite suit sitting at the sushi bar. He seemed busy examining a bottle of sake celebrity chef Mesahiro Hikuyama was showing him—damn, that guy looked even balder than on *Top Master Chef.*

I stole a glance at March and Alex. They looked cool as cucumbers, whereas my palms were getting clammy and my stomach was doing flips. When our host turned to acknowledge our presence and got down from his chair, I couldn't help but stare, trying to file every detail of what might be my only close encounter ever with my big boss.

In my mind, Hadrian Ellingham had always been more or less a stock photo: some aristocratic Ken doll, smoothed by makeup and studio lighting. I thought it made sense that he looked like a Nazi cyborg, since everybody said the guy had this terrifying aura about him—think Max Zorin minus the creepy mental illness. Even the Bad Sex Sloth meme hadn't been able to help that part of his image, and that's saying something.

So, imagine my shock to discover a mere mortal in his late thirties, with dark circles under somewhat downturned blue eyes, and a few wrinkles in what was no doubt an Egyptian-cotton shirt. My gaze lingered on the faint oblique scar linking the underside of a straight nose to his upper lip. Prince had once told me that the guy smiled so rarely that it wasn't his real mouth on those magazine covers: they always photoshopped some random model's smile on the pic so Ellingham would look more human. Well, here's a scoop: they didn't photoshop his mouth just because he looked too stern. They did it because the guy was born with a cleft lip. I wondered if he had a problem with it and asked for that particular retouch himself.

He extended his hand to March for a firm handshake. "It's a pleasure to see you again, Mr. November."

I thought his voice sounded a little deeper than on TV.

"And you are Mr. Morgan, I presume," he went on, greeting Alex in the same fashion.

Then it was my turn. And apparently regular employees didn't deserve a handshake. Had those blue eyes been that cold a second before? God, they were so pale they looked like ice. "Please sit down, Miss Chaptal. I've heard a lot about you in the past couple of days—perhaps more than I wished to."

I shuddered. Alex and March wouldn't have told him things about me . . . *right?* "I . . . uh . . . It's an honor to meet you, sir," I mumbled as March took the chair next to Ellingham's and I sat between him and Alex, safely away from our host.

As soon as we were seated, the young waiter in a black suit with a long white apron waltzed toward us, carrying four sake cups on a platter. Someone dimmed the lights in the restaurant, leaving only the large sushi bar under the spotlights, illuminated like a stage.

Chef Mesa, who had been chatting with Ellingham before our arrival and had since retreated into the kitchen, came back from the shadows. I realized that low atmospheric music was now filling the room, mixing notes of dramatic Japanese flute with birdcalls and the sound of water running. I looked at March and Alex alternately, in case either of them might have an idea what was going on.

"Making food."

I jumped at the ominous echo of Chef Mesa's thick Japanese accent. He stood before us, head bowed, arms along the sides of his body, legs apart. He looked like Madonna before starting a show. His bald skull shone bright under the ceiling's lights, his outfit and apron blinding white patches against the darkened background. Each crease and wrinkle on his solemn face was sculpted by the golden hue bathing him.

"I seek the essence of food. The life within the ingredients. The *shibui* sensory experience. *Tamashii. Umami!*"

I gawked as he struck a little ninja pose and grabbed a long kitchen knife with a beautiful Damascus steel blade. Behind us, I realized that the waiter and the young woman who had greeted us were applauding discreetly. Ellingham consented to a few lazy claps; March, Alex, and I took the hint and did the same too while Chef Mesa started slicing a horseradish in half, ignoring us to concentrate on his art.

"Now, I understand you haven't made any significant progress at all in your investigation?" The tone was cordial, the voice soulless, and Ellingham was looking at the three of us with a sort of rictus I think he had intended to be a smile.

"Actually, we *have* made some progress. We've yet to understand who engineered the theft and where the money was wired, but we now have a clearer understanding of the chain of events that led to Ruby's activation," Alex ventured, at the same time that the chef raised his knife with a dramatic gesture and grabbed a couple of bananas. I stared in confusion at the strange recipe being prepared before our eyes.

"But since the servers got destroyed, it's difficult to know what files were used and what happened to them. Ruby's code might have been replicated with the intent of being used again," I added, not daring to look at Ellingham, and instead focusing on the way Chef Mesa was superimposing millimeter-thin slices of horseradish and banana on large black plates.

Ellingham's fingers tightened around his chopsticks when the chef handed him the first plate and announced a "Vegetal Essence Carpaccio."

"When will you leave for Zürich? I've already warned Professor Premfield of your imminent visit. He's the head of research in our Swiss subsidiary."

Alex seemed a little taken aback, while my mouth just fell open. How *the hell* could he already know? "Sir, are there, like, bugs in our offices?"

"No, Miss Chaptal." Ellingham exchanged a smug look with March. "You might, however, want to invest in a metal case for your phone."

On the counter Alex's fists clenched. "She certainly will."

So that was how March had known about the progress of our investigation. As too often, I had no idea if I wanted to strangle him for his controlling streak or hug him for being my guardian angel. And it was neither the place nor the time for either. I let out a long, calming breath. "Can I ask you to refrain from accessing my personal devices in the future, *Mr. November*?"

March's eyes softened. "I'll see what I can do."

Seriously? Okay, next time we were alone together, he was definitely getting that slap.

Around us, the musical ambiance had changed to something more spa-ish, with light bells and shamisen. I looked down at the plate I had just been served, sighed, and grabbed my chopsticks. It wasn't awful, but the whole combination didn't work all that well, mostly because of the banana. I could tell Alex was a little resigned as well, whereas March sported a faint smile, no doubt due to the perfect organization of each element on his plate.

All three men were done with their carpaccio, but I was still toying with mine when I noticed the music had stopped. Above us, the spotlights turned red, and Chef Mesa moved to stand before us again in his Madonna position, while threatening Japanese flute notes rose in the darkened dining room. Two sous-chefs appeared from doors located at each end of the kitchen behind the sushi bar, scuttling toward their rock star. One was struggling with a couple of live eels, while the other carried . . . a Japanese sword? I cast an alarmed look at March, who responded with a reassuring smile. On his left, Ellingham seemed perfectly at ease with whatever the hell was going on.

Chef Mesa took a deep breath through his nose and extended both arms, receiving the unsheathed sword in one hand and a wiggling eel in the other. He spoke in a sepulchral voice. "The essence of life . . . is death. The beauty of death. *Unagi!*"

I bit back a scream and shielded my eyes when he secured the eel on the wooden counter with his left hand and brought the sword down with a battle cry to chop it in half. I think right afterward Alex leaned toward me to make sure I was okay, but I couldn't focus. Because in the dark, March was holding my hand, squeezing it tight, soothing me and wrecking my defenses at the same time. Neither Alex nor Ellingham seemed to have noticed, and while Chef Mesa cut his eel to pieces, I looked up at March. He still hadn't let go. His touch felt hot; his thumb kept drawing light circles on my knuckles. He glanced at me with a masterfully controlled poker smile, but the slow caress on my skin belied his mundane expression.

My breath was getting a little short, and I think time stopped. Until that obsequious waiter snuck between us to serve us glasses of mineral water from Easter Island or whatever, forcing March to let go with an imperceptible sigh. My cheeks felt on fire, and I registered Alex's questioning eyes when I fidgeted on my chair. I tried to concentrate on the way Chef Mesa was sprinkling cherry flower petals on what were essentially dices of raw eel, all while prattling about the beauty of birth and death. I didn't give a damn. All I knew was that for a few blissful seconds, my connection with March had returned.

But it was gone already. And now I had to eat raw eel and I wanted to cry.

Near us, Ellingham was digging into his plate with a feral expression. I shivered at the sight of him munching on the reddish dices. March and Alex ate quickly as well, but out of a clear intent to shorten this regrettable *shibui* experience. Alex drank from his sake to help the last mouthful of eel go down. He then peeked down at my plate, still full, and at Ellingham, who was watching me expectantly.

I'll never forget the expression on Alex's face. The look of a man sacrificing himself, championing a damsel in distress. "I'll take yours if you don't want it."

I gave a weak nod.

March stepped in. "It's all right; I'll have it. I can't get enough of such a delicacy."

Alex's hand had already moved to take my plate; his eyes narrowed in response. My eyes traveled back and forth between them; I swallowed pitifully. "You . . . you can share if you want."

I'm pretty sure neither wanted to both lose the cockfight *and* have to eat the beautiful dead eel, but they welcomed my offer like gentlemen and split the "delicacy" in half with tight jaws under Ellingham's amused gaze. The lights returned, and Chef Mesa retreated behind the kitchen doors, presumably to oversee preparations for his next performance. The waiter came back with an assortment of *tsukemono* for us to nibble on while we waited for the rest of the show; I was grateful, because those traditional Japanese pickles, while coming with tart and strong flavors, were okay. Alex and March seemed to share my relief: they raided the long rectangular plates with deadpan faces. Alex even ate the little blue flowers in his, even though I'm almost positive those were for decorative purposes.

"Mr. Morgan," Ellingham began, before biting on a crunchy piece of bright yellow *takuan*. "I was hoping you'd be able to enlighten me on a specific point."

Alex schooled his features in a good-cop smile. "I will if I can."

"I'm grateful—EMG is grateful—as you can imagine, that our government is helping us deal with this crisis. But I'm wondering why the CIA took over this particular case, rather than, say, the FBI."

On my left, I noticed March's shoulders straighten ever so slightly, and I realized that Ellingham's piercing aquamarine gaze was no longer set on Alex, but on me. I gulped down a bite of sour and salty *umeboshi* and responded with an uncomfortable grin.

"What do *you* think, Miss Chaptal? Are you, like I am, left in the dark? You, whom I was requested—I dare not say ordered—to allow to help Mr. Morgan in his investigation, during your work hours . . ." His eyes had narrowed as he said this, and the fingers of his right hand were rapping slowly against the wooden counter.

A sheen of hot sweat formed on my brow. "I-I'm really just helping Agent Morgan with technical stuff and—"

"I'm sorry, sir, Miss Chaptal's collaboration with our division entails high levels of confidentiality. I'm afraid we have to end this track of conversation."

Ellingham's eyebrows shot up—I bet it wasn't often that he heard someone telling him to get lost—before he regained his composure. "I see. Well, let us hope that the opacity in which you operate is not a mere guise for incompetence."

Ow. I practically heard that banderilla stab Alex in the face. Leaving his victim to nurse his ego, Ellingham then looked at March. "As for you, Mr. November, I count on your involvement to speed things up. Our mutual friend spoke greatly of your ability to . . . *solve* such issues."

March welcomed the compliment with the faintest smile creasing his dimples; my ears perked up. *Mutual friend?* What kind of friend? Could Ellingham know about March's old job? Alex looked interested too, but we weren't given the opportunity to further question Ellingham. Chef Mesa had returned, the lights were dimmed again, and this time, I got worried. I wasn't sure I wanted to eat something that came served with Albinoni's "Adagio" as a background soundtrack.

The chef brought his hands up, fingers curling and trembling, his face a mask of pain and concentration. "Life. The struggle for life. *Kodako!*" he roared, throwing his fists in the air.

Sweet fricking Jesus. I knew what *kodako* meant, but I had this moment of doubt when the waiter waited for the organ solo to bring four large black square plates. My mind couldn't reconcile their content with the notion of edible food. Not just because this sensory *shibui* experience seemed to be squirming quite a bit, but because I had never envisioned eating a live baby octopus before. Especially one wearing a delicate purple wig made of red beet shavings. It was so cute. It reminded me of Katy Perry's hairstyle.

I watched mine struggle to remove its wig, wading in what I understood to be a mixture of truffle oil and *sudachi* lime juice. March and Alex seemed just as disconcerted, but when Ellingham picked his up mercilessly and shoved it inside his mouth with a sinister gulp, they took the hint and imitated him.

Alex's wouldn't let go of the black plate, its suction cups sticking to the smooth material in a desperate fight for survival. He kept pulling, stretching the tiny white limbs like gooey elastics until they let go with a series of wet popping sounds, only to wrap themselves around his chopsticks instead. His eyes screwed shut as he gobbled the helpless creature, munching on it with the face of a man about to throw up.

I fought a wave of nausea of my own when I watched him swallow with difficulty, his left hand clenched into a fist on the wooden counter. March went through the ordeal with more grace—mostly because his baby octopus had tangled its arms in the beet shavings, and therefore posed less of a challenge. I didn't miss his trembling exhale as the invertebrate traveled down his esophagus, though.

"Won't you eat yours, Miss Chaptal?"

I stared past March's chalk-white face and into Ellingham's eyes and their satanic glint. I looked down at my plate and gulped.

Mine . . .

Mine was courageously sustaining my gaze with its tiny beady eyes, rocking its beet wig with dignity in spite of the horror of the situation. Until it tried to escape the plate. And all that lime juice made it look like it was crying. I poked it back in a few times with one of my chopsticks, but it was no use—I was already thinking of names for him. I think it was a he—feminine intuition.

I couldn't do it. My eyes fell on the glass of water the waiter had served me earlier; I made a lightning-quick decision. Grabbing Krakky—yeah, that was his name now—I pulled him out of the plate and threw him in my water glass, watching with relief as he settled there.

"I-I'm saving mine for later."

That earned me perplexed looks from March and Alex, and a raised eyebrow from Ellingham. Which was nothing compared to the glare I got from the waiter when I stopped him from taking the glass away. I glared back. In that price range, I was entitled to do whatever I pleased with my life essence food.

I can't describe the amount of joy I experienced when I saw Ellingham bow to Chef Mesa with his palms pressed together, soon imitated by pretty much everyone in the dining room, including me. The waiter came back a few minutes later with strawberry and eggplant *granités*, indicating that the meal had reached its end. I finished mine down to the last drop, having reached a point where eating raw mixed eggplant was more or less an antechamber to heaven.

After he was done with his own *granité*, Ellingham clasped his hands together and looked at us. "Well, I'm pleased we were able to have this conversation. I'll leave you, lady and gentlemen, to your investigation."

As if on a cue, the young Asian woman who had greeted us and had been waiting in a corner of the dining room with Ellingham's bodyguards walked toward us, presumably to show us out. I took my glass—and Krakky—with me under the scandalized stare of our waiter. I hoped Ellingham wouldn't tip that douche.

Our host cast the baby octopus a scornful look. Then his icy gaze traveled up, stabbing me like a million tiny daggers. "Miss Chaptal, you intend to keep this creature, don't you?"

I took a step back, seeking refuge between March and Alex's solid frames. "Maybe . . . I don't know. I've heard they're extremely smart and—"

Without a word, Ellingham took the glass from my hands. I let go with difficulty and cast a pleading look at March, while that monster held the glass in front of his eyes and examined Krakky with pursed lips.

"Denise."

The elegant assistant nodded.

"Do you remember that octopus who could aptly predict soccer results? What was his name? Patrick?"

"Paul, sir."

Ellingham frowned. "Yes, *Paul.* Do you believe we could perhaps train this one to anticipate market trends?"

"We'll hire the best zoological specialists, sir."

"Excellent. Find a suitable tank for it and put it in my office."

Part of me wanted to protest, but being a good parent is also wanting what's best for your kids, and I couldn't deprive Krakky of this opportunity to slither up the corporate ladder. I watched with a heavy heart as he pressed his little tentacles against Ellingham's fingers on the other side of the glass. He had probably already forgotten about me, and it was better this way. Hadrian Ellingham would be his new family. Which was really horrible if you think about it, since the man had eaten one of his siblings not so long ago. Such is the harrowing journey of a young octopus in this cruel world.

Ellingham handed the glass to his assistant and seemed ready to take his leave when I remembered something. This might, after all, prove my only chance to pierce the darkest secrets of a man who sent me quarterly e-mailings to remind me that he and I were working together as a team to build the future, because with EM Group, "Tomorrow Comes Today."

"Sir, can I ask you a question?"

A contemptuous sigh escaped him. "You can always try."

"What's her name? Your new girlfriend?"

Behind me, March and Alex cleared their throats in unison. To my amazement, Ellingham sort of blushed. Not a full blush high on the cheeks—that would have looked very weird on him—more like a diffuse pinkness in his neck and ears. Then it was gone, replaced by flaring nostrils and arctic blue eyes.

"Out of my sight, Miss Chaptal."

FOURTEEN

The Limbos

"They collided together like fiery particles, their joining a passionate fusion of every single atom in their bodies."

—Christie Dolan, *Physical: A Hopegrove Nuclear Plant Novelette*

"God, I need a cup of black to wash that stuff down!"

I would have agreed with Alex if I liked coffee; I personally contemplated forgetting the Mesa experience with a two-dollar cream cheese bagel. As for March, he had been silent ever since leaving the restaurant, lost in his own thoughts. I knew for a fact that he was almost as addicted to coffee as he was to mints, though, so I suspected he shared Alex's opinion.

"So, are we still going to visit Thom's place?" I asked Alex as we stepped out of the Time Warner Center.

"Yes, we'll go there immediately," March announced.

I looked up at him in mild surprise, and Alex cocked an eyebrow in a fashion I understood to mean "Who the hell put you in charge?"

"Follow me," March ordered.

Alex and I exchanged puzzled looks but complied, allowing him to lead us around the building and to a line of cars parked on West Fifty-Eighth Street. He pulled out a key fob from his right pocket, pressed it, and the lights of a gray Lexus sedan flashed twice.

"What happened to the Mercedes?" I asked.

March let out an irritated sigh as he opened the driver's door. "I understand that room must be made for Mr. Morgan."

I fought a grin. "Thank you."

"But you really didn't have to," Alex said.

The passenger door clicked open—for me, I assumed. I had a moment of hesitation. I gathered March expected me to sit up front with him, but I figured it would only piss off Alex further, especially after what March had done to his car. I shook my head with an apologetic look, and climbed into the backseat under March's displeased gaze.

Alex was about to follow me when his head jerked up. A smile lit up his face at the sight of a tiny food truck parked a few yards away from us. "I'll go get myself that coffee before we go. You guys want anything? Island?"

Oh. In the mirror, I saw March's eyes turn to slits. "Um, Alex . . . maybe we can stop for drinks later?"

He shook his head. "Don't worry, I'll drink it in the car."

March's tongue clicked in rising aggravation; I grabbed Alex's sleeve before he could leave. "You can't really do that in March's car."

His brow twitched, and he stared past my shoulder at March, but said nothing otherwise, consenting to get into the car. I gave him a thankful smile, buckled up, and . . . the car didn't start.

God. Mr. Clean was giving us the full Monty. I winced at the sight of March's obstinate blue eyes in the mirror. "Alex, your seat belt," I whispered as the stickman light kept blinking on the dashboard.

Alex's mouth formed a little O of perplexity before he submitted to March's iron rule with a diplomatic smile. I relaxed in my seat when the engine finally hummed to life, at the same time that the first notes of a neurasthenic country guitar rose in the car.

"Is that the only kind of music you have?"

I rubbed the bridge of my nose with trembling fingers. *"Alex . . ."*

"Conway Twitty earned forty number one Billboard country hits. He was a *genius*," March hissed as he drove us toward the monumental steel frame of Queensboro Bridge.

I saw Alex's mouth open, ready to discuss the merits of Conway Twitty's musical contributions. I grabbed his right arm and squeezed it, shaking my head with a warning look. He nodded in understanding and took my hand, his thumb grazing the underside of my wrist.

In the mirror, March was observing us. I snatched my hand away with a faint blush and ignored Alex to focus on the traffic surrounding us, and Manhattan's skyline stretching along the East River.

———

I'm gonna sound a little dramatic, but our arrival on Roosevelt Island struck me as a plunge into another world, the harsh red lines of the bridge a gate to quiet limbos where time had stopped. It probably had something to do with the dark clouds growing in the sky above our heads, and also it was only quarter to three, so everyone was either at work, school, or safely inside their apartments. There was something eerie about those deserted streets and parks, the lines of identical brick buildings. No passersby, not a sound except for an occasional birdcall echoing in the distance. The colors themselves seemed faded, blending into the ashen sky and giving me the impression that the entire place was shrouded in a gray veil. Granted, the fact that we were there to visit a dead man's place didn't help.

The Lexus glided down Main Street. I checked the numbers on each building. "465. March, it's this one."

He parked a little farther down the street, and the three of us stepped out. The spacious and brightly lit lobby was a sharp contrast with the dull external appearance of this soulless LEGO, with its white walls and wooden panels. Spotting Thom's name on the intercom, I exchanged looks with March and Alex, silently asking for permission to ring. The jerk of Alex's chin was my cue; I pressed the button and waited. In vain.

"They're gone, you know—staying with the grandparents in Fort Lee."

At the other end of the hall, the door to the super's office had opened and a fiftysomething man with graying hair now stood in front of us. He scratched his beer belly absently through a brown plaid knit vest.

"Mr. Degraeves?" Alex asked with a friendly smile.

"The one and only."

"You saw my colleagues yesterday."

"You one of those Feds again?"

"I'm Agent Morgan—" He flashed his badge briefly, not long enough for the man to figure he wasn't FBI, I thought. Then he pointed to March and me. "And these people are consultants working with me."

There was some more scratching, and the super stared at us for a little while, cocking his head as if to better assess who he was dealing with. He pointed at the ceiling with his index finger. "You need to go up there again?"

"Yes," Alex confirmed. "Can I ask you to open the apartment for us?"

"Sure. Come with me."

Degraeves called the elevator, and we all joined him inside while he pressed the button for the tenth floor.

Now that I was standing so close to him, it was becoming obvious that the guy's belly was, indeed, full of beer. From the corner of my eye, I registered March's lips pressing in disapproval. "So, Emma and Tobias are staying with Thom's parents?" I asked.

"Yeah. It's been tough. You know, all those cops, neighbors talking . . ."

"I understand," I said.

The car stopped, its doors opening on a long white hallway lined with dark doors.

Degraeves pointed to the left. "This way."

It was hard for me to place the feeling, but I experienced a sort of guilt when the super unlocked the door to Thom's apartment. I had been there a few times, for dinner or the last-minute wrap-up of an important presentation. Now that he was gone, though, being there in his living room, surrounded by his son's toys, his family pictures . . . it felt like invading his privacy, forcefully taking something he hadn't offered this time. I looked around, filled by a sense of familiarity that was now laced with grief. Thom's place reminded me of Joy's and mine, only bigger. It was a heteroclite mix of styles and colors betraying a series of genuine attempts at interior design thwarted by the purchase of an eighties leather La-Z-Boy and *Star Wars* figurines.

Degraeves stood in the apartment's doorway while March and Alex started examining the furniture, the lamps, the windowpanes, dissecting every detail of Thom's life with practiced eyes. I left the living room in search of any computer or connected devices he might have kept at home. A pang of sadness tugged at my heart upon passing the door to little Tobias's bedroom. It was slightly ajar, allowing me to glimpse a heap of stuffed toys and a few crayons on the floor. Next was a large bathroom with blue tiling, facing Thom's bedroom—I didn't enter either of them. There was something disturbingly intimate about touching anything in there while Emma and her son were away; I chose to leave that to March and Alex.

At the end of the hallway, a third door led to Thom's office, with its shelves crammed full of programming books and, sitting majestically on the old black desk, an unfinished LEGO model of CERN's large hadron collider—his latest magnum opus. I hoped Tobias would grow up knowing just how cool his dad had been.

I sank in the large blue gamer chair facing the desk. It was weird to see it empty like that. There would usually be at least two old Macs,

Thom's huge PC tower, several external hard drives, and an entire cardboard box of wires and mystery tech junk in a corner of the room. But I gathered Alex's colleagues had taken all that stuff during their previous visit. I doubted they'd find anything, though, save for the most heavily modded install of *Skyrim* any mortal had ever witnessed.

My fingers played absently with the LEGO model in front of me. Something had happened in the past weeks, which had culminated last night, and led us here and now. Thom had been standing on the edge of a cliff, while I was too preoccupied about that stupid date to reach out to him.

I picked a blue LEGO plate to complete the dodecagonal barrel hosting the collider. What was I missing this time?

———

We've all been there: someone enters the kitchen, you're standing near the oven with your sweatpants down, chocolate cake batter everywhere, a mixer in one hand, your stepmom's cat in the other, and all you can say is "It's not what it looks like."

I kind of felt like this when March and Alex entered Thom's office ten minutes later, followed by Degraeves, while I was sitting at Thom's desk in front of several boxes of LEGOs, wires, batteries, and LEDs—I was almost done completing the circular particle tracker.

I looked up at them. Alex was scratching his chin, one eyebrow raised, while March's hands had clenched into fists and his breath was getting a little short, like he was hyperventilating.

"It's because it helps me think—" I whined, letting go of Thom's LEGOs.

"Have you found anything yet?" March asked, scanning the mess on Thom's desk with a frown.

I shrugged and shook my head. "No. Your colleagues took everything. If it's not on his devices, I don't think it'll be anywhere in here."

March pointed at the LEGOs scattered on the desk. "Do we still need these?"

"Not really, they're—"

Before I had the time to finish, he had already moved, and the desk's surface was being cleared at a surprising speed. Bricks were sorted by shape, size, and color, wires were untangled and coiled into neat bundles, and everything was stacked in the corresponding box. Once he was done, a contented smile stirred March's lips.

Alex, on the other hand, seemed deflated; his "ace," as he had called me, had ultimately proved useless. Well, almost, I thought, as I inserted a button cell in Thom's LEGO model. The large hadron collider was complete.

"Check this," I announced, watching the inside of the barrel light up thanks to an ingenious system of pink and orange LEDs. Very movie-like. I could tell March and Alex weren't impressed yet, though.

I grabbed some small plastic pearls in one of the LEGO boxes and loaded them on each side of the barrel. "Then I think you press here to fire them against each other—haven't tested it yet."

While Alex watched with an expression of incredulity, March bent toward the LEGO model to press on the block I was pointing at. A small click resounded, and indeed the two plastic pearls were released and collided in the barrel. At the same time a small piece fell off.

"Is it broken already?" March asked anxiously.

"I don't know," I said, reaching inside the barrel to retrieve the piece. "It doesn't look like a LEGO brick. I'm not sure where it goes."

Once I held the tiny object in front of my eyes, I realized it wasn't a LEGO, but rather a micro SD card.

"That's MacGyver shit!"

The three of us turned to look at Degraeves, who had been watching the whole operation with undisguised interest.

March gave him the cold-killer look. "Can you wait in the living room, please?"

Degraeves padded away reluctantly. "You the boss, sir."

Once the guy's back was turned to us, March and Alex moved closer to examine the SD card.

"I'll plug it in my phone and check what's on it," I said, hardly able to contain the excitement in my voice.

I went to get my phone in my bag and sank back in the gamer chair's soft blue leather while March and Alex stood on each side, leaning against its back to better watch the screen. Two perfectly timed sighs of annoyance caressed my hair when a password prompt popped up on the screen. Of course the data was protected. But thanks to Colin's efforts, I was pretty sure I knew what to type in that field.

My doom has come upon me.

"Is this that quote he used as a password to protect his files at EMT?" Alex asked as my fingers danced on the glass screen.

"Yes." I pressed Enter, only to deflate instantly when a red window appeared on the screen. "Dammit. We don't have time for this!"

"Twice the same password . . . that would have been too much luck," Alex commented grimly.

My fingers rapped on the desk as I went through my options. We could just take the drive and abandon decrypting its content for now; there was no telling what sort of secondary protection protocol might start if I entered one too many wrong passwords. But just one last try—surely we could afford that. My eyes searched his desk for a hint, anything that might sound like the perfect password. No, Thom had probably stuck to using a full sentence; staring at his stapler wouldn't help.

March, at least, had refrained from commenting on my failure. But, above me, his breath was a little unsteady. I didn't want to disappoint him—to disappoint anyone. I didn't want to lose. I stared at the screen. In my mind, flashes of conversations replayed, a kaleidoscope of words, memories I had with Thom, of Colin and me cracking his password.

This is taken from Homer's Iliad. *It's the part where Hector is about to die.*

"I want to make one last try," I mumbled as I typed the sentence, praying my brain cells wouldn't betray me. "But we'll probably need Colin again."

It wasn't actual joy, but when on the screen the window's fire-engine red faded to a welcoming green, I laughed. I watched my phone grant us access to the SD card's content, a series of nervous chortles shaking my frame. It was so logical, so . . . beautiful, in a way.

"Sometimes I wish I had a flashlight and could take a trek in there," March said in a tender, almost reverent tone, tapping his index finger against my skull gently. "What was it?"

I looked up. "Back at EMT, we found that Thom had used a famous line from *The Iliad* to encrypt his code: *My doom has come upon me. I thought maybe I'd try the second part of that line: Let me not then die ingloriously and without a struggle.*"

As it was, Thom's choice of password didn't leave much doubt regarding the circumstances of his involvement in the Ruby scheme, and the pictures he had scanned and stored on this card only drove this point home. They were a little grainy, likely taken with a telephoto lens: his wife and son at the park, the three of them in their living room, Thom leaving EMT's building. Someone had threatened him and made it clear that he had nowhere to hide.

On my right shoulder, I felt a warm touch—Alex's hand. "You were right. He was trapped, and he tried to leave bread crumbs."

A little huff escaped March. "Island, is there anything else on the drive? What's this file?" He pointed to a text file, among the images.

I tapped to open it. One line of code. A bit underwhelming, if you ask me.

```
RR extends coreLaunch {}
```

"What is that?" Alex inquired.

"No idea . . . coreLaunch is one of Ruby's classes. It basically gathers all the necessary configuration info, checks that all the files are ready, and launches the program. But I'm pretty sure we don't have any class called 'RR' extending this one. Maybe it's something Thom added to the version of Ruby that was on the servers he destroyed?"

Alex's hand finally slid away from my shoulder to point at the code. "You told Ellingham you were worried Ruby's code might have been stolen. Do you think Thom could have added this 'class' to help find it?"

"I don't know. Given what coreLaunch does, it's more likely that it's a set of hidden functions meant to tweak Ruby's launch parameters. Perhaps even make it crash entirely."

He winked at me. "I like the sound of that."

"So do I," March concurred. "Now what we need is to understand who recruited Roth. I'll ask Phyllis to arrange a flight to Zürich. Mr. Morgan, please warn your superior that Struthio will bill his division for any expense made on your behalf. Processing fees will apply."

A whiff of good-guy cologne reached my nose as Alex leaned forward. *"Processing fees?"*

"Yes."

"Let me make sure I get this right: You ruined my tires, and now you're going to bill the CIA 'processing fees' for the trip you're *already* billing them?"

"Yes. Five percent fixed rate." March typed something on his phone. "Would you like to subscribe to our options package? There's a supplement."

"What's in it?" Alex asked warily.

"Seat, parachute, light meal. Drinks not included."

I sprang up from the chair. "What the hell, *March?*"

"I'm sorry, Island, rates and packages are determined annually; this is out of my hands."

A destitute childhood had left March a bit of a tightwad in some regards, and I remembered one of his friends once telling me that he negotiated his flights from Paulie, a rather nice mobster operating an illegal private airline in Pennsylvania. Squaring my shoulders, I glared at him. "What about the Paulie Airlines discount?"

March's jaw ticked. "I don't think Mr. Morgan qualifies for this program."

"But *I* do?"

His features relaxed. "Of course." He reached inside his jacket for a small leather wallet, from which he pulled a golden rectangular plastic chip with a little plane engraved on it. He placed it in my hand. "Free flights. Free drinks. It's yours."

I held the coupon in my hands for a few seconds, looking into March's eyes, in that ocean of blue. And I wondered if he understood that I didn't care about free flights, that I didn't need him to make Alex miserable in order to assert some sort of virile superiority. Apparently not.

I handed him the golden chip back with a sigh. "I'm redeeming it; I want a seat for Alex. And a parachute."

Ever a master of self-control, March took the chip with a curt nod, the rise of his chest and the tightening of his lips the only hints that he was, in fact, seething.

A cocky smile tugged at the corners of Alex's lips, while March reached inside his jacket for a tube of extra-strong mints and poured a couple into his hand. Oh, I knew this posture, this face—the slanting of his eyes, the way his molars ground the candy with muted sounds. The last time March had looked at me like this, I had ended up in his trunk as retribution for a similar display of insubordination.

FIFTEEN

The Medal

"Book your tickets to hell."

—*Quasimodo d'El Paris*, 1999

When we stepped out on Main Street, the sky had turned a dark gray, and a light drizzle had started to fall, the characteristic scent of rain on grass and asphalt permeating the air. I saw a couple of passersby in the park facing the waterfront, but other than that, the area was still as deserted as ever. Maybe it'd get a little better after five, when people would come home. Along the Queensboro Bridge, I could see the Roosevelt Tram approaching the island, its red car dangling from its cable a measly 250 feet above the East River. I had never taken it. Never needed to, for one, and, well, the idea of being trapped up there made me feel a little queasy. As one of my dad's friends put it: "They had it renovated by the French. French cars. French cables. Cables that surrender! Would you ride in a tram that surrenders? I sure as hell wouldn't!"

Alex's palm on my chest took me by surprise. Don't get ideas: he was merely blocking me, and I realized March had frozen as well. Both men's jaws were set, their upper bodies imperceptibly leaning forward as they gazed at the Lexus twenty yards away.

"Not like you to litter, Mr. November," Alex said in a low voice.

"Indeed, Mr. Morgan."

I squinted at the car. Alex was right. *I* would never have noticed, but less than an inch away from March's visible front tire lay some kind of discarded burger wrapper, which could have, indeed, been the result of a random act of littering, but, with the right amount of paranoia, it almost looked like it had been placed . . . with the clear intent for the car to drive on it. My eyes traveled back and forth between the two of them. "What is it? What's wrong with the car?"

March stepped in front of me. "Island, stay back, please."

A chill coursed through my body. My eyes never left his gloved hands as he pushed back his left sleeve to reveal a high-end black chronograph I knew. He pressed a button on the side, turning the glass into an LCD screen. Would he use it to text someone, like I had seen him do in Tokyo? He seemed busy rotating the bezel ring instead. Lights flashed twice in the distance. I refrained from applauding when the Lexus's engine started, because judging from the looks on March and Alex's faces, this was not the time to imitate a sea lion—I do it well, though.

Alex's hand sneaked around my waist, pulling me backward and against him. I fidgeted a bit at his sudden closeness. March's eyes were locked on the car. He started rotating the ring again slowly, commanding the front wheels. The car moved a few inches.

I felt the explosion as much as I heard it—a deafening boom thundering through my rib cage at the same instant Alex gathered me in his arms and shielded my head with his hand. The Lexus was propelled in the air by the force of the blast, before being swallowed by a cloud of flames and smoke, debris flying all the way in our direction as the charred carcass crashed back on the ground.

The seconds after were a blur. My ears were buzzing, making March's and Alex's voices sound muted, distant. There were burning fragments of plastic and metal everywhere, and I could see both men had pulled out their guns. I registered a sort of hum coming from our right, getting closer. I know it's stupid, but the first thing I connected it with was a chain saw, and my legs nearly gave way. How angry do you have to be to blow up someone's car and go after them with a chain saw right afterward?

I was wrong. The hum morphed into a roar, and two bikes tore through the acrid smoke, their riders' faces concealed by dark helmets. Oh God, I knew where this was headed. Alex dragged me behind one of the thick concrete columns flanking the building's entrance; March imitated him and took cover behind the other. Blood rushed and pounded fast in my temples. One of the bikers drifted to a stop and raised something that looked bigger than a gun in our direction. A machine pistol. He fired at us, sending a round of bullets smashing against the walls and pavement with earsplitting cracks. Alex squeezed me against his body so hard it hurt, while around us chunks of concrete exploded under the force of each impact. Somewhere nearby I heard screaming; the passersby I had noticed were running away toward a building to shield themselves.

A beat of silence followed the last shot. Could be that the gun's magazine was empty. There was no second round, though. Before our attacker had the time to see him through the thick cloud of dust enveloping us, March stepped out. There was something surreal, I now realized, about the calm fluidity of his movements. Always so precise, so focused amidst the chaos surrounding him. One shot. All he needed. I saw our assailant collapse, his helmet visor shattered by the star-shaped impact.

I think March and I had the same idea; he spun around, gun still firmly in hand, looking for the second biker. There was a roar coming from the left; Alex shoved me to the ground when the guy raced toward us. March shot twice in the bike's rear wheel, causing it to somersault. Alex finished the job, firing four bullets at the unfortunate biker without hesitation as he tumbled forward.

My fingers were still gripping Alex's leather jacket; I felt his free hand stroke my back. I stared at the two dead men at our feet. The one Alex had killed was bleeding on the pavement, a thin layer of dust absorbing the growing red stain like a blotter. I took a deep breath to block the nausea churning in my stomach and let go of Alex, stepping closer to March. He seemed nearly unruffled, when I knew I must have looked haggard.

I wasn't given time to think about it any further. "We need to move," March said as he grabbed my hand and signaled for Alex to follow with a jerk of his chin. Next thing I knew, the three of us were running fast down Main Street toward the Queensboro Bridge, and my feet were barely touching the ground. My mind was spinning, fueled by adrenaline. Between two choked intakes of air, I blurted out the first coherent thought I could hold on to. "March! Y-Your leaflet talked about nonlethal methods!"

"There's some fine print on the last page."

"I knew it," Alex snapped.

We kept running, even as on the bridge police cars could be seen approaching, sirens blaring. We were almost at the tram station. I gathered March intended for us to seek refuge under its massive triangular hangar. Screams echoed from the station's entrance, and a group of panicked people hurried down the ramp leading to the cars—random explosions and gunshots tend to do that.

I had already been picturing myself safely inside the hangar, but my relief was short-lived. Above us, a new detonation tore through the air. I screamed, certain for a split second that I had been shot. I was still alive, but near us, Alex had stumbled and fallen to the ground. On his left shoulder, something had torn his jacket, and a dark, wet stain was rapidly forming on the worn leather. I freed myself from March's grip to lunge toward him. "Alex! March, Alex is—"

"Superficial," Alex groaned as he struggled to get up.

I offered him my arm, but March shoved my head down at the same time that two new shots were fired in our direction. Where *the hell* from? We were well away from Thom's residence. There was only one brick building left behind us, and its windows all seemed closed. Everything else was just vast empty lawns, and the waterfront. I saw March look up with a snarl as he hauled a wincing Alex up. I followed the direction of his gaze.

Seriously?

Now at least I understood why those people had fled the tram station. Alone in a rapidly rising car stood a guy with a sniper rifle. The double doors that would normally prevent passengers from shooting fellow commuters were half open, and he was still aiming at us. I watched the car shake as it passed the first tower base, forcing him to postpone his killing spree.

Alex was able to cover the last yards to the hangar with March and me, but his face was ashen, and beads of sweat had formed on his temples. We hid behind one of the large steel pillars supporting the structure.

"Stay with him, and for the love of God, don't try anything," March ordered, tapping the tip of my nose—a habit he had taken up on our first encounter, because he seemed to believe it held the power to shut me both up and down.

Next to me, Alex managed a smirk. "I'll keep an eye on her."

March nodded and retreated further inside the hangar. There, a deserted control room overlooked the red doors of the tram departure ramp, on which an empty car still waited.

"What are you doing?" I hissed, seeing him climb up the metal stairs leading to the control room.

He didn't bother with a reply and kicked the door open before lunging at the dashboard. *Oh God.* There were at least two things I knew for sure about March: he was *not* an accredited tram operator . . . and he never gave up.

I have no idea what he touched—what he broke—but after a couple of seconds, the huge cables hauling the cars started to vibrate and creak ominously above our heads. I craned my neck to see that the small wheels rolling on the track cable now seemed to be spinning backward.

That asshole in the red car was being hauled back toward the island at the same time that the second car was starting to move.

I felt Alex's amazed gasp against my ear. "Oh shit, he's got some balls."

March stormed out of the control room and jumped down to the first floor, not even bothering with the stairs, just in time to force the second car's doors open and get in.

"Oh no . . . Oh *nononono* . . . March! Please *stop this*!" I yelled in vain as the car sped away and toward its evil twin.

Against me, Alex shifted a little to see what was going on. The movement caused a renewed trickle of blood to appear on his jacket, which he ignored with clenched teeth. I searched my pockets for tissues and pressed several on the wound, my stomach heaving when I saw the sticky red coating my fingers. For a moment I could no longer focus, and a long, painful shudder shook my frame. Alex was bleeding in my arms, while in the distance, March's car was about to reach that horrible sniper guy's car, traveling in the opposite direction. I tried to breathe through my nose, concentrated on pressing my hands to Alex's shoulder.

In my throat, air wheezed. March was climbing on the car's roof, his jacket flapping in a rising wind that seemed to hinder his progress. "Alex, he's gonna kill himself!"

"Maybe. That looks like a ten-foot jump with a one-, maybe two-second window, though. His odds aren't that bad," Alex said, his eyes locked on the two cars and the dwindling distance between them.

"But there's a guy with a rifle in there!" I squeaked.

Indeed, the other car's occupant had no intention of getting caught. He leaned precariously against the half-open doors and attempted to fire at March. The wind carried the sound of a first gunshot; I squeezed Alex's hand harder. Thankfully, for the particular task of hanging from a tram car like a monkey and shooting people, a handgun would have been more practical than the heavy rifle that guy carried. I jumped and breathed shivering sighs of relief with every shot that missed March, who was shielding himself behind the steel arm securing his own tram car to the cable.

"He's doing well so far. He can still survive the jump and die later," Alex commented in a conversational tone, while we could make out March's silhouette standing on the tram car, an ink stroke against the low clouds engulfing Manhattan's skyline. The cars were now too close to each other for the other guy to shoot at March, who stood legs and arms slightly apart, body projecting forward. He was getting ready to jump.

I struggled for air in a series of panicked pants and squeezed my eyes shut; I couldn't look. I couldn't.

"Island, you can open your eyes."

Alex's hand squeezed mine. My eyelids fluttered open. *Thank you, Raptor Jesus. Owe you one.* March was still alive, now kneeling on the roof of the opposite car. Several seconds passed, during which the car approached the first base tower it had passed earlier, and again it struck me how feline, how unhurried his movements were when March did his "job." He was now closer than ever to the car's opening, hands resting on the edge of the roof. The shooter apparently wouldn't take the risk to come up, and had opted to retreat to the corner farthest from the door, his back to the windows. Waiting.

March chose the moment the car was passing over the first base tower. The steel structure trembled; I saw him leap forward and rotate his body around the roof's edge, agile as a big cat. He was inside the car before I could even understand how he had done that, and if enough gym hours could teach me the same trick. Several gunshots echoed in the dark, then only silence. I couldn't make out the inside of the car clearly. I'm pretty sure I forgot to breathe.

"March . . ." I whispered.

At my side, Alex didn't seem convinced that "Mr. November" had survived the fight. He placed his index finger on the black Glock's trigger, ready to welcome the shooter if need be.

The car was still moving, getting closer and closer.

A cold sweat broke on my back. "A-Alex . . . isn't it supposed to slow down?"

"Oh *shit*."

That wasn't the answer I expected, not when I could see and hear the cables vibrate under the weight of the car racing toward us without giving any sign of stopping. Alex pulled me out of the way, dragging me with him. The metallic noises coming from the car were getting louder and louder. We rushed away from the departure ramp, desperate to escape the tram station. My heart was beating painfully fast, and I had this petrifying feeling that I was racing against the limits of my own body, that I wasn't running fast enough, like I was struggling in quicksand.

If you think the Lexus exploding was bad, wait until you sit on the front row while a ten-ton cable car crashes at thirty miles per hour against a concrete-and-metal hangar. My last clear memory is a threatening rumble and a few seconds of weightlessness, before the car hit the ramp, destroying everything in its wake with a terrifying din. Metal bent with long howls, the wall supporting the control room collapsed, sparks and debris flew in all directions, some hitting the police cars that were coming from Main Street and surrounding the tram station. Alex and I crashed face-first into the wet patch of grass in front of the hangar; I felt the weight of his body on mine, crushing me as much as he was shielding me from flying fragments of concrete.

Praise French technology after all—the eight-cable ropeway didn't rupture . . . entirely. I registered the low, ominous moan of the cable structure when the tram's engines stopped and the tension became unbearable. One of them did give, snapping with a loud noise and lashing at the lampposts and trees around us like a several-inch-thick whip, before ending its course on the hood of a police car.

After it was over, thirty seconds or so passed during which I was shaking so much I couldn't move. The rain was seeping through my clothes, cold and wet, and in contrast, Alex's breath burned against the nape of my neck, his stubble rasping my skin. His embrace finally loosened; I rolled away in panic.

"March! March! *Oh God—*"

"I'm good, biscuit."

What the . . . ?

Okay, he wasn't good. This time March looked ruffled. Really ruffled. Like a man who had taken a twenty-foot jump off a tram car in extremis. A few yards away from us, he was trying to sit up with slow movements. There were bruises on his face, and his jacket was a mess. I scrambled to him. I got close, but I didn't dare touch him. You always hear that people need air and space and all that stuff when they're wounded. "Oh my God, are you sure you're okay? Your *shoulder*!"

That I didn't dare to touch either. I gathered he had landed on his side, thus sustaining the minimum possible damage, but his left shoulder looked . . . wrong. Like it was slumping. Dislocated, very likely. Behind me, policemen had gotten out of their cars and were running toward us, some asking if we were okay, another talking in his radio about a possible terrorist attack. I heard sirens. "March, there's an ambulance coming, don't move!"

"It's all right, biscuit. I just need—"

"Allow me."

I looked up to see Alex's frame hovering over us. His own shoulder had stopped bleeding. A faint smirk twisted his lips as he looked at March. "I'm probably in no condition to do this, but it's gonna be my pleasure entirely."

The muscles in March's jaw tightened. "I'm certain it will."

I stared at the two of them in confusion. Alex had knelt by March's side; he circled him with his arms as if he was going to hug him, positioned one hand on his shoulder, the other under his armpit, and pulled, eliciting a low groan from his nemesis. It was over in a second, and afterward March massaged the area, his eyes closed under a creased brow. "Thank you, Mr. Morgan."

I dusted grass and gravel from March's hair gingerly. "Let's get you both to the hospital."

"All right," he said, a tender expression softening his previous grimace.

Above us, Alex sounded almost amused. "Mr. November, you destroyed the Roosevelt Tram. I'm afraid I'm gonna have to report this."

March's features hardened into a poker smile. "Make sure Mr. Erwin enjoys every single detail, Mr. Morgan."

I froze. This was something I knew already, but hearing March pronounce the Caterpillar's name suddenly gave me a new perspective. This job, me, Alex . . . The Ruby case was a battlefield for these two, a clash between the Caterpillar's intention to retain control over his precious "South African" and March's equally strong will to turn that page for good.

Except I stood in the middle, and given my unfortunate family tree, I feared I was a pawn the Caterpillar wouldn't let go of so easily.

Before I could further my descent into such gloomy thoughts, March fished a small object from inside his jacket. Alex knelt again, and I scooted closer to look as well. It looked like a bloodstained medal in the shape of a shield, depicting a parachute with a sword in its center and some details I couldn't make out in the dark. There was also something engraved.

"*Numquam Retro,*" Alex read out loud.

I translated with a frown. "*Never retreat?* What is it? Was it on that guy?"

"Yes. You might want to translate it as '*Niemals Züruck,*' in German," March explained.

"You know German?" I asked, still trying to figure out where he was going with this.

His eyes narrowed at the bloody medal. "Not that well, but I know the Jagdkommando—the Austrian special forces."

Alex took it from his hands to examine it. "Austria . . . interesting. A stone's throw from German-speaking Switzerland—"

"And Zürich," I concluded, pulling out from my pocket the micro SD card we had found hidden in Thom's apartment. "Whoever manipulated Thom was ready to kill anyone for this, so let's go find Ruby and discover what that code does to it."

SIXTEEN
The PJs

"There's only one treatment I can inject you with, Peyton: love!"

—Izzie Shepherd, *The Cardiologist's Christmas Surprise*

I've never been a fan of hospitals. The medicinal smell, doors slamming, hushed voices—it reminds me of my mom's accident, of that split second when I woke up in a foreign bed with tubes lodged in my throat, and my dad was smiling at me while I thought I was dying.

For ten years after that, it was the only memory I had of the day of her death, until Rislow tried to extract my kneecaps on an operating table in an abandoned French hospital. There, suffocated by the most intense terror I had ever experienced, I remembered her murder. I saw it all over again: her body going limp in front of the wheel after a single bullet had traversed her skull, her long auburn curls matted with crimson blood against the white of her blouse. I heard my own screams, in that car that wouldn't stop.

I remembered the crash, how everything had become loud and white.

Then tearing through the mist, through the flames rising from the hood and the panicked shrieks of onlookers, had been March, the little black knife he had used to cut the seat belt, his arms around me for the first time. The scent of the mints.

Him, in the shadows. Since that day, and for all those years.

And even now, ever present in my thoughts.

I was sitting on a bed in a room at Bellevue Hospital, facing Murrell and that older blond agent I had seen with Colin the day prior. March and Alex had been taken to different rooms to be examined, and my own doctor had left ten minutes ago with a statement that I was fine, save for a few bruises and the promise of some degree of PTSD.

I don't think Murrell cared about such issues, though. At the moment he looked pissed. Or maybe it was just his normal face. He adjusted the cuffs of that (really) classy trench coat, speaking in a slow baritone voice. "Once again, so I'm sure we get this right: *at no time* did you see Mr. 'November' engage in *any kind* of reckless behavior that might have precipitated this collision, Miss Chaptal?"

I cleared my throat and avoided their unwavering gazes, my finger-tips rubbing the kind of cool, scratchy sheets hospitals seem to special-ize in—no idea where they got them. Was there a place that specifically sold scratchy linen? Could you apply for a refund if it was too soft after all? "Well, he did climb in the car at the same time that Austrian guy did. But it was only to stop him. Then those little wheels on the cables started rolling backward and the car was coming down toward us. That guy must have touched the tram's buttons, sir."

Murrell's eyes narrowed. "Now, did you see him do that?"

"Not exactly, but he was there first. Also the tram was French, so—"

That seemed to catch the attention of the stoic blond agent. He scratched his sort hair, and a frown deepened the creases around his mouth. "French?"

"Yeah. They had it renovated by Poma. Everything was French in there: French cables, French cars . . ."

He seemed appalled. "*Damn!* Even the little wheels?"

"Yeah."

Murrell raised a doubtful eyebrow at his colleague, who kept mumbling something under his breath about this shocking news. A southern drawl had insinuated itself in the guy's expletives, perhaps due to the emotion. Murrell sighed. "Miss Chaptal, security cameras contradict your version."

I gulped. "Oh God. This time it's Guantanamo, right?"

"Do we have orange PJs that small?" the blond guy asked Murrell, with what sounded like genuine curiosity.

He rubbed his eyes between his thumb and forefinger in response. "I don't know, Stiles. I don't know . . . Why don't you go get yourself a coffee while I finish with your soul mate here."

The guy's perplexed stare traveled back and forth between me and his partner for a couple seconds, and he eventually headed for the door, flashing me the hint of a smile before closing it behind himself.

My eyes slanted toward Murrell. "What was that supposed to mean?"

"Did you think about the PJs?"

"Of course not!" Of course I had.

He seemed to be fighting a smile. "I think we're done for tonight. You remain under the supervision of Agent Morgan. You're not permitted to leave this hospital without him."

Knots formed in my stomach at the memory of Alex's injury. "Where is he? Is he okay?"

Murrell pointed to his left with his thumb. "Next room."

"And . . . Mr. November?"

"He seemed well enough. We had a few questions for him as well," he said, his tone suddenly a notch cooler.

My chest tightened. "What's going to happen to him? To me?"

"That's something you should ask Agent Morgan."

Murrell gestured for me to follow him with a little jerk of his chin. I hopped down from the hospital bed, grabbed my sweater and bag that a thoughtful nurse had gathered for me on a chair, and we exited the room together. In the dimly lit hallway, the clock on the wall indicated ten fifteen; I gathered patients were sleeping. He opened the next door and ushered me in before closing it behind me.

The room was very similar to mine, with muted lights and a large window overlooking the East River and the Queens skyline under a starless night sky. Alex was sitting on the edge of his white hospital bed, shirtless. On his left shoulder, a thick bandage now covered the wound inflicted by the Austrian guy. Remembering the wisdom of those old Wonderbra ads, I struggled to focus on his peaceful smile rather than the ripped torso I was seeing for the first time. I tried. I really tried. But the various material I had gathered on my favorite research subject was quickly filling my mind and rewiring my neurons. I *had* to study Alex's androgenic hair.

So here goes. Alex was a CS (circumareolo-sternal), which is acceptable, but somewhat underwhelming. My eyes scanned the faint brown line between his pectorals and those questionable little rings of hair around his nipples. There was also a pencil-thin dusting of hair under his navel, but overall the skin covering his muscles seemed very smooth, making me suspect some sort of partial shaving business. It was a far call from March's glorious PSI pattern, which formed a satisfying golden chestnut rug across his chest, right up to his clavicles, and ran down his stomach in a narrowing line. *PSI*, as in "pecto-sterno-infraclavicular." A synonym for super manly, especially when combined with the abs of a superhero.

And by the way, yes, people were paid actual money to conduct studies regarding the subject and establish a precise chart and terminology system. I wish I had been part of that scientific adventure. I *so* wish I had.

"Are you all right? You seem distracted."

That was as good as him saying, "Hey, my eyes are up here." I self-combusted. "Y-yeah. Sorry. I zoned out for a second."

There was a mischievous glint in Alex's eyes as he spoke. "It's okay. Oh, and I meant to tell you I like your version of the tram collision. Very creative."

I'm almost positive I heard my heart plop down into my stomach with a splattering sound. How the hell could he already know? Had they tapped my room or something?

Alex seemed to read my mind. He gave me a little wink. "Island, Murrell and Stiles work with me, you know."

I winced.

"Anyway, we're keeping that version. Very dramatic, excellent for journalists."

I walked to the bed. "You mean March won't get in trouble? We'll blame it all on the other guy?"

"He won't. Regarding the second point, however—" His gaze hardened. "I'm obliged to inform you that the details of what happened on Roosevelt Island are *absolutely* confidential."

"I know that, I'm just wondering how you guys will explain it to the public."

He dismissed my concern with a shrug of his good shoulder. "It's already been taken care of. There's no shortage of supplies in our cold rooms."

As he said this, he pulled his phone from his back pocket, swiped across the screen, and handed it to me. In the browser, the Fox News home page was open, with a series of blaring headlines about a victimless terrorist attack led by an Algerian jihadist named Mohamed Nabil Nachour. He was described as a lone wolf, trained in Afghanistan and Syria, and the journalists claimed his body had been retrieved from the wreckage. A series of sickening pics corroborated this thesis, where Nachour's lifeless, bruised body could be identified among the tram's debris.

Right below was a video of Hadrian Ellingham making a stilted speech about the fight for freedom, his love of New York, and how EM Group would donate thirty million dollars to the mayor's office to rebuild the tram in exchange for some pimping of EMG's leper kids foundation. Behind him, a giant screen displayed a hasty photo montage of the future project: "Roosevelt 3000," a futuristic aerial tramway—made in America—whose cars would sport giant pics of smiling leper kids, along with EMG's logo.

I handed Alex his phone back with a grim expression. "I don't like that. This isn't right, and you know it."

His lips curved in a rueful smile. "It's just politics, Island. That way everybody wins."

"And that guy, Nachour, does he win too?"

"You have no idea who he was, what he did to end up like this."

In Alex's eyes I could read nothing but a gentle weariness, a silent plea to let go of a cause neither of us had any control over anyway. I thought of Antonio Romos, a Mexican killer I had freed from March's trunk—where he awaited certain death—and whose case I had pleaded until March gave him a second chance. Antonio had ultimately helped us beat Dries's plans as a way to pay his debt, and he proved to be a loyal and reliable partner. But no one would ever know whether Nachour had it in him to accomplish something good.

I looked down at the mice decorating my ballet flats. "I don't care who he was. I believe everyone can change, at some point in their lives."

I registered the rustle of the sheets, saw his bare feet on the blue linoleum as he got up. "You're wrong. And still naïve. But I wouldn't want *that* to change."

I hadn't realized I was standing so close to the bed. So close to him. His right hand grazed mine tentatively, fingertips traveling up, tracing my shoulder, reaching the nape of my neck. I stood petrified, my feet glued to the floor when every ounce of rationality in me told me to stop him, that our situation was complicated enough as it was.

The silence in the room made everything louder, each quiet breath, the sound of his tongue darting to wet his lips. I thought the whole hospital might hear us. He had to be hypnotizing me. That's why those cinnamon eyes weren't blinking, staring into mine until I couldn't sustain the intensity of his gaze any longer and my eyelids fluttered shut.

And then the brush of lips on my forehead. I shouldn't be there, I thought. I needed to think this through, figure out what was left of . . . us. But I stayed, and he kissed me again, pressing a tender peck on the tip of my nose this time. I couldn't see his smile, but somehow I guessed it, pictured it in my mind. The third kiss landed on my jaw, and when his fingers laced with mine, I gripped them instinctively. Because otherwise I think my knees would have given up on me.

When had he moved even closer? My eyes snapped open at the feeling of his chest, his entire body pressed against mine, warming it fast past any acceptable temperature. I couldn't see more than shadows, not when a mere inch separated my nose from his clavicle and I was trying hard not to meet his eyes anyway. I breathed in the good-guy cologne, dissected its soapy notes mingled with his own scent—skin, sweat, and the medical smell of antiseptic on his wound. Our fingers were still intertwined, but I was no longer in control. *His* hands were gripping *mine*, gentle but firm, his palms unexpectedly hot.

My breathing grew uneven, answering his own intake of air as he bent his head to take what he had meant to all along. It was all new and familiar. I knew the brush of his lips, the stubble under my fingertips as my hands reached for his face, when and how he'd tilt his head . . . It was Alex. And it was someone else as well, holding my waist, pressing me against his body. Not so much a stranger—as I had first feared—than a different man, one whose kisses were more intense, more aggressive. Each nip, each tug at my lips spoke of an urgency that I found a little frightening, but at the same time, seemed to free something within me. My palms settled on exploring the smooth planes of his back, and I responded with some clumsy Frenching, punctuated by a couple of perhaps miscalculated nips.

I read somewhere that your body releases adrenaline during a kiss, which is how humans manage to overlook most practicalities when engaging in tonsil hockey—also it's apparently excellent for your heart. When Alex broke our kiss to press his forehead against mine, the lust bubble popped, and I was engulfed back into reality. A reality in which the status of our relationship remained unclear, and where even in Alex's arms I still couldn't stop thinking of March.

Alex's hands cupped my cheeks with a tenderness that was almost at odds with the animalistic exchange of saliva we had been engaged in mere seconds prior. I could feel my face scrunching already; I bit on my lower lip hard, willing my emotions back under control.

"Baby, I know this is my fault," he cooed, his breath fanning over my lips. "I hate feeling you drift away like that."

God, not the mind reading. Not now, not when my brain was yelling at me to take a step back and *fricking think.* "Alex—"

"I don't want to lose you."

This was too much for me to handle. I inched back. "Alex, I think we both need—"

"I love you."

To take a break.

We needed to take a break. And he had just fired the L-bomb into my unsuspecting face. On my cheeks, his touch now felt white-hot, and to tell it all, I was way out of my depth.

Maybe the mind reading was a good thing after all; his eyes studied me with a knowing glint, and he pulled back, leaving me room to breathe, to think. His lips curved into a hopeful smile. A goddamn puppy smile. "It's okay. I can be patient."

Now, there was a lot packed in those words that I didn't yet feel ready to deal with. I nodded weakly, and he reached for his shirt on a nearby chair, only to be interrupted by a knock on the door. Alex didn't reply; he pulled out his smartphone again, and his fingers danced on the screen. I saw black-and-white shapes moving on the tilted glass surface. Could he check the hospital's security cameras with that thing?

His index finger tapped once in the middle of the screen; I spun on my heel at the sound of the door unlocking. Hold on. Had we—had *I*—been locked in there with him?

"Come in, Mr. November," he said in his best good-cop voice.

I couldn't really place why, but seeing March's tall figure in the door-frame brought me a sense of relief. Even if the slanting of his eyes as he took in Alex's state of undress announced some imminent retribution.

"You might want to finish dressing, Mr. Morgan. A cold can happen so quickly . . ."

Ouch. I had heard him address guys he had been about to kill with a warmer voice.

Alex welcomed the unspoken threat with a good-natured smile. "I'm touched by your concern."

March's brow lowered for a second, but he managed to rein in the volcanic temper I knew to be sleeping under the surface of his usually cool exterior. Meanwhile Alex finished buttoning his shirt and shrugged his jacket on.

"Island," March began, sending a wary look in Alex's direction. "Before we leave for Zürich, there are things I would like . . . things *I know you* would like to discuss."

"Can you elaborate?" Alex asked, replacing his Glock in the waist-band holder at his back.

No, he couldn't. March's dark blue gaze met mine, a silent under-standing passing between us. "Maybe we could go to your office with Alex? That way he can wait for me while we talk." My eyes darted to Alex. "Agent Murrell said I'm still sort of under surveillance."

Blue eyes darkened at this. "If that's what you're worried about, I'm certain we can put an end to this ridiculous—"

"Mr. November, if you could get rid of me, I'd have gotten a call already." Alex had shelved the good-cop act for a moment, and there was a determination in his own gaze that made me wonder just how deep his motivations went in this mess.

In any case, he was right. March produced the precious tube of mints from his crumpled jacket's inner pocket, gobbled two, and adjusted his black leather gloves. "It will be my pleasure to welcome you to our office, Mr. Morgan."

SEVENTEEN

The Skittles

"Green like his eyes, red like the fire of his passion, orange like his tan: on his silky lips, Candice was tasting the rainbow."

—Carrie Aznable, *White House, Dark Needs*

Stiles was kind enough to give us a lift to Struthio in a black CIA minivan—I'm not entirely sure he had a say in the matter, though—and thus, I spent the fifteen-minute ride sandwiched between a brooding March and a smug Alex in one of the backseats. I mostly ignored them: I was too busy texting Joy and coming up with a bunch of lies about some unexpected work meeting. She texted back that I was a liar, that my pants were on fire, and asked if I was in Alex's bed. I sighed.

Around eleven thirty, the black minivan slowed down in front of an elegant brick building facing the park, the kind of place that makes you fear you'll get booted by security as soon as you walk in. March stepped out of the car first, holding the door for me; Alex followed. Both men seemed to be taken aback when Stiles waved good-bye at me with an earnest grin. I bit back a laugh; nothing worse for control freaks than not knowing everything that goes on behind their backs.

Once we had passed the revolving doors, I could tell Alex and I were being watched closely as March led us through the silent marble lobby. I looked up to examine the chandelier hanging fifteen feet or so above our heads, and I think it gave the old concierge sitting behind a wooden desk the wrong idea. His eyes narrowed, appraising me as if I was there to steal the lightbulbs. Behind him, a service door opened. A young black guy in his late teens and sporting a short Mohawk hopped into view and walked toward us. I immediately felt at ease around him, because much like me, he looked like he had ended up here based on some kind of misunderstanding. His gray uniform was a little too big for him, and those were sneakers on his feet. Pink and yellow sneakers.

He looked the three of us up and down before greeting March with a wide grin and a strong Caribbean accent. "Hey, rough night, Mr. November?"

March dusted his jacket as the guy followed us to the elevator. "Yes, Delroy, you could say that."

"Got chased by the ladies?"

"Not exactly."

That earned him a wink from Delroy, who drew his thumb and forefinger across his lips in a zipping gesture.

March acquiesced, while above the brass doors the antique floor indicator's arrow bounced to a stop, signaling that the car had reached the lobby. "By the way, did you take care of—"

"I parked it just the way you like, really parallel to the paint lines." Delroy mimicked two straight lines with his hands, before searching his pocket for a key that he dropped in March's palm with a contented sigh. I checked the logo—Mercedes.

"You need anything else? Sushi? *Crosswords?*" That last word was whispered in a way that suggested the boy regarded March's taste for crosswords as some kind of filthy sexual fetish.

Said fetishist pulled out a few bills from his wallet and gave them to Delroy. "No, no sushi, thank you. Perhaps some chicken and salads?" He turned to Alex and me and tilted his head, waiting for us to confirm the order.

I gave Delroy a sheepish smile. "That would be wonderful. And maybe a blueberry muffin if they have any?"

The boy took the bills with a firm nod. "Chicken and salads for four. Blueberry muffin for the miss, you got it!"

"And get something for yourself as well," March said as we stepped into the elevator and watched Delroy race out of the building.

March punched a seven-digit code on a small screen near the elevator buttons, and the doors closed. I studied him while the car took us to the fourteenth and penultimate floor. "He seems to really like you."

"I suppose so. He needed a little help with finding a job for his probation. I pushed his résumé here."

I arched an eyebrow. *"Probation?"*

"Well, Delroy used to sell . . . medical marijuana in Central Park." March cleared his throat. "There might've also been a few misunderstandings involving cars and personal items."

I blinked. Alex's lips pressed together in a visible effort not to laugh.

"He's a good kid," March added, as if in afterthought, when the elevator doors opened.

A sad tenderness warmed my chest upon hearing this. Back in Tokyo, Dries had told me a little about March's past. His mother had died when he was still young, and he had been "raised" by his father, a small-time British drug dealer operating his business in Cape Town's slums. Growing up neglected and left to cope alone with his anxiety issues and obsessive-compulsive disorder, March had soon dropped out of school and resorted to the same survival tactics Delroy had, turning into a violent thug breaking into villas for cash and jewelry. By the time he was seventeen, he had earned himself an eight-month ticket to one of South Africa's worst juvenile prisons. He had met Dries after that, who had given him his "chance"—a mold to be shaped into, a way out of this hopeless life, a fraternity to welcome him, where he'd finally become someone. But at the price of his very soul.

I gathered March saw himself in Delroy and wanted to help him find his way out of the street, hopefully with a regular job rather than by becoming a hit man. Those were the thoughts I entertained when the elevator doors parted, revealing a long hallway whose cream walls were covered halfway up with wooden panels. My eyes darted left and right; there were two double doors on the opposite wall, both closed. A hint of oil soap lingered in the air; the whole place was perfectly clean and silent.

"Does anyone else work here?" I asked, as March led us down the hallway.

"No. I purchased the top two floors, and for now it's only Phyllis and me."

I gawked. "That's a lot of space for two."

March shrugged. "Phyllis believed I was saving too much and needed to diversify my assets. New York real estate seemed like a stable investment, and the previous owner was in a hurry to sell. I think we made a satisfying deal."

I looked around. "So you're planning on renting part of it?"

His lips twisted sideways. "Hmm, I'm not certain. This is admittedly too much space, but I don't like the idea of sharing my premises with strangers."

"Then let's rent to people we already know instead."

My gaze shifted from March's peaceful smile to the door that had just opened in front of us. Leaning against its wooden frame was a woman in her early forties. A pink silk blouse and black cigarette pants clung to her lean, athletic figure. Long red curls fell over her shoulders, which she pushed back as she showed us into a large office with a breathtaking view of Central Park. Once I stood next to her, I realized that her stilettos made her almost as tall as March. And by the way, I was grinning so madly she probably thought I was going to propose.

"You're Phyllis!" I squeaked, overexcited to meet March's top-notch assistant at long last. There was a face to go with that sultry voice now!

She wiggled her hips and struck a little pose. "The one and only."

Alex, who had been silently scanning the nearly empty office until now, stepped forward and extended his hand to her. "Pleased to meet you, I'm Agent—"

"Alexander Morgan," she finished for him, plum lips curving in a mysterious smile.

"You can call me Alex."

"Sounds good," she said, walking around a smoked glass desk and over to a long gray sideboard. There, next to a minimalist paper lamp, sat a midnight-blue lacquered box. She opened it. "So, Island, Alex, Skittles? We also have coffee and tea, if you'd like."

The two of us stared down at the box's contents. Someone—couldn't imagine who—had sorted the candy by color, in perfectly straight lines. Also, that someone apparently only ate the strawberry one. I picked a grape Skittle carefully, feeling March's anxious stare digging holes in my back. Alex seemed to hesitate and, after two seconds or so during which his hand hovered over the candy, chose a lemon one. Now, I'm sure it was an accident when his fingers trembled. He didn't mean to mess up the lemon and green apple lines.

March was at our side in an instant, slamming the box shut with a sharp intake of air. "Delroy is going to bring us dinner; that's enough Skittles for you two."

I winced. "Sorry about that."

"It's all right; I'll reorganize them later." He shot Alex a withering glare. "You're not responsible."

The culprit rolled his eyes at March's antics, and I couldn't restrain a chuckle. Then the laugh died in my throat, because on the desk I saw something. Phyllis, Alex, and March seem to notice the shift in my expression, the three of them sobering as I approached the sleek surface hesitantly.

The coupons were stacked next to a pile of various documents all labeled with colored Post-its depending on their category. Orange was apparently for bills, turquoise for tax-deductible receipts, and so forth. I took the incomplete coupon book and examined the pink logo featuring a little maid silhouette.

It was stupid, in a way. I mean, I had suspected he was behind it, and I had been through so much already—the car chase, the shootings, the explosions, the baby octopus. And then there had been those few minutes with Alex. "Not on the same page" didn't even begin to describe our current situation. So you'd think I could hold my ground in the face of a free cleaning hours program. But that's what did it for me. After this exhausting day, seeing the coupons, feeling them in my hand, crumpling them with a trembling fist . . . It was a tangible reminder of just how close and yet so far March had been for all those months—a ghost hovering above me, tinkering with my life, when I missed him so much I sometimes couldn't sleep. And he was still here, standing a few feet away from me. Frustratingly out of reach.

I knew his attitude owed a lot to Alex's presence, but it was only part of the issue. No, the root of the problem was March's—or was it Hedwardh's?—need for *control*. Control of the Skittles, of my apartment, of my feelings . . . of his. Control of fricking *everything* and *everyone*, at any cost.

I massaged the dull ache I could feel rising in my temples. "March, can we go somewhere to talk?"

From the corner of my eye I saw Phyllis cringe.

"Yes, let's go into my office," he said, gesturing to a closed door behind Phyllis's desk. His eyes slanted in Alex's direction. "Alone."

Alex sustained March's glare with one of his own. "She doesn't leave my sight."

My last nerve snapped at this unbidden display of male territoriality. I straightened my shoulders and attempted to outglare them both, like I had once seen March's flamboyant ex do. "I'm not a package!

You"—I pointed a finger at Alex—"will let me *fucking breathe* for once! If I want to talk to March, I *will!* And you"—I turned to face March— "need to stop playing with me! I. Am. Not. A. Fucking. *Sim!*"

"I know that. I know it all too well!"

Shivers cascaded down my spine at the barely repressed fury in his voice. Hot, cold, like thousands of needles in my shoulders, then my neck, my head.

"I-I—" As I tried to form a coherent sentence through all that confusion and anger, the buzzing in my temples turned into a pounding that seemed to resonate inside my skull in painful waves. I buried my face in my hands; I could no longer stand the blinding white of the room's lighting, and around me the walls were spinning. I remember the way my knees shook, while a little voice in my head noted that it was a miracle my brain had waited so long to take revenge for all the stress it had been subjected to over the past twenty-four hours.

I didn't fall. I saw Alex lunge forward to catch me, but March was quicker, and in a split second I was nestled in his arms, my fingers gripping his jacket. And my eyeballs hurt so much I wanted to scream. A big thank-you to Dries's goon—not only had that asswipe killed my mother, but the resulting car accident had left me with "minor cerebrovascular sequels," as in a two-week coma and occasional but debilitating migraines for the rest of my life.

I vaguely heard March say something to Alex and Phyllis before my feet left the ground. I know he carried me up a flight of stairs, but I had resorted to covering my throbbing forehead with my forearm, so the whole trip felt like riding on a boat swaying in the dark.

There were more stairs, and I was laid on a bed on a darkened mezzanine, registered the weight of a comforter covering me. On the pillow lingered a fragrance I knew: a combination of laundry, some kind of lemony soap, and the indefinable musk of another human being. March's scent.

He left for a while and came back with some kind of meds. Halfway passed out in the haze of my pain, buried under the covers, I registered his fingers threading in my hair as he held a glass of water to my lips. I swallowed the caplet and sipped the cool liquid with difficulty, a trickle running down my chin—which he wiped diligently.

My eyes had already closed when I felt him readjust the comforter. A long sigh breezed against my cheek, followed by a soft contact. March had pressed a kiss to my temple.

At last, I welcomed the viscous night engulfing me.

EIGHTEEN
The Tea

"He will destroy me like he destroyed all the other girls who ended up in his playroom. Yet I know I'll sign his contract. Because it's the only way this gorgeous, dark billionaire will be mine. I look him in the eyes, my jaw set. "'We need to clarify a few terms.'"

"He crosses his arms over his $50,000 silk suit.

"I point at the first page. 'What do you mean by *teabagging?*'"

—P. G. Edwards, *Roped and Broken*

I'm not proud of myself—when I finally cracked an eye open to stare at the ceiling, it was past noon. Way to go when the clock was ticking and we couldn't afford to waste any time. I did feel better, and I hadn't thrown up in spite of the nausea that often came as a bonus with my migraines. So, apart from the burning shame of waking up in March's bed at lunchtime, things were great. I pushed aside his plain white comforter to sit up, and I looked around the sparsely furnished mezzanine overlooking the living room. I gathered that this was the fifteenth floor's penthouse, right above his office. On the wall across from the mezzanine were the same type of windows I had seen downstairs, bathing the place in a dull light and showcasing the silhouettes of Central Park's trees.

I carefully slid out of the bed. My feet grazed something soft on the wooden floor. There was a pair of white terry hotel slippers waiting for me next to my ballet flats, which he had removed—and cleaned, it seemed. I fought a smile. Housekeeping level: over 9000.

After some lengthy stretching, I padded down the stairs. Under the mezzanine was one of those sleek gray modern kitchens that look like it's forbidden to eat in them. No sign of life on the stone counters; a long teak table; one chair—this particular detail tugged at my heart a little.

Across the room, and forming what I understood to be the bulk of March's furniture, were a dark upholstered leather couch facing away from the kitchen and a couple of wooden shelves where he seemed to store books and an intriguing collection of colorful African tin cars. Other than that, I was more or less standing in the middle of two thousand square feet of nothing. Plain walls, no rugs, no photos, no paintings, not even a TV.

"Are you feeling better?"

I jumped at the sound of March's voice behind me. I turned to find him standing in the penthouse's doorway—which meant he had somehow known I was awake. I shuddered at the idea that the place might be riddled with cameras and he had seen me scratch my butt when getting up.

I gave him a thumbs-up and yawned. "Peachy."

He held a paper bag in his hands. "You missed dinner, but I kept your blueberry muffin."

Guarded, secretive, but ever thoughtful—March in a nutshell. My eyes performed a quick scan of his body. Clean jeans and a white shirt had replaced the clothes he had ruined during his fall from the tram. He had rolled his sleeves on his forearms with great care to form flat and even folds. No wrinkles anywhere, of course. Dammit, how did he even do that? I could still see faint bruises on the bridge of his nose and on his brow, but overall he seemed fine.

"Thank you for last night. I'm sorry I lost my temper like that. It's been a difficult day," I mumbled.

A gentle smile creased his dimples. "Don't apologize. Would you like something to drink?"

I scratched my head. "Why not."

"Tea?"

"Tea sounds good."

Now that I was more or less focused, I noticed a patch of green near one of the windows. I sauntered across the room. "Is this Gerald?"

March nodded while filling a kettle with water.

Gerald. The legendary roommate. Also an orange tree.

Back during our date in Tokyo, March had opened up to me about their twisted relationship and his constant horticultural efforts to per-haps, someday, get decent oranges, instead of the botanical insult I was currently beholding. Gracing the branches was a grand total of three greenish lumps whose shape suggested Gerald had been recently raped by a gingerroot. They were hardly bigger than tangerines, and one of them threatened to fall off any moment. I scanned the tree's surround-ings: from the soft carpet on which its pot rested, to the water spray bottles and Superthrive plant vitamins, March had tried everything to please his bitter friend, including the purchase of a small UV lamp, and music, if that mini speaker was any indication.

Maybe Gerald didn't like Conway Twitty.

Behind me, I heard the faint clatter of cups being set on the kitch-en's island. I watched him pour boiling water into each of them with practiced gestures, and a wooden, smoky aroma soon filled the air.

"Lapsang souchong," I said, joining him.

"Would you prefer something lighter?"

"No." I leaned against the island and took one of the cups, holding it in my hands and breathing in the peculiar blend of smoked tea. "March. Are we gonna talk?"

He took a long sip of his tea, dark blue eyes never leaving me. After he was done, he deliberately placed his cup back on the counter. "How did you hear about I2000009?"

Oh.

The way I had envisioned it, I'd be the one asking the questions and grilling him until he fell to his knees and told me all the things I wanted to hear. Except now it was *my* heart racing, and I knew my ears were turning a guilty shade of burgundy, while I was almost certain color had otherwise drained from the rest of my face.

I had been just as unworthy of March's trust as he had been of mine. I wasn't sure why I hadn't told him back in Paris. Perhaps because it had made no sense at the time. We had been looking for Mr. Étienne, my mother's "notary"—not really a licensed professional, but close enough, I guess—and found him in a strip club. Then guys had started shooting at us, so it wasn't the best time to tell March. Then . . . then it had just become my secret, something warm that I cherished and kept jealously because it was all I had left from my mother.

My two fathers had wiped almost every single trace of her, but I had this—the secret my mother's notary had whispered in my ear before being shot.

I2000009. I two million nine.

And I had no idea what it meant or what to do with it. Innumerable Internet searches and hours spent torturing my brain had brought no results—and here I was, in front of a cup of tea, hearing March basically admit that he knew about it already.

"How . . . How did *you* learn about that? I never discussed it with you."

On the counter, March's fist clenched. "Indeed. If you intended to keep this secret, you should have perhaps better protected your online activity. A shame for an engineer of your caliber, I must say."

My first instinct was to ask him if he read my Facebook posts as well, or what he thought of my new shower gel—I knew he liked strawberries. Exploding and yelling that he was an overcontrolling douche doubled with a goddamn stalker wouldn't help me out of that particular pinch, though. I took a deep breath and sustained his hard gaze. "I think my mom was trying to tell me something. She's the one who gave that code to Étienne, and he whispered it to me at the Rose Paradise."

"I suspected so."

I went on excitedly. "She said in her letter that she'd made a huge mistake, but that Dries would never betray his brothers for her. So maybe this was her way of—"

"Hold on a second. Her *letter*? I thought Dries's men had stolen it in Paris. How have you read it?"

Oh. Yeah . . . That's the detail I forgot to mention. Against the rules of every single rom-com ever written, it wasn't March who had caught me on my way to Narita Airport to patch things up after our adventures in Tokyo and his dumping me. It was Dries.

There's this old cliché dictating that whatever criminals do, they never do so for personal reasons, that they have this uncanny ability to compartmentalize all aspects of their lives. Richard Kuklinski posing with his kids in family pictures at the same time that he killed two hundred guys for the Mafia is a good example of that, and Dries undoubtedly fit the profile as well. Never mind that he had kidnapped me and tried to beat March to death fifteen hours prior. The incident being over and the battle lost—his own words—he saw no wrong in spending some time with his daughter.

It went sort of okay, and for all his parental shortcomings, Dries gave me two things that day that I would treasure for the rest of my life: a hug, and my mother's last letter, which she had written before her death. The hug was everything you'd expect from a man more used to crushing people's vertebrae than dispensing comfort to newly found family members. Awkward, a little emotional. Weird, I guess. The letter . . . honestly,

I didn't expect he'd hand it back to me. It was my mother's good-bye, a short and pragmatic confession lifting a tiny bit of the veil under which her many secrets rested. A tale of love and regrets.

She made no mystery of her real job, although she remained—intentionally?—vague about the details of her résumé, and trusted my adoptive father would fill me in; he never did. That wound between us eventually healed, but for a while after the Cullinan affair, I felt like my dad had stolen something from me by hiding my mother's past and emptying our apartment in Tokyo. He had almost erased her in a way.

The letter also contained explicit warnings against Dries. For reasons even he himself couldn't seem to fathom, my mother had grown scared of him, and by the time we had arrived in Japan, she believed he might kill her—kill *us*. Every word on the crumpled paper had spoken of this urgency, this race against time. She had known something was coming, had meant to warn me, to make sure I'd be safe . . . before the inevitable.

That letter had left me with more questions than answers, had broken my heart and patched it up in the same moment. Changed me. Even more so than March had. I looked down at the dark amber swirling in my cup, unable to meet his gaze now that my own secrets were bubbling to the surface. "Dries gave me her letter."

I peeked up to see his Adam's apple move in his throat, but no sound came out. I wasn't sure I had ever seen March's eyes so wide.

I soldiered on. "After you left Tokyo, the morning before I took my flight, he followed me into a *combini*. He bought me ice cream, and we went to a park so we could talk . . . like father and daughter."

March slammed his palms on the stone counter, making me jump. "Do you even realize what kind of risks you took?"

God. I could count on the fingers of one hand the number of times I had heard him raise his voice like this. I took a swig of my tea, mostly to hide behind my cup. "It wasn't so bad. We made peace."

He ran his hand over his face. "Island, he's the Lions' vice commander; I don't think that word bears the same meaning to him it does to you."

"And he's also my father," I said in a warning tone.

"I'm sorry. I know how difficult this is for you."

Upon hearing March say this, I thought of all the Kleenexes I had gone through after Tokyo, and a surge of anger rose inside me. "No, you don't." I breathed my temper out. "So, I2000009, what is it? I'm all ears."

He sighed. "Island, I'm not allowed to tell you that. I have no idea how your mother learned about that number, but it could have been enough for her to lose her life."

I inhaled sharply. "Is it related to the Lions? Are you saying that they killed her?"

Here came the two-billion-dollar question . . . After the Cullinan affair, I had spent quite a few sleepless nights shifting the pieces of the puzzle in my head over and over again. At first, the obvious explanation had been that my mother had been killed by her "employer"—the Board—as a punishment for having betrayed them and plotted to hand the diamond to Dries.

Problem was, those Board guys would have done anything to get their diamond back, and according to one of my mom's accomplices, after changing her mind and making the decision to stay clear from Dries's toxic influence, she had intended to return the stone to the Board. Except she had been killed before she could safely do so. So it wouldn't have made any sense for them to eliminate her, at least not at the time; they still needed her.

Technically, the one to shoot her had been one of Dries's men, a Lion, like him. But Dries had been adamant he hadn't given the order, leading me to think that someone else had hired that sniper and made the guy circumvent his loyalty to his "brothers." Until now, I hadn't considered the possibility that this someone might have been another

Lion, who would have engineered my mother's assassination against Dries's orders. I mean, March had called Dries a vice commander, which confirmed my suspicion that he was a bigwig—a bigmane, if you prefer—in the organization. Also, here again, same conundrum: no Léa Chaptal, no diamond.

So, Board or Lions, whoever had decided to eliminate my mom hadn't cared that the Cullinan might be lost forever. None of this, however, told me why she had chosen to bail on Dries, too, and wanted to make so certain that the Lions would never get a hold of the stone. Furthermore, why had she been so utterly convinced that Dries would never betray his brotherhood to protect her, when he himself hadn't seemed so sure of that?

March probably picked up on the frustration building inside me. He resumed speaking in a soft, coaxing tone. "Biscuit, listen to me, please. This is not your world. I understand how you feel about your mother's death, and I—" He stopped, raking a hand in his hair. "I don't have the answers you're looking for. We'll never know if our teammate truly shot her by error, or if someone engineered this. Dries had his doubts; that's why he killed that man. And I had mine too. But you need to stay away from the Lions and Erwin. You *have* to let go, Island."

"Says the man who'd rather destroy an entire tramway than let go," I gritted out.

He finished his tea and treated me to a self-righteous snort. "Those were different circumstances and—"

"It was exactly the same! You put your life on the line because you wouldn't let him get away. Well, allow me to decide what's worth risking my own life for!"

March had started to move toward the sink to clean our dishes. I heard them hit the gray stone surface with a clang, and in a second he was against me, his hands gripping my shoulders with controlled strength. "Have you lost your mind? Do you hear yourself talking? *How long* do you think you'd last against a Lion?"

I shivered as much from his unexpected outburst as the close proximity of our bodies.

"I'll answer that one for you: *one second.* That's how long it'd take him to grab your neck"—his right hand wrapped around my nape, and goose bumps bloomed across my skin—"and snap it like a twig."

From a purely rational point of view, he was right—as he often was. But rationality can only get you so far. I relaxed in his arms, stifling a sigh of disappointment when I felt his hands release me. I shook my head. "It's too easy. You can't expect me to just go on with my life knowing—"

"That men like us exist? Island, you led a happy life before all this happened, and all I want is for that life to resume. You have your friends, a wonderful job . . ."

One of my eyebrows rose at his evocation of my so-called wonderful job; he seemed to realize how unfortunate a choice of words that was. "We'll solve that case, and once it's done, you'll be able to live your life."

"Under whose surveillance? Yours or Erwin's?" I asked with a derisive smile.

March stepped back to lean against the island, arms crossed. The mere mention of the Caterpillar's name had morphed his gentle expression into a harsh and guarded one. "I did not expect him to use the Ruby incident as an excuse to recruit you."

"So you came back to help us find that money and force Erwin to leave me alone?"

"Yes. Hadrian Ellingham's late father was a friend of the Queen. She recommended me to his son."

The Queen, aka Guita. A really nice woman who read *Elle,* liked cats . . . and ruled over the Board. Needless to say, nice Guita had been pretty pissed when my mom had vanished with the diamond, and I could testify that when the Queen really wanted something, shit could get real fast. She had spent a decade obstinately looking for "her" stone, allowing her goons to kill and torture without hesitation to this end.

Until one of my mother's old accomplices had been caught and revealed that I was the key to finding the Cullinan. I didn't want to think about what would have happened to me if March hadn't stepped in . . . Anyway, as far as I knew, Guita was now primarily concerned with pureeing Dries for betraying the Board.

Ellingham's words replayed in my mind: *our mutual friend.* So, March had requested a favor from the Queen for me. Again. At what cost? Much like Erwin, Guita didn't always play fair—if she ever did at all—and I didn't dare to imagine what March would have to do to repay her.

"I see. That favor is gonna cost you, right? And your plan isn't working so well," I said grimly.

"I'd say we've made some good progress."

"March, you know I'm not talking about Ruby. Alex said you didn't have the power to get rid of him."

His nostrils flared. "A highly debatable statement. I registered for a Twitter account." A malevolent flame lit up in his eyes. "And I won't hesitate to use it . . ."

Sweet Jesus. Not the Ukrainian Twitter bazooka. State-of-the-art villain technology. March had bought it in Paris to use on Dries—yeah, he had been pretty pissed at the time—and if properly configured, the weapon allowed for its user to post a tweet that said "Boom" every time you fired it. Antonio loved that thing.

"*Please* don't shoot Alex with a bazooka."

"I won't. Unless there's a pressing need to."

A pressing need?

"As for *you*—" His gaze slanted. "You must stay away from Erwin." I took a wary step back. "I didn't exactly ask to meet him."

"You know what I mean, Island," March said, his tone suddenly cutting. "He baited you, didn't he? He told you about your mother?"

It took me a second to process his words. March *knew*? No, I realized. He had guessed. Because he knew Erwin's tricks already. "Well, he—"

"And it worked," March went on, his voice deepening with anger. "Erwin knows what he's doing, Island. If you let him, he'll tell you everything you want to hear, and—" He paused and shook his head, almost as if talking to himself. "No. I won't allow that. Just keep your distance, and if he ever tries to contact you again, tell me immediately."

Wouldn't allow what? For the Caterpillar to recruit me . . . Like Charlotte? My skin prickled at the idea. I could tell that guy was playing me, but I had no idea to what end. Was he looking to pierce my mother's secrets? Or was it just about March? About making sure that *he* would never leave that same pool I had been dragged into.

As for Alex . . . he was perhaps the biggest mystery. Even now that his mask was off, I still couldn't tell what he really wanted from me. Had it all been just a job for him? No. Whenever he looked at me, I had this intuition that his interest stemmed from something deeper. There was a glint in his eyes sometimes. Not just a lustful or even a loving one. The best way I could describe it is that Alex looked at me the same way Dries had looked at the Ghost Cullinan.

March had calmed down, but he now seemed distant. I bit one of my nails absently, searching his shuttered expression for a sign that this wasn't it, that he wasn't just here with me to win a chess game against Erwin. A thick silence stretched between us. It's hard to explain, but I could physically feel us drifting apart from each other. I wrapped my arms around my body; I realized I was cold. "I want to go home. I need a shower, and I have to pack before we leave for Zürich."

His gaze avoided mine. "Mr. Morgan is waiting for you. I understand he recovered his car early this morning."

"Good."

He was telling me to leave him—leave him and return to Alex. Each word felt like a slap. I gritted my teeth and went back upstairs to get my shoes. There, I stood for a few seconds in front of March's bed. My fingertips lingered on the lone pillow, still wrinkled from my night's sleep. I closed my eyes and thought of his body against mine in that bed in Tokyo, of how warm, how right it had felt. Until he had rejected me. There was this ache in my chest, and I felt completely empty, almost seasick. I swallowed the tears I could feel coming.

Back in the living room, March was done cleaning our cups. The counter had been wiped, as had the sink. Once the bed was done, there'd be no trace that I had ever been there. We headed together toward a set of double doors I assumed was the apartment's entrance.

When I saw his hand on the doorknob, something squeezed my heart; I stopped and looked up at him. "If none of that stuff with Ruby had happened, would you have come back?"

I didn't give him the time to answer. I went on, my voice brittle, desperate. "Would you have, like, called and said, 'Hey, it's me. I was trying to sneak this cleaning lady into your apartment because it's a mess, and I thought we could go for a drink and, you know, catch up.'"

"Island, it was a little more complicated than that."

I stared down at the tip of my shoes. Spit-shined. "I thought so."

"Biscuit—"

"Don't call me that," I snapped.

Above me, I felt the faint breeze of a huff of aggravation. "Is this what you're making me pay for? Not coming to you sooner?"

I pushed him away to walk through the door and looked back one last time. "I'm not making you pay for anything, March. Comme on fait son lit on se couche." *As you make your bed, so you must lie on it.*

NINETEEN

The Bagel

"His finger traced the hole slowly. 'I like my bagels with lots of cream cheese, Diana.'"

—Terry Robs, *Glazed by the Cook #2: Catering to Her Needs*

March had been right: earlier, Stiles—whom I now understood to be some sort of fairy godmother for the rest of Alex's division—had delivered the Corvette, obviously fresh out of the car wash, and with four brand-new tires. Alex seemed pleased as we sat together in the car—that is, until he turned on the MP3 player and was greeted by Céline Dion instead of Metallica.

"Stiles . . ." He sighed as under my butt, the engine's powerful vibrations rose.

I didn't mind. Honestly, *who* doesn't like "My Heart Will Go On"?

The ride from Struthio to West Eighty-First Street was a short one, and we flew more than we drove through New York's streets. Probably in part because Alex was happy to be reunited with his baby and abused the hell out of the gas pedal whenever traffic allowed it. Boys and their toys . . . He seemed relaxed enough, but every time we stopped at a red light, he'd turn his head and stare at me with that tranquil smile of his, wordlessly hammering at the same question over and over again.

When we reached the front of my building and the Corvette slowed down, I finally snapped. He was still giving me that gentle, inquisitive look as I undid my seat belt. I took a deep breath and looked him in the eyes. "I just had a migraine, and I slept it off. *Nothing* happened up there, okay?"

"I didn't ask."

"Yes, you did. You did that . . . thing, with your face." I made a wide-eyed grimace, attempting to imitate the mysterious good-guy smile that forced people to spill their guts.

He laughed. "I had no idea I was so terrifying."

"You are." I sighed as I got out of the car.

Alex seemed to sober, tilting his head as if to better read me. "Phyllis arranged a flight with 'Paulie Airlines.' We'll take off at three from Teterboro. It's already one, which means you have"—he shot a glance at the dashboard clock—"a maximum of thirty minutes to pack and refresh. Any questions?"

"No, I'm good. Are you—" Here came the awkward part. "Are you going to wait down the street while I do that?"

He pointed at Broadway with his chin. "Actually, I was thinking of going to Starbucks. I need a coffee, and I could do with something to eat."

I debated with myself whether I should offer this. I did want to end things with Alex. I knew I had to. But at the same time, it sounded callous to just act like we were strangers until either he got the hint or I mustered the courage to talk to him. I took a deep breath and managed a confident smile. "Can I interest you in stale bagels and an espresso instead?"

"I'm sold."

We climbed up the stairs; that sign on the building's broken elevator had been there for so long it was starting to look like an old friend. Alex followed me to the door, and as my key turned in the lock, a strange nervousness crawled up my spine, making my body tingle. He had been here before, a couple of times, when picking me up for a date. But back then, he had been Alex the insurance guy, the Yaycupid guy. For some reason, being here with CIA Alex felt like that time when I had come home to find March searching my tax returns. Just like him at the time, Alex was now somewhere he didn't belong, a wolf trying to casually fit into a sheepfold.

Upon pushing the door open, I realized I had forgotten a minor detail when inviting him up: today was a Tuesday, and therefore a West Eighty-First Street and Broadway Neighborhood Committee day—WEFBNC, for short.

And Joy stood in the doorway.

Because she was home, hanging around the apartment in yoga pants, and making phone calls to the mayor's office regarding the organization of a sack race down the street on the Fourth of July.

Well, not anymore.

She stared past me at Alex. Then her eyes settled back on me, a smirk forming on her lips. "Hey, hey, someone's in need of fresh clothes."

"How have you been, Joy?" Alex asked with a congenial smile.

"Pretty good, lover boy."

I cleared my throat several times. The lump wouldn't go down. "Um, yeah. I needed to pick up some stuff. I had forgotten that you—"

"No problem. I'll make Alex some coffee meanwhile. That way we can talk, right?" she asked him. Dammit, I knew that face, when her cheeks would get round and pink from the effort not to laugh. *Oh no* . . . At least she wasn't calling him Jesus to his face and cracking that horrible joke about him parting the Red Sea—I kept telling her it was Moses anyway.

Alex welcomed the offer with a good-natured shrug. "Sounds good." He then looked at me. "Will you need any help packing, baby?"

I'm pretty sure I saw a red glint appear in Joy's eyes, like in *Terminator.* "Packing?"

"We-we're going to Switzerland for a few days . . . for work."

Her hands flew to her mouth, and for a couple of seconds she was speechless. "Are you doing it again?"

"Doing what?" I asked, inching away from her.

"A BDSM getaway!"

Behind me, I heard Alex's sharp intake of breath, but he didn't comment.

Joy gazed at him with a mixture of surprise and awe before turning to me. "Change of plan. I'm helping you pack."

"It's okay, I can—"

She ignored my protest and flashed Alex her warmest smile. "You know where the kitchen is, lover boy!"

———

"So, what's up with the impromptu getaway?"

I sighed. The red digits on my alarm clock indicated 1:35; I was late already, trying to simultaneously put on a blue cotton sweater dress as fast as possible and shove clothes in my suitcase, while on my bed Joy hopped up and down furiously. In the living room, Alex was sitting on our couch, watching the news and drinking his coffee, a ten-day-old bagel in hand.

I dodged the pillow that had been fired at me; she reloaded. "Earth to Island. I asked you a question."

"Joy. Alex isn't here for that. This is about my job . . . it's complicated."

She took one of my hands, dropping her playful act. "Go on."

"Thom is dead." I paused upon seeing blood drain from her face. "And something happened with Ruby. I can't say much, but it's a security issue, and I need to go to Zürich to work with EMT's local subsidiary."

She looked down at our joined hands for a moment before pulling me into a tight hug. "I'm so, so sorry."

"It's okay," I rasped out.

She stroked my hair with a confused frown. "But this is . . . What's Alex got to do with it?"

And one more lie coming up for table two! "He . . . he's just taking me to the airport."

"Okay. It's good that he's here for you," she said wistfully. "That's when you know it's serious."

You know what the problem is when you're lying all the time? You get tangled up in those lies. That's one thing. But it's not the worst part. The worst part is that you end up feeling completely alone in the middle of a crowd of friends and family, because you can never have any kind of sincere, meaningful exchange with them. I had spent the past six months telling a variety of lies to Joy, all woven together in an intricate and barely credible web.

I was tired. So tired that a handful of half-truths sounded better than weaving another single lie into my masterpiece to make it all hold together a little longer.

I averted my eyes and clenched my fists. "I've seen March again. He's in New York."

Joy's mouth tightened in a thin line into which her usually full lips seemed to disappear. I kept talking in a hurried voice before she could react. "And I swear it's got nothing to do with him, but things are different . . . and Alex and I—"

"Please don't tell me that you cheated on *Jesus* with . . . with that rotten fucking piece of . . . of *shit!*"

My hands flew to her mouth to cover it. "Nothing happened!" I hissed. "March isn't like that! I'm not cheating on Alex. I think we're just . . . done."

She jumped up and another pillow flew in my direction, hitting me square in the chest this time. "For the love of God, Island, this is Relationships 101: don't ditch the good guy for the sexy asshole!"

"Maybe Alex is a little more complicated than that," I snapped, placing the pillow back on my bed.

Joy sat back down, her expression turning serious. "What do you mean by that?"

"Nothing. He's . . . nice. But he's just not who I thought he was, and I have no idea how to tell him I want out."

A brief silence followed as she studied my features. I tried my best to look relaxed, but I could tell she had picked up on my unease. "Did he, like, hit you or something?"

"Of course not!"

"Because if he did, you tell me. I know people who know people, and I can—"

My palms rose in an appeasing gesture. "No! It wasn't anything like that. Also, when did you start hanging around the mob?"

"Not the mob." Joy scooted closer to me and lowered her voice to a conspiratorial whisper. "But I know this girl who slept with the bouncer at the Silknight Lounge, and she told me he's into underground fighting and that sort of stuff, and that he'll even mess people up for money, like kicking them in the balls and breaking their legs," she explained, mimicking a few punches.

I rolled my eyes. "You'd seriously send someone to break Alex's legs?" Not that it would work, I reminded myself.

"If he had beaten you, yes. Why?"

"But you're a lawyer!"

My outrage was welcomed with a faint shrug. "Island, the first thing you learn in law school is that law and justice aren't the same thing."

"In any case, Alex didn't hurt me. He just isn't the right guy for me," I said tartly, slamming my suitcase shut.

Heavy blonde curls sprang around her face as she shook her head. "As opposed to *Valmont*?" She nearly spat the word, as if pronouncing March's actual name might brand her tongue. "I don't get it. This is . . . This is masochism. The truth is, you *want* to agonize in frustration and pain and whatever."

I curled into a ball, pretending to be busy checking my passport. Yes, I could have argued that the whole BDSM thing was a complete misunderstanding, and that March, with his single dining chair and passive-aggressive orange tree, was in fact as far as you could get from the manipulative womanizer type. But so many expletives had been uttered already that I didn't feel ready to try and plead "Valmont's" case to Joy. Even more so since I myself had no idea what March really wanted, or if he'd ever graduate from the I'm-stalking-you-but-that's-it-no-touching stage.

Joy shook her head at me. "I don't recognize you. Swear to me that you won't do something stupid."

"Don't be so melodramatic!" I groaned.

I couldn't fight the blush that spread on my cheeks, though, and Joy's eagle eyes didn't miss it, turning to accusing slits. She could tell. Maybe she couldn't read my exact thoughts and see that vision of March dressed like the pirate hero of *Winds of Passion*, getting on one knee and promising that he'd lay his heart in my palms if I followed him across the seven seas, but she could definitely tell I would do something stupid if influenced by a combination of sufficient and specific factors. And by that I mean if he asked nicely.

"Don't even think about it," Joy said.

I shrugged and marched to the living room, dragging my suitcase behind me. She followed, sulking all the way there.

"I'm ready," I announced.

Alex sipped the last drop of his espresso and stretched his legs before getting up. "Fantastic. Let me get this for you."

I pulled the suitcase away from him. "No, it's okay. Your shoulder—"

"It's the left one. Let me pretend I'm a gentleman," he said with a wink.

I reluctantly allowed him to help me. As we headed to the door, I waved good-bye to Joy and tried to block her heated glare and the sight of her pointing her index and middle finger to her eyes in a V-sign before pointing them in my direction. If Alex saw it, he didn't react, and I was grateful for that small blessing.

———

I have to say I was surprised when Alex and I arrived on Teterboro's humid tarmac. Ever since embarking secretly with March on a flight for Paris with a fake passport from a tiny airfield in Pennsylvania, I had assumed Paulie's services revolved exclusively around arranging illegal flights. The jet with a royal-blue logo waiting for us challenged this theory; there *was* such a thing as Paulie Airlines. And I was pretty sure that Pan Am would have sued regarding the use of the aforementioned logo, had they still been in business.

I spotted March already waiting near the plane with his magic suitcase—not really magic, but with an awesome fingerprint lock system, and always full of perfectly folded things and guns. The short, stout man with a charcoal beard and a receding hairline standing next to him looked familiar. I waved at Paulie. He saw it and strode toward us with his arms wide open. His mouth stretched into a wide grin, revealing his secret weapon: large, square, and blindingly white veneers that might have looked like a malpractice suit waiting to happen, if it hadn't been for his girlfriend, who actually loved them.

Did I say he was coming to greet *us*? Typo, sorry. Paulie was coming to greet *me*. I was pulled into a heartfelt hug, received overstated compliments regarding my beauty, a kiss on each cheek, and Alex got . . . an icy glare.

"You the snitch?" Paulie grunted in lieu of a welcome.

Alex made a brave attempt at good-cop-smiling him. "I'm Agent Morgan. Always a pleasure to meet a businessman of your . . . caliber, Mr. Strozzi."

Paulie's veneers disappeared under a tight-lipped frown. "Sounds like snitch talk to me."

Alex shrugged it off and pointed to the airstair deployed at the front of the jet. "I'm sure it does. Can we embark?"

Paulie made an evasive gesture with his hand. "Yeah."

March moved toward the airstair, but stopped in his tracks when he noticed Alex and I weren't following. His eyes met mine. I responded with an uneasy smile, and he disappeared inside the cabin with one last peek at us. We were about to embark when Alex reached inside his jacket's inner pocket; his phone was buzzing. Nodding for me to get on the plane, he walked away to answer the call.

I'd have complied, but I was curious. I took a few cautious steps in his direction, trying to get close enough to hear at least part of his conversation. Alex's back was turned to me, but whatever was going on sounded serious enough that he was raising his voice, in spite of his obvious attempts at keeping it down to an exasperated hiss.

"No . . . *No!* . . . Listen to me, all that kid's got going for him are straight Fs. He should be studying, and *you* should be avoiding him . . . Yes . . . I hear you, and if you want to go see *Rome and Julie*, I'll take you when I get back, but you are *not* allowed to go out with Scott. Am I making myself clear? . . . Poppy, I don't care that school is closed tomorrow. It's *no*."

Poppy was at it again, and she treated Alex to a long rant, punctuated by his own sighs. "Pass me Irene . . . Hey, Irene, is everything all right? . . . Yes, she told me; I said no." His voice dropped to a threatening whisper; I had to strain my ears to listen. "Irene, you know where the paint gun is. If you see that boy anywhere near our apartment, you shoot him. I'm counting on you . . . Good . . . Good. Yes, thank you. I'll see you in a few days."

Alex hung up, and I watched with amusement as he raked a nervous hand in his messy brown locks.

"Boy troubles again?" I asked.

He shook his head. "Yeah. I'm being told that my 'vision of a patri-archal system in which women would be tradable goods under the authority of their brothers is inherited from the Middle Ages.'"

I shrugged. "She's kind of right."

"She's also sixteen, and therefore a tradable good under my medi-eval authority."

My shoulders shook with quiet laughter as we climbed into the plane. Once we were in, Alex ducked his head to acknowledge March—who was sitting near a window with a crosswords magazine on his lap—and went to sit at the back of the plane. I hesitated, searching March's impassive expression for a second. Finding no sign that I was welcome to sit near him, I managed a polite smile and walked past him to go settle in a large cream seat at Alex's side.

A light drizzle had started falling on the tarmac, dusting Alex's window with diamond-like drops. The plane started moving. He stared through the thick glass, his eyes locked on the horizon. "You never asked about my parents."

An unpleasant pressure built up in my chest, only made worse by the cabin's vibrations as we took off. I had hoped for a friendly breakup, and the last thing I wished was for him to be reminded about his par-ents' gruesome death while sitting on a plane. We were off to a bad start. "Alex, I just didn't think it was my place to—"

"But you looked it up. You did research on the crash without tell-ing me."

I glanced at March's seat at the other end of the cabin. His back was turned to me. Could he hear our conversation? I lowered my voice to a whisper. "I'm sorry, I just wanted to understand."

He shrugged. "It's okay. I know every detail of your file; it's only fair you get a peek at mine."

"I don't know the details, Alex. I just looked up crashes in Egypt for that year, and there was only one involving American victims. I had read that the government wouldn't release their names, so, after I learned about your real job, I figured . . ."

"That my father was an agent too?"

"Yes."

He didn't look at me as he spoke, his eyes still lost in the ashen clouds now surrounding us. "Six years ago, he was stationed in Cairo for several months. I was still in college, and my mother thought Poppy was too young for that kind of trip. She went to visit him alone for their wedding anniversary. He had to accompany local officials on a trip to Luxor around that time." Alex paused, his throat tightening imperceptibly. "My mother wasn't supposed to be on that plane, but officially it was just a routine business trip, and my father made a last-minute decision to take her to visit Esna after his mission. Their plane was shot down over the Eastern Desert. There were no survivors."

"Is . . . is this why you followed in his footsteps?"

He nodded. "I guess."

I was tempted to tell him that it was unhealthy, that he might someday meet the same fate as his father, but I thought of my conversation with March about my mother, and realized I was no better. I fidgeted in my seat. "Do you know who they were, the people who killed your parents?"

"Yes."

"Did you . . . did someone catch them?"

"No." He stared at me, something unreadable in his eyes. "But I'm close."

For a moment, I had this terrifying thought that maybe March had something to do with the incident and that it was the reason Alex was so wary and confrontational around him. March didn't fit the profile, though. He hated side casualties, and judging from my previous experience as his client, he favored covert assassinations—the type of guy to spend one bullet wisely rather than blow up an entire plane. The Roosevelt Tram and Dries's lair didn't count because he'd been pissed; we all have our bad days.

I glanced at him. He was still immersed in his crosswords, but he'd turn to check on us every now and then. When his eyes met mine, my heart skipped a beat. What if I was wrong? What if . . . A painful knot formed in my throat. Anything but this. I didn't even want to consider the possibility.

Alex leaned closer, and one of his hands started to move to cover mine on the armrest; I pretended to readjust my dress to avoid the contact.

"I'm sorry, Island. I shouldn't have brought this up," he said.

"No, it's okay. I'm the one who asked."

God, how was I going to get out of this? *I'm sorry for the brutal murder of your family, Alex. By the way, I know you're a little depressed at the moment, but I have to tell you I'm thinking of breaking up with you.* Yeah . . . no.

Next to me, his voice dropped to a murmur. "Thank you for listening."

"Thank you for trusting me with this story, I guess."

"We're in the same boat."

No, we weren't. I averted my gaze. "I'm going to get myself some water. Do you want something? A Coke, maybe?"

"Yeah, thanks."

I got up and searched the galley's mini fridge while behind me Alex rose as well to retrieve a small laptop from his travel bag. I grabbed his Coke and a plastic cup. When he took them, I glanced to the front of the cabin.

March had abandoned his crosswords, and his eyes were set on me, radiating anger.

TWENTY

Boy Toy

"You see the gear lever here? Well, if you take the top off, you'll find a little red button. Whatever you do, don't touch it."

—*Goldfinger*, 1964

It could have been worse. It was overall an awkward flight, filled with reproachful glances and unspoken tension, but with Alex and me busy on our respective laptops and March eventually opting to resume his crosswords and check his smartphone instead of staring at me, there was enough fubbing going on in the plane to keep the storm at bay.

We landed in Zürich before dawn. Local time was six a.m., and a light breeze welcomed us upon stepping out of the plane. In the distance stood the massive skein of glass and metal of the terminal's hall, casting a bright light on the darkened tarmac. This time our passports were real—even March's—and I experienced an odd sense of satisfaction upon entering a foreign country legally, waving my precious sesame in front of the customs officers with a regal gesture. I *did* notice the way March's magic suitcase and Alex's black travel bag seemed to be cleared without much effort, even when I knew what rested in them. I chose to look the other way. Given my recent troubles, I wasn't going to get all picky just because we were relying on corrupt customs officers to sneak a few guns into a neutral country.

There was some fuss over who'd receive the honor of carrying my suitcase for me—proof if need be that you can be both a gentleman *and* a red-ass baboon. I decided to drag it myself.

"I'll see you two at the Eden au Lac in thirty-five minutes," March announced as we strolled through the terminal and passed a group of tourists struggling with the self-check-in kiosks.

March didn't look at Alex as he said this; he looked at *me*. More passive-aggressive vibes, huh? I was torn between guilt and anger, and I didn't want him to witness either. I dusted imaginary lint from my sweater dress and looked down at my loafers. "Fine. I'll see you at the hotel, Mr. November."

His jaw ticked. "Excellent."

I kept telling myself that, after all, I was being handed yet another opportunity to come clean, and that a bazillion girls had dumped a guy before me—how hard could it be to just say no?—but in that moment, following Alex to the elevators, I just felt a little nauseated.

He led us down to an underground garage. There he pulled a key from his pocket, which he pressed. At the other end of the aisle, two beeps resounded and lights flashed; a boyish smile lit up his features. We walked toward the source of the noise, and I have to say I was a little disconcerted when we reached the vehicle, like there'd been an error or something. Alex, on the other hand, seemed increasingly pleased, circling the simple white urban SUV with his hands on his hips, inspecting it.

Honestly, those sleek lines were so generic I couldn't even identify the model. The only odd detail was perhaps the lights, with their unusual bluish hue. I stepped closer to the round hood, examining the T-shaped logo in its center. "Tesla? An electric car?"

"Yes, it is," Alex replied with a carnivorous grin, grazing the handle to unlock the driver's door. Okay, that was a little cool.

"Why this one?" I asked as I buckled my seat belt, staring at the tactile dashboard.

"Because I wanted to verify the rumors."

"What rumors?"

His answer came at the same time that my body was propelled backward—I hadn't even heard the engine start. "That it'll pin you to your seat."

———

We made it to Zürich in one piece, but as the Tesla slowed down, I was pretty sure some of my internal organs were now stuck in places they shouldn't be. All those accelerations had to be messing with my anatomy. The sun hadn't risen yet, and we were driving on the Utoquai, along the shores of Lake Zürich, a dark, quiet immensity stretching for twenty-five miles in a valley guarded on each side by chains of snowy mountains. On our left, an endless ribbon of elegant nineteenth-century buildings flew past the car. Once refuges for rich landowners able to afford a chunk of the lake's scenery for their private enjoyment, most of them had been turned into hotels welcoming an international clientele.

My breakup with Alex had gone well. I had just said, "Sorry, we're done, please don't touch me anymore because it makes things weird between us," and he had said, "Yeah, sure."

Okay, I'm lying. Alex seemed in such a good mood, and delighted with his new toy, that the words had remained stuck in my throat. I had spent half an hour trying to come up with appropriate lines for a gentle breakup, stuff like "Things are too complicated between us," or "I have to let go for your own sake," and . . . nope, I had nothing good, and I was still chickening my way out of this.

I sighed in resignation as we stopped in front of the Eden au Lac hotel's neo-baroque façade. Greco-Roman columns and sculptures, vegetal patterns—the ensemble was gorgeous, and perhaps a bit too much.

Very European. I thought of Thom. He had been here, seen the same façade—this was precisely why we had chosen this hotel for our stay. Something had happened within those walls that had changed his life. I needed to stop wallowing in self-pity and work on understanding what.

Alex took a left turn to access the hotel's parking lot. He glanced in the mirror at the black BMW about to enter the parking lot as well. No need to see through the tinted windshield—March had been following us all along.

Much like the flight, the few yards from the parking lot to the hotel's lobby were spent in tense silence, and I pretended to be fascinated by the ceiling's moldings while March took care of check-in. I can't overstate how relieved I was when he handed me a key of my own. At this point, the last thing I wanted was to share a room with either of them.

———

I plead guilty of filling my plate with a mountain of food at breakfast that morning, but that nice waitress in the dining room forced me. Like a pusher in a dark alley, every time I moved away from the gargantuan buffet, she'd show me something new and delicious I hadn't seen yet. It went very fast, and before I could fully understand what had happened, I was sitting at our table, in the middle of that Versailles-like room, surrounded by gold-leafed stuff and big chandeliers. And there was approximately a pound of brioche, cake, cheese, ham, eggs, and jam in front of me.

Alex raised an eyebrow at my plate before resuming his explanations. "I received our tram enthusiast's identification during the flight. His name was Karsten Salzgeber. Thirty-eight. Born in Feldkirch, Austria. Good career in the Austrian army, with five years in the special forces—"

"Until he received a dishonorable discharge following a disastrous raid in Afghanistan," March completed, as if to drive home the point that *he* had read the file too.

I took a swig of my hot cocoa. "But you don't usually get a dishonorable discharge just because a mission went badly. Right?"

"You do if you try to set a Taliban's fifteen-year-old son on fire to make his father talk. Five members of the unit were tried. That's the magic of combat stress and peer pressure, I guess," Alex said, looking down at his cup of coffee. "Following his discharge, he became a mercenary. According to our data, he joined a Vienna-based private security company about a year ago. That's when he kind of vanished from our radar."

"Why is that?"

"The question you want to ask is: Who did that? After that date, we have no records whatsoever—no credit card logs, no medical expenses, no flights . . . nothing."

"Someone was paying it all for him? Like, keeping him in some sort of bubble?" I asked.

"Yes. A pattern typically seen when one joins the service of a powerful employer," March explained.

I chewed on my brioche. "He and those guys with the motorbikes were watching Thom's place. They probably wanted to make sure there would be no loose ends. Do you think Thom met him here in Zürich?"

March confirmed, cutting his slice of cake in even pieces. "Very likely."

Alex watched him do so with a curious stare. "We could try to question employees here at the hotel, but I'm not really fond of that kind of direct approach. They're used to keeping their clients' secrets, so we'll mostly get lies."

"What about the security cameras? Thom was here less than four weeks ago, and many systems can store logs for up to a month. Can't the NSA, like, hack into those? Or maybe Colin?" I inquired while stuffing my face with French cheese.

"Probably, but I'll need an authorization before they do it for us." Alex smiled. "What about you? Could you?"

I laughed at first, because I thought he was joking. "Of course, network security is IT's biggest joke. But I don't do that kind of stuff; I never had the mindset for that."

Next to me, I hadn't noticed the way March's lips had curled into a predatory smile. "Don't sell yourself short, Island."

TWENTY-ONE

The Chihuahua

"We need you to get back in the game, Samantha! You're the only hacker hot enough to infiltrate Andreï Preskovic's sex club and break into his computers."

—Abby Chuman, *Fatal and Sensual Ukrainian Nights II: Bound Forever*

"Swear again!"

Alex rose from the white Louis XVI armchair in which he had been listening to my complaints until now. He flattened his right palm over his heart. "Island, I swear that if you get caught, I'll cover for you. You won't go to jail."

Sitting cross-legged on my bed, I cast a wary glance at my unopened laptop. In a corner of my room, March was leaning against the wall with his arms crossed, and watched the negotiation unfolding before his eyes in silence.

"I won't get disavowed?"

"You won't. You're not even an agent. Worst-case scenario, you'll get a call and your phone will explode, along with you." Alex grinned.

"Oh my God!"

He doubled over with laughter when I scrambled up from the bed. "Just kidding! Now can you please . . . ?"

I searched March's expressionless features for some sort of actual reassurance. He answered my silent plea with the arching of a haughty chestnut eyebrow. "You wanted to be a spy. Congratulations on becoming one."

I drew a resigned breath and grabbed my laptop. Alex sat on the bed next to me, and when I launched the command line and started typing, March joined us, sitting on my other side.

"What are you doing?" he asked, watching the colorful lines of code scroll on the black screen.

"I'm inside their router's admin. That was the easy part, because their password is super weak. This, here"—I pointed at a particular block of text—"is the list of all devices connected to their network. Mostly phones and laptops, so it's not really interesting. What I'd like to check is this . . ." My index finger stopped on a specific entry, an old-ass Windows server that seemed like the perfect candidate for hosting temporary video surveillance archives, but it also looked ripe for the taking. There were dozens of critical vulnerabilities to be found in a nearly ten-year-old server, and someone who named their machine *"IchliebeRösti"*—I love rösti (a kind of Germanic hash browns)—couldn't be trusted to properly install security updates in a timely manner.

I cracked my fingers and set about exploiting a well-documented vulnerability. It was nothing incredibly elaborate, in the end: just a few remote requests in ASP that would mess with IchliebeRösti's web applications, granting us total access to the server. Hacking is bad, and I should have felt bad, but I have to confess that a thrill of impish excitement sent tingles through my body. There was a joy to be found in sin that I couldn't deny.

Soon, I was scouring its drives for video files. A long list of results appeared. Now, Alex and March might have cared little for computer shenanigans, but they knew what a several-gigabyte ".avi" file meant.

"Great, can you isolate the recordings for March 13, the day before he came back to New York?" Alex said, placing a hand on my shoulder. March clicked his tongue, but said nothing otherwise.

I was all too aware of the warmth radiating from Alex's palm as I selected a group of files. "There you go. Are we going to watch them all?"

"No," Alex said. "According to his agenda, Roth spent most of the day at Machina Tomorrow and came back to the hotel around six. Show me the lobby, starting from five thirty."

I double-clicked on the file, and we watched as an accelerated ballet of guests, visitors, and employees appeared on my laptop's screen. The recordings were in black-and-white, but the resolution was decent, allowing us to distinguish faces and some level of detail.

"Look!" I paused the video and pointed at the lean silhouette of a balding blond man walking through the front door. Long gray coat, always that same old backpack. Thom. There was something eerie in seeing him alive again, real and unreal. I felt my heart tighten, watching him cross the lobby and climb the marble stairs. It was hard to see his expression clearly, but I thought he didn't look particularly stressed.

On my shoulder, Alex's hand tightened.

March cleared his throat. "Can you show us his floor?"

I squirmed away from Alex's hand as I searched for the second floor's security recordings. There were several files, one for each camera. I opened them all, creating a black-and-white mosaic on my screen. As you'd expect from cameras filming an empty hallway, there was nothing remarkable about that particular tape. Thom could be seen reaching the top of the stairs, strolling on the thick carpet, and entering his room—end of story.

The three of us looked at each other, then at the screen. I sped up the video again, watching the hours tick by in each window's lower right corner. People coming and going, room service, a couple fighting . . . no Thom, who appeared to be still in his room. March's hand suddenly pressed mine.

"Stop, please."

My heart jolted: he was right. At 2:17, Thom had come out of his room. His posture, the way his shoulders hunched as he fumbled with his room key—something was wrong. This had clearly marked the start of his descent into the pit. Before our eyes, Thom walked down the stairs and into the lobby. I loaded the lobby's security recordings. He was leaving the hotel in a hurry, without his precious backpack. Behind the glass of the entrance door, a man in a black parka was waiting for him in the street.

"Salzgeber."

I paused the video and turned to Alex. He was staring at the still with a dark expression, his forefinger rubbing his chin mechanically. "Keep playing it, please."

As soon as I pressed Enter, a visibly shaken Thom followed the Austrian mercenary outside the hotel. The last that could be seen of them were their backs as they climbed into a dark Mercedes.

"They contacted him. Somewhere between six and two that night," March concluded.

"But we checked his phone calls, his e-mails, and nothing came up," Alex countered.

"It doesn't mean anything," I said. "You know better than I do that it's easy to reroute a phone call and mask its origin."

He nodded, brown eyes still locked on the screen. "Could you do the same for the street cameras? Tell us where they went?"

"I'm not sure. I have no idea if they even store the files for that long, and we're talking about hacking dozens of different cameras in order to re-create their path. I don't think I'm qualified for this, Alex."

I saw the disappointment in his and March's faces, and I kinda felt like a loser because I wasn't the badass hacker they had imagined. I offered Alex a rueful smile. "You're gonna have to call for help after all."

He patted my shoulder. "Don't worry, I'll ask the NSA to lend me Colin again. Let's just hope they cooperate quickly."

"How long will it take?" March asked.

"Twenty-four hours max, if their boss really wants to test Erwin."

March's eyes narrowed. "That 'boss' is the handler for the young hacker you're talking about, correct?"

"Correct."

"And he's on bad terms with Mr. Erwin? What's his name?"

Alex shot a suspicious glance at me. "I'm afraid this is not something I can disclose, Mr. November."

March indulged in a huff of exasperation. "For God's sake, stop these pathetic games. We're obviously talking about Mr. Hendry."

"I can't confirm—"

"Save your breath, Mr. Morgan. I'll call him. He knows me."

Alex and I blinked like owls while March got up from the bed and pulled out his phone. He seemed to look up a number, his fingers scrolling and tapping on the screen repeatedly. Several seconds passed, during which he waited for someone to pick up. They did.

"Good morning, Mr. Hendry, I'm sorry to wake you up. I'm with Mr. Morgan, whom I'm certain you already know operates under the supervision of Mr. Erwin. I took the liberty to contact you because I believe you might be able to help us with an urgent matter."

I had no idea what the other guy was saying, but I gathered it had to be something along the lines of "Who are you and how the hell did you get this number?" When March spoke again, his voice exuded the icy cordiality I knew he reserved for clients. "*Who am I?* Well, I'm Mr. November, and I used to kill people for a living. And *you* are the man who shared a photomontage based on what I understand to be a popular children's movie. A photomontage describing me as *the Tomato Guy.*"

I could hear the daggers in each syllable as March gritted out the nickname Hendry had once given him. If phone calls could kill, that guy would have been dead, and I think he knew it. The exchange lasted for another minute, during which I heard March tell Hendry that, indeed, each life was a sail on a sea of regrets, before inquiring about the well-being of his grandma—who was apparently retired in Miami and had a Chihuahua named Edgar. Once he was satisfied that, on the other end of the line, his victim was pissing himself in terror, he voiced our demand regarding the surveillance camera recordings.

In the end, I think March didn't care if the NSA could actually fulfill his request. This was about a man to whom life had offered an opportunity for revenge. And it was about a Chihuahua too.

Of course, I cannot condone those thinly veiled threats to shoot Hendry's grandma and her dog, but I have to admit they did the job. Less than twenty minutes later, the guy sent us a nifty 3D map designed from the partial logs of thousands of various unsecured cameras and security devices in the area—gotta praise how the NSA really is *everywhere*.

We gathered around my laptop again to examine the map. According to this data, the Mercedes had taken Thom for a seventy-minute trip past Lake Zürich and its smaller sibling, the Walensee, and through the border to Liechtenstein. The vehicle had reached its microscopic capital, Vaduz. It had then left the well-lit and camera-monitored streets to drive north toward the Alpspitz—a 6,300-foot peak overlooking the city. The glowing blue line depicting Thom's trip stopped there, because once on the mountain road, there had no longer been any external device capable of recording the vehicle's presence.

Thom had been brought back to the Eden au Lac around six thirty, something confirmed by the hotel's own surveillance recordings.

"So, Vaduz it is," Alex said, his eyes set on the interrupted line on the screen.

"A charming city," March remarked.

I closed my laptop. "What's next?"

Alex looked past me and at March. "I suggest we split. Island and I will go to EMT Switzerland to question Professor Premfield. I gather he knew Roth well. Meanwhile, Mr. November, you could put your knowledge of Liechtenstein to good use and see if you can find where they took him after the car left Vaduz."

The plan made sense—and there was a good-cop smile to help the medicine go down—but it was obvious in the way his shoulders stiffened that, for March, the very notion of receiving an order from Alex was akin to eating an apple Skittle. Obscene.

"I'll make sure to let you know if your opinion is needed, Mr. Morgan," he retorted coolly. I saw the way his fingers were drumming on his thigh, though. Alex's plan was the best one and he knew it.

"March, I think Alex is right. I won't be of any use to you in Vaduz, and maybe Premfield can tell us more about what happened during Thom's trip."

That one earned me a Tomato glare as he produced his precious tube of mints from one of his pockets. The only answer I received was the ominous sound of the candy being ground in his mouth as March got up and left the room.

TWENTY-TWO

The Beacon of Tomorrow's Science

"I can't reveal anything yet, but we're working on something you'll find under all Christmas trees next year!"

—Kerri Lavalle, *EMG Mag*, March 2014 issue

By the time Alex and I reached the small municipality of Tuggen, at the other end of Lake Zürich, it was past ten, and I was seriously considering asking for a transfer to EMT Switzerland. The headquarters of this local division exclusively dedicated to R&D had been built on the outskirts of the town in a postcard setting, nestled between the lake's shore and the mountains and surrounded by lush greenery where a few cows grazed lazily. There was even a golf course and a steakhouse nearby, dammit!

Alex took a right turn to enter the enclosed facility, and the curve of the building's roof appeared, like a smooth, white shell protecting a low structure made of wood and glass. After we had identified ourselves and parked, we made our way toward some sort of futuristic banana-shaped awning that guarded the building's entrance. A wave of hot air hit me when we entered the lobby, which carried a whiff of pinewood, no doubt from the tangle of curved beams supporting the ceiling.

Alex approached the desk behind which two receptionists chatted in German. He good-cop-smiled at them and they exchanged a few words. "Professor Premfield will be here in a moment," one of the girls announced, batting her eyelashes at him under her colleague's amused gaze.

"You're making friends," I said with a chuckle, leafing through an issue of *EMG Mag* featuring Ellingham on its cover.

Alex cocked his head. "I didn't picture you as the jealous type."

I was about to jump on this opportunity and tell him that I actually didn't mind at all if he turned to new horizons, but I never had the time to. A croaky laugh echoed through the lobby, and an elderly voice greeted us with a British accent. "Hey, hey, hey, welcome to the Matrix, my friends!"

We turned at the same time to see a *fricking metalhead* walking toward us. I had never seen any pictures of Prentis Premfield, and nothing in his scientific papers hinted at this sort of commitment. Or maybe those frequent references to Norse mythology and Nietzsche should have tipped me. Anyway, his gray hair was gathered in a long ponytail, a fierce beard covered most of his face, and the guy wore a Black Sabbath T-shirt over worn jeans. And spiked wristbands. And green flip-flops. So, a metalhead, indeed. Except for the shoes, but maybe it was because they heated the building so much—I didn't dare ask.

Alex introduced himself with a firm handshake, and it seemed an immediate understanding passed between the two men when they took in their mutual state of careful disarray.

Premfield extended his hand to me as well. "Ah, nice bird you brought, brother," he said, addressing Alex while he crushed my fingers in his wrinkled ones.

"Not like them tarts over there." He shot a slanted look in the direction of the receptionists' desk; the blonde one returned the favor, burying her head in her shoulders and narrowing her blue eyes at him. He grabbed Alex's arm, his voice dropping to a low hiss. "Don't waste your time with them. You're gonna buy 'em chocolate, flowers and shit, and you'll never see a tit!"

"Thanks for the heads-up, man," Alex whispered. "Can we talk somewhere private?"

"Yeah, come with me."

I rolled my eyes at their antics and followed Premfield's lead through quiet hallways and open spaces in which dozens of nerds worked hunched over their keyboards. The sound of a *Star Wars* ringtone or Techno Chicken video occasionally tore through the silence, punctuated by adolescent snickers. As we progressed into the facility, security door after security door, the atmosphere turned colder. There were no longer any wooden inserts on the white walls, and behind the windows, most of the employees wore lab coats, or even white coveralls sometimes.

Premfield noticed the direction of my gaze. "Nanoprocessors. One grain of dust and you're bloody fucked."

"I see."

I should mention that while the horned skull on the front of his T-shirt might have been misleading, Premfield was in fact a world-class authority on a variety of computer-engineering-related areas, and the mastermind behind EMT Switzerland's research facility. The giant lab was his love child, an incubator for the best and worst promises of digital hardware, and he had been overseeing its futuristic projects for more than three decades. From actually useful projects like nanomachines capable of destroying cancerous cells, to perhaps supererogatory ones, such as the fridge that tells you you're too fat and shocks you if you grab ice cream, Prentis Premfield was shaping our future.

He led us to a cluttered office with an extraordinary view of the lake and Swiss Alps. His desk reminded me of Thom's; it was covered with papers and computer parts, as were the floor and chairs. Premfield made room on two metal armchairs, stopped to blow his nose with a large tartan handkerchief, and eventually sat across from us.

"So," Alex began. "Do you know why we're here?"

"Because Thom jumped headfirst into a shit pool without a life jacket?"

Alex cocked an eyebrow but said nothing otherwise, allowing him to go on.

"Listen, brother, I don't put my nose in Hadrian's business, but I know shit when I smell it, and that shit with Thom stinks real bad. He was a good chap, brilliant one too. Didn't deserve to bite the dust—not with a wife and kid."

I nodded, my chest tight, fighting the pain I could feel reawaken as Premfield talked about Emma and little Tobias. Two details stood out from his tirade: First, the man liked to say *shit*. A lot. Second, he called Ellingham by his first name. I had never known the two were this close.

"Did you speak to Thom during his stay in Zürich? Did he come to you?" Alex inquired.

"Yeah, of course. We both had a speech slot at MT, so we talked about work, life . . . went to grab a bite. He was still fine, at the time."

"*Still?* What about *after* the conference?"

"He called. About a week after that. That's when I knew something was wrong. He wouldn't say, but he kept saying shit like 'Maybe I won't stay with EMT for that long.' I thought he meant he had gotten an offer somewhere else, that maybe he didn't know what to do with his life." Premfield bowed his head, and in his tired gray eyes, I read that all the metal bravado was probably an act to some extent. Like me, he blamed himself for what had happened, for having failed to understand the kind of hell Thom had been trapped into.

"Did he say anything else?" Alex insisted.

"Well, we talked about work. He was interested in one of our nano-technology projects," Premfield said with an evasive gesture.

I leaned on his desk. "What kind of stuff, exactly?"

"Hot stuff. I'll show you."

Alex and I exchanged looks and followed him out of the office and down the hallway. Security appeared to be reinforced in this area of the facility. We passed through two thick steel double doors with finger-print authentication.

Premfield beckoned us with a wave of his arm. "You're gonna love this little asshole."

This . . . what?

He brought us into an empty lab that seemed a little different from the other ones. On the long metal tables lay some tubes and syringes still wrapped in plastic, what looked like meds, but also half-chewed dog toys—the damage had been considerable. I looked around. There was a fridge filled with colorful tubes, but also chicories and carrots.

I heard a rustling sound behind me. The noise had come from a long cage lined with straw, inside which stood a pink rodent house.

Premfield opened the fridge and took out a few leaves of chicory. A series of increasingly loud wheeks rising from the little house answered this initiative.

"Come out. Come out, you little piece of shit!"

I imitated Alex as he bent toward the cage with a childish grin. "It's a cavy?"

A tiny, quivering pink nose darted out, confirming his diagnostic.

"Yeah. Careful, fucker's been biting lately. He's depressed or some shit."

"He's in a cage, and you're experimenting on him—of course he's depressed," I huffed, taking one of the chicory leaves to bait the creature.

Soon, a ball of golden and white fur waddled out of its shelter, call-ing me—or the chicory—with enthusiastic squeaks. He looked almost normal. Almost. Save for the fact his eyes were glowing blue.

Premfield opened the cage and lifted the struggling cavy with a level of care that belied the many expletives he used against the animal. "This," he said, rubbing the rodent's back while I fed it one of the leaves, "is the beacon of tomorrow's science. It's the fucking future."

"What's up with his eyes?" I asked.

"MicroLEDs. That way the owner knows if he's connected or his batteries are low."

Alex poked the cavy's forehead gingerly. "His batteries?"

Our host looked jubilant as he presented his creation. "We call him Ricardo3000. He's fifty percent wireless server and fifty percent guinea pig. This is the most advanced nanotechnology in the world as I'm speaking. And it's happening here, at EMT Switz! Right, little twat?" He patted Ricardo's butt affectionately.

I fed the rodent another leaf. "But what's the point?"

"You're asking me that? When all the good families in the world only want two things: to store entertainment shit on portable devices and to have a pet to love! Well, I give you a user-friendly custom Linux distribution with a two-terabyte server *and* a best friend for your kids!"

Next to me, Alex's mouth hung open in horrified awe. "How does it work? Do you . . . don't you need to plug it in to something?"

Premfield made room on one of the tables to lay down Ricardo. "Watch this." He started fiddling with the cavy, who remained surprisingly impassive. "You tug on the left ear to turn the Wi-Fi on and detect devices; right ear to turn it off. Scratch his butt to scroll, like that, you see?"

Alex and I watched in fascinated horror as Ricardo's eyes flashed successively red, green, and purple.

"What about the server's batteries?" I murmured.

Premfield held the small furry butt with a firm hand. "I'll show you. You just plug it in here—"

Alex lunged to pull Ricardo away from the alimentation cable just in time. "It's okay! We get the general idea!"

I helped him put the poor thing back in his cage. "So it's still at the experimental stage, right?"

"Yeah. EMT pulled the plug on the project. Got cold feet."

I cleared my throat. "Wow . . . it's . . . super unfortunate."

"Right, huh? They whined about 'concerns regarding animal cruelty and marketability,'" Premfield said in a grating falsetto voice, complete with air quotes. "They don't know shit. Thom found him great, and Ricardo liked him."

He let out a weary sigh and looked at Alex. "Sometimes I don't get this world, brother."

I smiled. "So you're not really experimenting on him anymore—you're just keeping him?"

A gruff tenderness filled Premfield's eyes as showed us out of the lab. "Yeah, you could say that."

Once we reached the lobby, Premfield exchanged a virile handshake with Alex, and his hand landed on my shoulder. "Sorry I couldn't help you catch Hadrian's dough."

I stared at him, my eyes wide. "Oh my God, you know about this?"

He just blinked. "Did you two really think I didn't know? Nana always tells me everything she hears."

"Who's that?" I asked.

Behind me, Alex was scratching his chin until I feared it would fall off. The situation had to be critical. "I'm sorry, Island, I should have briefed you—"

I held my hands up in the air. "Hold on a second. Who's *Nana*? And what did you forget to tell me?"

"Nana is Hadrian's mom. She's my little sister." Premfield shrugged.

I'd have been less surprised if they had told me that N = NP, after all. I gaped at Premfield, at the ponytail, the Black Sabbath T-shirt, the green flip-flops. "You're Hadrian Ellingham's *uncle*? On his mother's side?"

He drummed his palms on his stomach proudly. "In person!"

"Wow, I would have never guessed." I winced as soon as the words left my mouth.

He just laughed it off before his lips pursed in apparent respect. "Yeah, his old man and me, we had a hard time getting on. But he had a good vision for this place, and that brought us together. The man knew his beer too."

I responded with an awkward smile. Indeed, it was difficult to imagine the late Marcus Ellingham III—ten times the iceberg his son would ever be, according to the rumors—sharing a beer with Premfield.

Oh well. I'd have to text Prince as soon I had a moment for that.

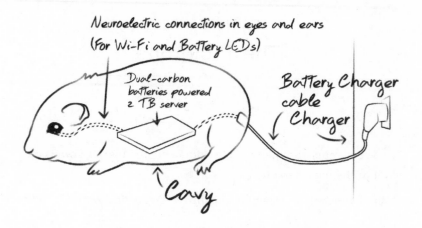

TWENTY-THREE

The Toblerone

"And remember that in a couple's darkest hour, there's always a
light at the end of the tunnel: divorce."

—Aurelia Nichols & Jillie Bean, *101 Tips to Catch Mr. Right*

"That was weird," I announced as we exited the building.

Alex shrugged. "I think he's a pretty nice guy."

"It's the bromance talking."

He laughed. "Maybe. What do you say we call Mr. November to
see if he's found anything interesting?" As he said this, he pulled out his
phone and started dialing. March picked up.

There were no pleasantries exchanged; Alex went to the point
immediately. "Anything new?"

I scooted closer to listen as, on the other end of the line, March
spoke. "Based on Mr. Hendry's map, I played tourist on the mountain
roads surrounding Vaduz. I'm almost certain that they took Roth to
Gaflei, a charming hamlet northeast of the city. There's a closed trail
leading to a manor higher in the woods. It's a private property owned

by Platt Paradise Limited, a Bahamas holding, and quite obviously a shell company."

"Good, I'll have my colleagues do a search to find out who's hiding behind it," Alex replied.

I performed a fist pump. Now we were getting somewhere! One thing nagged at me, though: March didn't like his partner much, that I knew already, but there was an edge to his voice that I didn't think had anything to do with their feud. "March? Is there anything else? You sound a little preoccupied."

He remained silent for a couple of seconds before answering. "I believe I've seen faces I know, guarding the access to that trail."

Alex's jaw tensed. "Can you elaborate?"

"No. Not until I've figured what it means myself. I'll see you in Vaduz, Mr. Morgan," March concluded in a cutting tone.

I grabbed the phone. "Wait a second!"

All I got in response was a beeping sound. He had hung up on us, reminding me of just how frustrating he could get when he switched to his secretive douche mode.

I sighed and looked at Alex. "Sorry about that."

"I'm getting used to it. He'll tell us when we get there." Alex pulled out his car keys. "Looks like we'll be spending the night in Liechtenstein after all. Let's go get our bags."

My shoulders slumped. "That hotel had such a nice breakfast, though."

———

"Be careful, there's a speed limit."

I thought Alex was exaggerating. We had already covered more than thirty miles on the freeway in the direction of Vaduz, I was in the driver's seat, and we were still alive. So, did his hand really need to hover around the steering wheel like that?

"Oh, come on! This car is magic! It's even following the white lines—I don't even have to do anything!"

I pulled my hands off the Tesla's wheel to demonstrate; Alex's immediately moved to replace them. "I should have never let you drive. You're a road hazard, Island."

I rolled my eyes. "You can't be serious. I never raced with anyone the way you did with March. I haven't driven since I got my license!"

His breath caught in his throat. "You *what*?"

"Well, not exactly. My dad has this old Plymouth he keeps at his Hamptons house, and sometimes, when we go there for the weekend, he lets me drive it in the alley."

Alex performed a slow facepalm with his right hand; the left one never left the wheel. "You told me you knew exactly what you were doing!"

"Theoretically."

"You said—and I quote you—'Electric cars have no secrets for me.'"

"I read Wikipedia a lot." I hit the blinker as I said this, watching with an ecstatic grin as the car did a lane change on its own.

"Well, enjoy it while it lasts," Alex announced in an ominous voice. "Because you are *never* touching this wheel again after today."

"You're sounding like March."

"It's because you need discipline." He sighed.

On my right, the large touch screen serving as a dashboard started beeping. "You have an incoming call."

Alex tapped the screen. "It's Murrell."

Indeed, as soon as he had accepted the call, Agent Murrell's face appeared on screen. He was sitting at a desk, and I could see computers and people behind him. I realized it was the first time I was seeing him without his trench coat.

Possibly even more exciting, the hint of a smile danced on his lips. "Good morning, Morgan. How's the weather in Switzerland?"

"Lovely. Do you have anything for me?"

"Don't I always?" Murrell smirked as a secondary window appeared on screen, displaying several pictures of a middle-aged guy with short sandy-blond hair and deep bags under his eyes. "Our analysts traced Platt Paradise back to an Austrian investment advisor named Niklas Van Kreft. Born in 1967 in Vienna, graduated from the London School of Economics in 1981, joined J. P. Morgan and married Nancy Lyles, a British dermatologist, that same year. Divorced three years later, no children.

"In 2009, following an investigation for insider trading, he left his position in the firm as a partner to fund his own investment company based in Vaduz: Adventia AG. It's mostly been a succession of shady but profitable deals and long-simmering lawsuits, since. He's banned from operating a business in most of the United States and in three European countries."

Alex nodded. "Okay, and beyond that? What's your feeling about him?"

Murrell leaned back in his chair and crossed his arms. "I'd say Van Kreft doesn't fit the profile. He's made some exceptional deals, also sold a lot of junk to his clients. Still, he was never really big enough or connected enough to interest us.

"Never been linked to any homicide before, no significant ties to any government, and the amounts he lost or swindled from his clients remain within an acceptable range for a financial advisor: less than twenty million worldwide in six years, for a ninety-seven million net benefit over the same period. The guy is sketchy, but he's solvent, and he doesn't play in the big leagues."

"Well, maybe he decided to up his game. All our evidence points to him, so far."

"Or maybe he's not acting alone," I suggested. "Maybe he's doing the thinking, and someone else is handling the killing."

On the screen, Murrell's lips pursed. "Would make sense, Miss Chaptal. Van Kreft lives in the manor most of the time. Are you planning on paying him a visit, Morgan?"

"I certainly am."

"What about—" Murrell paused, his eyes darted to me. "Mr. November? He's not with you?"

"He's in Vaduz already. He had some input of his own regarding Van Kreft's crib, which I have yet to hear," Alex said, his tone cooler.

"All right, just be careful."

With this, the call window turned black, indicating that Murrell had hung up.

I drove for a while in silence afterward—yes, *the autopilot* was driving, shut up—pondering our conversation with Murrell. Alex seemed just as deep in thought. We were entering a tunnel when I had an idea. "Alex, what sort of stuff do you need to make someone think you're rich? Would it work if someone showed up with, say, really expensive jewelry and a suitcase full of cash?"

He shifted to look at me in the darkness, the tunnel's lighting casting golden flashes of light across his face. "I'm not sure where you're going with this."

"Well, I was thinking that breaking into that manor would be difficult and maybe even dangerous if it's well guarded. So maybe one of us could pretend to be a potential client, you know, to get invited there."

"Island, the CIA doesn't send us undercover with millions of dollars to blow as we please. That's in *James Bond*."

"But what if someone used their own money?" I risked.

He chuckled and shook his head. "It's a terrible idea, and I don't think your savings account will be enough for that. Were you planning on asking March?"

No, I was actually planning on using my own money—just some real estate here and there, and a few million euros my mom had hidden in various offshore bank accounts before her death, and which I had inherited from her at the same time I discovered the Cullinan's existence. Not much, really. It dawned on me, though, that Alex's lack of reaction suggested that this was not in the CIA's files, maybe because I had been so uncomfortable with all that money until now that I hadn't dared touch it, or even contact those banks, for that matter. I decided against telling him.

My fingers tightened on the wheel. "No, I meant . . . Sorry, I guess that was a stupid idea."

He chuckled. "Infiltration is a bit more difficult than you imagine, but don't worry, we'll find a way to meet Van Kreft. For now . . . how about we take a lunch break, baby?"

I flinched upon hearing the b-word. Carried away by our investigation, I had allowed myself to once again postpone the inevitable. "I'll take the next exit, Walenstadt. We can probably grab a sandwich there."

Alex stretched in his seat. "Sounds great!"

———

After we had bought cheese sandwiches and some Toblerone in a bakery, we both leaned against the car on the side of the road and ate in silence. Alex had confiscated the car keys from me—because I was apparently undeserving of my driver's license—and gazed at the grandiose scenery of the Swiss Alps surrounding us as he finished his chocolate bar.

I was nibbling on the last bite of my Toblerone as well. The sound of his voice startled me. "What's the deal between you and March?"

I breathed deeply. *Here we are. Breakup talk in three, two, one . . .* "Alex, listen—"

He shifted to face me, perusing me with a sudden intensity that raised goose bumps on my forearms. "Did you lie to me? When you said you hadn't slept with him?"

"No!"

I was taken aback not so much by his blunt approach but by the lack of emotion in his voice. As if it didn't matter either way. When he spoke again, I could no longer meet his eyes. "So? I'm all ears, Island."

"He helped me find the Ghost Cullinan that my mother had stolen.

I'm sure you already know that. We gave it back to . . . the person who wanted it." One more word and we'd have to discuss the Board, or Dries's implication in the theft. I chose to stop there.

A bitter smile appeared on Alex's lips. "He came to help you, just like that? Out of nowhere? And as soon as Erwin strikes a deal with you, he's back in the picture. I suppose that's a coincidence as well?"

My fingers dug into the cotton of my dress. "Alex, it's a little complicated, even for me. There are . . . things from the past tying me to him. And when we were looking for the Cullinan—" I tried to ruffle my hair so it'd conceal my ears. I could tell they were on fire and that the rest of my face would follow soon.

"He's the ex you told me about."

There was no questioning in voice, just a calm certainty. His tone was light, conversational. He wasn't even looking at me anymore; his gaze focused on a point in the horizon, far beyond me. His eyes had never been so cold, not even when he had questioned me back at EMT.

I managed to get the words out of my throat, struggling to form each syllable. "Alex, I'm sorry. I don't think we're good for each other. I want to stop . . . I want to stop for good."

I'm not sure what reaction I expected, but I stared at him in incomprehension when he ducked his head and I heard a dry chuckle. "Oh fuck. Did you just dump me for him?"

I didn't like this—his tone, his apparent indifference, the nervous laugh. I took a step back. "It's not about March." Yes, that *was* a lie.

Alex moved fast, much faster than I could process, and in a split second my back hit the side of the car hard as he flattened me against it. His hands locked my wrists alongside my body in a bruising grip. Air escaped my lungs in a brutal rush as the pain registered in my ribs and shoulder blades. I think I cried out, but the sound died in my throat when he pressed his forehead to mine. A feverish breath traveled between us that carried the sweet smell of chocolate as his lips moved closer. There was a little sweat on his brow, matting his brown curls to my skin; my stomach heaved at the cool, sticky wetness connecting us. I gritted my teeth and tried to turn my head away to escape this sudden invasion.

My heart was beating so loud I could barely hear my own voice over the thumping in my eardrums. "Alex, please, calm down!"

"This is too easy, baby. You get caught up in your own game, things get tough, and you dump me on the side of a road to escape the shit you got yourself into. It doesn't work like that, Island!" he shouted, his face close enough for me to feel the rasp of his stubble on my cheek. My brain conjured that scene in *Alien 3*, where the xenomorph is inching closer and threatening to drool all over a terrified Ripley's face. In that moment, I wondered how I had ever allowed this guy—whoever he was—to touch me.

I squeezed my eyes shut and one of my legs jerked in a futile attempt to kick him off me. He dodged it and pressed his thigh between mine, blocking me completely.

"Let me go! I said we're done! We're done!" I wished it would have come out as a roar, to free the fear and rage building in my chest, but in truth I was begging, and that near sob sounded foreign even to my own ears.

Around my wrists, his fingers tightened. Pain shot up my arm. "That's *my* call. And I'll be sure to let you know when we're done."

With this, at last, he let go, leaving me panting and shaking against the Tesla's door.

"Now get in," he ordered, his voice softening.

I looked at him with uncertainty, trying to catch my breath with a series of gasps.

I think Alex finally figured just how badly he had screwed up. Warmth returned to his eyes, and along with it a spark of distress. He shook his head, raking a hand through his hair. "Baby, I'm sorry. I shouldn't have. I just think you're making a mistake."

I wasn't sure what to think of this typical wife-beating pattern of unexpected violence followed by a—no doubt sincere—apology. *Tamed by the Lone Wolf* would have equated it to a display of alpha male amorous frustration, something along the lines of "Babe, you drive me crazy. I brutally banged you in my cabin in spite of your explicit protests because it was the only way I could express my feelings." How romantic. In any case, I didn't want to discuss the incident further and see just how much worse things could get. I climbed in the passenger seat with slow, controlled movements, my eyes never leaving him in case he lost it again.

TWENTY-FOUR

The Rendezvous

"Don't lie to yourself, babe, your body wanted this! You say no, but your tits say yes."

—Azure Typhoon, *Tamed by the Lone Wolf*

The rest of the ride to Vaduz was mostly silent. And awkward. As awkward as it gets when your ex who just turned Mr. Hyde on you half an hour ago is now attempting to make small talk to ease the atmosphere, only to earn monosyllabic responses and the occasional nod. My wrists still hurt, and reddish-blue bruises had appeared on my skin, like ugly bracelets. I pulled my dress's sleeves over them and looked at the scenery to distract me, blocking Alex's voice as he commented on the beauty of the Alps.

I had never visited an actual tax haven, even during those years traveling with my mom, and I sort of expected that everything would be different the second we crossed the border to Liechtenstein. Like Marco Polo sailing across the oceans, I in my cool electric car, dreamed of the golden roofs of Cipango. Vaduz wasn't like that. It looked in fact more like a village than an actual city—or even a capital—and possessed the same quiet alpine charm that could be found in the Swiss villages we had driven through. A flock of tiled roofs encased in a valley, scattered among pine trees, church steeples, and traditional half-timbered buildings—not what you'd imagine for a country boasting one of the highest GDP per capita in the world. Perched on a hilltop and overlooking the city was the medieval castle, a massive and somewhat random stack of ancient stone towers.

"March texted me that he's waiting for us at the Sonnenhof Hotel. Phyllis took care of the rooms," Alex announced, typing the hotel's name in the GPS.

I acquiesced. March. Could I tell him what had happened? God, I wanted to. I wanted to be the five-year-old who points at the bully who hit her and asks an adult to avenge her. But I knew what it would entail, and I didn't want any more violence. It was best I popped back into my shell and bore Alex's presence until this investigation was over and I was able to put a galaxy or two between us.

The Sonnenhof Hotel was on the outskirts of the city, facing the still, white summit of the Alpspitz. I wished we had actually been there on a vacation, because its chalet-inspired design and the lush scenery of its garden made the whole place look like a fairy tale.

Alex was opening the trunk to retrieve our luggage when March's voice echoed behind us. "I wouldn't call this proper parallel parking."

The single wrinkle on his brow was self-explanatory. Those few hours spent alone had done little to improve his mood.

I cast him a pleading look. "Not now—I promise to bring a protractor next time."

"You won't have to," he said in a lofty tone.

My mouth fell open in a scandalized O when he pulled out his phone from his pocket and aimed the screen at our car briefly.

"Thirteen degrees. Would you like help with your suitcase while Mr. Morgan fixes this?"

I had no idea what to answer to that, so I just let him pick up my suitcase and followed him toward the ivy-covered arch leading to the hotel entrance. Behind me, I heard Alex mutter that March needed professional help as he opened the driver's door. Mr. Clean ignored his diagnosis to follow me into the lobby.

Once we were alone, he seemed to relax a little. "Phyllis booked you a very nice room. I think you'll like it."

"Thank you," I mumbled.

"There's a table waiting for us at the restaurant. We can discuss our next course of action over lunch."

Lunch. The very word brought up the memory of Alex's body pressed against mine, of his hands crunching my wrists. Blood started pulsing rapidly in my neck; I felt dizzy. "I-I'm sorry, we already ate on the road. But maybe we can have a drink?"

On March's forehead, the creases reappeared, this time out of concern. He removed one of his black gloves, and his hand rose to graze my cheek with the back of his knuckles. "Biscuit, are you all right?"

"I'm good. It's just that I'm exhausted and—" My voice faltered, and in spite of myself, March's touch made me flinch. "I'll go unpack; I won't be long."

He fitted back his glove with doubtful eyes. "Very well. Take your time; I'll see you at the bar."

I rubbed my temples tiredly and followed a young hostess to my room on the hotel's first floor. Once in, I let go of my suitcase and opened the bay window to stand on the balcony, staring at the view for a while. I could see the castle well, its outline sharp against the blue sky and frothy white clouds. The slope of the hill it stood atop was covered with bright green fields and blooming trees, creating a soothing postcard.

March had been right—the room itself was really nice, brightly lit, with its warm wooden furniture and white linen enlivened by black strip cushions here and there. I briefly contemplated slipping into a bathrobe, turning the TV on, and calling him and Alex to inform them that I had changed my mind and no longer cared about finding Thom's killers or Ellingham's money, because I had no energy left for either. A rage-quit, if you will.

I didn't. Because there was too much at stake. I needed to clear Thom's name. So I took a gianduiotti from the minibar to give myself some courage, brushed my teeth because I didn't want to get diabetes *and* cavities, and left the room like the winner I was.

———

Alex's spoon tinkled against the porcelain of his cup as he twirled it in his Vienna coffee. "This is all we've got so far. We need to approach Van Kreft carefully. If he's our guy, after what happened on Roosevelt Island, it's a given that he knows someone is on his track."

"I know you didn't take my idea seriously," I said between two sips of hot chocolate, looking at Alex. "But, like I said, I could go undercover and pretend to be a potential client."

"Island, we've talked about this already—" He sighed.

March glanced at me over his coffee cup. "Agreed. There will indeed be no undercover mission involving Island."

I raised a finger. "I think we should take the time to discuss the pros and cons—"

For a second, I thought I had gotten through to March. His features had lit up, and he was looking at me intently. He squinted his eyes in apparent incomprehension, before his expression morphed into something complicated that I wasn't sure how to interpret—worry, disbelief . . . rage.

And I understood. Upon raising my hand to defend the merits of my plan, my sleeve had been pulled back, revealing the purple imprints of Alex's fingers on my skin.

Across the rustic wooden table, March was very still, and his gaze was now set on Alex, unblinking. "Mr. Morgan, will you follow me outside?"

I winced at his velvety tone. Polite as the invitation might have been, his clenched fists and flaring nostrils promised a world of hurt. I shook my head in a silent plea. He didn't listen—probably couldn't, at this point.

Alex's glare suggested he believed himself to be up to the challenge. "Certainly, Mr. November."

I should have felt vindicated that Alex was about to learn a painful lesson in not handling a breakup like the Hulk, but I found the idea brought me no comfort, filling me instead with an asphyxiating sense of guilt. *I* was the one who had allowed the tension to escalate between the three of us . . . until this. A distant part of me was able to analyze the situation rationally and conclude that Alex had brought this on his sorry ass, and that March wouldn't kill him anyway—that was no longer who he wanted to be. But I couldn't shake off that damn guilt, and I watched, petrified, as they both got up and left the table.

I thought of going after them, even started to get up as well, but then I caught my own reflection in the window, and I realized how pale I was, how hollow my eyes looked. I looked like Dobby the fricking house elf. This wasn't me. I needed to get over this, find myself again, and it dawned on me that the best way to accomplish that wouldn't be to stand and watch while those two fought. It was to act!

Master is busy beating the shit out of Alex! Dobby is free!

I took out my phone, following from the corner of my eye until they had disappeared behind a wall and, I gathered, inside the garden.

It was a little weird for me to call Valorbank for the first time and give my client code. My personal set of moral values was still fairly traditional, making me feel bad for calling a Liechtenstein bank where I supposedly had a couple million dollars stashed. In any case, there's no problem a well-stocked bank account can't solve, and when I told my newfound financial advisor—a charming guy named Anders—that I was looking to invest my money and asked him what he thought of Adventia AG, he was all too happy to offer to call them for me and see if a meeting could be arranged. Of course, confidentiality being a chief concern in Valor's particular field of business, I was assured that my identity would not be disclosed. I was a nameless, faceless client looking to purchase stock with cash currently sleeping in a dozen different tax havens, and everybody here was just fine with that concept.

After he had hung up, I lapped at the remaining whipped cream topping my hot chocolate, while outside a few onlookers and a waiter hurried toward the gardens to get a better view of whatever drama was unfolding there.

Mmm . . . Maybe I should have stopped March and Alex after all. I paid for our drinks and barged out of the bar and toward the gardens. On my way, I passed an old lady covering her mouth with her hand, wide-eyed.

Okay, on a scale of one to total tram destruction, it wasn't that bad. There were bloody noses, ruffled hair, and March was close to victory, slowly choking Alex on a wooden table. Or not. Alex's left leg managed to swing and send a powerful kick that made his adversary let go and double over. I'll spare you the details, gentlemen: you know where it hurts the most. March quickly recovered, though, and in the blink of an eye grabbed Alex again in a powerful neck hold.

"Stop it!" I yelled, raising my arms in the air.

Around Alex's neck I saw March's hold loosen, and they moved away from each other, eyes still smoldering with anger, chests heaving with exertion.

I lowered my arms. "That's enough."

To my surprise, March apologized first, his voice tight. "I'm sorry, Island. I believe Mr. Morgan and I have worked out our differences."

Alex rubbed his throat gingerly. In his features, rage receded, leaving behind something I couldn't decipher. A sense of emptiness, of quiet reproach. His gaze traveled back and forth between me and March.

"I'm here to do a job," he eventually said, his eyes set on March. "And so are you, Mr. November. I agree we should focus on this instead."

March gave a slight nod. Alex wouldn't look at me—I gathered our mutual wounds were still a bit too raw for that, in every sense of the word—but it seemed that a sense of understanding passed between the two men, a nonaggression pact of sorts.

The tension in my limbs ebbed.

"Good, now we can—" I stopped midsentence when my phone chimed again. I couldn't suppress a grin. Anders was offering to arrange a meeting with a certain Hannes Wille, senior advisor for Adventia—and Van Kreft's right-hand man. Would I enjoy a dinner tonight at the Sonnenhof's restaurant? Why, yes, of course I would! My fingers fluttered on the screen's glass surface under March and Alex's inquisitive stares.

I raised a victorious fist in the air. "I'm having dinner with one of Van Kreft's advisors at eight tonight!"

"You're not."

"This is unacceptable."

Great. Those two finally agreed on something without needing any prior negotiation. I glowered at them and turned my back on them with a light shrug, making a show of walking away.

"Island, where are you going?" Alex groaned.

"I've got some errands to run before tonight's dinner."

March's sigh reached me as I turned my back on them. "Biscuit, you won't play spy."

Ignoring him, I squared my shoulders and puffed up like a pigeon, walking toward the chair on which he had laid out his jacket before beating Alex up. *Watch me.* I fished in his inner pocket for a small black key fob. "I'm taking your keys; I need a car to go downtown."

"Let's calm down and discuss this," he said, aggravation filtering through his words as he walked toward me.

Alex was quicker to figure out that the fight had been lost already. He picked up his leather jacket from the ground and dusted it roughly. "All right, is a debrief too much to ask for?"

I proceeded to recap my exchanges with Anders to them. By the time I was done, he was dragging his palm across his face in a visible effort to digest the news. "Okay. So, you used some secret offshore account to bait Van Kreft's most trusted advisor and arrange a meeting. Is there anything else we should know before we proceed any further?"

March appeared equally shocked and displeased, and to be honest, I didn't understand them. It wasn't like they had any better lead to offer, and I felt in fact quite proud of myself.

"I'll need a cover," I announced. "A fake identity, and some online tracks, in case they look me up. Alex, do you think the NSA could help with this, now that we're best friends with that Hendry guy?"

"*Best friends,*" Alex repeated, enunciating each word slowly as he looked at March. His attention returned to me. "I can make a few phone calls."

March crossed his arms and towered over me with a stern expression. "You're unqualified for such a mission." I straightened, readying myself for the upcoming battle. "But what is done is done. I'll take you downtown to shop for a proper dress."

My eyes scanned his dirty, bloody shirt and the split on his lip. I gave him a rueful smile. "Okay. But first we need to take care of you."

TWENTY-FIVE

Book of Island

"Island rose from the ground, and although her eyes were opened,
she saw nothing: she didn't get men yet."

—*The Book of Island: Spiritual Teachings for the Dating-Impaired*
(Possibly borrowed from Acts 9:8 of the Bible)

"You shouldn't have fought with Alex. But . . . thank you." I sighed,
dabbing at the cut on March's lower lip with an antiseptic swab.

"It was my pleasure entirely."

I smiled. I had no doubt he could have taken care of himself, but I
suspected he enjoyed being pampered a little, and in his own room, no
less—no better way to assert that he had won, *Rawwrrr*. Once I was done,
I went to dispose of the bloody piece of gauze in the bathroom's trash can.

When I returned, March was still sitting on the bed, observing with
attentive, cat-like eyes. "You should have told me," he said.

"It was very sudden. I told him we were done, and I guess Alex . . .
He lost his temper."

March's nostrils flared upon hearing this. "Don't make any excuses
for him."

"I'm not. It's just that I wasn't sure what to say, and I was afraid that if I told you it would end . . . the way it did."

I knew that cool glare wasn't directed at me, but it made me shudder a bit. "My response was appropriate, and, dare I say, moderate," he said tightly.

"You reacted like a caveman."

At last, the harsh lines on his brow seemed to relax, and a boyish smile outlined his dimples. "Perhaps so."

Now, if this was the *Book of Island*, a faithful account of the many miracles she accomplished during her life as a prophet—let it be known that Joy would have never assembled those Billy shelves without my divine power—we would be at the part where Island is blessed by a vision from the gods and suddenly sees the truth of things.

She was blind, and then, *bam*! She figures out something that had been eluding her for years, ever since that day when she was fourteen and a bum flashed her his noodle in Pretoria, in broad daylight no less.

Women have power over men too. The power to make them do (stupid) things. Out of desire, most of the time. Out of spite too—Alex had taught me that. But also . . .

I gazed at March, still sitting on his bed. Drops of blood had stained his shirt, forming an oddly beautiful pattern on the pristine cotton, as if red chrysanthemums had been scattered on the collar and front. He'd need to change it.

He probably noticed that my expression had changed. His smile faded, replaced by a question in his eyes, in the slight tilt of his head. I stepped closer, until my knees were brushing his. He remained silent. All shields up, guarding himself carefully, as usual.

Funny how mere days ago, I'd have self-combusted with shame at the very idea of doing something like this. I placed my hands on his shoulders slowly, feeling his muscles coil at this first contact. My eyes never left his as I straddled him and sat on his lap. My dress was pulled back tight by this new position, baring my thighs as my legs landed on the comforter on each side of his body. Our faces now inches apart, I watched as his dark blue eyes widened and his breathing quickened. March's hands hadn't moved, but I noticed the way his fingers dug slightly into the white comforter. He felt it too, that heat where our bodies made contact with each other.

His tongue darted out to wet his lips before he spoke. "Island, what are you doing?"

My fingers tightened around his shoulders, and I had to close my eyes for a second because maybe the similar tension building within me was more than I could handle. "I want to talk."

One of his hands left the bed to graze my cheek. My toes curled. "Maybe we can do so . . . in a standing position."

I squirmed forward on his lap, closing what little distance remained between our bodies. A sharp exhale fanned over my face that carried the scent of the coffee he had been drinking at the bar. Between my thighs, his legs shifted a little, in a desperate attempt to prevent further intimate contact. I pressed my forehead against his, struggling to collect my thoughts when our lips could practically touch.

"I don't mind talking like this," I murmured.

The hand that had been hovering near my cheek traveled down to settle on the small of my back, pressing me even closer. "Biscuit, this isn't *talking* . . ."

While he was clearly affected by this sudden proximity, March was still capable of serving me some gentleman bullshit. I took it to mean he wasn't yet quite where I wanted him. I started unbuttoning his shirt with trembling hands. To my amazement, he didn't resist, the slight movement of his Adam's apple as he swallowed the only hint that I was, in fact, playing with the limits of his self-control.

Emboldened, I pushed away the dark chrysanthemums of dried blood to reveal skin. And so much fuzzy, curly, silky chest hair. When my fingers abandoned their task to caress his chest and lose themselves in that wonderful rug, he wavered. His head lolled as if he had meant to bury his face in my neck, but he seemed to catch himself, merely grazing the shell of my ear with his lips, his breath hot and uneven. "This is a bad idea."

"What do you want?" I asked in what I hoped was a sultry voice, at the same time that my palms found their way under his shirt.

"Island . . . You know exactly what I want right now."

My eyes darted to his left hand, still clenching the comforter in a white-knuckled grip. "But you won't take it. You could have slept with me in Tokyo, but you didn't. And yet—" I pushed the shirt off his shoulders, only to be rewarded by a furtive nip on my neck that nearly derailed my thoughts. "You're back. And you want something else. What do you *want*, March?"

He pressed a line of kisses along my jaw, his mouth searching mine. "I just want you to be safe. To be happy."

"I'm not!"

My cry of frustration echoed in the room. He wrapped his arms around me, locking me into a tight embrace, and straightened on the bed to balance us in this new position. When his lips brushed the tip of my nose, I thought he was at last going to kiss me, but he maintained a "safe" distance between our mouths.

"Biscuit, it's always perfect in the beginning." He searched for his words in between breaths. I waited for him to go on, each second ticking between us an eternity. "But in the long run, no one ever changes, and you won't want to be there—"

"I've been in your trunk. I've been on Rislow's table. Don't tell me what I can handle or not."

One of his hands moved to cradle the back of my head, his fingers threading through my hair. "I need to wash everything at least twice. Sometimes I wake up at night to check if objects are in place. There's a rifle under my couch and a gun under my pillow because I never know when someone might come knocking at my door to settle an old score."

I listened to him, basking in the heat of his skin, the way our scents mingled, his soap, my perfume, earth, grass. I felt powerful, almost light-headed, because for once I understood things he didn't. My palms splayed on his chest; I pressed a single kiss on the pulse beating fast in his neck. "But you're not checking anything right now. Your shirt is dirty and you're not doing anything about it. Tell me why you came back," I insisted.

In my arms, March seemed to slump a little; his grip on me relaxed. "Because I thought I could change . . . for you."

For you. I pressed my forehead to his and took a deep breath. It took me a few vertiginous seconds to process his words, let them flow through me.

His face moved away, though, just enough to look into my eyes, as if trying to pierce a mystery. "But I was wrong. You need someone normal, with a stable job, a name, a phone number, papers—someone safe."

My chest tightened as I thought of Struthio, of the office, the emu on the brochure. March had tried his best to become a good citizen, had turned his entire life upside down in a matter of months, but he still believed it wasn't enough. That *he* wasn't enough. I bit my lower lip hard. Already, I could feel my eyes and nose prickling.

He cupped my cheek with his hand, his thumb wiping a lone tear I hadn't felt roll down my cheek. "Biscuit, please don't cry."

I sniffed. "I-I think my dad would like it if I dated a guy who has his own brochure."

March hugged me tight. The sexual tension between us seemed to have now evaporated—no doubt because I had ended up sobbing like a kid. He combed his fingers through the wild curls in my hair as he spoke. "But I haven't found a good first name yet, and I'm not safe for you."

"Why don't you have a first name?" I mewled into his shoulder.

"I didn't know what to put in that field, so I just left it blank."

Renewed tears built up in my eyes at this. Somewhere along the course of those fifteen years spent killing, March had truly, completely lost himself, to the point where he wasn't capable of writing down his birth name anymore. I straightened in his arms to cradle his face, traced each angle, each line. "I like 'March.' You don't need to find another name; I don't care."

"Just March?" he asked quietly.

"Just March."

His eyelids dropped; he seemed conflicted, even as his hands roamed down my sides and settled on my thighs, making the decision his cautious, rational mind couldn't. When he opened his eyes again, there was a new determination in those dark blue irises.

Slowly, March brought his head down until our mouths were brushing each other. His lips parted, and with my first taste of him since that night in Tokyo came a sense of being home. Hesitant yet thorough, hungry but never wild—a kiss like no other, the sum of his flaws and qualities. I realized there was something sweet laced with the coffee on his tongue; I remembered the little Swiss chocolate that had been sitting on his saucer and smiled against his mouth before resuming kissing him eagerly.

A sigh of disappointment escaped me when he pulled away with a final tug at my lower lip. His dimples appeared, framing an impish grin. "A point well made, Miss Chaptal. But we still have a lot to do before tonight's dinner."

My love bubble burst with a resounding pop. Why was it *never* the right time to be swept off my feet in a passionate storm and all? I pushed on March's chest with all my strength in an attempt to force him down. It worked, but I think it was because he let himself fall on the fluffy comforter with a chuckle, without offering any resistance. I followed him, lying by his side, my right hand never leaving his chest. Because now, all that *precious* hair was *mine*.

"We need to set some rules," he said, his eyes on the ceiling, half closed.

I groaned. "Already?"

"Rule number one: from now on you'll be honest with me, as I'll be with you."

My mouth opened to make some snide comment about this statement, but he took me by surprise. "When we're done beating Ruby, I'll tell you about the code your mother left for you. But I'd like to tackle one issue at a time, if you don't mind."

Past the shock, I rested my cheek against his chest, reveling in the simple, evident connection between us as his arms wrapped around me. "Okay, you win this round; I won't pester you until we're done. For now I've got some shopping to do to look my best tonight. I need to go downtown."

I felt the peaceful rise and fall of his rib cage, heard the smile in his voice as he answered. "Just let me change and I'll take you there."

"Can I drive?"

He rubbed the top of my head absently. "Depends. What's the speed limit in town?"

"I'm sure it's written on the signs."

"Wrong answer. I'm sorry, biscuit. Maybe next time."

Dammit!

TWENTY-SIX

The Socks

"Sometimes I actually stare at your eyes instead of your rack, baby. That's how fucking much I love you."

—Piper Nightwings, *Renegade Rider from Hell*

Seven fifteen . . .

March was supposed to show up to take me downstairs in less than thirty minutes. I had just gotten out of the shower. My hair was a mess, I was still wearing a towel, I couldn't find my body lotion . . . but what I *had* found were more gianduiotti in the minibar, so we were getting somewhere.

A ring came from my laptop. I checked the caller ID: Phyllis. Perfect. I sat on the bed, a chocolate candy in hand, while her smiling face and flaming curls appeared on the screen.

"Good evening, Island, are you getting ready?"

"Yup, almost done." Okay, maybe not almost.

"Fantastic. We're done setting you up for tonight. That Hendry guy is actually a sweetie. I think March is too harsh on him, you know," she said, shaking her head.

I couldn't suppress a chuckle. "Those tomatoes won't go down."

In the chat window, Phyllis dissolved into laughter. "Yeah, my boss can be a little stubborn sometimes."

"What about my cover? Can you brief me?"

She started reading the file to me. "You are now Maeva Rochebresse. You were born on May 6, 1991, daughter to Chiara Lisi and Bernard Rochebresse. Both deceased, no living relatives—makes it easier for us to weave some secret child into the picture. Your father served seventeen years in a French maximum-security prison for a series of bank robberies. He died there five years ago. The cash from the robberies was never found, and you miraculously inherited twenty million euros on your eighteenth birthday." Phyllis paused in her debrief; over the line, I heard some typing. "Hendry had his guy set up a social security number and a birth certificate for you. What about those web pages you told me about?"

I checked the chat window on my laptop, in which Colin had just posted a Victory Baby meme to indicate he was done. "All the pages are online, and they've been pushed to the top of a dozen search engines' results. Crawling bots work fast and they're pretty smart, so these won't last very long. They'll quickly figure out our websites are nothing but copies of the real ones with some DNS spoofing. But it should be enough for now. If Van Kreft's employees look me up in the next few days, they'll get a consistent profile with social presence, school alumni, and even a mention on Wikipedia!" I said triumphantly.

"Awesome! Did you get yourself something sexy?"

I flushed at the memory of my shopping trip, and the way March had insisted on checking every detail of the gray silk dress I had bought. In the changing room. Needless to say, the saleswoman had imagined the worst, when he had in fact been examining the dress's cut and seams, with, say, 90 percent pure intentions. "Yeah, I found a nice silk dress. I think I won't look too bad."

"Don't forget the makeup. Your strong points are your eyes and those baby lips. Two coats of mascara; easy on the gloss. Sexy, but natural," Phyllis instructed.

"Okay. Should I—" I cleared my throat. "Do you think I should pad my bra?"

Her lips twisted into a pout. "Permission to speak frankly?"

"Yes."

"Two pairs of socks. In each cup."

Ouch. Straight in the feels. "Okay."

"Relax, it's gonna be just fine. March won't leave you for a second."

"I know, but we only have tonight. I have to get something out of Wille."

"And you will. Go kill it!" With this, Phyllis hung up, and I winced at the idea of her encouraging March with those same words.

The next half an hour was a storm during which underwear, shoes, and beauty products flew all over the place. Once I was done, my room looked like it had been rented by Keith Moon. I checked myself in the wardrobe mirror and was satisfied with the results of my efforts. I had only balled one pair of socks in each cup of my bra, though, and the feather-light silk gray dress was a little too short for my taste. It hadn't seemed that bad in the dressing room, but now that I stood perched atop black stilettos, I had no doubt my thighs were visible from space. I frowned at my short auburn locks. Nope. I was starting to come to terms with the fact that I was born disheveled and would die so.

I took a selfie, which I sent to Phyllis for validation purposes. Never in my life had I felt more like those gorgeous and insecure girls wearing napkins to go clubbing, who end up throwing up their cosmo(s) on the sidewalk, with a stranger holding their hair and offering them an Alka-Seltzer and some BDSM at his place. Wait, wasn't that from somewhere?

Phyllis texted back her approval. I frowned at my reflection. No cosmos tonight.

A knock at the door forced my mind away from creepy visions of floggers and handcuffs. I hastily shoved my lingerie back in my suitcase and staggered across the room, struggling to get used to the pumps. Maybe I should have gone for lower heels after all.

Our recent adventures had made me cautious. I didn't open the door immediately, waiting for my visitor to identify himself.

"Island? Are you ready?"

March. I looked around the room. That wouldn't do. Not for him. "I . . . Uh . . . Just a moment!"

I scrambled to pick up a dozen gianduiotti wrappers from my nightstand and the clothes lying on various pieces of furniture. I spotted the towel I had thrown across the room and folded it carefully, before placing back on its shelf in the bathroom.

Another impatient knock. "Biscuit, are you all right?"

"Yes . . . Just—yes!" I unlocked the door with a flushed face, allowing him in.

Damn. I had forgotten just how good he looked in a tux. I treated myself to a couple of seconds of shameless ogling. The cut was impeccable; not a single wrinkle on his white shirt, and of course, no tie. I had never seen March wear one, and I was starting to wonder if there was a reason behind this particular fashion choice. I smiled. He smiled. And then he didn't. I followed the direction of his gaze, taking in the slight flaring of his nostrils.

"I have *no* idea how that got there!"

I'd have run to retrieve the pair of frilly panties currently hanging from the lampshade sitting on my nightstand, but March outsped me. He walked to the bed, took the offending garment with a sigh, and moved toward my suitcase.

I lunged to stop him before he could open it. "No!"

"Biscuit, I'll just—"

"Trust me. You *don't* want to open this suitcase," I said, taking the panties from him.

I guess March remembered the state of my apartment: realization dawned on his face. He paled. "I give you five seconds." With this, he averted his gaze.

It was all I needed to shove the panties in my suitcase and slam it back shut. For good.

When I turned to him, he seemed to have relaxed, but a threatening glint lingered in his eyes. "We'll talk about that suitcase again . . ."

I acknowledged his warning with a wince, and my attention returned to his tux, remembering the way he had dressed the same for our date in Tokyo. "Not bad, Mr. November."

He ducked his head, a genuine grin chasing the sanctimonious scowl. "You don't look too bad yourself, Miss Chaptal."

My body warmed up a little at the way his heavy-lidded gaze ostentatiously checked the silk dress, lingering on the hem that almost revealed the top of my thighs, before traveling back up. He blinked and opened his mouth, but no sound came out.

Holy. Fucking. Raptor. Jesus.

The shaming session wasn't over, after all. My hands fumbled up to cover my chest. I think you could have fried an egg on my cheeks at that point. "It's . . . Phyllis said I should put socks, for the seduction job!"

I could see he was battling his own facial muscles not to laugh. A chortle escaped him, though. "Biscuit, I'm not sure that those . . ."

My nose bunched; he hastily completed his assessment. "I meant that they're . . . fine. I think they're remarkably fine without the socks."

"Thank you." I relaxed. "But I'm keeping the socks. Dries once told me that there's business and there's pleasure. The socks are for business."

"Is that to say"—March moved closer, wrapping his arms loosely around my waist—"that I'll be allowed to remove them later, for my own pleasure?"

Oh, that deep, velvety voice almost made me want to take them out right this instant. I inched closer, resting my cheek against his chest, and breathed in the hint of citrus and spice floating around him. Soap and aftershave, no cologne. Typical March.

"Maybe . . ."

His voice dropped to a suggestive whisper. "I look forward to it."

So do I . . . I looked away to smooth nonexistent wrinkles in my dress. "Business first, though!"

"Business first," he confirmed, before glancing at the laptop on my bed. "Is everything ready for tonight?"

"Yes, Phyllis briefed me and Colin, and helped us set up a consistent online identity in case they look me up."

"Excellent. Once you're with the target, the most important thing is not to try too hard. Just let him talk, nudge him in the right direction when you can, but avoid any direct questions."

I gave a firm nod.

A chime interrupted us. I took out my phone from my bag and checked the caller ID: Premfield. March observed me while I took the call.

"Hey! How you doing, little bird?"

"Fine. Do you have any news?"

"Oh yeah! Had my little anoraks check recent activity on our servers. Wanted to make sure again, you know."

Around the phone, my fingers tightened. "So?"

"I think Thom actually managed to connect to Ricardo the night he died, around three. That sneaky bastard accessed Ricardo's server with the test credentials he had seen me use during his visit. Used a proxy too; never realized there was something wrong with that log entry until we checked the time."

"That's when he transferred the money with Ruby! What did he do on Ricardo?"

March stepped closer to listen to Premfield's answer.

"He copied one file. Encrypted. We're working on cracking it."

If the code Thom had copied on Ricardo had been meant to rectify what he had done, then I could now easily guess what would constitute the last piece of his password system. "Professor, try this: *But let me first do some great thing that shall be told among men hereafter*," I suggested.

March and I waited as on the other end of the line, some furious typing took place, until Premfield spoke again. "Was that totally random?" he asked, amazement clear in his voice.

"Not really," I conceded. "Can you tell me what's on the file?"

"Some code. A class, actually, named, uhm, *RR*."

I performed a silent fist pump and felt March's hand squeeze my shoulder. I looked up to see his smile. He was proud of me, and it was all it took for me to fly to cloud nine.

I took a shaky breath to try to contain my excitement. "Professor, can you give me access to Ricardo? I think we're gonna need that code."

TWENTY-SEVEN
Delicatessen

"The blood he had just drank from her beautiful neck rushed directly to his crotch, stirring his sinister salami to life."

—Muffin Thorpe, *Slave to the Rich and Sexy Vampire*

As I walked down the hallway leading to the hotel's restaurant, my heels clicking on the floor, a thrill of excitement raced down my spine. This might, after all, be the closest thing to the spy life I'd ever experience.

Oh yeah, I'm talking about the small pearl pendant that Alex had secured around my neck, under March's wary gaze, which concealed a fricking itsy bitsy tiny microphone. And I had a spy earplug too! I don't think they call it that, by the way. March noted with a scornful shrug that it wasn't that amazing, and anyone could buy that stuff on eBay nowadays. Some derogatory comments regarding the CIA's budgets followed—likely a form of catharsis for the earlier incident, one that would not involve pummeling Alex into a bloody pulp again.

When the restaurant's red carpet and golden chandeliers came into view, I took a calming breath and imagined that I was on a catwalk. Miss J's teachings on *America's Next Top Model* had to come in handy some day. An uptight maître d'hôtel welcomed us, informing me that my guest had already arrived. He gestured to an isolated table around which two baroque armchairs covered in red damask had been set. In one of them sat a blond guy in his midforties, lean, almost wiry, and wearing a super-elegant tux. I waved a timid hand at him, and he got up immediately, a radiant smile lighting his sharp features.

He greeted me with a soft voice that I found hard to reconcile with his harsh German accent. "Mademoiselle Rochebresse, je présume?"

I batted my two coats of mascara at him. "Yes, and you're Mr. Wille? I'm delighted to meet you. Your French is excellent!"

I extended my hand for him to shake, but to my surprise, he bowed and took it for an old-fashioned *baisemain*. Behind me, I felt March and Alex stiffen at the sight of his lips grazing the back of my hand. I wanted to snatch it back; I didn't. This was too important for me to chicken out because of one mildly disgusting physical contact.

Wille seemed to at last acknowledge my two bodyguards and examined them, perhaps waiting for some sort of introductions to be made. I responded with a giggle and slapped both men's arms playfully. "I'm so sorry about that. A young woman needs her gorillas to keep her safe these days. But I think I couldn't be safer than with you, Mr. Wille. I'll send them away, right, boys?"

You could have cut the tension between the three of us with a (Swiss) cheese wire, and I'm pretty sure March and Alex both glared at me when Wille turned to speak to our waiter. Still, they walked away to sit at a nearby table, their eyes never leaving me as I sat down with my guest.

Soon afterward, the waiter came back with two plates of a yummy-looking grilled foie gras and a bottle of Château d'Yquem Wille had chosen to complement it.

Once his glass had been filled, Wille picked it up and swirled the golden liquid inside with a flick of his wrist. "So, I understand you're looking for some investment advice, Miss Rochebresse?"

I imitated him, but some drops landed on my plate, which I tried to wipe with my napkin. "Please call me Maeva. Yes, I received a . . . certain amount of money from my late father—such a good man, God bless his soul—but for now, it's just sleeping in several bank accounts, and I read in *Forbes* that some hedge funds returned more than twenty percent last year. So I told myself, 'You have to do something with all that money, or else it's gonna, like, melt, because of the inflation,' you know?"

His blue eyes lingered on my socks insistently. "Yes, yes, the inflation, of course."

"And my advisor at Valorbank said Mr. Van Kreft was this total genius, and he offered to arrange a meeting with you, and here we are!" I concluded, spreading my foie gras on a slice of bread.

"He is, indeed, a genius, you can trust me, Maeva." He raised his glass with a relaxed smile. "Allow me to call a toast to our chance encounter."

"To our chance encounter! What about you, Mr. Wille, can you tell me more about yourself?"

"You can call me Hannes. Well, I'm but a humble financial advisor and, I believe, a man of my time, who seeks beauty wherever he can," he said, tilting his head with a smile oozing fake modesty.

I encouraged him to elaborate, and there followed nearly half an hour of brain-melting crap about golf, yachting, ornithology, and his opinion regarding the situation in the Middle East. Then came an in-depth study of the intellectual chasm that led proletarians to rebel against a system that nourished them, and without which they wouldn't be able to survive because their unfathomable stupidity would drive them to devour each other—literally speaking. The guy quoted Plautus's proverb, *"Homo homini lupus est,"* and offered cannibalism as an example of what poor people do when you don't watch them closely.

I didn't talk much, just nodded and spurred him toward any subject that might lead the conversation back to Van Kreft. Fortunately—or not—Wille didn't expect his dates to say anything.

Dates . . .

God, this had actually turned into some sort of *date*, right?

This particular point was clarified when he started fondling my hand, while the waiter brought us two . . . octopus risottos. I thought of Krakky, alone in Hadrian Ellingham's office, crying perhaps. I couldn't touch mine. Which didn't bother Wille either. He was now telling me about the joys of skiing in the Alps, and I just wanted his bony fingers around mine gone. Funny how it had been so different during my date with March in Tokyo. He had done the same—the hand touching, I mean, not the asinine rants—but his caresses had made me melt like butter on a pancake, pleasant jolts of electricity dancing on my skin and up my arm with every contact.

"Island, focus!"

"Maeva? *Maeva?*"

I jumped a little on my chair. In my ear, Alex's voice had covered Wille's, reminding me that it wasn't okay to zone out during a seduction mission, even if your date was super boring and somewhat creepy.

Dammit, I needed to get something out of that guy, because we were reaching dessert already, and so far I had no lead.

"So, you were saying you love skiing? Where do you ski?"

"Well, the Alps have no shortage of exceptional stations, but I must confess to being a bit of a wild man." Yeah, he was. Like, crazy wild.

I made a show of touching my hair to send him a signal that I found him irresistible. "So where do wild men ski?"

"Backcountry. You can enjoy some exceptional trails on the other side of the border, in Austria. I'm also a hiking enthusiast. The Gafleispitz, for example, is a lovely area."

My ears perked up. Gafleispitz? As in Gaflei, the place where they had taken Thom? "That sounds incredible! So you, um, go there often?"

"Well, Mr. Van Kreft possesses a residence in Gaflei. We have easy access to the mountain from there," he explained as the waiter brought us strawberry-ginger gratins and some sorbet.

My eyes darted to Alex and March's table. Their intense gaze told me everything I needed to know: we had an opening. I counted on all that ginger on Wille's plate to help me, and I shunned every single drop of modesty I possessed. Swallowing back a wince, I trailed a tentative caress on his hand the same way he had done to me. A slow smile stirred his lips.

I looked at him through heavy-lidded eyes and bit my lower lip for good measure. "I'd love for you to take me—"

Wille leaned toward me, resting his chin on his left hand.

". . . hiking there. Is Mr. Van Kreft's manor nice?" I inquired innocently.

On the table, his hand left mine so he could take a bite of his strawberry gratin. He tilted his head, his eyes gleaming with something familiar. I took in the crinkles at the corners of his eyes, the lazy, lopsided smile. Knots formed in my stomach when I realized that Alex had sometimes looked at me like that. Like he understood things I didn't . . . like I was dessert.

I pursed my lips as Wille answered. "Well, the manor is what you'd call a *gentilhommière*, dating back to the seventeenth century. Legend has it that it was built around 1680 by an Austrian nobleman as a hideaway for his wife, who had been accused of witchcraft during a widespread hunt."

"Oh my God, I love these stories! I *have* to see this place!"

He gave me an apologetic smile. "Mr. Van Kreft doesn't usually receive visitors."

Too bad, because I *really* wanted Mr. Van Kreft to receive me. I slipped off one of my pumps under the table. In my ear, I heard March's angry hiss. "Is this absolutely necessary?"

Pretending to rearrange my hair, I turned the spy earplug thing off. I didn't need his input. Not on what I was about to do. In the twitch of Wille's brow, I could read the exact instant my bare foot touched his calf. I was fascinated, in a clinical sort of way, by the way his features froze, the knowing smile morphing into an intense, lustful stare. He then resumed eating his strawberry gratin, looking every bit like this was an ordinary business dinner.

"You like experienced men?" he asked casually, his voice low.

I felt my cheeks redden, and I could tell what little foundation I had put on wouldn't conceal it. The worst part was that, on a rational level, I was mentally cheering at how well the seduction job was going. Not in the way I had imagined, but I had his attention all right.

"Yes," I breathed out, at the same time that under the table my leg moved up and down with excruciating care, feeling unpleasant chills run down my spine with every awkward caress. I tried to focus on the strategy I had in mind. Never had I been so glad to have read *Slave to the Rich and Sexy Vampire*. Twice. "Hannes, I've never . . . done it in a castle. I kind of like, you know, the whole dungeon atmosphere, and the idea of doing . . . *different* kinds of things," I whispered.

He took my hand again, but this time his fingers curled around mine with quiet urgency. "It might be difficult to arrange. Mr. Van Kreft works a lot."

Not good enough an answer. I clenched my teeth and kept exploring upward, until, through his pants, my big toe met something that wasn't his thigh—that wasn't even his leg, and felt like . . . like raw turkey sausage. Not really soft, not rock-hard like in my Aloha's Cave books. Just . . . *icky*. Wille's eyes screwed shut in apparent delight. I jerked my leg back, gripping the edge of the table. His breath was a little short, his smile more carnal than ever, and, help me, Raptor Jesus, he was staring at my socks again.

He took his glass and finished the wine there in one gulp. "Well, Maeva, I will talk to Mr. Van Kreft, and I'm sure we can arrange to see each other at the manor on Friday. I'll be . . . delighted to see you there."

As the tension receded, I schooled my features into a childish pout. "Only Friday?"

He grabbed my hand and pressed it feverishly. His palm was sweaty;

I fought a gag. "I'm so sorry, but Mr. Van Kreft is hosting a professional event tomorrow, an auction of sorts. You'd find it extremely boring."

An auction? "Wow, Mr. Van Kreft also sells art? He's such an unpredictable man!"

"No, not art. I'm sorry, my dear, these are matters requiring a high level of confidentiality," Wille said.

"No, I'm the one who should apologize. I didn't mean to make you uncomfortable, Hannes. I'll see you at the manor on Friday, then." I squirmed on my chair and bit my lip a little. "Will you text me tomorrow?"

"Of course! And I'll arrange for my chauffeur to pick you up on Friday morning."

The contented sigh that escaped me as he sipped his coffee was almost genuine, even though I could feel March and Alex's blistering gazes on us. I worried about Wille spontaneously combusting when he walked past their table, after having said his good-byes with a long, ambiguous *baisemain* on my knuckles.

I waited for the man to be gone, and got up as well. My knees were shaking a little—and the five-inch heels didn't help. I passed their table without sparing them a glance, not to attract anyone's suspicion. I didn't want to risk anyone who might have accompanied Wille seeing us debrief the dinner.

I sensed their presence behind me, getting up to follow me toward the hallway.

The second we were safely shielded from prying eyes, all hell broke loose. "What was that?" March seethed, struggling to control his strength as he wrapped a possessive arm around my shoulders.

Alex seemed just as pissed. "Island. Never, and I do mean *never* break contact when you're in the field!"

"I needed to focus without you two complaining in my ear." I wiggled my right foot, which had touched Wille. "All I want right now is some soap!"

March's brow shot up. "*Soap?* Island, what happened? *What* did you do under that table?"

"It was an accident! I think I touched his . . . his—"

"Jesus Christ!" March immediately reached inside his jacket. Gotta love a man who carried a mini bottle of antibacterial gel wherever he went. I took it, removed my shoe, and leaned on his forearm while I squeezed some on my toes and frantically cleaned them.

Good news is that I didn't catch any kind of exotic venereal disease from my brief indirect contact with Wille's turkey sausage. As March and Alex escorted me back to my room to debrief, however, I decided that I would retire from the spy game after we were done clearing Thom's name and retrieving Ruby. My career as an operative, albeit a short one, had already taught me that sometimes, in order to fight for those who can't fight back, you gotta step on more than just toes.

TWENTY-EIGHT

The Candles

"There was no stopping him now. She was a vodka-soaked rag he would set on fire."

—Lacey Black, *The Fireman's Searing Touch*

I sat curled in a large cream armchair, drained, and feeling like Cinderella after midnight—mostly because my shoes lay at the other end of the room, and I had gotten rid of those ridiculous socks in the bathroom a few minutes earlier. March was leaning against a wooden desk, his arms crossed, and Alex stood near the bed while I summarized Premfield's call and Wille's revelations for them.

"So you think Van Kreft could be planning on auctioning Ruby?" Alex asked.

I scratched my nose in concentration. "Maybe. He could have stolen Ellingham's money because it was the most easily accessible. With EMT's mainframe at his disposal, and Ruby's help, it probably wasn't difficult for Thom to break into EMG's systems and locate the target accounts. Plus, Van Kreft had to know Ellingham wouldn't go public about losing money sleeping in tax havens. The way I see it, what we've perceived as the end of the operation until now might have just been a test, something to prove potential buyers what Ruby could do."

"Then there's only one thing left to do," March announced coldly, moving away from the wall toward the door.

Alex followed him. "Wait a second, where are you going?"

"I believe, Mr. Morgan, that our collaboration is over now that we've identified the target."

A smirk formed on Alex's lips. "Very funny. I'm going with you. Your arrangement with Erwin doesn't allow you to kick me out of this investigation."

"If only . . ." March growled.

This time I got up too, barring their way with more than a hundred pounds of fierce determination. "I'm coming too. And March, you still haven't told us about those faces you saw around Van Kreft's manor!"

March's features hardened, and for the first time in six months I was standing again in front of the icy professional who had once broken into my apartment and put me in his trunk. "You're staying here."

My hands balled into fists. "Wait a minute, we need to discuss this."

March's index finger landed on the tip of my nose, the cool warning in his eyes knotting my vocal cords. He removed it after a second to check his watch. There was some sort of red LED blinking on the bezel ring. He rotated it, turning the glass into an LCD screen. His brow furrowed.

I had no idea what was going on, but Alex apparently did. "You set a tracker on one of the cars you saw in Gaflei?"

"Yes." March said, taking another step toward the room's door.

I needed to act quickly. I went for the first plan that crossed my mind. Jumping around his neck without warning, I pressed my lips to his. I felt him startle at first, then respond, gathering me in his arms and allowing himself the brief delight of a French kiss.

"You can be such a douche," I whispered.

March responded with an unapologetic quirk of his lips and a brush of his fingers in my hair. I was very aware of Alex's gaze on us, but I figured that, beyond the initial purpose of the kiss, maybe Alex and I needed this—a final statement that things were over for good.

There were a few tense seconds, heated glances were exchanged between the two men, and at last, the door slammed shut behind them.

As soon as I was certain they were far enough away, I lunged at my laptop and set it to track the whereabouts of my precious CIA pendant, which I had "inadvertently" slipped inside March's jacket pocket while kissing him. I was grateful for all that chatting with Colin; I had picked up a few things along the way. With the help of his expert advice and some of the tools he had recommended to me—he was somehow persuaded that I had some sort of future as a hacker—the device proved surprisingly easy to trace. March and Alex hadn't made it far; the little red dot on my map had stopped moving already, somewhere on the outskirts of Vaduz.

I called reception, asking for a cab. There was no time to change. I just slipped on my regular sweater dress over the flimsy silk one and hopped into a pair of sneakers. I was running across the hotel's lobby when in my bag my phone started to vibrate. I picked it up while waiting for the cab.

Phyllis's voice greeted me. "Good evening, Island. I need to reach March, and none of my calls are making it through. Is he with you?"

"No, he took off with Alex. March said he had seen people he knew around Van Kreft's manor, and he set a tracker on one of the cars. The car moved, and they went after it. I know where they are, though. I'm on my way there."

"Okay, but be careful, spygirl. What I needed to tell him is that something is off with Van Kreft. I'm not sure we're looking in the right direction," she said, clucking her tongue in what I understood to be equal measure worry and annoyance.

In front of me, a white Volvo with a taxi sign had stopped. I waved at the driver, and when he nodded back, got in. Once I had given him the address, I tried to focus on Phyllis's words rather than the strong smell of tobacco surrounding me. "What do you mean? One of Alex's colleagues sort of said that too. Is it because of his background?"

"No, more like the lack of recent background," she said, while the car glided past Vaduz's low buildings to reach a quiet residential area. I could make out dark roofs concealed behind high hedges. "Our man hasn't made any credit card purchases for months, other than some auto-renewals of online services. He hasn't been seen in public either, and—wait for it—I dug up medical results from a seven-month-old cardiologist appointment, along with several prescriptions, and Van Kreft never had his MRI, never bought any meds . . ."

I frowned. "Um, are you saying he's . . ."

"Your guess is as good as mine."

"Okay, I'll make sure to let them know. I gotta go," I concluded, seeing a familiar black BMW a few yards away from the cab.

I called to the driver in (likely broken) German. "Bitte halten Sie hier an!" *Stop here, please!*

He parked next to the BMW. I fished some cash from my wallet in a hurry and stepped out. The street was quiet, snoozing under a starless sky. The place the magic necklace had led me to looked like a nice villa. One of those high, neatly trimmed hedgerows enclosed the place, and lanterns lit the path toward a massive wooden entrance door. Two big guys in dark suits stood guard. I walked toward them on unsteady legs, mentally reviewing every single pickup line I knew. As I got closer, I registered a dull, distant noise, halfway between a hum and a rhythmic pounding. Some sort of club? If so, how would I get in?

Dobby will improvise!

Indeed. Once I was facing those beefy bouncers with shaved and tattooed skulls, it became clear I'd have to come up with something good—it says something about a guy, I believe, when he wears sunglasses after midnight.

"Guten Abend," I said.

A slight twitch of the tallest one's fingers. No sign they had even heard me.

This wasn't the way. I had been challenged by enough bouncers and barmen in my short time on this earth to know that the dynamics regulating nightlife were somewhat different from those regulating, say, a library. And I was in a foreign, Germanic land, a place where nothing mattered more than order. What I needed was to show these gentlemen that I understood the social etiquette ruling this mysterious den and therefore belonged among their guests.

I lifted my sweater dress to reveal the short silk dress underneath. Ignoring the cool night breeze whose embarrassing effects I could already feel—should have kept the damn socks—I cleared my throat and searched for memories of that German extracurricular class I had taken in high school. Yes, I was very lonely at the time. "Guten Abend, meine herren. Ich bin sehr reich, ich bin kaum bekleidet, und ich habe sehr geringes Selbstwertgefühl. Kann ich mich bewegen bitte?" *Good evening, sirs. I'm very rich, I'm barely dressed, and I have very low self-esteem. Can I please come in?*

There were a few seconds of silence, troubled only by the imperceptible thrumming reaching us from inside the villa. One of the bouncers seemed to listen to someone talking to him in a tiny earpiece, adjusted his glasses, and broke down into a gravelly laugh, holding his stomach. The other one seemed on the verge of cracking up as well, but he held on to his composure better than his colleague did.

I blinked. "I . . . Uh . . ."

After a few seconds, the man calmed down and slammed a snake-shaped door knocker twice.

The doors opened with an ominous creaking sound.

I looked up at the bouncers. There was no explanation to be read on those stony faces; I went in.

The doors were closed behind me, and I was plunged into complete darkness, save for a line of tiny candles on the floor, meant, I supposed, to guide me into this strange place. At first, I feared there had been a huge misunderstanding and I had accidentally stepped into some sort of Satanist party where I'd be offered a martini with an eye in the glass instead of the traditional olive.

"Wilkommen." *Welcome.*

I jumped and looked around. Something—or rather someone—had popped up a few feet away from me. A lean female silhouette, outlined by the golden candlelight. She came forward, and when a green glow came to life in her hands, I realized she had turned on a credit card terminal. Maybe they were pragmatic Satanists, after all. I pulled out my wallet again from one of my dress's pockets and handed her my credit card. I cringed at the amount that appeared on screen. No Sabbath, even the most hardcore one, was worth a thousand Swiss francs entrance fee.

The worst part was that she didn't even thank me! Once I had been billed, she pressed a stamp to the back of my right hand, leaving the imprint of a snake head glowing on my skin in the dark. Then without a word, she retreated into the pitch-black she had emerged from.

I took a few cautious steps down the shimmering path laid out for me, and I reached the end of a long hallway, guided by the beat of music, which seemed to be getting louder. On my left was a flight of stairs. By then, I could feel the bass of a popular electronic hit song vibrating through my rib cage. A little candle on each step still showed the way, but a cautious mind had made sure to also line their edges with a thin golden neon light—I figured even super-secret Satanist clubs didn't want guests to trip and fall.

The stairs turned twice at small landings. The temperature had progressively risen, and the music was becoming too loud. Finally, I made out some sort of thick, dark curtain ahead of me. My hand rose to push it, but before I could, a giggling woman waltzed through, shrouded in a cloud of alcohol and perfume. I let her run past me and made a second attempt at parting the curtain. I was assaulted by a burst of colorful lights tearing through the darkness, and a wave of hot, humid air carrying more scents than I could count.

What lay before my eyes was something halfway between a club and a lounge. A few dozen people swayed and rubbed against each other in the middle of a dance floor, while all around the vast room, others appeared to be drinking themselves silly in alcoves where backlit cubes served as low tables. Those half-dressed girls kissing their partners with fluorescent cocktails in their hands made my own look seem conservative in comparison. Then again, there's this rumor in Europe that for all their apparent rigidity, Germans are completely decadent behind closed doors. Two words: *German porn.*

I frowned at the long, dark lines I could make out on some cubes. There was more than just weird booze making the rounds in there. Half-blinded by the tangle of stroboscopic lights stabbing my eyeballs, I staggered my way through the partying crowd, wincing when I noticed that some guys had opened their shirts. Yucky sweaty chests, no hair—nothing to see there.

What the hell were March and Alex doing in a place like this? Did they need to unwind? No, March, at the least, wasn't like that. He had once forbidden me to smoke a mere joint, so I assumed that the very sight of a coke line would cause him to shoot the offender on sight. My ears were ringing from the deafening beat filling the place; I was so confused that I almost missed the tall silhouette wandering along the alcoves. Bright blue and pink lights flashed across his face, highlighting a strong jaw and a slightly aquiline nose.

"March!" I yelled through the noise.

He turned to acknowledge me with a frown, standing still while I struggled across the dance floor. Behind him, Alex had emerged from the crowd as well. As I reached them, something moved at the edge of my field of vision. All I saw clearly was a silvery flash tearing through the crowd and latching onto March. Well, onto his lips, in fact.

I think I gritted my teeth so hard I could have shattered them. Some—admittedly beautiful—skank had grabbed March by the collar and was kissing the living breath out of him. I gaped at the hourglass figure hugged by a tight, silvery tube dress. Long black curls cascaded down her back, dyed bright blue at their extremities. That wasn't the detail I paid the most attention to, though. What I doubt I'll ever forget was her hands, the way they held on to his shoulders with a sense of desperation. I understood that, for her, it wasn't just a kiss.

March, for his part, didn't seem very responsive, and he was actually trying to disentangle himself from his enthusiastic partner, coaxing her hands off his shoulders, drawing his lips away from hers with patient, gentle movements. He gave her a sad, almost apologetic smile. He knew that girl.

She let go with reluctance and tucked a long lock behind her ear before looking at me. Whatever she saw, she didn't like it. Coal-black almond-shaped eyes appraised me and narrowed in suspicion. "Is that her? Is that the Frenchwoman's daughter?"

I staggered back in shock and bumped against Alex's chest. At some point while I had been watching the newcomer kiss March, he had navigated through the inebriated fauna surrounding us and reached me. I moved away before any level of awkwardness could set in.

March laid a hand on the girl's bare shoulder. "Please, Sahar, that's enough."

Her cherry-lacquered lips twisted in disdain. "It's just that I thought she was hot."

I clenched my fists. *Oh, bitch, you didn't!*

March probably read on my face that a comeback was on its way; he dragged her away. "Why don't we find a quiet place to talk?"

"Great idea," Alex cheered.

We followed March and Sahar to a back room whose white upholstered walls I thought gave off a claustrophobic feeling. I sat on one of the long black velvet couches next to Alex. Sahar and March settled across from us. I worried my lower lip in aggravation when she sank into the opposite couch's cushions and rested a possessive hand on March's thigh, which he guided away discreetly.

"So?" I asked, mimicking the haughty expression on the girl's face.

"Sahar is the youngest sister of a friend of mine." March said, sending me a pointed look that I tried to decipher. "A friend I am very loyal to."

I scanned her high cheekbones, straight nose, and thick, well-defined eyebrows. There was indeed something familiar in her features. Oh God. *Guita.* That girl looked exactly like a younger version of the Queen. My eyes widened. March didn't say anything, but gave an imperceptible nod.

What was it that March had said, back in Zürich? A "powerful employer" handling the killing for Van Kreft? Van Kreft, who, by the way, seemed to have practically vanished . . . and now entered someone with ties to the Board. Next to me, Alex leaned back on the leather cushions, his arms crossed.

"So, what are you doing here?" Sahar asked March, snuggling back against him.

"Well, I'm in Vaduz for professional reasons, but I stumbled on a couple of your men in town and thought that it'd be a shame not to see you." He winked at her. My skin prickled with something that was *not* jealousy. Righteous indignation, that's the term.

"You're so sweet!" She rested her cheek against his shoulder. "You were always like that—my knight in shining armor."

I played with my fingers, cracking my joints. "*Wow*, how long have you two known each other?"

March shot me a warning look that I sustained with a stiff smile. I gathered he was merely doing his job, but if it entailed allowing that hussy to cling to him like this, I'd rather he become unemployed.

Sahar ignored the silent war raging between the couches. "Ten years.

I was a wild teen, and he'd always watch out for me. You know, flying to the rescue whenever things got out of control."

Alex cocked a suspicious eyebrow. "Out of control?"

"Well—" March began. "Some of Sahar's past dates were . . . inadequate. And I was summoned on a few occasions to help rectify that."

She broke down into a fit of giggles. "Oh my God, you seriously rectified Yuen! You know that he still has a limp? The surgeons can't fix that." She seemed to notice the look of horror on my face and deemed it useful to elaborate. "March shot him in the knees with dum-dums."

"Dum-dums?" I asked.

"Expanding bullets," Alex clarified with a smirk.

March sighed. "There were very specific circumstances."

"It was in Macau. Yuen and I launched a business together, but then he started to say he wanted me to sleep with some fat-ass casino owner to pay a debt. March saved me," Sahar said with dreamy eyes.

"How romantic," I squeaked out.

"Movie material, no doubt. Now, tell me, Sahar, what brings you to Liechtenstein?" March asked, slaloming away from the icy trail of his past exploits.

In the space of an instant, all childish playfulness vanished from Sahar's features. She had seemed very young to me, but I now realized she might be around my age, if not a little older. She leaned and crossed her legs deliberately—yes, she *was* wearing underwear. I checked.

"You already know why I'm here, March."

She looked so smug, so goddamn pleased with herself, and all I could think about was Thom. A surge of burning anger ripped through me. I felt Alex's hand move to stop me, but I jumped to my feet before he could. "You helped Van Kreft steal Ruby! You *murdered* Thom!"

March had tensed as well; he seemed mad at me, and ready to intervene if I touched Sahar.

And she . . . just blinked. "I have no idea who you're talking about.

I didn't steal Ruby." Her eyes lit up with a knowing glint. "I'm only here to buy it from him."

The auction Wille had been talking about. My intuition had been right: robbing Ellingham had just been a warm-up. Someone—the Board—would buy Ruby's code from Van Kreft, and there was no telling what they'd do with it.

My eyes met March's. The message in them was clear: *Calm down and don't say a word.* I sat back, struggling to stay still.

He brought his attention back to Sahar, gazing at her with what seemed tender amusement. "I'm afraid you'd be making a terrible mistake."

She smirked. "Would I? Because you're here to recover it for Hadrian Ellingham?"

So she knew. I looked at the wall, past her shoulder, trying not to react to this new piece of intel.

March only smiled. "Sahar, you and I know that my loyalty will always go to the Board first. No, the reason I would advise you not to purchase Ruby is that we've made some unfortunate discoveries over the course of our investigation. Miss Chaptal here, whom you apparently already know, took part in the software's development. She can confirm this."

Near me, Alex kept quiet, as if there was a silent agreement between the two men. I cast March a questioning look. Why would he share anything with her? What was I supposed to confirm?

He ignored me and went on, looking at Sahar. "Roth tampered with the copy of Ruby he stole for Van Kreft. There's a virus in it. Whoever uses this software will see it turn against their own system and compromise their financial data—greatly so."

My mouth hung open in silent admiration. I never knew he had it in him to bullshit someone so well where IT was concerned. Sahar's nostrils flared; her fingers twitched. She was swallowing March's tale, hook, line, and sinker.

He affected a sorrowful expression. "I'm sorry, Sahar. I'm just glad we were able to warn you in time."

She frowned. "So you're here to neutralize Van Kreft?"

"Yes. But given my ties to the Board, I intend to spare all parties involved. We need to return Ruby to EM Tech without harming any of the potential buyers in the process," he said, his eyes set on Alex.

Pretending to score against his own team to better serve Guita—well done. If I hadn't been so irritated, I'd have been impressed. By now, Sahar appeared to be completely under his spell, her body becoming lax, her eyes searching his, filled with gratitude and unspoken feelings. "I'm here with one of our financial advisors. He was supposed to negotiate for us during the auction." She shook her head. "I'll send him back. I don't want to take any risks."

The corners of March's lips curled up. "Has he met Van Kreft yet?"

"No, he's an incredibly secretive guy, always sending us his own advisors. Even I haven't met him."

"Excellent. Sahar"—I bristled when he took her hand in his, lowering his face to hers—"would you allow me to take your advisor's place at tomorrow's auction?"

She blushed a little. "Anything for you. But I'm not sure he'll agree."

March's smile turned feral as he looked down at her long indigo nails. "Is that your usual nightclubbing nail polish? The one that, if I remember well, 'sends losers to the toilets'?"

TWENTY-NINE

The Nail Polish

"She wanted nothing more than to rake her nails all over his rock-hard, perfectly chiseled, and tattooed biker body, but she knew she could never give in to this burning hot and incredibly torrid temptation."

—Lizzy Dare, *Savage Biker SEAL Stepbrothers #1: Ryder*

Wow. Sahar had only dipped one pinkie in the Board emissary's martini, and now three brawny bodyguards barred access to the restrooms, crossing their arms over their chests menacingly whenever a drunk guest stumbled too close. Curled in one of our alcove's seats, I observed the strange ballet taking place in front of the black upholstered doors across the room. A fourth guy had just shoved his way through the dancing crowd to bring a jumbo TP roll. One of the bodyguards sneaked it into the toilet. Whatever was going on in there had to be pretty serious. A Poopmaggedon of sorts.

I poured into a glass the orange juice can March had insisted I choose—a not so subtle way to emphasize the point that most if not all alcoholic drinks might be spiked in here. Next to me, Alex was taking slow sips of his mojito and observing the drama unfolding before our eyes with equal interest, while Sahar and March didn't give a damn about their own drinks, because we were seconds away from public intercourse here!

Did she have to constantly touch his arm and whisper stuff in his ear like that? And March wasn't doing anything about it. More like encouraging her with a lazy smile and whispering back, allowing his lips to hover inches from her skin as he did so.

My skin prickled with every featherlike contact, and the hair on my nape stood on end whenever his eyes met mine, warning me not to react to their little game. Alex was watching my growing irritation with a knowing gaze, and offered to order me another drink. After twenty minutes spent alternatively brooding and sipping an overly sweet Peach Fizz, one of Sahar's goons came to us. This one didn't wear sunglasses inside, and his build seemed lighter than that of the gorillas guarding the restrooms. I examined his dark suit and heavily gelled black hair; he had to be some kind of assistant.

March, at long last, put some distance between him and his conquest. *Man whore!* I listened as the newcomer confirmed to Sahar that the Board's emissary would not be able to leave at dawn for the manor as planned—due to a minor case of "fatigue."

"What a regrettable turn of events. Sahar, can I be of any assistance?" March asked, watching the messenger from the corner of his eye.

She landed a playful kiss on his cheek—Alex's fingers blocked my wrist just in time before I could give her a Peach Fizz shower—and she turned to her guard, beckoning him closer. She tilted her head, pointing at March. "Do you know who this man is?"

He gave a nervous nod.

"Good. Then go tell the others that he'll be accompanying us to the auction."

I thought I saw a flash of doubt in his black irises; I figured March's reputation preceded him, like Alex had said upon meeting him for the first time. The guy nodded again, this time more firmly. "Yes, ma'am."

"I'll be joining you, if you don't mind," Alex said, as if in afterthought.

Sahar acknowledged him with surprise—she had probably thought he was part of the furniture until now.

On the backlit cube where our drinks rested, March's fingers curled into a fist. "That won't be necessary, Mr. Morgan."

"Allow me to insist."

I fidgeted at the edge in Alex's voice.

Sahar's voice cut through the rising tension, light and friendly as she spoke to March. "I don't mind your American friend coming with us. What about you, Island, will you join us too?"

I stared at her in mild shock. I hadn't expected her to be so nice to me. The hint of a smile tugged at the corners of my lips. "Yes, I'd like to. I want to see Van Kreft bite the dust." If he even had anything to do with all this, I reminded myself. Could Wille and his turkey sausage be pulling the strings, after all?

"Out of the question."

I glared daggers at March, ready to pounce and scratch his face off.

Alex backed him. "He's right. Your job as a consultant ends here. You're not trained—"

I got up abruptly. "I get it!"

I was exhausted; in my skull blood pounded in tune with the music, clouding my thinking; and I couldn't stand March's little game with Sahar anymore. I needed some calm to reflect on the night's events, make some sense of Sahar's sudden appearance, and most of all, of the shroud of mystery surrounding Van Kreft. "I'd like to go back to the hotel, since I'm no longer needed."

"I'll drive you back," Alex said, getting up.

I held my breath—I'd have preferred a taxi, or even a walk alone in the dark. With rocks in my shoes.

Across the table, March had stilled. His eyes were set on Alex and me, and the faint tic in his jaw spoke volumes: he was enraged. Sprawled in the couch's cushions, Sahar observed the tension between him and Alex with undisguised interest.

Talk about being in a pinch. Option A: Allow Alex to drive me back to the hotel, knowing that he might lose his shit again once we were alone. If what had happened on the road to Vaduz was any indication, I wouldn't see it coming, and a repeat might earn me more than just a few bruises.

Option B: March could interfere, and thus lose his grip on Sahar. At least she'd stop rubbing herself against him like a cat in heat. But then she'd probably turn on us, and there went our best chance to get into Van Kreft's manor and find out what that auction was about.

Option C: I could make the decision for March.

I offered Alex my largest, fakest smile, whose meaning I was certain he'd get. "Great, thank you." *Don't get any ideas. I'm only doing this because we need Sahar. If you touch me, I'll tear your balls off!*

I glanced at March. I knew he couldn't acknowledge me, not with Sahar leaning on his shoulder. His eyes plunged into Alex's, though, narrowing to dark slits. "Very well." He paused to hand his car keys to Alex. "Be *extremely careful* with my car, though. I value it very much, and I doubt I could stand to find even the *slightest scrape* on its body."

I was pretty sure we were not talking about the BMW. Alex acquiesced with a faint smirk. In the club's changing lights, I couldn't read his expression well, and that alone made me shudder. I hoped all that strangling back at the hotel had talked some sense into him.

As Sahar shifted away to take the fluorescent cocktail a waiter was offering her, my eyes met March's, and for a split second I felt our bond, like an invisible silvery thread between us. He knew I hated his game with Sahar; I knew he hated to have to trust Alex alone with me. But soon this would be behind us. I smiled. "I'll see you later."

His eyes shone with determination. "You will."

I turned away and followed Alex toward the thick velvet curtain at the entrance. The second the heavy drapes fell back into place and engulfed us in darkness, his breath fanned over the nape of my neck. "It's okay if you're upset."

A chill raked down my back. "I'm not upset."

"Evidence to the contrary."

I could hear the smugness in his voice. I grimaced in the dark. I knew he could see it, because *I* could make out the creases around the corners of his mouth, gilded by candlelight.

"Baby, I hate to see you like this, but you made a choice. You wanted the South African—well, you got him," he said.

A tiny spark of fear burst in my chest as he used the b-word. He still wasn't done. I started moving toward the first candlelit step, my head down. "I think you're reading too much into March's strategy. You of all people know that seduction can be part of the job," I snapped.

His drawn-out sigh resounded against the walls. "It can. And I, of all people, know how dangerous that game is."

I didn't look back, afraid he'd see his words had hit very close to home. "A *game*, huh?"

All my senses were on high alert, with Alex climbing the stairs behind me, a shadow close enough to touch me, but whose face I couldn't see. When he spoke again, though, there was no trace of anger, or even spite, in his voice. All that was left seemed to be a form of weariness. Perhaps even regret. "Figure of speech. Don't play dumb. You know you meant more than that. It was never a game for me, Island."

This time I did look back. And the peaceful, gentle guy I had once tried to love was there. Or was he? Perhaps that was Alex's problem—I wondered if he even knew who he really was. Maybe someday the right girl would come and tell him. I wouldn't. I knew I couldn't fix him; there was no point in trying. Instead, I allowed myself to hope that his prior outburst had drained an abscess he would now recover from. We were almost at the top of the stairs when I noticed there were other footsteps echoing behind ours. Alex froze. The footsteps stopped as well.

I turned to him, my heart racing. "What's going on?"

On one of the walls, the candles and the neon light cast barely visible shadows. Concealed by the turn of the stairs, someone had followed us. I heard a rustle of fabric, a metallic sound. Alex had pulled his gun.

"Island, get down!"

I didn't even have to. When bright blue beams appeared out of nowhere and outlined the dark figure lunging at us, my legs simply gave way. I fell on my ass and curled into a ball as Alex shot twice. The silhouette fell with a groan. I realized that the light came from his gun, on which a tiny laser lamp mounted under the barrel streaked the walls around us with a bluish glow.

Above me someone pulled at my arm. I shrieked, my arms flailing in all directions to escape the newcomer's grasp, while a third figure seemed to have emerged as well, in front of Alex this time. The hands reaching out for me let go, leaving a smarting sensation where long nails had scraped my skin. A familiar perfume floated in the air, something flowery. The girl with the credit card terminal—the nails that had dug into my flesh were hers.

More gunshots resounded, silenced this time, and Alex started fighting with our pursuer. Terrifying shadows danced on the walls, and I could hear grunts and punches, along with the sharp clatter of shoes slamming on the stone steps. Alex and his adversary tumbled together, sending candles flying everywhere. Drops of molten wax splattered on my legs, leaving a burning sensation in their wake. I scrambled away with a scream of alarm.

Amid the growls and dull thuds of bodies hitting the walls, a noise suddenly reached my ears that I didn't recognize. Like a low rush of air and some crackling, followed by a harsh acidic smell. Someone howled, and Alex raced back toward me. Then, like they say in the Bible, there was light. Or more exactly, the blaze of an acrylic suit catching fire and lighting up the stairway. The man who had tried to kill Alex staggered on the stairs with desperate moans that turned into blood-chilling screams.

Behind him, a shadow moved, shielding himself with his arms. In a split second I recognized March's tall frame and black tux—I gathered he had heard the gunshots and come to our rescue. He shoved the human torch out of the way, making me guess, with no small amount of horrified awe, that his own jacket was *not* acrylic, and possibly fire-proof. A practical demonstration that smart fashion choices are, indeed, a matter of life and death.

Both men hauled me up by the shoulders, and we ran up the stairs so fast I wasn't even sure my feet were touching the ground. We reached the top of the stairs, and Alex slammed shut the security door behind us, leaving the torch guy to his misery. I could still hear his cries through the heavy steel, still smelled burned flesh and fabric, and I wanted to throw up. I clutched my stomach in an effort not to.

Ahead of us, the hallway had been deserted. Credit-card girl appeared to have vanished, leaving the dozens of tiny candles to burn in a silence troubled by the low hum and sinister groans rising from the entrails of the club.

"They're waiting outside. They won't let us get away," March said, pulling out a gun from his jacket.

I gripped his arm harder. "What the hell is going on? Are we . . . are we trapped in here?"

Alex smirked. "I guess Sahar didn't like March's little tale."

"What do you mean?"

I was stopped by March's hand on my shoulder. "They're here."

"They" announced themselves with thin rays of red light piercing the darkness at the end of the hallway. One, then two, then too many for me to count. Ten, at least, maybe more. Soon, the candlelight gilded leather boots, combat gear, and the harsh lines of rifles and guns.

Alex raised his Glock in their direction. "Mr. November? Any immediate suggestions?"

It was when March did the exact opposite and lowered his own weapon that I understood just how profoundly screwed we were.

"No. Not for now."

THIRTY

The Price

"Gianni had paid the price to rise to the top of the Risoli family. His heart was a calzone the Mafia's oven had burned to ashes."

—Kerry-Lee Storm, *Gods of Darkness #4: Gianni*

It's probably gonna sound weird, but when we came out of the villa, escorted by a small army of terrifying guys who seemed straight out of *Call of Duty: Black Ops*, I thought about yoga pants. About how I should have put some on before leaving the hotel, since goose bumps were forming on my legs.

The two guards who had allowed us in earlier were nowhere in sight, replaced by a second group of five armed men—less equipped than their little friends surrounding us, so good news, right? March and Alex had handed their guns to our captors; the three of us stood perfectly still for what seemed like ages—waiting for Sahar, I assumed. I felt March's hand brush mine, like a silent reassurance that we'd be okay somehow. I had no idea how he could remain so calm, so focused when all *I* wanted was to piss myself.

At some point I rubbed my palms together because I was getting cold and my entire body was shaking, but one of the black-ops guys pointed his rifle at my head and barked, "Freeze!" Which was precisely what I was doing, in fact. That earned him a cold-killer glare from March, who removed his jacket to place it on my shoulders, without so much as a glance at the long, silenced barrel our host was pointing at us. Once I felt the garment's weight, I wrapped it tight around my body, folding my arms to hold on to its precious warmth.

Behind us, the villa's front door creaked open. We all turned to look at the newcomers. Sahar stood in the doorway, flanked by that assistant with the slicked-back hair, and one of the bodyguards I had seen in the club.

She snuggled into a white coat concealing her silvery dress and took a few steps toward us, smugness oozing from her every pore. "I'm sorry for all this. You guys jostled my schedule a bit."

March still appeared cool and controlled, but I knew those little signs—the twitch in his jaw muscles, the intensity in his gaze. Rage. "Does Guita know?"

"Know what?"

"That Van Kreft is dead and she's going to buy Ruby from *you*."

I startled upon hearing him say it out loud. That being said, I had already been suspecting Van Kreft was either gone or dead, so learning that Sahar was in fact a manipulative bitch on top of that almost sounded like old news. "So Van Kreft did die? When?" I asked.

"I'd say six months ago or so," Alex said, a cold smile on his lips.

Around the same time Phyllis said he had vanished from the radar. Figured. My eyes darted between the three of them while Alex went on. "Murrell had his doubts about Van Kreft's profile; he told us that. He called me back later today—"

"To tell you that no one had seen Van Kreft in public for months, and that he was no longer using his credit cards or seeing his doctor?"

I completed, almost certain Murrell and Phyllis had come to similar conclusions.

"Yes," Alex admitted, his voice tinted with mild surprise.

March locked eyes with Sahar. "You put Wille in charge of running Van Kreft's business, and your men secured all access to the manor. You made him a scapegoat for the Ruby operation and hired Austrian mercenaries so all evidence would point to him."

She tucked a long strand of black-and-turquoise hair behind her ear and applauded mockingly. "My God, when did you become so smart? Is it all those crosswords? I was so sure you'd end up breaking into the manor and destroying everything in your wake to find that insignificant piece of shit."

Alex shook his head. "Get over yourself. Do you want to know what tipped us off so easily? It's that at *no point* during this entire operation did you act like Van Kreft would have. You're an average mind with considerable means. You're not your sister, Sahar."

Each of his word rang in my ears, like water drops troubling the surface of a black lake. Just how much did Alex know about Guita and the Board to have seen through Sahar so easily? I thought of March's strange arrangement with Erwin, of the way the CIA seemed well aware of the Cullinan affair and my subsequent kidnapping, but they were okay with that, and they didn't mind that the Board got to keep the diamond. The word *ecosystem* came to mind: a vast gray area where players could neither publicly acknowledge nor genuinely fight each other. An ecosystem into which Sahar, with her brutal ways and selfish ambitions had fired like a loose cannon.

At any rate, Alex's severe assessment of her criminal skills struck a chord. She looked up to the night sky for a second, and the way her lips were trembling, I thought she was going to cry.

"Shoot that fucker in the face."

One of the henchmen raised his rifle, and I jumped in front of Alex. "No!"

"Island!" March had moved as well, quick as an arrow. He was now in front of us, while Alex's hands were on my shoulders, hauling me back.

Sahar walked up to March until she stood mere inches from him. "I'm tired of waiting in the shadows. I'm fucking tired of waiting for someone to *notice* what I'm capable of." Her voice broke as she brought a hand to caress his cheek. "And you don't understand. I know you don't."

March pushed her hand away. "I lied to you. There's no virus in Ruby. Let them go. They're Erwin's assets. If you kill them, you'll find yourself biting off more than you can chew, Sahar."

She bit her lower lip, and her shoulders shook in quiet laughter. "You're so sweet. I don't need you to tell me what Roth did or didn't do to Ruby. I *know* he tried to screw me and that you guys found something in his apartment."

Maybe she wasn't so stupid after all . . .

March flashed her the hint of a poker smile as he shielded me and Alex. "You're giving us too much credit. Not even the NSA could find anything on Roth's computers."

Sahar looked away, shaking her head in mock disappointment, before she jerked her head as a signal to one of her guards. Two of them punched and shoved Alex away. He knelt down in the gravel, clutching his stomach with a muffled grunt. March spun around, but by the time he turned to face us another guy had drawn out his gun, and it was now pressing . . . against my temple.

Trust me, if this had been a game of red light, green light, I would have won. I was so damn petrified I could hardly breathe. My heart was thumping in my rib cage, and the ground under my feet felt like cotton, like it would give way any second and swallow me into a bottomless pit. The cold contact of the barrel, the slight pain as the guy pushed as if to drill into my skull. That was all I could think about. A few feet away, March stood equally still, his hands raised in a pacifying gesture. Dark blue eyes stared directly into my captor's.

Sahar treaded past him and to me. She grabbed my chin. "My sister says that whoever pulls your strings gets to pull March's." Her fingers dug harder into my cheeks. "We'll see about that. Get her into my car; she'll ride with me."

She turned to March one last time. "That way I know you'll behave."

———

It's so difficult to find a suitable conversation topic when you're sitting in the back of a limo across from a beginner female supervillain who's got you handcuffed, sandwiched between two armed men, and who's taking you to a secluded manor on a mountain to do God knows what. I was tempted to talk to Sahar about Guita, the Queen, and how it seemed that organized crime was yet another sector where women defied the odds and excelled. She seemed, however, to be lost in her own thoughts, curled in that big wool coat on her leather seat, staring through the window.

I decided to shut up for now.

Behind my back, the handcuffs were starting to chafe my skin. I squirmed, struggling to balance myself every time the car took a sharp turn. My eyes darted to the men sharing my seat. I examined the large "88" tattooed on the older one's skull—there was probably something to be said about his political views, but I didn't dare bring it up, because he had a Desert Eagle and I didn't. I gulped, a bead of cold sweat rolling down my neck and raising goose bumps in its path.

The one on my left seemed about my age, maybe even younger. I studied him as we drove through the deserted streets of Vaduz. Brown hair, handsome Hispanic features, very soft brown eyes—not exactly your typical brute. I tried to focus on him to keep my fear at bay; he didn't seem as scary as his neo-Nazi colleague. I wondered if he would become like March some day—if his face would age gracefully, but his eyes would turn cold, concealing some secret wound.

Thinking of March, I felt my chest tighten. I wanted to turn in my seat to look through the rear windshield and see the other car, just to know that it was there—that *he* was there. I didn't dare, though. For one, I had no idea how my captors would react if I moved, but I also figured that seeing me crumble into an emotional mess would give Sahar even more ammo against March. I tried to relax and breathe at least part of my fear out.

We left town at some point and started driving up a narrow mountain road, which confirmed my earlier impression that if things went wrong, I'd be done for good. Miles were rapidly piling up, and I'd never make it back to Vaduz on my own, should I manage to run the hell away.

In front of us, Sahar shifted to look at me. Her silent appraisal had me fidgeting on my seat. After a couple of minutes I couldn't take it anymore. Consequences be damned, I opened my mouth to speak. "Aren't you scared of what will happen if Guita finds out what you've done?"

She straightened in her seat, and for an instant I thought I glimpsed something genuine, almost childish in her big coal eyes. "No. I know she'll be pissed at first, but once she realizes what I'm giving her, it won't matter anymore. She's like that, all about business."

"But why *sell* Ruby to her, then? Why take the Board's money? Isn't Ellingham's money enough for you?"

A bitter smile twisted her mouth. "You don't understand. I need my own wings to fly. I don't want to serve her well; I want to make my own way and rise above her."

I looked down at my lap. "How much will that dream cost?"

She smirked. "Nine zeros."

My head lolled back; I stared at the roof light. Judging from her answer, it was obvious Sahar hadn't understood my question.

THIRTY-ONE
The Tub

"Emerging from the water, covered in a light, fragrant foam,
Bradley's lighthouse stood proud, tall in the storm of his desire."

—Gem Windcrest, *The Cowboy of Clam Beach*

After nearly half an hour of driving, we reached a large metal gate barring access to a small trail. Fifty yards down the trail stood a seventeenth-century stone-and-brick manor consisting of a long main building and two towers. The left one was flanked by a second wing, built in the late eighteenth century, judging by its neo-classic architecture and the presence of what appeared to be a vast greenhouse. Thirty yards away or so, a much smaller building lay half-hidden by pine trees. Stables, I supposed.

Small in-ground lights drew a path to the entrance door, framed by two large lanterns. Wille had been right—this was, indeed, a typical *gentilhommière*, as the French would say, except I was pretty sure there were no gentlemen in there. Several unfunny-looking men guarded the entrance, and I heard some barking in the distance, which suggested that someone patrolled the compound with dogs—no doubt equally unfunny dogs, like rottweilers, as opposed to dachshunds.

Whether Guita's theory regarding March's strings was right or not, Sahar's prediction proved true. When we stepped out of the car and the doors to the black SUV following us opened as well, March and Alex appeared, handcuffed as I was, and compliant. No one had been killed, no car had been blown up, and I suspected none would be, as long as that neo-Nazi with the 88 tattoo held me at gunpoint.

She gestured to me. "Get her downstairs and take these two into the dining room."

March shrugged his captor's hand off and took a step forward. "Sahar—"

"She'll speak to us alone. Now, you can either cooperate and get her back in one piece, or keep fucking with me, and I swear, March, that I'll cut off bits she doesn't need to talk."

What kind of bits were we talking about? My teeth chattered, and I clenched my jaw as hard as I could to stop it.

March didn't say a word, but the look in his and Alex's eyes sort of reassured me—a silent promise that if anyone chopped any bit off me, not even Guita could save Sahar's ass. She shrugged the unspoken threat off, a cue for my new Nazi friend and the younger guy to drag me toward the entrance door, followed by several guards, while a second group escorted March and Alex.

Behind me, I heard Alex's voice. "It's gonna be okay, Island. Tell her everything she wants to know."

I tried to look back at him and March, but my captors wouldn't let me. Once inside, we were greeted by the sight of a magnificent lobby decorated with antique statues and Renaissance-style tapestries—Van Kreft had obviously been an art enthusiast. I watched in dismay as March and Alex were led toward a set of French doors on our left. Casting one last look at them, I tried to smile. *Don't worry*, I mouthed.

To be honest, I wasn't so sure things were gonna be okay, but no point in sobbing like a chicken when they were powerless to help me at the moment. I heard the clatter of heels on the stone floor; Sahar had removed her coat and joined us. Across the hall, a guard whispered something in one of his colleagues' ear. The other goon nodded in response and pointed to a small wooden door, almost hidden under a double flight of stairs.

It looked a lot like I was being taken to the basement, and well, I had qualms about this. Legitimately so. After the old door had slammed shut behind us, the bright chandeliers and limestone walls of the lobby were replaced by dark stone and a persistent scent of mold. Leading our procession, Sahar didn't seem disturbed in the least by this haunted-house vibe. I staggered down a dingy corridor lined with ancient wooden doors, sandwiched between Baldie and his partner, until we reached a large room that could have been an ancient wine cellar.

A single bulb hung from the low, vaulted ceiling, and the room was nearly empty, save for a couple of empty wood barrels, a few old barreling tools lying around in the dirt, and—oddly—a tub. I could see something shimmering inside it—water, if the long hose lying on the ground was any indication. At any rate, it looked like they weren't finished with the plumbing, and the floor needed some work too, but the place had great potential.

I was trying hard to distract myself from the inhospitable atmosphere, when the younger guy reached behind me to undo the handcuffs. For a moment there, I actually thought things were looking up. Wait. *No.* The young one had pulled out a hunting knife at the same time that Baldie tore March's jacket away from my body. As soon as it hit the ground, he grabbed my arms, and locked them in place. I screamed and jerked against his grip, sweat matting my hair to my forehead. I squeezed my eyes shut when the long blade made contact with my sweater dress. He ripped the front with a single gesture, tearing a few inches from the top of the silk dress I wore underneath as well. I tried to curl my body with a yelp of shame and horror, now that I stood in that cold cellar with my bra visible. I saw the corners of the younger guy's lips curl into a salacious smile. Anywhere, anytime, show a man a glimpse of lace underwear and he'll be happy.

The part of my brain that was busy leafing through all possible scenarios warned me that we might be looking at rape in the immediate future. Yet they had done no effort to undress me any further . . . Sahar seemed pleased with the way things were going so far and watched with a catlike smile as Baldie's palm connected with the side of my face without warning. The gesture had been meant as a slap, but given his strength it felt more like a punch. I fell to the ground, tasting blood in my mouth.

My ears were ringing so loud I barely registered Sahar's voice. "What did you find in Roth's apartment? What did he *do* to Ruby?"

I remember Alex advising me to tell her everything. Part of me wanted to. My cheek hurt, my knees too, that had been bruised upon hitting the ground. But the pain seemed to simmer out of control inside me, boiling, overflowing in a surge of rage. If I told her about the code Thom had hidden in Ricardo, she'd kill us anyway, and he would have died in vain, like Van Kreft.

"There were only pictures that you sent him to threaten his family," I rasped. "He wanted to let someone know he had been forced into this."

A few inches from my face, one of her silvery heels tapped the floor impatiently. "Keep going."

I thought she had been addressing me, but the order had in fact been directed to Baldie, who dragged me to that tub. I couldn't believe how loud I was screaming, how much strength I still had in my legs as I kicked the ground helplessly. His hand fisted in my hair, and he hauled me with an iron grip. Pain exploded in my skull. I saw the layer of ice cubes, a shadow underneath, and my entire upper body was forced into the water.

I wasn't prepared for anything like this—the temperature shock, the burning sensation in my lungs, feeling myself drowning. That wasn't what ultimately caused me to lose it and inhale a huge gulp of icy water, though. I opened my eyes for a second, not even long enough to be sure

I wasn't dreaming. A ghost lay underneath the ice. Ashen, bruised skin, blond hair. Wille . . . Wille was in the tub.

Baldie pulled me out. Water had made it inside my nose, probably in my lungs as well, since I was choking, coughing a string of drool, and gasping for air. I could feel my heart beating everywhere in my body—in my chest, my head, my ears. I couldn't see very well, and I was shaking too much to even scream anymore. My teeth were chattering uncontrollably; I bit my tongue hard, drawing some more blood.

Sahar walked to the tub and knelt near me. The material of her silvery dress was a shimmering blur before my eyes. "You see, I have my own little nerd up there, and he's working on scouring every single line of code in Ruby. And he, too, says that March was lying, that there is no virus meant to turn Ruby against us."

"Then . . . then . . . why are you . . . doing this?" I stuttered, feeling, with a modicum of relief, Baldie's grip on my hair lessen.

"Because I don't like you, for one. And because I had my men pay a visit to a certain Mr. Degraeves after March destroyed everything there." A smirk revealed her incisors, the same pointy shape as Guita's. "I *know* you found something in Roth's apartment, and I *want it*, whatever it is," she said, grinding out each word through those sharp teeth.

"He didn't . . . It was just pictures." I thought I must have sounded convincing, since the part about the pictures, at least, was true.

Maybe not that much. Or maybe it didn't matter to them. Baldie hauled me up and plunged me back into the tub. Stupidly, I had thought it would be more bearable the second time; if anything, it was worse. More painful, more terrifying. When my lungs started struggling for air, I think I went into shock for good. I opened my eyes again, and this time it was okay. I was able to accept what I was seeing, and Wille's lifeless features brought me a disturbing sense of peace.

I surfaced back to reality when my body hit the ground, dirt sticking to my drenched skin. Every breath was a painful spasm that ended in a shivering hiss. I wanted to tell them to go die, or something badass like that, but I could hardly speak. My throat was sore, and I coughed the words more than I spoke them. "You killed Wille . . ."

"He wasn't really useful anymore, and he couldn't think with anything else than his dick anyway. I was furious when he told me he had mentioned the auction to you, but in the end it turned out for the best, right?"

Tears rolled silently on my temples. "There was nothing . . ."

I heard Sahar snap her fingers, and the younger guy, who had been watching the scene silently so far, came to help his colleague bring me to my feet. I was little more than a marionette at this point, shaking like a leaf, and standing only because they had locked their hands under my armpits to hold me upright.

She cupped the side of my face. "I know March. I know him well. He's a great pro, but not exactly a genius. And maybe you don't want to talk, but he will, because he's just a *fucking lackey*, whereas *I* brought a Fortune 500 company to its knees!"

"No . . ." I murmured, allowing my head to loll down.

At this point, I honestly thought Raptor Jesus had abandoned me, or that maybe, like with Job, he was testing my faith and allowing Satanasaurus Rex to persecute me. Meanwhile, I registered Sahar speaking to those guards in the corridor. "Bring them down here."

She turned to me with a sardonic grin. "I'll show you that with the right move, there's no intel you can't obtain."

A pitiful sneeze shook my frame in response. I closed my eyes. Footsteps were echoing outside of the room, male voices. I could feel some strength return to my legs, but I chose to hang limply in Baldie's grasp, to spare whatever energy I had left. Door hinges groaned and a cool breeze hit me, leaving an icy sensation in its wake wherever it licked my naked skin.

My lids fluttered open. March and Alex stood in front of us, still handcuffed. Behind them, the wooden door had been closed again, and two armed guards stood on each end of the room. I recognized their black combat gear, but they wore less equipment than they had back at the club, probably because they thought their prisoners now posed less of a threat. Had I been the one in charge of overseeing supervillain activities in Sahar's lair, I'd have made my goons keep their weird goggles and rifles. The quiet fury in both men's eyes as they took in my sorry state boded no good.

A snarl revealed March's teeth. "Sahar, I'm extremely worried for you."

She giggled and bent down to pick up an old rusty hammer lying in the dirt. "You're worried? For *me*? March, have you seen *Hostel*?"

Oh God. The last thing you want to hear when someone hell-bent on torturing you is holding a hammer is a reference to a torture-snuff movie where people get their toes broken one by one by a maniac with a hammer. In my sneakers, my toes curled of their own will, as if to escape the prospect of getting squished into a bloody pulp. I stared at March and Alex in growing panic. Their shoulders seemed to be twitching, beads of sweat pearled on their brows in spite of the cold, and there was the same expression of intense concentration on their faces. Not just anger, but rather a frightening determination.

Alex looked me in the eyes, a smile forming on his lips. I understood that he wanted me to focus on *him*, not the rest of this nightmare. "What about you, Island, have you seen it?"

I let out a quivering breath. "Not really—I closed my eyes."

Sahar laughed. "I know, right? It fascinated me, the idea that money could buy something like that." She ducked her head, and in an instant all amusement vanished from her features, leaving only a stony mask. She walked up to March, waving the dusty hammer inches from his face. "You're going to tell me what was in Roth's apartment and if that asshole rigged Ruby. I know you are, because if you don't, it's not *your* legs I'll break."

He didn't react to her threat, just looked straight ahead at me, and his lips pursed. I realized that seconds ago, Alex had made a similar face. As March would later teach me, there are a few things a gentleman should never forget when getting ready for work: a small knife strapped to your ankle; mini antibacterial wipes in your pocket—that one might have been a matter of personal taste; and, of course, a couple of steel pins in your cuffs, in case of an emergency. Even then, getting rid of hinged handcuffs remained a somewhat tedious business, especially under watch. Nothing more annoying than having to interrupt your efforts constantly. Thank God, Sahar's evil little show did a great job capturing her audience's attention . . .

In any case, she hadn't expected March to grab the hammer from her, with a right hand that should have been still properly handcuffed behind his back. He didn't strike her, though; Alex did. Here again, I'm pretty sure she hadn't anticipated receiving a brutal punch in the face at the same time that the hammer flew across the room and rammed between Baldie's eyes. His head was thrown back under the force of the impact, blood splattered on me, on the floor, and I felt his grip around my arms weaken as he tumbled backward into the tub.

The whole thing had occurred in the space of a heartbeat, and the three remaining men in the room looked completely disoriented for a couple of seconds at the sight of their dead colleague's upper body sinking into the reddened water, while Sahar sat on her ass and clutched her jaw with a loud wail. I knew from prior experience that those two seconds were more time than March needed to start a bloodbath. I heard Alex yell for me to get down. I crawled as best I could as someone started firing, and the last thing I saw clearly was March taking a silenced gun from the younger guy, who lay on the ground, his own hunting knife planted in his bloody throat.

I guess Sahar and her goons had missed another critical point. Here in this confined space, and with their colleagues on the other side of a closed door, it wasn't March trapped with them—it was them trapped with March . . . and Alex, who had gotten rid of his remaining handcuff bracelet and helped himself to Baldie's gun as well. By then, it was too late for the two remaining guards. There were more gunshots, one of the guys was hit in the stomach with some kind of sharp barrel-making tool, and it was over.

Loud thumps echoed on the other side of the door, making it tremble and creak. I figured the rest of Sahar's men were trying to come to the rescue. Either March or Alex had turned the iron key in the door's ancient bar lock, momentarily blocking access to the cellar. I saw Sahar crawl on the floor, trying to reach for the key and unlock the door. I scrambled toward her, pulling on one of her ankles to stop her. Her other leg flew to kick me, and I rolled away just in time to avoid getting stabbed in the face with a five-inch heel. Alex saw us and lunged at Sahar, shoving her away from the door while March picked up his bulletproof jacket off the floor and threw it on me.

Blood pumped so fast in my veins that I thought I was seconds away from heart failure. I so wished there'd been time for him to hug me, tell me everything was going to be okay, but someone shot repeatedly into the door's aged wood with an automatic rifle and it burst open, several men barging in with a terrible din. I curled up in my corner, shielding myself under March's jacket, and saw little of the chaos that followed.

There were gunshots, screams, the sounds of bodies being rammed against the walls. I only peeked a few times, but all I caught were scenes I'd rather forget: Alex wrestling with one of Sahar's guards, the muscles in his forearms straining as he drowned the guy in the tub's reddish water with loud, sickening bubbling sounds; then knees, knees that dropped to the ground before the rest of the body followed, and wide-open, teary eyes gazing at me. A guard was dying, a pool of dark blood growing on the ground under his chest, and he was watching me. Or was he already dead? Part of me knew that this was an ill time for sentimentalism, but I couldn't help the chill that spread through my body, carrying a wave of nausea.

When March and Alex finally helped me up, the room spun for a while. I eventually looked around. There were now eight, maybe nine bodies on the ground. So much for March's retirement projects. Cries and barking sounds reached us from a tiny cellar window above us.

I gripped his arm. "Sahar? Where is she?"

"She got away," Alex said, picking up a magazine and a rifle from one of the dead men.

March's hands cupped my face, his thumbs wiping dirt from my cheeks. "Can you walk?"

"Yeah, I'm good." *Not really, no.*

"Take this." Alex handed me a semiautomatic pistol.

March glowered at him but made no attempt to take the gun from me. I didn't want to use it either—and had no idea how to—but I could understand Alex's decision, given the circumstances. I took it, shoving it in one of March's jacket pockets.

"They'll be here soon. We need to go!" he hissed.

We ran through the cellar doorway and into the corridor that led to it. Above our heads, heavy footsteps were already echoing on the floor, along with orders in German. I didn't understand everything, but I gathered that Sahar wanted me alive to tell her about Thom's plans, whereas a deep voice discussed the merits of making *"Jagd-Trophäen"* of March and Alex's heads—that's hunting trophies, for those of you who chose to have sex in high school rather than taking German.

March shot the lock to one of the corridor's doors and kicked it open, sending shards of rotten wood flying all around us; Alex and I followed him into a darkened room. This part of the basement was just as humid and moldy, only much more cluttered. Discarded paintings rested against the stone walls, there were spiderwebs and sheet-covered furniture everywhere, along with an incredible amount of bric-a-brac, ranging from dusty tankard-shaped lamps to Dschinghis Khan vinyl discs dating back to the eighties. A pleasant smell of detergent floated in the air, which I connected with an old washing machine, apparently still used to clean those sheets and some worn gardening clothes.

I think the three of us experienced the same sort of relief when it became clear, judging by the narrow windows, that this part of the basement granted access to the gardens. Behind us, though, beams of white light tore through the darkness. Voices. The sound of guns being armed. The lights vanished; I figured they counted on their night goggles to help them.

Alex pulled me against him to hide behind a huge portrait, while March glided toward our assailants like a shadow. I saw him disappear between two sheets, a ghost among ghosts. The men started spreading out in the room, making little hand gestures to each other. One of them walked right past Alex and me, so close I could see the pockets on his combat gear and smell some sort of smoky cologne. A squeak almost escaped me, but Alex's hand clasped over my mouth before it could come out.

I'm not much of an expert at these things, but by then I more or less understood March's tactics of choice. For example, he'd often rely on surprise—such as smashing a guy's face with a hammer to spark the chaos in which he swam like a shark in water. In here, however, outnumbered and with limited visibility, he'd probably wait and let the guards place themselves where he needed them for an optimal shooting angle.

My heart skipped a beat when I saw one of the guards approaching the long sheet hanging from a canopy bed. He hadn't realized that March stood behind it, right next to the statue. I experienced an odd combined feeling of power and helplessness when I realized this guy would be the first to be shot, no matter what happened. This was like looking into one very dark crystal ball. I knew he was going to die, and he didn't.

Alex's hand had let go of my mouth, but all I could produce were shallow intakes of air anyway. A muted thump resounded in the room, at the same time that the man near the statue fell to the ground, as expected. My chest tightened, but I held on to Alex and struggled not to make a sound when the rest of the guard's teammates started firing relentlessly at the canopy bed. I covered my ears, watching the bed disintegrate into a haze of shredded white fabric and wood splinters. Alex pulled me down and forced me to crouch, to avoid getting hit by a random bullet.

All that shooting was useless anyway. March hadn't been facing the guard he had killed, he had been on his side, and he'd already flitted farther away, somewhere on the group's right flank. Unfortunately for those guys, two of them had to reload, and they stopped firing. Not the kind of luxury you can afford when you're standing less than three feet away from "the South African."

Across the room, I saw the sheet covering a long table billow slightly, as if caressed by a gentle breeze. Several black holes appeared one after another in the pristine sheet, at the same time that three men fell to the ground. The fourth and last guard took cover behind a wardrobe and started firing in March's direction, reducing the table to the same shredded mess the canopy bed had been turned into earlier.

The shooting stopped as March's adversary adjusted his goggles to search the room. He hadn't noticed us yet. Against me, I felt Alex shift.

"Hey!"

His gun wasn't silenced, and the single detonation rattled down my spine. The man collapsed before I could fully process that Alex had leaped out from our hiding spot and killed him.

A shadow rushed between a bookshelf and a medieval wooden statue. March appeared. "Thank you, Mr. Morgan," he whispered, as we made our way through destroyed furniture and lifeless bodies.

Near the washing machine I had noticed earlier was a small wooden door. March opened it, revealing a dank passage at the end of which the garden's lights shone bright in the darkness, casting a faint golden hue on the darkened lawn. There was a recess in the stone wall, leading to a small room that was used to store gardening tools and some chemical products. The three of us hid in there, enjoying a brief reprieve until Sahar's goons found us. Some barking echoed in the distance.

"That could be a problem," Alex said.

"Two dogs," March confirmed.

I shrank, shielding myself behind their broad backs in case yet again another overequipped guy popped up, intent on stuffing our heads and hanging them in his living room.

"They took Sahar to safety. Second floor, maybe?" Alex mused.

March nodded. "Possibly."

"She told me that she had her own nerd 'up there,'" I ventured.

Amazing how those two ignored me while playing super tough pro or whatever. Alex spoke to March, without even sparing me a glance. "Worth a try. What about Island? We can't leave her alone."

March turned to Alex and for the first time addressed him as he would have a partner. "Can I entrust her to you while I go entertain these gentlemen?"

"You can."

Spurred by frustration, I felt my energy come back. I kicked Alex's leg to finally gain both men's attention. "No, you won't! You two have lost your minds!"

"Baby—"

"Biscuit—"

"I'm no one's baby or biscuit!" I hissed. "And if you're seriously thinking of taking on the rest of these guys, at least be efficient: do it together. We're right under the left wing; I could go hide in the greenhouse. It looked empty when we came in, and they're all focused on the garden and the upper floors. That way, even if they catch you, Sahar still won't have me."

I had a point. I could tell by the frowns on their faces.

March shook his head. "It's too dangerous—"

"You mean, *more dangerous* than following you guys in your shooting spree? Or *more dangerous* than wrestling with dogs and paramilitary clowns on your own out there?" I said with a heartfelt glare.

Alex's hand squeezed my shoulder. "All right. Once you're outside, we'll distract them. Run to your left. Don't stop; don't look back. Use your gun if you have to, but mostly, just *stay hidden*."

"And for the love of God, do *not* try anything!" March added.

In the jacket pocket, my fingers gripped the handle of the semiautomatic pistol. "Got it."

THIRTY-TWO

Beaks

"This thing is gonna bite us, and we're all gonna die a horrible death!"

—*Uninvited*, 1988

Honestly, I had no idea Alex was so much into gardening, and when he said he'd distract Sahar's men, I hadn't imagined it would involve using a bag of nitrate fertilizer and an old lawn mower's gas tank to construct a homemade bomb.

It did work, though.

There certainly was a lot of distraction when the powerful explosion destroyed most of the lobby's windows and sent half a dozen men flying to the ground, some severely burned. I covered my ears with my hands and raced toward the greenhouse door without looking back. It was unlocked. I tiptoed in and knelt behind some kind of exotic plant in the darkness, watching the wreckage of Alex's bomb burn on the lawn, my breath coming in short pants.

He and March had benefitted from this "distraction" as well. Gunshots had started to resound near the manor's entrance, and whatever they were doing, I just prayed they'd make it out alive. I could hear windows breaking, men screaming, dogs barking—no doubt after Alex's balls for unearthing some of the bones they had hoarded. I sat crouched in soft earth, shivering with every distant detonation, and reconsidering my promise to not leave the safety of the greenhouse. I knew I'd be useless on such a battlefield, though. I curled into a ball and waited.

After a few minutes, I gathered March and Alex had made it inside, since the garden had become quiet, and the gunshots now seemed to be coming from inside the manor. I had been too focused on the rampage outside to notice until now, but a variety of strange sounds echoed in the deserted greenhouse. Some rustling, water splashing—and something halfway between cooing and groaning.

I got up and looked around the dark jungle of plants and flowers surrounding me. The noises seemed to be coming from the other end of the greenhouse. I padded toward their source, stopping every now and then to listen for potential danger, every sense on high alert. As I walked through what I recognized as rosebushes, the splashing sounds became louder. I inched closer, until my knees met something hard. Glass. I laid my hands on the glass balcony circling a huge pool. Maybe the sounds came from some sort of fountain? No. Something was moving in there, alternatively wriggling and slithering. I squinted my eyes, making out one, two, then an entire group of slick, dark shapes, the size of small dogs.

I bent over the balcony to take a better look . . . and nearly fell into the water when all the lights came on. Once I had recovered my balance, I got a better view of the strange creatures frolicking down there. Platypuses. Dozens of them, swimming, playing in a well-landscaped pool, surrounded by nice flat rocks, plants, small trees. I looked up at the ceiling in mild panic. Had someone turned on the lights accidentally? Had I been found?

"Stay where you are, bitch!"

Sahar. I stepped away from the balcony slowly. Indeed, standing in a small clearing, among banana trees and exotic flowers, was her curvy silhouette. Her black and blue hair was a mess, the silvery dress had been torn in several places, and she was pointing a gun at me. I gulped. I could see no guards with her. Maybe March and Alex had wreaked such havoc in the manor that she had lost her personal guard in the process? Or had she been looking for me? Over her head, in a corner of the ceiling, the blinking of a red light I hadn't noticed before tipped me off: there were goddamn security cameras in that greenhouse!

"You're coming with me," she announced, her index finger tightening on the trigger.

I thought of my own gun, still tucked in March's jacket pocket. She'd kill me if I tried to aim it at her, right? Without thinking, I staggered back and reached in the pocket. Either she saw the gun or she guessed its presence, because she marched toward me and the pool.

"I told you to stay the fuck where you are! Pull out the gun—slowly, or I'm blowing your face off!"

I knew that technique—I had witnessed March use it on other guys. She was shouting at me to increase my stress levels and make me do something stupid. It worked. I pulled out the small black pistol and held it out by the barrel in what I hoped was a gesture of appeasement.

"Throw it in the pool!"

"W-What if one of the platypuses gets smacked on the head and—"

"Stop *fucking* with me or you'll be their next meal!"

Fear thrummed in my ears and temples, making my skull hurt. I threw the gun as I had been instructed, hearing it land in the pool with a splash. A few platypuses grunted at the intrusion. No, it was more like . . . *growls*. "D-Did you say they were going to eat me?"

She cocked the gun with a sneer. "They're carnivorous."

"I know . . . they eat worms and shrimp—"

"Look closer," she ordered.

I glanced at the pool, never daring to lose sight of the gun Sahar was still pointing at me.

Shit. Bones. Or more exactly ribs, and possibly a femur. There were goddamn *human bones* lying on the rocks. And a shoe. I clenched my fists as hard as I could in an effort not to tremble.

She let out a cruel laugh. "It took them a week to completely finish Van Kreft."

"But th-they're not supposed to have teeth! It's just the spurs, right?"

She shrugged. "Van Kreft said it was an incredibly rare subspecies. They were his passion, and Wille was kind of obsessed with them too."

I racked my brain for memories of my dinner with Wille. I think he had talked about ornithology and Australian endemic species, but I had been zoning out at the time. I should have listened. I so should have. Because I was now facing the horrifying truth: there *was* such a thing as killer platypuses. I knew about the poisonous spur on their leg already, how a single sting could cause unbearable pain that would last for months, even years. But teeth. These monsters had killed their own master and eaten him! And eaten his shoe too.

"You said that it took a week for them to finish Van Kreft. Was he . . . alive?"

Sahar sighed dispassionately. "No. The venom killed him after a few hours. But their teeth are really small, so it takes a while for them to eat their prey. I'm planning on having them trashed. I prefer sharks."

Sh-sharks? . . . By then I was completely petrified, and my breathing had all but stopped. My knees were shaking, and I dared neither run away nor follow her as she had requested. All I could see was a choice between getting shot or getting eaten alive by a pack of bloodthirsty platypuses.

"Now come here—we don't have all night," Sahar ordered.

There was nothing rational about my decision. But then again, was there anything rational about this whole situation? My legs stopped shaking for a second, which was all I needed to flee in terror. Of course she shot at me, as I ran along the pool's balcony and toward the greenhouse's garden door. With each detonation resounding behind me, I envisioned myself collapsing to the ground in a pool of my own blood.

She was taller than me, with a more powerful build, and even as she swore and almost stumbled because of her heels, I could feel her closing on me. I registered a whiff of overly sweet perfume and acrid sweat, and her body rammed into mine, flattening me to the ground.

Her nails dug into my sides, my arms, and I just fought back for my life, driven by pure adrenaline. I kicked and scraped and bit and screamed, wiggling under her weight, batting her hands every time she tried to pin me. She lost the gun at some point; I saw it fly and land somewhere on our right, near the pool. I rolled away and crawled to reach it, my arms straining desperately toward its barrel. Sahar was quicker, dashing to pick it up and aim it at my head.

She leaned against the balcony with a smirk, her breath coming in short pants. "I can't wait until you've talked . . . so I can finally get rid of you."

This statement triggered my most primal instincts. I was cornered; she'd torture me and kill me anyway. Nothing mattered but survival. Under my right palm, I felt for one of the many decorative stones peppering the greenhouse's ground. When my fingers met a particularly large one, I grabbed it. With the war cry of a prehistoric beast, I jumped to my feet and threw it at Sahar, at the same time that she fired.

The bullet missed me, landing in a banana tree a few feet behind. My stone, however, hit her square on the forehead, and to my horror she staggered backward. I saw her eyes widen as she lost her balance, her hand reaching out for me in a silent call for help. My brain told me to grab on to her fingers, in spite of everything, but my feet remained glued to the ground under the effect of stress. She fell over the balcony and into the pool.

There was this huge splashing sound, her yelp of surprise, then, right afterward, the ghastly swarming of an entire pack of hungry platypuses charging her. I managed to overcome my fear and ran toward the balcony. There are no accurate words to describe what I witnessed: Sahar's face looking up at me, like reddish putty distorted by a grimace of agony, her screams of anguish, all the blood tainting the once clear water as the creatures plunged their—admittedly small—teeth into her flesh. I feared it might already be too late, but I decided to help. I couldn't watch this abomination without doing anything. I removed March's jacket, and, under it, what was left of the dress one of her men had cut in half: a damp rag. With great caution, I approached the balcony and threw the garment in her direction, holding on to the end of one sleeve and hoping she'd manage to catch the other so I could pull her up. She couldn't even seem to reach her end of this improvised rope. I watch her struggle toward it, one of her arms rising weakly out of the water.

Now, I'd like to stop right here and seize the opportunity to praise the remarkable training provided by both the Lions and the CIA to their professionals. When March and Alex burst into the greenhouse via a second door, guns in hand, they demonstrated a level of focus and self-control that was simply superhuman. They saw me half-naked trying to pull Sahar out of a pool of berserk platypuses trying to devour her, and they barely blinked before running to our aid with cold-blooded efficiency. March jumped on the rocks and pulled Sahar out of the pool, while Alex shot twice into the water to disperse the platypuses—for some reason he didn't seem to want to harm them.

March cradled Sahar's trembling, bruised body in his arms and hauled her back to safety, assisted by Alex. They laid her on the ground. She had bites everywhere, but also large patches of crimson, swollen flesh on her arms and legs where the platypuses had stung her. She had stopped screaming—probably no longer could—and emitted a series of whimpers, lolling her head softly.

March placed a hand on her forehead. "She needs medical attention. When will they be here?"

"Less than an hour or so," Alex said, before turning to me. "What about you? Are you all right?"

"Yes . . . just cold. Who are you talking about?"

March examined my body anxiously—perhaps looking for platypus bites—as he spoke. "Mr. Morgan was able to contact his colleagues stationed in Geneva. They're coming to clean up."

"And we found something you'll like in Sahar's bedroom," Alex added with a wink.

March's lips quirked. "Indeed. Let's take her to the second floor with us. We're going to need your help, biscuit."

THIRTY-THREE
The Bonsai

"My doom has come upon me; let me not then die ingloriously and without a struggle, but let me first do some great thing that shall be told among men hereafter."

—Homer, *The Iliad*

Once March had picked up Sahar, I followed him and Alex through the greenhouse, then the left wing of the house. There, an apocalyptic mess awaited, made of half-destroyed baroque furniture, tangled curtains, and dead bodies. At the end of the building, a stone staircase led to the manor's second floor. There, too, among Renaissance tapestries, damask sofas, and classic paintings, shit had gotten very real, and I didn't dare to ask why a pair of legs dangled from under the lid of that black grand piano. March's nostrils flared at the sight of a shattered vase, and I gathered he'd need to sort a thousand Skittles to recover from this adventure.

We reached a vast bedroom with a view on the park. The two men who had been guarding its doors were dead, but here, at least, the furniture was untouched, suggesting that no brutality had occurred. March laid Sahar's prone body on the bed, wrapping her in the comforter with careful gestures. She seemed to have finally passed out.

After Sahar had been taken care of, two details struck me: several laptops sat on a Napoleon III desk, along with a surprising number of chocolate milk cartons. A nerd had been here. The second point was that low, insistent moan coming from an antique Chinese wardrobe. Alex walked toward the source of the noise with a contented smile and opened the heavy wooden doors to reveal a quite young, chubby blond guy, who sat gagged, tied, and handcuffed. Tears streaked down his cheeks, and his expression was that of a man who had stared death in the face. Alex pulled him out, along with a camel cashmere coat, which he handed to me. He helped the hostage to his feet while I shrugged the coat on, shaking away the strange guilt I experienced upon wearing something that was obviously Sahar's.

Much like me back in the cellar, the guy's legs were shaking so badly he was having a hard time standing up. A blue *Avatar* shirt suggested that he was the troglodyte creature who had consumed all that chocolate milk. Also, one of his hands looked a little red . . . and weird.

March noticed the direction of my gaze. "It's nothing, just the left hand. He still has his right one to type."

The guy whimpered.

My hands flew to my mouth. "You *broke* his hand?"

"Just twisted a couple of fingers."

"March, it looks like a bonsai!"

"Now you're being dramatic! Mr. Morgan, hold him for me, please. We'll put these back in place."

The victim welcomed March's treatment plan with a muted scream while Alex locked an arm around his shoulders with a good-natured smile.

"Hmm! Hmmggnnmm!"

My body jolted as the swollen articulations snapped back in place.

Something halfway between a groan and a gurgling sound erupted from the guy's throat.

March patted his back. "See? He's just fine."

My heart went out to this fellow IT enthusiast. "Can we at least remove his gag?"

Alex complied, untying the piece of fabric that had been used to silence the guy.

"Please! Don't kill me!" he squeaked in a broken sob.

"Not if you help us, young man," March said coolly.

"He's the one who supervised the final transfers for Sahar. He can wire the money back," Alex explained. "We were going to make him, but we heard Sahar's screams, saw the lights on, and came to help you."

March narrowed his eyes at the crying boy. "We have, however, returned to finish what we started."

His victim cowered in fear. "I'll do anything you want! But please don't torture me again!"

"Then put that right hand to good use," March instructed the guy, removing his handcuffs and the rest of his bonds before helping him sit on the chair.

Alex turned to me and pointed at the screens with his chin. "Can you check that he's not playing us?"

"Yes."

I think March's abuse had made a lasting impression on the guy. He diligently went through a list of accounts located in every single tax haven you could think of—and some you wouldn't think of—and got down to business. Soon the transfers were starting, and we all watched as $698,473,510.82 changed hands in less than a minute.

Once the young hacker was done, I placed a hand on his shoulder. "There's one last thing I need to do. Can I use your laptop?"

Truth be told, there was no need to ask politely, because, had our victim refused, *March* would have asked. And we no longer needed that right hand. But I thought even the criminal underworld needs a little humanity. The guy nodded and left me his chair. I sat down and reveled in the simple luxury of a soft cushion under my butt and an untouched can of Cacolac waiting in a USB fridge. Heaven.

My eyes started scanning the endless stack of code lines in front of me. Sahar had told the truth—this guy had been performing various tests on his copy of Ruby in order to verify March's claim. I browsed through the files and opened the coreLaunch class. Time to test Thom's last trick.

"What are you doing?" Alex asked, moving closer to check the screen, while behind us, I could hear March's low voice admonishing the young hacker about the risks of working for a criminal organization.

"I'm connecting to Ricardo to retrieve Thom's code, and I'm updating this version of Ruby with it. We'll see what it does."

"Is it working yet?" March asked, simultaneously babysitting the young hacker and Sahar's prone body.

"Wait a second, I'm committing. You're worse than some of our clients."

As soon as the code had been updated, I relaunched Ruby. The laptops' screens turned black, before an animated ruby appeared, glowing and spinning to signal the application's imminent launch.

Alex's fingers curled around the back of my chair. March held his breath.

Frankly, after everything we had been through, when the first notes rose in the air I thought Alex and March wouldn't take the joke well. But next to me, I heard Alex's nervous chuckle, which turned into a genuine laugh as the laptop's speaker blared Rick Astley's "Never Gonna Give You Up," while files started disappearing from the young hacker's servers at a surprising speed.

March tilted his head, blue eyes full of boyish wonderment. "It's a very nice song, but what is that machine doing?"

"It's . . . It's destroying our entire install of Ruby," chubby boy sniffed.

"No," I corrected. "I think it's also getting me fired."

Alex cocked an eyebrow; March frowned.

"It's . . . um . . . It's also destroying what was left of Ruby on EMT's servers," I clarified.

March abandoned his wards to look at the screen. "It's destroying it all?"

I shrugged in confirmation. "I thought Thom would have created this code to help us retrieve the money or something like that. But now that I think about it, that just wasn't the way he functioned. He figured that what was happening to him would happen again to someone else, because you simply shouldn't create a weapon like Ruby, even if it's just for testing purposes and you think you've secured it perfectly. He meant to kill his chef d'œuvre; he just wasn't given enough time to do so."

March seemed thoughtful. "He was a wise man. And it takes courage to wipe out everything you've built without looking back."

His words lingered in my mind. Did March feel the same? That he had, as Rudyard Kipling would say, watched the things he had given his life to being broken, and that he was now building a new life back up?

I bobbed my head to the rhythm of the music. Ellingham would fire me for this, no doubt. And if word got out—although I couldn't imagine *who* might gossip about me destroying the entire Ruby program with Thom's help—my career in IT at large was over, nipped in the bud. Would I have to find a new purpose in life as well?

The three of us stared at the screens for a while, allowing Rick's mantra to slowly brainwash us, until all loading bars had reached 100 percent. The screens went black. I scrunched my nose at the smell of burned plastic, which I connected with the sparks and white smoke coming from the laptops.

March pulled me back.

Hacker boy wailed. "Oh shit! It's killing all my stuff."

"Don't be sad. It's a glorious death," I told him, even though I knew he couldn't understand.

Outside, the sky had turned a dark blue against which the gray clouds looked almost black. Dawn was coming. I heard the hum of a helicopter in the distance. Alex's colleagues were finally here.

He moved to one of the windows to watch the aircraft approach. "*Shit!* It's not ours!"

His gun was armed and ready in his right hand before he had even finished speaking the words, and my heart rate was speeding up again, the flutter in my temples increasing to a painful pounding.

Near hacker boy, March stood perfectly calm. "Calm down, Mr. Morgan. Everything will be all right."

My gaze caught his. I saw the fleeting shadow in his eyes, the hint of a sad smile. I understood.

Alex didn't. He pointed his gun at March, causing hacker boy to fall to his knees and resume his whimpering.

"What the fuck did you do? *Who* did you call?"

I shook my head in a silent plea. "Alex, it's for Sahar."

Anger darkened his eyes. "You *knew*?"

I shook my head, fighting the stinging in my eyes. How could Alex understand? How could he fathom the reasons March had decided to free Sahar? Ten years. Thirty-six thousand and five hundred and thirty days. Almost a third of his life. That's how long March had killed for the Board. Killed for the Queen. It had earned him his deepest scars, but also made him who he was. Even now that he had decided to tread a new path, this bond, he could never put behind him. I wondered how I had missed this—in a twisted, unconventional way, March and Guita were friends.

And so he had called the Board, to spare Guita the humiliation and the inextricable mess of seeing her sister fall into the CIA's hands.

My lips parted to say something, to find the words to explain the situation to Alex, but March spoke first. "Call Mr. Erwin if you want— he would have done the same." He said, looking at Alex wearily. "You and I know that the Board's business with the Agency won't allow otherwise. Sahar is a diplomatic asset."

Alex lowered his gun, while through the window I watched the black helicopter blow leaves and dirt away as it landed softly on the lawn.

"What if I refuse?"

March's eyes closed for an instant; Alex's resistance was testing his patience. "Then it will merely be our collective loss. Yours. Erwin's. Mine. Your colleagues', a handful of whom will have to pay a hefty price for such an affront to Sahar's sister."

At last, Alex's posture relaxed, and his lips quirked. "You really think I'm an idiot, don't you?"

One of March's eyelids twitched.

Alex tucked the gun back in his waistline. "You could have just shown a minimum of courtesy and warned me of your decision, Mr. November."

My eyes traveled back and forth between the two of them. A game. Alex had feigned outrage to test March. To prove what? Probably that March's loyalty still went to the Board and the CIA would always come second.

March walked to the bed to pick up Sahar, and we all left the bedroom, Alex escorting the young hacker with a firm hand on his shoulder. On our way out of the manor, I couldn't help stealing a glance at Alex, searching his tranquil expression for answers. I felt so stupid for having bought into his little indignation act. It was all he had been doing since the very first day, I realized. Testing, stirring, prodding, studying. Me, March, the inextricable knot tying us together with the Board, the Lions, Erwin. Because gathering intel was his job? Of course. But I was now certain it went deeper than that. Alex wanted something from us. I thought of my conversation with him back in the plane.

"Do you know who they were, the people who killed your parents?"

"No, but I'm close."

I still didn't believe March to be the one. There had been countless opportunities for Alex to try to get rid of him since their first encounter, but he hadn't acted on any of those. One could even say Alex had teamed up with his nemesis with surprisingly good grace, given the tension between the three of us, going so far as to play along and cover for March after the tram incident, when he could have leaked Struthio's name to the press and forced March back into the shadows.

No, much like me, March was just a means to an end for Agent Morgan, nothing more. Alex apparently knew the Board well, and I gathered he understood the depth and complexity of March's ties to Guita, more than I had given him credit for. Was this why he had first gotten angry upon realizing March had arranged for Sahar to be extracted? Maybe Alex had been hoping that the "diplomatic asset" would remain his to use as he pleased. Against Guita?

When we reached the gardens, the helicopter had stopped, the rotor blades slowing down to a lazy spin while several men dressed in dark coveralls jumped out. For now, it seemed the Board had won.

As usual.

THIRTY-FOUR

The Start

"Standing alone in the ashes of his compound, Ramirez picked up the torn lace panties from the blackened ground and pressed them to his nose, inhaling deeply. 'It's not over, Rica! You can run, but you can never hide from your destiny . . . Our destiny!'"

—Kerry-Lee Storm, *The Cost of Rica II: Ramirez Strikes Back*

I snuggled in the cashmere coat while two paramedics carried Sahar on a stretcher toward the Board's black helicopter, escorted by heavily armed men. They left as they had come, without a word, and once the long blades had all but disappeared into the mountains, swallowed by dawn's mist, I let out a breath I didn't know I had been holding.

The CIA cleaners from Geneva showed up twenty minutes later, in a white-and-gray aircraft, indeed. I'm not sure what became of hacker boy. I never heard of any sort of public trial after the Ruby affair. Alex seemed confident that the cleaning team would take him to "safety," where they'd take the time to assess what kind of services they could squeeze out of him in exchange for some relative freedom and a chance at a longer life.

I have to admit that I did entertain some level of morbid curiosity, because I had never seen an actual cleaning team in action before. When I saw guys in dark coveralls bring out bottles of chemicals and body bags, however, I decided I could live without this particular bit of knowledge. I allowed March to take me away in one of the cars Sahar's goons had brought us in. I think it was better this way.

March had unlocked the doors to a black SUV, and I was about to get into it when I saw him stiffen and glare past my shoulder. I turned to find Alex standing a few feet away from us. Seeing him like this, in his wrinkled shirt and tux pants, covered with cuts and bruises, exhausted but alive, and radiating that peaceful warmth I now knew to be only a small part of the puzzle of his true self, a pang of nostalgia tugged at my heart. Ours was a story that couldn't have worked in the long run, shouldn't have been written in the first place, but I had felt something for the gentle guy who had talked to me on Yaycupid and taken me to the Museum of Natural History. I wished Alex would find him again, someday, and let him take the wheel.

Behind me, March was already walking around the car and closer to me; I signaled to him that things were okay with a jerk of my hand.

When Alex spoke, there was a rueful tenderness in his eyes. "You're leaving."

"Yes. I think it's time."

He took a few steps forward under March's tense gaze, until he was standing inches from me. His hand rose to touch my hair. I fought the reflex to flinch. This was good-bye; no need to make things any worse between us. I steeled myself when he lowered his head to whisper in my ear. If Alex wanted to apologize, I wouldn't ruin those last moments.

"I told you I'll be the one to decide when we're done," he began. Ice crackled down my spine as he went on. "So you tell Dries this for me: We're *not* done. We're only getting started."

I stood stunned, willing my heart to slow down. Behind me, I heard rapid footsteps crushing the gravel as March moved toward us. The cleaning team had interrupted their work and several men were now staring at us, ready to intervene.

Alex's lips tugged to the side in a strange grimace that I couldn't reconcile with a smile; an adolescent laugh burst out of him. "We're good," he said out loud for his colleagues to hear as he walked away, his hands up in mock surrender.

———

Once the adrenaline rush had receded, I realized that there were very few parts of my body that didn't hurt. I was covered in scrapes and bruises, my scalp still throbbed where Sahar's henchman had pulled my hair, and I prayed that the slight headache wouldn't turn into a migraine . . .

Even so, I was grateful for the way March held me for a while afterward. He didn't say anything, didn't ask; he just got me into the car, welcomed me in his arms, and enveloped me in a warm, protective bubble. He was just as battered as Alex, smelled of smoke, gunpowder, and sweat, but I didn't care; the way he rocked us tenderly and kept kissing the top of my hair was worth a thousand showers.

After a few minutes, I felt the rise of his chest as he sighed. I knew he wouldn't force me to talk if I didn't want to, but his words back at the Sonnenhof echoed in my ears. *Rule number one: from now on, you'll be honest with me.* I would. I snuggled even closer, as if I could merge my body into his and forget all this. "It was about Dries. I think Alex is after him . . . because of what happened to his parents."

"I thought so."

My head shot up, and I escaped his hold. "You knew?"

"Not exactly. After I discovered he worked for Erwin I made some calls, because I was—"

"Jealous."

"I was *concerned*. I wanted to understand who I was dealing with. I found out about the attack in Egypt, the plane crash. I knew for a fact that the Lions had been hired for that particular job, so I started to suspect something like this."

"Is it true? Did Dries murder Alex's parents?"

March shook his head sadly as he started the engine. "I don't know. But even if he didn't carry out the operation himself, he's the vice commander—he's responsible all the same."

I thought of my mother's assassination. Dries's confession, back in Tokyo, that one of his men had shot her against his orders had come as a bittersweet relief, making the disfigured family portrait I had been painted into a bit brighter. My biological father hadn't killed my mother, after all.

I knew her death had affected Dries more than he let on, but only now that I listened to March did I understand the extent of my father's grief. He had been forced to take responsibility for that man's actions. Because that's what bosses do. He may have executed the guy, but that didn't absolve him. I was struck by the realization that Dries hadn't returned my mother's letter to me because he no longer had any use for it—as he claimed—but because ten years later, he still couldn't shake off his guilt. I wondered whether he felt the same about Alex's parents. How many ghosts did men like Dries and March sleep with?

I curled in my seat, watching pine trees fly past us down the mountain road. "Do you think Alex can find Dries?"

"Possibly. What Mr. Morgan did—" March's fingers drummed on the wheel. "What he did to you speaks of his determination."

A cold sweat made the silk dress stick to my back. My biological father was no choirboy, but I certainly didn't want anyone killing him. "Will you warn Dries?" I asked.

"No." He sighed. "I refuse to stand in the middle of these two. There's no good side."

March cast me an anxious look as he drove. I squeezed his forearm as a silent reassurance that I understood what he meant. I remembered my last conversation with Dries in Tokyo. Back then, he had suspected

March of having slept with me, and expressed clear disapproval. Like I said earlier, even supervillains are actually regular parents under the three-piece suits and the big guns. I didn't want to imagine what Dries might do if he heard that Alex had tried to seduce me to get to him. I thought of Poppy; Alex was all she had left. Bringing Dries's attention to Alex would endanger her as well.

"Thank you," I murmured.

"It's only a temporary reprieve. If Mr. Morgan chooses to pursue his vendetta, the price will be high."

I slumped in my seat. What could I do? Warn Alex that Dries was dangerous and revenge was a bad idea? He'd laugh in my face, like he had minutes ago. As for Dries . . . He just wasn't the sort of man with whom you could have a conversation that would start with "I have to tell you something, but please don't get mad."

March glanced at me while he drove. "I'm sure we'll find a solution, but before that, we need a little rest. How about I kidnap you again, Miss Chaptal?"

I stretched with a smile. "Dammit, am I going in the trunk again?"

That earned one of his rare grins. "I can think of a trunk-free special offer for returning clients."

"So where are we going?"

"I'm sorry, I can't tell you that. Rule number one of a successful kidnapping."

We passed a road sign; we'd be at the Sonnenhof in a few minutes. "Can I at least call Joy and my dad to tell them I've decided to run off with my fortysomething dom again?"

His lips pressed together; his cheeks were trembling. I could tell he was trying hard not to laugh. "Thirty-three, please."

I almost missed that detail, but as the SUV stopped in front of the hotel's entrance, I realized that sometime between October 28 of last year and today, March had celebrated his birthday.

THIRTY-FIVE

H.

"**IMPORTANT**: If you checked items **#7** (he's in his thirties and still on the market) **and** #13 (he suffers from either psychiatric and/or cognitive troubles), we must advise you to reconsider your choice. **Unless** you've also checked **#2, #5, and #17**, in which case your insane boyfriend is rich, good-looking, and capable of sustaining an erection without medical help. Keep him."

—Aurelia Nichols & Jillie Bean, *101 Tips to Catch Mr. Right*

It took almost twenty hours of flying and driving to reach our final destination, the dark dungeon inside which I would be held captive by March for an undetermined amount of time. Okay, the tiny dark dungeon. Also it wasn't really dark, because it faced the South Atlantic Ocean and there was pretty much nothing around. March liked his privacy; his closest neighbors lived nearly a mile away.

You guessed it: I was in March's legendary cubicle house in Cape Saint Francis, in South Africa. It was my new domain. All four hundred square feet of it. This isolated brick house was, indeed, more or less a cubicle standing fifty yards away from a long croissant-shaped beach of rock and sand. The place consisted of one small bedroom, a bathroom, a spotless kitchenette, and a living room where March stored his books. To my surprise, there was also a surfboard standing near the window. I hadn't pictured him as a surf enthusiast, but he explained to me that the area was in fact a renowned surfing spot, and that it was one of the many reasons why he had chosen to buy there.

Maybe I should mention that there was also a huge basement. If you guessed that March's basement doubled as a fallout shelter and was ten times bigger than his home because there were enough weapons and military equipment inside to take over a small country, you won.

A wooden porch circled the house, on which Gerald had once stood. Perfect place to put a rocking chair, by the way. After a day spent sleeping the jet lag off and recovering from my romp in Sahar's basement, I could think of no better way to end the afternoon than gazing at the powerful waves rolling and crashing on the beach in foamy white splashes. Standing next to me and leaning against the brick wall, March seemed just as content, a beer in hand—he apparently indulged once in a while—while the navy linen shirt he had changed into billowed under a cool and strong breeze.

I snuggled into the white cotton sweater I had borrowed—yeah, "stolen"—from his closet to wear over my T-shirt and shorts. "Will you tell me now? About the code?"

His lips curved into a resigned smile. "I had hoped you'd be busy enough to forget about this."

"You underestimate me. I *will* touch and examine everything in your house, but only after you've kept your promise."

"Let's get inside, then."

I followed him into the living room, sizzling with curiosity, and watched in confusion as he took off his shirt.

"It's on my Lion," he began, his voice suddenly lower, colored perhaps by a touch of anxiety. "The outward circle, on the bottom."

I approached him gingerly, torn between my need to learn more and, might as well admit it, different and somewhat baser emotions. It had been six months since I had seen him bare himself like this, but you know what they say—absence makes the heart grow fonder. And, indeed, I could feel my heart growing fonder by the second as my gaze traveled up the landscape of corded muscles and innumerable scars that was March's body. And *God*, I would *never* tire of that chest hair. Each golden curl beckoned me, tempted me to fondle his pecs, trace every vein running under his skin, and perhaps take a closer look at that wonderful navel.

But we weren't here for that. *Yet.* I walked around him, moving closer, and one of his hands grazed mine in silent encouragement to follow his instructions. Rediscovering March's Lion scarification, I was overwhelmed by the same blend of awe and distress I had experienced in the past. My stomach heaved at the sight of the large disk of tortured flesh stretching across the muscles of his back, covering most of his left shoulder all the way to the valley of his spine. "Carved," to quote Dries; a fierce lion head, surrounded by a complex African pattern, as a testimony to the fact that March had once pledged his life to his "brothers."

Once I was done reacquainting myself with the design, my eyes focused on the outer line of ridged flesh delimiting the disk, as he had told me to. I noticed the pattern was different there; it no longer looked like a group of identical, geometrical, and repetitive incisions in the skin, but rather various specific signs. I read the rough canvas with my fingertips, struggling to focus on the symbols rather than the way his muscles bunched under my touch, or the pleasant, soapy scent of him.

"Are you familiar with cuneiform?" March asked.

I nodded. "A little. It's a very ancient writing system, used in Meso-potamia?"

"In short, yes. What you see here is—" He paused, and I heard him swallow. "My number. H2014867."

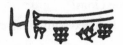

My fingers never leaving his skin, I let that new piece of information sink in. March's number . . . which probably meant that I2000009 was another Lion's number. That didn't tell me why or by whom my mother had been killed, but now I had a lead. I traced each line, as if I could make them speak and tell me all their secrets.

"Yours starts with an H. Why?"

"The number is a very ancient tradition. It's probably been around since the Lions were formed, twenty-five hundred years ago. The original founders were Romans and Persian warriors," he explained.

"So they kept the single Roman letter and used cuneiform numerals to identify their members?"

"Exactly. When you join the Lions, you agree to lose everything from your former life, starting with your name. All you're allowed to keep is the initial of your former name. First, last—you get to choose that."

I leaned my forehead against his back and molded my body against his, drawing strength from his warmth. "March. Who's I2000009?"

He went rigid. "He's the current commander of the Lions. His name is Anies. He's Dries's elder brother."

And therefore my uncle, I realized, holding on to March to fight the tremors in my knees.

When March spoke again, his tone was softer. "Do you understand now why I said you need to let go?"

I lowered my arms, for them to find their way around his waist. I focused on his feverish exhale as my fingers explored the line of hair running down his stomach. His hands covered mine.

"I'm not ready to give up yet. I need to understand," I said. "But if he's the one . . . I'm gonna need to take up self-defense classes."

Under my palms, a chuckle rumbled through March's abs. "You'll be the death of me, biscuit. Am I allowed a few days of rest before singlehandedly taking on the Lions?"

"I give you a week," I replied with mock authority.

The moment I said this, he spun around and pulled me into a tight hug. I was a little dizzy, and still bruised, but I ignored it and buried my face in that goddamn soft hair, listening to his heartbeat.

As I nuzzled the Promised Land, I registered his hands moving down my back. Then the most wonderful thing happened: my feet left the ground. I allowed March to lift me up, wrapping my legs around his waist to better support myself. My fingers threaded in his hair, and I felt his lips graze my neck as he spoke. "Why don't we take this somewhere more comfortable?"

Oh . . . Yes!

My mouth searched his, lavishing it with little pecks as he carried me toward his bedroom. I remember that I looked up, and above us, there were angel babies with little wings and harps playing Beethoven's "Ode to Joy"—true story.

For the sake of full disclosure, the bed's linen was a dark shade of indigo, and it carried a faint smell of detergent—no doubt it had been laundered recently. March laid me on the mattress like I was made of glass. I had no idea if it was the best moment, but when he covered my body with his, there was something so open, so vulnerable in his eyes, that I asked.

"H . . . It's not the initial of a month."

I noticed the way the muscles in his arms contracted. I brought my hands around his neck, stroking it soothingly.

"H was the initial of my last name," he said.

Once again, I could hear Dries telling me about March, mocking the boy who wanted to escape his miserable life, escape his own self. I pulled away to look him in the eyes. "It's your choice, whether you want to be H, whether you want me to know him. I'll never ask again, and maybe one day, if you're ready, you'll tell me."

He rolled us around the bed to gather me in his arms, and against my ear, I heard his murmur. "Thank you."

"You're welcome," I managed to breathe out.

So, so welcome!

That's more or less the point where I stopped thinking. The way his body molded against mine gave me those little chills of excitement that would travel from the top of my scalp to the tip of my toes. Observing my reactions under heavy-lidded eyes, March pulled me against him, placed one of his hands around the back of my neck while the other cupped my chin, and proceeded to knock my proverbial socks off—I was actually barefoot, if it's of any importance—with a deep kiss. He hadn't eaten any mints for a little while, and I found it made me more aware of his own taste, laced with beer. I locked my ankles around his legs as our hips met and ground together in a fashion that Corinthians 6:9 sternly proscribes. At the moment, however, I couldn't care less that I wouldn't inherit the Kingdom of Heaven. Breaking our kiss long enough for us to gasp for air, I looked at him. His pupils were dilated, black pools swallowing the blue in his eyes, and that single detail was making me regress to an animalistic state.

His Adam's apple rolled in his throat. "Biscuit, we need to slow down a little."

A bubbly laugh escaped me. "Hilarious . . . but you shouldn't joke about that. You have no idea how frustrated you got me back in Paris!"

He responded with an uncertain smile, and I realized, with no small amount of panic, that he was maneuvering his hips *away* from mine. "I'm serious."

Clinging to him, I bit his earlobe. "You're really milking that joke, aren't you?"

"Biscuit, I don't have condoms."

Oh.

"I'm sorry," he went on, stroking my hair. "It's been a little while, and it would seem that the ones I kept in the bathroom are expired."

My lips pressed together in a quivering pout. "Maybe it's like bagels—they never go bad, they just dry up a little."

He laughed against my cheek and untangled us, bringing our level of promiscuity back to that of a *clean* hug. "I promise I'll go buy some in Saint Francis Bay tomorrow."

My nose bunched. Scammed again. By a man I now understood to be a tease and denial fetishist. I wasn't going to cry; I would face the new lemon life had just fired in my face with dignity. I squirmed away from him. "I understand."

The worst part was that I *could see* the faint smile playing on March's lips. "Come back here, biscuit. I'll make it up to you," he said, wrapping his arms around me and pulling me back against his chest.

I fought him with a little grunt. "I know it's another trap!"

My accusations were met with a chortle as he drew the comforter over us.

Now . . . I won't get into a graphic account of the things he did to my socks—or the rest of my anatomy for that matter—but as it turned out, there's a surprising amount of exquisite exploration you could accomplish, short of the whole LEGO business.

So yes, in the end, he did make it up to me. Thoroughly so . . .

ACKNOWLEDGMENTS

First and foremost, I would like to thank my fantastic team of beta readers, and the fellow authors and readers who support me every day in my grotesque literary endeavors: Katerina, Roberta, Corinne, Carmen, Marie, Taylor, Becca, Arletta, Niahm, Amber, Hilda, Anna, Elizabeth, Erica, Kellen, Fathima, Laura, Malina, Jaycelle, Beth . . . and all the people I'm ashamed to forget.

Ladies, I love you. I'm one step away from creepy stalking and sexually ambiguous Facebook messages.

More thanks fired in the general direction of Tiffany Yates Martin, my beloved developmental editor, who works hard to make sense of the incoherent soup I send her, JoVon Sotak and Anh Schluep, who made this book happen, and of course Sharon Belcastro and Ella Marie Mohan Shupe, who put up with me.

Finally, I'd like to remind anyone who still has some amount of faith in humanity left, that I got paid money to write about killer platypuses. I live the dream.

ABOUT THE AUTHOR

Camilla Monk is a French native who grew up in a Franco-American family. After finishing her studies, she taught English and French in Tokyo before returning to France to work in advertising. Today, she's a managing partner in a small ad agency, where her job is to handle all things web-related and make silly drawings on the whiteboard when no one is looking. Her writing credits include the English résumés and cover letters of a great many French friends, and some essays as well. She's also the critically acclaimed author of a few passive-aggressive notes pasted in her building's elevator.